For Joe

The Gunnysack Castle

by

Julian Silva

with fond memories
of my favorite class.

Julian Silva

Typesetting and layout by
Prepress Advertising
Denver, Colorado

Part I

Chapter One

1

He built his castle against a backdrop of horse chestnuts that lined the banks of the creek. It began as a simple teepee of burlap over a frame of grapestakes. With a turkey feather in his hair, like some Indian chief in solitary glory, he contemplated his creation. But the supply of gunnysacks had not been depleted and he was too restless to limit his dreams. He continued to build.

Room by small room the teepee grew, each sack carefully unstitched and the hempen string saved for resewing the stretched burlap. He gathered wood from the creekbed — bits of old lumber and branches from fallen trees stripped of their bark and hewed into posts. Stitch by slow stitch the complex of tiny rooms multiplied, each connected to the others by a network of covered tunnels. A wooden sword replaced the turkey feather and the Indian chief became a king.

But what is a king without subjects? He wouldn't be satisfied with the immigrant hordes, their very gait branded with the stamp of peonage. He must win the allegiance of the whey-faced Anglos whose fathers had founded the town — though its name was a legacy from the Spanish. As were the two highways whose intersection marked the geographical center, one following the east shore of the Bay, the other leading from the salt flats toward the Altamont Pass and into the San Joaquin Valley. Meeks Landing was built in the 1850s, and those in search of a sunny retreat from the bustling, fog-bound city could travel — leisurely and luxuriously — from San Francisco to San Oriel by boat. A series of great houses rose, each vying with the others in the splendor of its ornament and the size of its park.

But fashions change rapidly in frontier states. Before San Oriel finished celebrating its first decade, the Peninsula had

3

already replaced it as the favorite haven for the City's new rich. The first Portuguese arrived in the eighteen sixties, but not until the early seventies did the dribbling influx become an invasion. The abandoned parks of the old estates were transformed into orchards, and for at least one generation English ceased to be the dominant language. There were then two San Oriels — one "American," the other "Portaghee."

Unlike his fellow Ports, he would not cling to the old ways and the old language. He had cast off the foreign-sounding Vicente for the simple Vince. Still his pallid American classmates remained obstinately unmately, and he spent his childhood in a no-man's land, no longer a true Portaghee, yet only a token American. He would command respect with the splendor of his sack city on the shores of the creek.

It was, he realized almost immediately, a mistake. Dreams cannot be shared.

"So what's so great about a pile of gunnysacks?"

The speaker's hair was carrot-orange and his sickly white face was blotched with brown freckles. But his father owned the Aiken Salt Works out on the marshes of the Bay, and the stout Robert — the third Aiken to bear the name — was a molder of fashions. His contempt signaled the sneers that banished the envy on his companions' faces.

"Let's see *you* build something better."

"Well, you can be sure of one thing: it won't be made out of sacks."

"What then — salt?"

There were snickers. The face of Robert III flamed as red as his hair.

Vince knew that he had won no more than a mere skirmish, and as he waited the next afternoon squatted before his castle, his stomach was tight and his black eyes burned. The stillness was eerie. He listened.

He smelled them before he spied them. The odor of kerosene was pungent in the clean air. Their pale faces were streaked with mud as they emerged from the cover of shrubbery and crossed the dry creekbed. In their upraised hands they carried poles tipped with dried corncobs. A match was struck and the corncobs flared.

4

There were five of them, but for an instant their courage faltered as they confronted the slender Vince, fiercely clutching his wooden sword. Then Robert III, his hair as fiery as his torch, gave a savage cry. The marauders descended upon the frail fortress. In a minute it was over.

Great defeats are not measured in time and the deepest scars remain invisible. Vince did not shed a tear. Build big, he thought. Amid the smell of smoldering burlap, he promised himself that next time he would build big enough to outface them all.

And so he had.

2

By the turn of the century, the mansions of the founding fathers were little more than decaying relics, and Wood Acres was San Oriel's pride. A double row of date palms still too young for majesty lined the approach to the dazzling white house. A large carp pond with an island of lilies dominated the front lawn, but initial efforts to give form to the garden had been overwhelmed by the wild growth of vegetation — a formless mass of flowers and vines, colorful in summer and vibrantly green in winter. A pair of monkey trees set in a circle of lawn flanked the front stairs, which mounted with modest breadth to a long veranda of fluted columns. Formality gave way to fantasy in the upper stories, the symmetry offset by a fanciful tower with four oval windows and a mansard cap of shingles. A wrought-iron coronet sat on top like a cherry on an ice-cream sundae.

From the west tower window one could watch the paddle-wheel ferries ease their way into the dock at Meeks Landing. But yearly the travelers grew fewer, and by 1910 the emerging automobile, making the Peninsula more accessible than ever, put an end to the last remaining pretensions that San Oriel was ever to be anything but a community of farmers.

That was just fine with Vince Woods. Unlike his sometime neighbors, he never apologized for his calling by prefixing it with a gratuitous "gentlemen." He had, however, Anglicized his name and restricted the use of his ancestral tongue to his hired hands. Vince purged his children of the last remaining taints of a foreign heritage. None of them understood more than a dozen words of Portuguese, most of those unsuitable for polite use.

For them it was a language of mysteries and taboos, its peculiar rhythms a signal that the forbidden was about to be broached. They had only to enter a room of laughing adults to inspire a whispered warning. The sudden switch of language, mounting on a swell of laughter, piqued their curiousity — but never enough for any of them to pick up a viable vocabulary from the field-hands. Thus they listened in blank-eyed silence as their mother switched suddenly in the midst of her interview from English to Portuguese, and Sarah Cabral answered in kind.

Sarah's round, plump figure presented a coarse contrast to the party picnicking on the front lawn, like some Brobding-nagian caricature plopped in the middle of an Impressionist landscape, all white lace, pink ribbons and dappled light. Even in the open-air confrontation she came swathed in a heady mix-ture of glandular excretions. But her arms were strong and her back, Clara observed, had clearly been constructed to bear bur-dens. Her manner also commended her.

There was something close to religious awe in the way her eyes lit upon the beautiful young boy lounging against Clara, his head pillowed in the lace of his mother's lap. Through eyes creamily brown as melted fudge, he studied the homely Sarah, with her kinky hair and bulbous nose and the large wart on her left jowl, as though she were some rare specimen of a beetle fit to be added to his collection — if only he had the energy to catch and mount it.

At fifteen, Sarah had not acquired the art of dissembling. There were no hidden depths to her character. Her emotions rose to the surface like so many carbonated bubbles, beyond her power to will or control them, but bursting with the salubrious satisfaction of an afternoon belch. Her face was far more elo-quent than her command of language, and her expression now transcended all verbal flattery.

To adore her son was the surest way to Clara's affections. The girl would do. There were, after all, considerations more compelling than the all too familiar stench of poverty. The maid's room came equipped with a shower stall, and the girl could very well be taught the rudiments of hygiene along with her chores.

As incapable of subtlety as her prospective maid, Clara was apt to be grander in gesture and manner than any grande dame outside the boards of a provincial theatre. The travesty of her performance — and she was always onstage — was saved from producing more laughter than respect by the simple fact that she was indeed playing to the provinces.

The success of a play depends on its public reception, and here as well Sarah did not fail. Credulous to the point of flattery, she was also so authentically, so indisputably, and best of all, so contentedly common, that her presence made Clara feel more than ever to the manor born. Not an actress at all, but a lady indeed.

Nor was Clara a fanatic about hygiene. She did, of course, draw the line at having the same finger that had just probed a scabby nostril sample a sauce, but such strictures had more to do with aesthetics than with health. If the rich were different, Clara had learned, it was because they smelled sweeter. And not even a fairy princess could smell like a rose garden without the luxury of privacy — of which there had been precious little in the house of her birth. There every act was a public act. When the original outhouse had been replaced with indoor plumbing, the only available space had been the hallway leading from the pantry to the downstairs bedrooms. Here the necessary appliances had been stretched out in a doordodging row, making it impossible to go from the kitchen to the bedrooms without first weaving a path around the commode and the sink and the huge enameled-iron tub, its lion claws sunk into the sagging softwood floor. There had never been any need to inquire if bowels were too loose or too firm. One's every evacuation was broadcast to the entire house. There was no muffled laughter from behind closed doors that did not reverberate throughout every room, no intimate confessions confided across shared pillows that were not shared by the entire family. Eleven surviving Bettencourt children clustered tightly together. Not particularly snug and warm. Merely close, so close that the air they breathed could scarcely be called their own. Not until she had been rescued from it had

Clara felt the full brunt of this stifling lack of privacy.

Thus the room in her own house that best symbolized the change wrought in her life by her marriage was her bathroom: a paradise of mauve and yellow tile canopied with a stained-glass skylight. Here, amid the convoluted writhings of Art Nouveau tendrils, she stepped each morning into her bath, her tissue-white skin brindled in lavender and amber, her full breasts dappled with rainbows reflected from crystal prisms. It was, in more ways than one, her private throne room. Anyone who did not know what it replaced might have marveled at the extravagance.

Only Lorraine, the youngest of the three Woods children, remained impervious to its enchantment. Well past her third birthday, she stubbornly resisted all efforts at toilet training. Despite promises of rewards and threats of punishment, she seemed quite content, as the beatific smile that now swept across her face indicated, to let nature have its due whenever and wherever the impulse struck her, and not all her doll-like frilleries could conceal her all-too-mortal lack of refinement.

"Phew!" The lounging Arnie clutched his nose with one hand and with the other fanned the air, his features so comically crinkled that Sarah rocked the earth with her laugh as she stooped to pick up the offending child without waiting to be asked.

The nine-year-old Louise, whose austere beauty might have been more truly remarkable had it not been overwhelmed by her younger brother's Apollonian features, attempted to brazen out the awkward moment with an imperious lift of her chin.

"Don't you fret," Sarah chuckled, her whole body rippling. "I'll take care of her in a jiffy."

"Please," Clara responded, looking as though she wouldn't have known what to do had she been called upon to remedy the situation herself, and balancing her weight on her parasol, she rose. "You can meet me in the kitchen when you're through and I'll show you around."

And without a single backward glance, she moved across the lawn toward the house, oblivious to the howls of the terrified Lorraine. So impressed was the pampered child by the rude shock of icy water pumped onto her soiled backside that the very next day she was ready to call "potty."

"The Cabral girl? You can't be serious, Clara."

"Yes, Dear. Sarah Cabral."

Still slender at forty, Vince Woods smiled indulgently at his wife. His sun-bronzed face rose from the stiff pedestal of a paper collar like the bust of a Bedouin sheik, his finely chiseled features more Moorish than Latin. In his youth more than one local virgin had fended off proposals in the forlorn hope of catching his fancy, and when finally at thirty, right on schedule, he made his choice, their disappointment was tempered with wonder.

Clara Bettencourt! They shook their heads as their eyes searched the prospective bride for some overlooked virtue, some depth of passion, some secret talent. They found nothing. Not beauty, not brains, not charm. Not even the prospect of a piddling inheritance.

But Vince Woods was a man who smiled quietly while those about him shook the walls with their laughter, who could in the midst of the most abandoned festivities retain his sobriety, and in the very fever of intoxication, coolly measure the degradation of excess. Only then, when all others were lost, would he allow himself to savor his own superiority.

Though moon-faced Clara had not been the prettiest of the nine Bettencourt girls, she had qualities more promising than beauty. Fair-skinned and fair-haired, she was all soft curves, like some malleable clay that could be easily impressed, that would give way before the lightest touch, but once fired would retain its shape — which would be the imprint of his shape. From the first she had revealed all the earmarks of loyalty and grati- tude, two qualities to be prized above beauty; and though he had known as he held her trembling hand before the altar that she did not love him, did not even know what love was, he also knew she would feed his pride with adoration. Her worship transformed gratitude, and an awe that not even intimacy could altogether dim, into something finer and more absolute than mere love.

Nor were her disappointed competitors long resentful, for Clara's shortcomings were transfigured by the gleaming satin of her wedding gown into shimmering virtues. All smiles and grinning deference, their hands tucked into rubber aprons rolled about their waists, their heads bound with red bandanas, the women with whom she once had worked on the assembly line of Hunt's Cannery knew their place. And Clara Bettencourt very quickly became Mrs. Woods.

She saw them now only at Sunday mass, sitting respectfully in their back pews or walking resolutely along the palm-lined drive past the house and the barn to the sheds that covered the long troughs where the rhubarb was washed, trimmed, and crated. And their names too had undergone a change in the mist of a willfully short memory, but they never seemed to mind when Lena was mistaken for Mamie or Mamie for Stella. Clara Woods, formerly Clara Dear, was their undisputed princess, the lucky lottery winner transported by the wheel of chance from a shack to a palace. The heights to which she had risen seemed to them proof enough of paradise, and no one begrudged her her great fortune — which in its reflected glory brightened their own: though they might themselves forever remain peasants, their daughters yet could become queens.

"She's moving in tomorrow."

Suddenly alert, Vince's eyes made a quick sweep of the table.

"Who? Old Frogface?"

"Please, Dear — the children! You want they should pick it up even before she's had a chance to get used to our ways?"

"Oh, I beg your pardon." He dabbed his lips with his napkin, winked at his son, and assumed a mockingly contrite manner. "Can't have them taking after their old man, now, can we?"

"I do wish you wouldn't use that expression. You're their *father*. Not their 'old man.'" She dropped the phrase like some slimy intruder found crawling on her plate. "I don't know why the expression annoys me so, but it does. And I won't have it used in my house. At my table."

Again he smiled, his wink this time encompassing all three of his offspring. Though they were expected to join him in his gentle mockery of his wife, not one of them would have dared demonstrate disrespect for her person or her authority. The only time that Arnie had ever felt the sting of his father's hand had followed a smart retort to one of his mother's requests. Both the violence and the suddenness of that slap discouraged repetition.

"Since your mother insists upon playing the lady, I suppose I've no choice but to try and act like a gentleman. All right then," he continued, pushing his chair away from the table and rising. "Your father's going to retire to your mother's parlor to smoke one of his cigars. If one of you children can manage a glass of brandy without spilling half the bottle, he'd be most grateful."

The sudden scramble for the liquor cabinet terminated in a tangle of limbs from which Louise emerged as victor. Not, however, before her disappointed brother had left the red imprint of his pinch upon her forearm.

His revenge accomplished, Arnie darted through the swinging door into the kitchen to answer a knock at the backdoor. A moment later he returned to announce in stentorian tones deliberately pitched to fall at the feet of their visitor:

"It's Frogface."

"You see, Dear," Clara spoke to the empty table, "how he picks up everything you say." Then turning to her son: "Her name is Sarah," she remonstrated. "Not Frogface. And I don't want to hear you — or anyone else around here — using that expression again. Do you understand? All of you?"

Then rising grandly from her seat, Clara first paused to insert her rolled napkin into a silver ring before sweeping majestically through the swinging door.

"Why, Sarah, I wasn't expecting you till morning."

Her voice took on the fluttering tremolo reserved for menials.

"I know you said tomorrow," Sarah began, tentatively. The bundle of rags clutched in her hands indicated she fully intended to stay the night. "But since I was doing nothing special, I thought I might just as well come on over right now and do the evening dishes so's you wouldn't have to fret yourself. And I could begin my regular chores tomorrow. Fresh and early."

Not altogether lacking in either heart or perception, Clara knew there was more to Sarah's sudden appearance than an overwhelming desire to accommodate.

"Have you had anything to eat yourself, Sarah?"

"No, M'am, now you mention it. There wasn't much in the house, and Pa — well, he said, long as I was a working girl now,

11

he didn't see no reason why I couldn't fend for myself.''

"You mean the rascal threw you out? On an empty stomach! His own daughter!''

"So people say,'' Sarah answered, though the toss of her head indicated *she* preferred to believe otherwise, and since her mother, who had died shortly after childbirth, was no longer around to bear witness, she felt she was entitled to the benefit of the doubt.

"Sounds just like the old codger.'' Clutching the evening paper, Vince inspected their new girl of all chores from the kitchen doorway. "But I'll wager there was money enough for the usual bottle of muscatel.''

A smile flashed from Sarah's crinkled face as her eyes met those of her new master. "You can bet your boots on that one without any fear a losing 'em.''

The pluckiness of her retort pleased him: anyone who could survive such a parent with spirit unbroken could weather any crisis.

"First things first, eh, Sarah? Always enough for a bottle of wine, but nothing left over for simple basics such as food. Or soap and water,'' he added, laughing as he fanned the air before him with the rolled newspaper.

"Oh, we got our own well,'' she answered.

"Yes, Dear, I'm sure you have,'' Clara interrupted with a frown at Vince, whose lack of delicacy in such matters might very well be suited to the fields but was certainly out of place in the house. "But sometimes it takes more than just a splash of cold water. I'm sure you've had an exhausting day, so why don't you have a shower and freshen up a bit while I try to scrounge up some leftovers for you? Have you something clean to put on?'' Clara did not wait for an answer. "Louise, Dear,'' she continued, turning to her daughter, whose eyes were riveted to the girl's enormous breasts, full and heavy and obviously unsupported by an undergarment, "Go up to Mother's closet and get her old kimono. The pink one with the coffee stain on it. You'll find it hanging on one of the back hooks.''

As Clara led Sarah down the three short steps into the maid's room, convenient to the kitchen, Louise trudged up the stairs to her mother's bedroom, her hands cupped to support the weight of

12

imaginary breasts against a chest as obstinately flat as her brother's.

A moment later, dragging the flowered kimono behind her like a limply gorgeous tail, she sashayed down the stairs with one hand on her slender hips. But before she could complete her dramatic pause on the first landing with one lingering backward glance at the disconsolate lover abandoned at the head of the stairs, the air was rent by a horrendous shriek. A slippery scuffle, like the flap of wet sails lashed by a sudden squall, followed the cry, and quickly forsaking dreams of romance for simple childish curiosity, Louise dashed into the kitchen to find the entire household in a state of hilarious upheaval.

Smack in the middle of the linoleum rug, like a great beached whale, stood a wet and dripping Sarah crying, "Sweet God-a-mercy!" over and over, her fulsome figure stippled with scarlet moles. Even Clara was too busy laughing to concern herself with anything else.

As the pain subsided, Sarah herself, more startled than scalded, joined in, her enormous breasts bouncing to the rhythm of her laugh.

The keen-eyed Arnie soon restored a sense of propriety to the gathering. "How come she's got whiskers down there?" he asked, pointing to the luxurious growth in the fork of the glistening thighs. And for one silent moment, all eyes, including Sarah's were fixed upon Sarah's pubic mound.

It was, Clara decided, clearly no laughing matter. Vince, suppressing a ribald chuckle, ushered his son away. Clara led the dripping Sarah back to her room for a more thorough lesson in modern plumbing.

4

Once she had made the startling discovery of instant hot water, it did not take much persuading to convince Sarah of the divine origin of personal hygiene. The experience seemed, initially, altogether too pleasant to be Christian. The first one up every morning, she could drain the tank cold before she finished, cupping her breasts in hands creamy with the perfume of violets and lifting huge nipples to be tickled by the warm spray. Tiny rivers

13

of soap ran down every crevice to gather in a torrent of suds over her slippery flanks, until blushing like a rosegarden and smelling almost as sweet, she stepped out onto the bathmat and a new day. If such were the rigors her betters required of her, who was she to object?

Within a matter of days the permanence of her position in the household seemed assured. The drying-up of Lorraine was the first indisputable triumph, and Clara, now that she had found the perfect servant, became the perfect mistress. She learned never to question the how of any success; the ends were all that interested her; and left up to Sarah, the ends, Clara soon discovered, always contrived to add to her own comfort. Lorraine's howls had been loud, but they had not lasted long. And the child, whose mother had been graciously spared the sight of her tears, seemed none the worse for the experience — seemed, in fact to take a special delight in the new frilled garments which promised to keep the family's attention focused upon her physical person.

Nor was the incident of Lorraine's toilet-training unique. Sarah, it soon seemed to Clara, was capable of unriddling every household mystery and steam-rolling her way across the roughest terrain. She was quite simply "a marvel." No challenge dismayed her, no task overwhelmed her.

And within a month's time Clara had added yet another touchstone phrase to the lexicon of soothing formulas with which she interpreted the wonder of her own life to herself and the world. Because such phrases required no thought and made the strange instantaneously familiar, this latest addition comforted Clara as much as it flattered Sarah, who found in its repetition the first promise of security she had ever known:

"I don't know how I ever managed without you!"

It was a promise almost immediately threatened by a rival and one whose claim could never be challenged. For even the most sterling of qualities were as tin when pitted against that sovereign word "family"; though her virtues were manifold, Sarah could scarcely yet lay claim to any privilege as sacred as that.

14

Chapter Two

1

"If there's anything I can do. Anything at all."

Licking a nicotine-stained tip of his white mustache, Joe Salazar pressed his black derby against his chest.

"No, Sal. Everything's already been taken care of."

The man's kindness made her so impatient she could not even add a gratuitous thank-you. She only wanted him to be done and gone. But clutching his hat in an agony of misspent emotions, he lingered, the mute stirrings of his heart doomed to expend themselves in flushed cheeks and rheumy eyes:

"Anything at all. You just let me know. If there's anything I can do."

"Yes, Sal . . . And thank you," Belle added as with a gentle hand on his shoulder, she guided him through the front door and then returned to confront her sister.

The dishes were already stacked in the kitchen sink, a few crumbs salted the rug of the Sunday parlor, a cake plate with a single tilting slab of angel food sat among the clutter of photographs — an hour's work. And then? She leaned against the door to steady herself.

"Poor Sal." She shook her head, her smile remote. "I thought we'd never be rid him."

"Like a bad tooth," her brother-in-law answered. "Never know he's there till it's time he was gone." And with a thumb and forefinger Vince reached into his vest pocket, sucking in his breath before he could extricate his gold watch. A diamond-studded elk's tooth dangled from the gold chain.

"I wonder why he bothers," Clara added, noting her husband's signal. She could not find the words to bring the afternoon to an end. "Coming to these affairs, I mean. Once he's here," she continued, borrowing her husband's simile as she borrowed all his ideas, "it's like pulling teeth to get a word out of him."

15

So smug and secure did they seem in their prosperity — Clara's extravagant mourning outfit more a pleasure of her buying power than of any grief she might feel for the loss of her mother — Belle felt a note of asperity returning to her voice:

"Maybe he just likes to be near us. Close enough to warm himself. Poor man," she added, the tremor in her voice not altogether selfless: "All alone."

"And whose fault is that?" Clara snapped, taking the old bachelor's rejection of marriage as a personal affront.

"Fault?" There was the ring of an old authority in Belle's voice: the sister who had herself been more mother than the woman now mourned. "Why must it be anyone's 'fault'?" Though she could, with a belligerent lift of her chin, give the impression of great size, she was neither tall nor stout, merely solid and unadorned.

But Clara was not intimidated: times and their relative positions had changed, and both radically.

"That's no life for a man to lead."

"Who are we to say it was a matter of his own choosing?" Aware of dangerous currents, Belle sank onto the edge of the nearest chair, but Clara was not to be mollified.

"He's a man, isn't he? And a man can always choose."

The implication was, of course, that Belle herself had never been granted a choice, and now that she had passed forty was well past all hope.

"Sometimes the choices are made for us. Even when we think we're making them ourselves," Belle added. She wanted to be left alone to find her own way through the chaos of her emotions. "Poor Pappa — he made his choice. And it wasn't Mamma — God rest her soul."

"Well, it worked out in the long run, didn't it?"

Clara rose abruptly and, picking up a picture from the cluttered table top, inspected it. It was unkind of Belle at such a moment, and particularly in front of the children, to bring up so bitter a portion of the past: the practices of an Old Country none of them had seen and all had foresworn. They were Americans now, thank God. Even the sound of Portuguese she found redolent of poverty, of cannery assembly lines and peach stains on scarred hands.

"Yes," Belle answered, her eyes lighting upon the last, limp piece of angel food, "it worked out. After a fashion." And for the first time all day she had to steel herself against tears.

On the corner of the sofa Arnie picked his nose. Beside him sat his older sister, prim in white. Too young at ten for the luxury of formal mourning, Louise had had to make do with her best party dress. A model of sober decorum, she continued to savor every nuance of the great day — her first funeral. She had never felt more than a baffled awe in the presence of the strange old woman who had been her grandmother. Now she felt compelled to grace the occasion with a suitably mournful mein. Not once through the morning and the long afternoon had a smile marred her perfect sobriety. She could sense the tension now, but she knew better than to interject herself into the conversation. If the mystery of her aunt's comment were to be solved, it would have to be pieced together on her own from just such indiscretions.

"How much longer we gonna stay?" The pouting Arnie ignored his sister's withering rebuke as he reached past her to grab the last piece of cake. He was not hungry, but he preferred the discomfort of surfeit to the pangs of regret.

"Sure now you wouldn't like us to help with the dishes?" Clara was already pinning on her hat.

Belle shook her head, and Clara, watching her in the mirror, wondered whether perhaps the poor thing had not already had all the feelings hammered out of her. Through the entire ordeal, no one had seen her shed a single tear. At such a time her sober efficiency didn't seem natural. So little regard did Belle have for public opinion, her behavior was sure to give new life to the rumors about their mother's last years. Soon people would be whispering how relieved she must be to be rid of the burden: free at last to lead her own life.

But something about Belle always put one off. Whatever it was, Clara feared, it was becoming ever more pronounced. Unyielding, Vince called her, and as usual he had hit the nail squarely on the head. There was no give to her. Right was right and wrong was wrong and there was never any question in her mind about which was which.

"I've nothing left but time, Clara. Nothing," she added with a tremor hinting at unshed tears — now that it was too late to matter, Clara noted, hardening herself against any countersurge of sympathy.

"I don't want you to make any hasty decisions you'll live to regret," Clara continued, drawing the veil over her face, "but you think about our proposal, Dear. We can easily let Sarah go — no problem there — and you can have her room. It isn't large, but it's comfortable. And you'd have your own bath. And heat, Belle. Central heating. No messy old kerosene stove to smell up the place."

Standing, Vince drew in his stomach and pulled down the edges of his vest. The house was Clara's domain, and though he did not relish the thought of his sister-in-law replacing the already comfortable Sarah, he would no more have told his wife how to run the household than he would have tolerated her telling him how to run his farms. There was something about the way the woman sat — forward on her seat, her back erect so that the chair carried as little of the burden as possible — that offended him. She did not know how to give herself to life. She never abandoned herself to enthusiasm or talk — or anything else. A proper old maid. Cold and withdrawn, her labors veiled in silence, her skimping and saving never lightened with a laugh.

Sometimes though, she smiled — as she did now at her sister's ingenuousness. For Belle knew full well who would be expected to feed the fires to furnish that central heat; who would be up at five so that those up at six would find a house already warm and a breakfast already spread.

"Oh, dear Clara, I'm not at the moment up to making decisions. It's too soon yet. Too soon for that."

Vince frowned. Though he did not relish having her live in his house, he did not like to see his generosity lightly valued. Since *he* had steeled himself to *her* presence, he could conceive of no objections she might have. A woman in her position.

"Well, of course, no one's going to *force* you . . ." The plumes of Clara's hat trembled with repressed indignation.

Belle blushed. She remained seated. The others standing about her made her feel like a prisoner under interrogation, but she had not the strength to rise.

Still stunned, not so much by her mother's death as by the

18

change in her own life, she needed time to order her thoughts. Only too well did she know what living with Clara would be like: a servant without wages forced to take her meals at the family table as if her due were alms. A life of continued drudgery. Cleaning up after Clara's children, who would always be just that — Clara's children. How easy it would have been to make her decision, a simple and firm no, if only there had been just a little money. The smallest legacy. But even the house was now in her brother-in-law's name, every penny of the rescued mortgage long since having been spent on doctors and food, and she could not, without some return, continue to accept his charity — even if the price of that return made her his indentured slave.

"Give me a few days. Please, Clara. A few days."

The break in the voice satisfied Clara. Knowing full well what the final answer must be, she was prepared now to be magnanimous:

"You take all the time you need, dear. All the time you need." And leaning forward, her hands on the older woman's shoulders, she kissed her sister's cold cheek.

2

The shades were still up in the Sunday parlor, but in the afternoon light the flocked paper seemed a blur of ornate frames. The bearded faces might have belonged to Old Testament prophets, stiff and humorless, their fierce eyes fixed upon the camera's lens with all the intensity of men obsessed by a single, consuming idea. Alongside them, with swelling busts pushed to chin level by waist armors of whalebone, their wives seemed every bit as formidable; taskmasters rather than lovers. The corner what-not shelves were burdened with a clutter of cutglass bowls, silver-plated trays, and glossy blue porcelains. Lace curtains yellowed with age and faded velvet drapes, traces of their original color buried deep in the dark folds, covered the windows. Clustered with needlepoint pillows and cuffed with crocheted doilies, the mohair sofa was large and cumbersome, the horsehair cushions packed hard, each one molded to the shape of its last occupant. In a cast iron umbrella stand stood the

19

S.P.R.S.I. banner with a portrait of the saint framed by the embroidered legend: SOCIEDADE PORTUGUEZA DA RAINHA SANTA ISABEL. An oleograph of the Holy Ghost, a white dove suspended in a golden aureole, hung above the fireplace. On a long table covered with a silk-fringed shawl stood a clutter of family pictures: all the children and grandchildren of the forbidding faces in the formal wedding portrait posed before a screen of painted palms. More than just a Sunday parlor, the room had been, since the beginning, a kind of family treasury, a ceremonial mask with which to confront strangers, and as such sacred to festive family occasions: baptisms, first communions, confirmations, weddings, and the lying-in-state of all the family dead.

But that was finished now. And as Belle turned the key in the lock, she felt a sudden chill at the meaninglessness of her action. What was there that anyone might want to steal? A few shining pieces of porcelain that were considerably more trouble than they were worth, to be dusted, but never used, to be seen, but never touched. Showpieces. And who was there left to show them to? Who would come to visit her now they were all married — or buried? Even Elsie, the youngest, in Turlock to help out her sister Nora, had found herself a beau. There was no one left but herself — the first born and the last survivor in the house of her ancestors. This honeycomb of tiny, ramshackle rooms that her father had built.

For it was he, strangely, whose presence she felt most keenly and not her mother, whose mind had been dead too long for fresh mourning. And with a ghostly calm, she wandered through his house. How he must have slaved, all alone, with few tools and even fewer skills, to build these poor rickety rooms! Years of solitude and work with no one to cook his meals, no one to wash his clothes, no one to hold his hand. Each precious penny hoarded to pay for their mother's passage from the Azores, only to be tricked, finally, by the same sly peasant's ruse that had been played on so many of the town's settlers.

Though he started late, Manuel Bettencourt had had fourteen children, eleven of whom, nine daughters and two sons, outlived him. And after the birth of his first, it scarcely mattered any longer that his wife was not the woman for whose picture he had bargained with the Portuguese sailors of a whaling ship docked for supplies in San Francisco Bay, but an older and less comely sister of the promised bride. Time and labor had inured him to shock. Despite the chicanery of her family, his wife had proved a good wife and the number of births had stopped at fourteen solely because Manuel himself died before there was time to conceive a fifteenth.

His death came too early to insure Belle's own marriage — not that she would have considered binding her self to any man who had to be thus intimidated into marriage. When, moreover, had there ever been time for courtship — time between her mother's extended confinements, each one of which left her weaker and less fit to cope? Someone had to feed and bathe the latest infant. Someone had to keep the pot of soup simmering on the stove, to boil the diapers in the tankhouse cauldron, to assist at birth and nurse each case of croup, to temper each fever and salve each rash. And when disaster had defeated all her best efforts, someone had to sit up sleepless in the Sunday parlor before the tiny, flower-decked coffins of the three brothers who, in three successive years, had succumbed to ailments known and unknown. Her assumption of the role of family drudge had been accepted by herself with the same sense of fateful inevitability as it had been accepted by the rest of the family. She was the oldest, she was the strongest. Who else might have taken her place? Nor did she cherish a grudge. So busy had her life been till now she had never had time for resentment. She had always been too much of a necessity for the luxury of being loved. She knew that. She had not complained. She had not thought of herself as ill-used. Only once had she been known to startle heaven with her cry of protest.

With the exception of chickens, whose necks she could ring with a stunning lack of sentimentality, she could not bear to see anything die. Stray cats were fed from the meager scrapings off the family table and whenever possible their numerous offspring rescued from drowning. Every broken branch of one of her begonias or coleuses was neatly trimmed, stuck into a jar of water to root, and later planted in some empty tin or crock. What was alive must be kept alive. And when the last infant, a blue, sickly twisted body whose last difficult breath was greeted with a general sigh from all but Belle, who had felt her finger caught in its tight grasp, who with infinite patience had forced it to swallow the tiny drops of gruel administered from a medicinal syringe, who had awakened from the soundest sleep at the first sign of its choking — when he had died, something inside of her gave way and a flood of resentment burst forth, more tears than she had shed in a lifetime — for the two otherwise whole and altogether splendid brothers, taken in the first flush of their youth, or for her father, dead before he could enjoy the fruits of his labor and reap the reward of his solitary youth. It had been so tiny, so frail a thing to fight so fiercely for each breath, so rejected by all save her.

"Poor little thing," she muttered, speaking to her own reflection in the hall mirror. "Poor little thing." She inspected the colorless face confronting her. It had been years since she had really looked at herself: hair pulled back and wound into a simple knot: gray eyes that might once have been brown but were now simply bleached and aged replicas of their former selves, faded like every other promise of beauty her face had ever possessed. Forty-one!

No longer was there that drastic shortage of women that had forced men such as her father to send to the Old Country for wives. The pioneer families had multiplied. New settlers had come. Men married outside their faith as well as their race. All the men her own age worthy of marriage were already married. Oh, yes, there were a few old widowers who would be more than willing to trade the use of their name for a cook and a nurse. But if she must take charity, she would take charity from her own. She was not past bearing, and marriage without the prospect of children would only be a continuation of her lifelong drudgery.

And suddenly opened before her was a world as infinite as hers had been limited and she was struck by a singular fact: for the first time in her life the decisions she must make would affect no one but herself. The thought made her giddy. She seemed to be standing all alone on the edge of an abyss. For the first time all day she felt the reality of her mother's death, remembering her as she could never possibly have known her except in reconstructed dreams: standing all alone on that ship crossing the vast oceans, all alone for months, knowing all along she was the wrong woman. Belle shivered. The vision had haunted her adolescence. Poor Mamma! Better solitude than degradation: to bare body and soul to any man with the price of one's passage around the Horn!

She at least was free! For the first time in her life she was free to do anything she liked. She could be as silly and as foolish. as she chose, and there would be no one but herself to suffer from her remissions. She might do anything, she might go anywhere. She could even — after all these years — give herself a holiday. In forty-one years she had never slept under another roof. She knew somewhere just across the Bay lay San Francisco. Along with the rest of the town, she had, one terrible April night, ridden out to Meek's Landing to witness God's gorgeous vengeance. A red glow on the horizon was all she had ever seen of the city. But now she was free to see a good deal more, if she so chose. And she did choose. She would take a trip. The blood rushing to her head made her so dizzy, she had to throw herself onto an easy chair before she crumbled to the floor, drunk from the sheer audacity of her decision.

In the Sunday parlor she sat, alone and laughing to herself, like a madwoman. Or a silly girl. The giggling, foolish young girl she had never had time to be. How her heart pounded and her head reeled! Until catching sight of the empty, crumb-filled plate, she had to bite her knuckles to stifle the sob.

"Oh, Mamma! Mamma! Mamma!" she cried, dropping her head to her knees for grief and shame.

Chapter Three

1

Perched on a modest knoll before a backdrop of eucalyptus and horse chestnuts at the first bend of the creek, the Bettencourt house had grown from three small rooms to an amalgam of uncoordinated bedrooms and parlors tilting at so many different angles that it seemed not so much a single house as a complex of tiny houses held together by a net of vines. The most striking architectural feature was a long, L-shaped backporch, the roof of which sagged under the weight of an ancient wisteria vine. The porch itself was a clutter of plants and crockery, of geraniums and begonias and coleuses growing from every conceivable container. At the foot of the stairs clusters of mint and rosemary hid the rotting supports. Red roses and purple bougainvillea, and on the western side an arbor of concord grapes, for most of the year disguised the fact that scarcely a flake of paint remained on the dry boards. Only the window frames were kept up, shining a glossy black in the first light of morning.

Gravel crushed and a horse neighed a welcome. The kitchen door opened and a figure all in black stepped out onto the porch. Pulling on her gloves, Belle inspected the carriage coming up the long drive past the cherry orchard. The morning sun was directly behind so that she could not see the driver, but she could tell from the elegant prance of the horse it was not the expected workmen coming to take her to the Melrose Station. For a moment she feared it was Vince himself making one last attempt to dissuade her from what his shocked wife had called "this shameful folly," and she braced herself for yet another confrontation; for despite all objections, she meant to have her way.

"Why, Sal!" she called out as the carriage pulled up before the porch to reveal a sombre Joe Salazar. "What in heaven's name brings you here so early?" Her quizzical glance brushed

24

past him as she peered up the sun-dazzled drive, too impatient to be gone to be truly curious about his answer.

"Well, Belle," he began, then instantly lost his way as his eyes met hers. Coughing out the initial H, he stumbled valiantly on: "Heard you was going to the City." Half hidden by brows that shot off in every direction, his tiny squirrel eyes watered from the strain, his hat held respectfully against his chest as though it had been nailed there.

"Yes, Sal, but I hardly expected . . . ."

He blushed before answering. "Had some business in Fruitvale and thought . . . a produce truck's no place for a lady."

He was wearing the same black best-suit he had worn to her mother's funeral. His high paper collar was bordered by a roll of flesh rubbed a particularly painful shade of red. The lapels of his jacket still smelled of the benzine with which they had been spot-cleaned, and his hair and mustache glistened with a balmy confection thick with aromatic oils.

"Well, that's mighty nice a you, Sal. And judging from the way you're dressed," she added, her eyes teasing him affectionately, "it's mighty important business, too. My, my!" she shook her head, her smile broadening. "Like a Christmas turkey already stuffed and waiting for the oven. Why, Sal, who's getting married?"

So rare were the town's bachelors and so touchingly incompetent his efforts to prove himself a master of the social graces, she could not forego teasing him, but as his face flared purple in an agony of confusion, she quickly repented.

"If you fetch my bag from the kitchen, we can be off," she said. With a change of color from purple to pink he put on his hat and skipped up the backstairs like a bumbling adolescent.

The morning was crisp and still. Cushioned by a silken carpet of dry grass, the sound of the carriage wheels seemed distant as they pulled off the side of the road to allow a car to pass, the sputtering intrusion answered by a frightened neigh. Tugging at the reins and talking to his horse with considerably more ease than he spoke to his passenger, Sal calmed the anxious beast.

"I'd get myself one," he said sullenly as they watched the third Model-T disappear before them in dust, "if I wasn't already too old to change my ways. No sir," he snorted, still shaking his head, "can't teach an old dog . . . . " He tried to cover his embarrassment by reaching for a cigar, but before he had it fully out of his pocket he stuffed it back in. Scowling furiously, his eyes buried beneath shaggy brows, he peered straight before him.

"Go ahead, Sal, if you like," Belle encouraged, "I don't mind. Rather like the smell, in fact. Always reminds me of Pappa."

But Sal was a man of principle, and one of his principles was that a gentleman does not smoke in the presence of a lady. So exalted was his view of women he could scarcely bring himself to use the word. He was a distant cousin of both her mother and her father, a not unusual occurence in San Oriel. Like most of the other Ports of the town, he had come from Fayal, an island so small that over a period of a few centuries everyone was bound to be everyone else's cousin. It had also, at one time, been a fief of Flanders, which accounted for a certain Nordic fairness and an asperity of feature as well as for family names — such as Bettencourt itself — not found on the mainland of Portugal.

They rode for a while in silence until Sal, speaking unnaturally loud, startled his companion with his question:

"Well, Belle, how does living alone suit you?"

It was clearly a rehearsed opening.

"Why, I can't say, Sal. Haven't had time yet," she answered, amused and somewhat baffled, though he was not, she knew, to be judged by ordinary standards. She liked him, and despite his own discomfort felt comfortable in his presence. She could not remember a time when she had not known him and she liked most what was familiar. "Mamma's scarcely been buried a week."

Her answer seemed to displease him, and he again took refuge in silence. His face grew disconsolate and his shoulders slumped forward so that he looked older than his sixty-some years. But he had determined to speak, and speak he would if each word seared his throat.

"Know it gets mighty lonesome sometimes, Belle," he began once again, speaking in fits and starts. "Even after all these years . . . . Was fourteen when I came over . . . . Fourteen . . . . A

26

good long time ago that was, Belle. A long time," he repeated, and for a moment he lost himself in his reminiscence, a nervous smile teasing the corners of his mouth, as with the back of his hand he smoothed the ends of his mustache. "Even after all these years . . . Yes, Belle . . . maybe you never thought of me any other way . . . but never quite got used to an empty house . . . Like an undertakin parlor with nobody round. No live body, anyways." And he chuckled joylessly at his little joke, which she suspected had also been rehearsed.

"Yes, Sal," she answered, though she was not sure what she was saying yes to. She had never before heard him speak so many words and she could not imagine what he was getting at.

"Well, Belle, you know — well, I wouldn't, naturally, a man at my age, be expectin . . . expect . . ." His voice wandered off in confusion, and she waited for a moment to learn what it was he wouldn't be expecting, until, with a sudden intuitive flash that made her want to laugh before it brought tears to her eyes, she realized he was about to propose to her. Her first impulse, as much a product of fright as of embarrassment, was to stop him while he could still extricate himself with some grace. To spare him as well as her. She could not understand why his words should make her heart suddenly pound so. She wanted nothing more than to return her pulse to normal. She did not want to be disturbed with decisions she was not up to facing.

"Not a poor man, Belle," he was saying. "Not much to look at — know that, but I could take care . . .''

"Please, Sal," she broke in, placing a gloved hand on his arm to prevent him from continuing as well as erase her rejection. "Don't say anymore. Why, you've always been almost like a second father to me, Sal. A second father."

Unable to determine whether her words were meant to encourage him or discourage him, he fumbled for a moment, more confused than ever. "Just thought, Belle — no offense — but since your ma was dead, you'd . . ." He floundered helplessly.

"I know, Sal," she continued, anxious to bring the painful scene to a hasty conclusion, "but no, Sal. No." She shook her head. "All I want right now is the peace and quiet to do a little thinking. I've never had time for that before, Sal. It's nothing to do with you, believe that. Oh, I'm touched, Sal. Touched. I can't tell you how . . . ." But shaken by what she herself could not distinguish as a laugh or a sob, she could not complete her thought. "I'll be grateful long as I live." She smiled, and with tears in her eyes she tried to turn the joke against herself: "No woman wants to go to the grave without at least one proposal to keep her company, Sal. No woman."

There was nothing more to be said that would not draw them both deeper into embarrassment. So they kept their silence, listening to the irregular noise of the iron-rimmed wheels, their bodies swaying slightly to the bounce of the springs, touching occasionally, but without adding to their discomfort. Through the bustle of San Leandro neither felt inclined to speak. It was not until they had passed the town and could already see the twin spires of the Elmurst church that Sal once again spoke, prefacing his words with a long and productive cough.

"You won't speak a this to anyone, will you, Belle?"

Again she laid her hand on his arm. "Not to a soul, Sal." And she shook her head to back up her words.

"To the family, or anyone," he continued as if he had not heard. It was clear whose scorn it was he most feared.

"Not for all the world," she reassured him, giving his arm an affectionate squeeze. So great was her sympathy at that moment that for the first time the idea of marriage to him did not seem ludicrous. "Not for all the world," she repeated, and once again they were silent.

2

Before it began her trip had become an anticlimax. Sal's proposal had opened doors she had hoped to keep shut a while longer. Without so much as the promise of a solution, it left her once again conscious of the dreadful void her life was about to enter, and she felt, as he handed her down her bag, a sudden panic at his imminent departure. With her hand out and her heart brimming, she saw him with a fresh clarity: a good man, a kind man, a lonely man; her father's friend and companion; a known quantity. Perhaps she had been too hasty in her refusal. If she had to be someone's nurse, why not his as well as another's? She was fond of him; familiarity had bred affection as well as

28

tolerance. Why not, then, companion his last years — though his timing had been disastrously wrong?

He seemed for a moment unsure what it was she expected him to do or say. Then awkwardly he leaned down to take her hand and became once again confused at the soft touch of her kid gloves.

"Thank you, Sal. For the ride. And Sal?"

A strange, childlike smile teased his lips as she held onto his hand.

"No hard feelings, Sal?"

The smile broadened, moving from his lips to his eyes. He seemed almost relieved that his ordeal was over.

"No hard feelings, Belle. Don't blame you at all. Not for a minute."

And once again touched by his modesty, his almost total avoidance of the first person, she watched his departure with mixed feelings. Then with her leather satchel in one hand, the beaver collar of Clara's cast-off coat turned up against the morning chill, she moved into the station.

"A round-trip ticket to San Francisco," she announced in a voice loud enough to draw every sleep-dimmed eye. Then, carefully fastening her ticket to the clasp of her coin purse, she dropped the smaller purse into the larger and sat on one of the oak benches to await the next train, her heart pounding with apprehension as well as anticipation.

Once the excitement and confusion of boarding were over, she was appalled by the filth of the train. The aisles were cluttered with crumbs and candy wrappers, with cigar butts and old newspapers. A wad of chewing gum was stuck onto the seat in front of her, and crumpled on the floor at her feet lay a discarded brown bag. Yet no one else seemed to mind or even notice, and she tried to distract herself by looking out the window. But that too was mottled with grime, and with such speed did the world move past, it made her dizzy. She was conscious only of an endless number of poles flashing before her measuring off the miles.

The instant she stepped into the smoky gray interior of the Oakland Mole, she felt herself coffined in her own foreboding. She had only to follow the ornamental arrows on the signs pointing to the FERRIES, but she was momentarily too be-wildered by the immensity of her surroundings to move at all. Never before had she seen so many men, all in black, with stiff paper collars and white-faced gold watches open in their hands. Everywhere she looked were men in a hurry, men with a pur-pose, all marching to their multifarious destinies. They brushed past, jostling her like some misplaced architectural detail. Occa-sionally one tipped a hat and with a brusque, "Pardon, Ma'am," withered her with eyes that challenged her right to clutter his path.

Numb with confusion she made her way onto the top level of the boat. Like a church, the ornate interior was lined with four rows of shining pews, and in the center, fronting the brass-railed stairway like an altar, was a bar paneled in dark wood and thick mirrors decorated with etched arabesques. She had to catch herself as she took a seat to keep from genuflecting. She noticed two smartly dressed women smiling at her, but when she returned their smile, their eyes went dead and their dull gazes passed through her. Baffled, she touched her hat, which like everything else she wore had come from Clara and was now at least ten years out of fashion. But fashion was a word she scarcely under-stood and certainly never used. She would have liked a second cup of coffee to brace herself, but the bar was lined with so many men standing with rolled newspapers before steaming cups she had not the courage to interject herself. Fascinated, she watched the long-cued cook pass orders through a steaming slot. A *Chinaman*. She had never seen one before and she was not sure why she knew that was what he was, for he was not, as she might have expected, any more yellow than she. Yet she did know, and that knowledge gave her the first lift of the morning. She felt suddenly older and wiser. A woman of the world.

There was an odd, almost imperceptible movement, a slight rolling sensation. When she looked up, she caught her face, sliced in half by the beveled edge of a mirror, bobbing seemingly in two different directions at once. Her stomach contracted. The air was thick with cigar smoke. It conjured memories of her father. He too was dead. They were all dead now. She was struck by the fact that she also would one day die. So forcefully did the thought hit her she could taste in her mouth the beginnings

30

of her own putrefaction. She had always before been too busy ministering to the demands of the living and the dying to give much thought to her own death, and though she had always known, as a rule of nature, that she too would one day die, she had never before felt that death as something already growing inside of her. She was going to die, and die before she had the chance to live. She leaned back against the bench and closed her eyes, but the darkness intensified the nausea. She looked about, longing for the sight of a familiar face, one face whose history might be a part of her own history, whose path might somewhere have crossed her path. Poor Sal. Maybe she had been too hasty. To be always alone — she could think of no prospect more dreadful. Not even death. Alone in a dead house with no one but the ghosts of the past to keep her company. They were all dead now. Or gone. And she was still young. Still too young. The nausea mounted. Soon, too soon, it would be her turn. She rose unsteadily, and with an occasional gorge-vaulting lurch, headed for the outside door.

On the deck she leaned against the rail. The wind blew brisk in her face. The fresh chill air calmed her stomach but not her heart. The picture of her mother standing just so came back to haunt her, and she tried again to imagine what it was like to be all alone on the rolling ship, day after day, torn from everything that was familiar and sent off to meet a stranger who was awaiting someone else. Did she never once fear there might be no one at all there to meet her? To be stranded, penniless, marooned in a strange land and speaking a language no one understood. Better to drown in the wide sea. What was a minute of agony measured against a lifetime of such uncertainty? And her eyes followed a piece of flotsam bobbing listlessly on the water.

Her pulse was pounding as though she had just awakened from a nightmare and could not rid herself of its inexplicable fears. She could see the City approaching, the white towers taller now. At first no more than a city of sandcastles rising on the beach of the Bay, it grew ever larger, tall and impregnable, and she must storm this fortress. Alone and unarmed.

She did not know what she had expected — a city of picturesque ruins; the blackened hulls of great buildings; a few, God-fearing survivors stumbling dazed over hills turned once again to pastures perhaps; but not, certainly, this bustling Babylon glaring white like polished marble in the morning sun. It was beautiful. It was majestic. It was terrifying. From the side of the ship the splash of a slop bucket startled her. A cloud of gulls descended in a rain of pecking beaks. In their sordid, gluttonous cries she could feel her courage ebb.

With a jarring thud the boat bumped against the wharf. The blackened poles bent groaning from the pressure like some living cry of pain. Ropes were hurled, the drawplank thundered down, an iron gate rose, and the crowd pushed its way toward the dark mouth of the Ferry Building and was swallowed whole by the city.

"Pardon, Ma'am. Something the matter?"

The voice she heard was kind, softly, gently solicitous, but the face from which it issued was only a blur. She could distinguish no more through her tears than two eyes, a mouth, a nose, and a hand touching a hat.

With her bag on her lap she sat, unable to move or speak, allowing strangers to see the tears she had always been forced to hide from her family for fear that if she ever gave way the very structure of the family would crumble, that if she ceased to be a pillar there would be nothing left to hold up the house. Well, the house had endured and now there was no one left to hold her up.

"Ma'am?"

She shook her head.

"If you're getting off . . . ." He seemed reluctant to leave her yet impatient to be gone.

"No, please." She shook her head and clutched tighter to the bag on her lap, her shoulders pressed in as if she would shrivel into herself like some mollusk retreating into its shell. "You're very kind, very kind, but please, I just want to be alone. Please. Oh, please, just let me be."

For a moment longer he hovered in the background protectively and then he too was gone, and she was free to weep unregarded.

Why had she come? What had she hoped to find here in this strange city that she could not find in her own backyard? She was too old, certainly, to begin anew. To change her ways. Too old. She marveled at the men, like her father, who had crossed

32

oceans to conquer the unknown. But she was a woman. And the women who had crossed those same oceans were transported as slaves, to be greeted, when they disembarked, with golden rings to circle their fingers. It might better have been soldered to their nose, so that they might be led like cattle into a future of servitude. Galley slaves and production mills. And though she had loved her gentle father far more than she had ever loved her fretful, waspish mother her heart swelled now with resentment at the shame of her mother's lot. Too frail and harried for a moment's peace she had been, until she had fled, finally, into that private world from which they had all been excluded.

The Oakland-bound passengers were already boarding. She took a handkerchief from her coat pocket and wiped her face. It was all right now. Perhaps that was all she had needed. Not a holiday, but a cry. She felt immeasureably better. Steadying herself with short, deep breaths, she stuffed her handkerchief back into her coat pocket and with one hand holding the top of her hat, she readjusted the pins with the other. Both her breathing and her pulse were once again normal. She might still have gotten off, but there was nothing she wanted to see.

On the voyage back she sat in the stern. Alone on the empty upper deck, she watched the City shrink until it was once again a city of sandcastles, a magical phantasm shimmering on the silver bay and no more real than any other place where children go to dream.

Chapter Four

"Just think, our world traveler here might've had him, the pot of gold right in her own backyard, if she hadn't been so busy off chasing rainbows."

Already at forty-two Vincent Woods had the look of an elder statesman. His face and figure were adorned with success: a tilt of the chin more telling than the expensive fabric of his expensively cut suits. He had the sleek, olive skin, the acquiline nose, the thin, sharply defined lips of a Bedouin tribesman, a handsome burnished arrogance that often confused cruelty with strength. His mockery, however, was too familiar to rouse more than a superficial blush; and nursing her secret with the faintest hint of a smile, Belle left her defense to her sister.

"But who would've thought, at his age, he was still in the market? Why, he must be old enough to be her father. Sixty-five if he's a day — wouldn't you say, Belle?"

"And at that still closer to Belle's age than to the spring chicken he's all set to marry. Why, I'll wager she hasn't seen twenty yet."

"Well, she couldn't be much of a catch," Clara snorted. "Any woman who'd marry a man old enough to be her own grandfather. But I still can't place her," she continued, turning to her sister for enlightenment. "Can you, Belle?"

"I think she's the one sits in the pew behind the Lopes. With the kinky hair."

"And the —?" Clara cupped her hands beneath her breasts.

Vince smiled. "You've got the one, all right."

"Sal? Our little Sal? Well, it just goes to show once again, as they always say: There's no fool like an old fool."

Even Belle was ready to concur. "But let's hope she makes her old fool a happy one. He's earned it. Poor Sal," she added, trying to imagine the agonies he must have endured during this second and even more improbable proposal.

"Earned himself an early grave, I should think." Vince's amusement was too vindictive to disguise the personal affront. With more craft than sentiment he had made the heirless, land-rich old bachelor Arnie's godfather only to find his well-laid plans upset by a scheming hussy whose sole claim to business acumen was a pair of bloated mammary glands. And since there was no one else to vent his chagrin upon, he continued to needle his sister-in-law as if she were to blame for allowing Sal's extensive real estate holdings to slip out of family hands. "And just think, Belle, it might all have been yours. Just for the asking. Enough land to keep you warm the rest of your days. And at his age." He chuckled too lewdly for Belle's comfort, "all you'd have had to do is keep the bed warm and the blood circulating. I don't imagine at sixty-five there's much else he'd need warming."

"Vince," Clara cautioned, chuckling in spite of herself. "In front of the children!"

Clara's concern spared Belle from any need to respond to her brother-in-law's ribaldry. "And besides," Clara continued, turning from the ominously silent children back to her sister, "Belle means to come keep house for us. Don't you, Dear?"

The entire evening had been planned to lead up to this question, and Belle, who had been patiently waiting for it, smug in the security of her many secrets, experienced now a thrill of triumph. She had become at last a part of the drama of life. No longer need she submit to a charity that always contrived to en-rich itself. For even the Sunday dinner she had just shared was the single meal of the week which Sarah was not there to pre-pare, and implicit in the invitation was the understanding that Belle would herself prepare it, serve it, and later, with the reluctant assistance of her two nieces, clear the table, wash the dishes, and tidy the kitchen. Nor would she have had it otherwise — for as long as she was still free, when the dinner was finished, her chores done, and the last dish put away, to say her thank-you's and leave, a free agent and nobody's slave.

"No, Clara." Belle shook her head. "I'm not coming to live with you."

"But Belle!" Clara flinched. "You don't mean to say you

intend to live alone in the old house? All by yourself?"

"That's exactly what I do mean."

She was clearly relishing the sensation her refusal had caused.

"But how will you manage? Certainly you don't think, now Mamma's dead, Vince can continue . . . ."

"Spare me, Clara!" With cleaver sharpness she cut her sister short. "Certainly you might have spared me that! When have I ever asked anything for myself? And if I thought for one minute I couldn't take care of myself, I'd be the first to . . . ."

"Take care of yourself!" Clara snorted. "And just how do you propose to do that?"

"With my salary, of course."

"Your salary!"

The sensation was now complete. Even the children — with the notable exception of Lorraine, studying her curls in the mantle mirror and still too intrigued with the wonder of her own person to be truly interested in anyone or anything else — were caught up in the drama of their drab aunt's totally unexpected answer.

"What salary, pray tell?"

Never expansive, Belle's smile remained under control. She would not gloat, though her eyes fairly danced with glee. "Why, from my new job, Clara. What else?"

"Job? What job?" Clara's voice grew shrill. "You don't mean to tell us you'd keep house for someone else wasn't your family. Belle, we won't stand for that, will we, Vince?" Trembling with indignation, she turned to her husband for support. "You want people to think we can't take care of our own?"

"Rest your mind, Clara. Rest your mind." With a composure that merely intensified the sting of her rejection, Belle attempted to mollify her sister. "I don't mean to keep house for anyone. 'Cept myself."

"Well, then —?"

Still Belle insisted upon being coaxed. It was not like her. But then everything about her since their mother's death seemed strange, and Clara wondered whether perhaps virgins did not enter upon The Change earlier than married women.

"My new job at the bank," she answered, and two blotches of red stained her cheeks.

"Bank!" It was Vince's turn to take over the inquisition.

"What bank?"

"Bank of Italy. Hayward Branch."

"Well," he huffed, "no one told *me*."

"I didn't mention you."

"What the hell's that to do with it? Bandini knows who you are, and he damn well knows who I am."

He made no effort to disguise or interpret his anger. He was not given to self-analysis. If he had needed a reason, he would have found it in the very unexpectedness of the announcement. He did not like to be taken by surprise. By all rights he should have been relieved that his dour sister-in-law was not coming to live with them. Yet anger predominated and found its expression in contempt:

"What the hell *you* know about banking?"

"Nothing, 'cept I can count and add and multiply, same as anyone else. And I guess you add money pretty much the same way you add pints and quarts."

Vince sniffed, and reaching into his tobacco cabinet took angry recourse to a cigar. If she had sought his advice, courted his influence, he might have felt different; but she had chosen to act on her own, trading on her relationship without granting him the courtesy that relationship demanded. Not for an instant did he doubt that she had been hired, not as Isabelle Bettencourt, but as Vincent Woods' sister-in-law.

"Mr. Bandini wants someone can speak Portuguese. Some of the oldtimers won't trust their money to anyone can't speak their language. You know that well as I do. He gave me a typewriting machine to keep home till I learn," she continued, feeling oddly like a child forced to justify an ill-considered act. "And a book to teach myself. Why, there's nothing to it, once you memorize the keys."

Vince restricted his answer to a few puffs on his cigar.

"But how'll you get there?" Clara broke in. "Walk in the rain? Five miles each way?"

"No," she answered and once again felt a giddy sense of her own daring. "I mean to drive myself."

"Now I've heard everything." Vince laughed. "Won't nobody be safe, horses or cars, with you on the road, Belle. Glory, Hallelujah! The corpses'll be strewn all the way from here to Hayward. Make Gettysburg look like a school playground.''

"That's all very well, Vince," Clara interrupted. "You can have your little joke, if you like, but what I want to know is what it is she means to drive."

"My new runabout," Belle answered. Already overheated from the intensity of the lights at stage center, she was eager now to have done with the scene as quickly as possible.

"And where, Belle Bettencourt, did you get yourself the money to buy a runabout?"

"Well," she began, less the mistress of herself than she had been all evening, "there was the three hundred dollars from the S.P.R.S.I. for Mamma's insurance policy, and," she continued, her blush searing her cheeks, as with a spasmodic jerk of her head, she lifted her chin as though offering it for a blow: "I sold Pappa's watch and chain.''

"Sold Pappa's watch!" Clara was clearly stunned. "His gold watch? From Lisbon?"

With a curt nod Belle sat forward on the edge of her chair. Her mouth was so dry her words seemed more abrasive than plaintive. "I didn't want to, Clara. I assure you it was the last thing I wanted to do. But you know Pappa left the watch to me as a keepsake. He mighta given it to one of the boys, but he didn't. He gave it to me instead. And I began to think, it wasn't the watch he wanted me to keep so much as his memory. And I didn't need a watch for that, Clara. No," she shook her head, and though her voice remained under control her eyes were moist. She was clumsily pleading for understanding. "I figured I could remember him best living in his house. And there wasn't any other way I coulda done that, Clara.''

"You might've asked us." Still too stunned for rancor, Clara could scarcely bring herself to answer. "We woulda been happy to buy it from you. To keep for Arnie so he'd have something from the Old Country.''

"No, Clara." Unable to bear the hurt in her sister's eyes, Belle rose, shaking her head as she prepared to leave. "You and Vince already done enough for me. I wanted to do this all on my own. So's I wouldn't be beholden to anyone. Even you. So please." She leaned forward to kiss her sister on the cheek and take her hand, but Clara made no attempt to respond. "Try to

39

understand. It wasn't easy." Then standing erect, she added softly, her eyes lost in the depths of the mantle mirror, "Nothing's been easy since Mamma died."

Part II

Chapter One

1

Spared eviction by the ungrateful Belle's blue-stocking rebellion, Sarah heaved a sigh and settled into her position. Her home now. The first real home she'd ever had. Her hours were long and her duties manifold, but she never complained. She seemed, in fact, to enjoy her labors as much as her leisure. She took pleasure in buffing the silver until she could see her own face mirrored in its surface, or ironing dresses the likes of which she herself had never been able to wear. When Lorraine's hair was curled, every ringlet in place, every ruffle of her newly laundered dress stiff with starch, until she stepped glistening like a porcelain doll onto the front lawn, Sarah clasped her hands before her with all the delight of a child playing with her own first doll. And when Clara, majestic in a knotted rope of pearls, smiled at her over the party crystal to compliment her on the excellence of a *creme caramel,* Sarah found the praise sweeter than the pudding.

But sweeter by far than her mistress's praise was Arnie's mere presence. Though he persisted out of his parents' hearing in calling her Frogface, she accepted the term as a lover's endearment, and she was soon indulging the young charmer with a shamelessness even his overindulgent parents might have balked at, stuffing him with treasures secreted from the family larder and the reserves of her own culinary triumphs. It was not long before his pockets as well as his stomach were making demands, and she found herself supplementing his already generous allowance out of her own meagre wages. For she was powerless to resist even the most blatantly insincere appeal of the fudge-brown eyes, as chillingly beautiful as those of a pampered Persian contemplating a mouse trapped beneath its velvet paw. Marvelously variable, they seemed capable of expressing almost any emotion except human sympathy.

His position as only son seemed at this date secure. For despite her buxom hips and full bosom, Clara proved unsuited to childbearing. She had no tolerance for pain. The ordeal, moreover, had been exacerbated by the spectre of her dotty old mother buried beneath a mound of crazy quilts and babbling away like a demented child. After fourteen confinements, who would be fit for anything but a madhouse? *Her* family, Clara was determined, would be fashionably small.

It was an attitude suited to the times and — once she had produced the required son — her husband's inclinations also. Large families were a thing of the past, of an earlier generation that had performed its duty too well. She could not count the times she had been slapped or pinched or screamed at for failing to respond to a name that was not hers, confusion merely adding sting to her harried mother's ire, until they had all finally been rechristened, "You-there." Only Belle as the family workhorse had been granted her own name, and Clara had not felt herself securely "Clara" until she had become Clara Woods. Safely, uniquely, and permanently herself, she determined that *her* children would never be so numerous that each would not have ample room, in her heart as well as her house, to be an individual.

And individuals her children were. But for some reason the smallness of her family did not increase its cohesion. The separate wheels were not parts of a single vehicle. More often than not, they seemed to be moving on different tracks in opposite directions. It was strange, since they had all sprung from the same seed germinated in the same womb, how different they could be, each from the other. They were emotionally, temperamentally, and intellectually, not simply different, but positively antagonistic, the strengths of each destined to affront the weaknesses of the others. Everything she did to draw them together seemed merely to drive the wedge of their differences deeper.

Clasping an injured arm against her chest, her wrists visibly encircled with welts, Louise ran down the stairs howling for justice. The lights from the stained-glass window cloaked her livid flesh in pink and amber. In the winter parlor a cherrywood fire burned in the grate. With a tearful howl, she hurled herself into her mother's arms and unleashed a torrent of words, her indictment stifled as she spied her brother outside in the hall, at the foot of the stairs, waiting, testing the field before he entered, *her* scarf defiantly furled about his neck.

"Look!" She pointed an accusing finger, exposing the arm braceleted with the welts he had inflicted. "There he is. With my scarf. Make him give it to me." Her slender figure quivered with the justice of her cause. "It's mine and not his. Mine! Mine! Mine!"

"Shush, Dear. Shush." Clara laid a cool hand on the inflamed arm. "That's no way to get anything. I can hear you very well without your shouting. Come here, Arnie, Love," she continued, beckoning.

And reluctantly, sliding his feet across the parquet floor in a kind of tauntingly slow tango, Arnie insinuated himself into the room, standing well out of arm's reach and poised for a quick retreat.

"You must play gently with girls," Clara cautioned, reaching out unsuccessfully to catch hold of him and draw him to her, her face slipping effortlessly into its mold of benign omniscience, her voice soothingly gentle, sweetly rational rather than admonitory. "You're a boy, and boys are supposed to protect their sisters. Take care of them. Not hurt them."

But their father had his own rougher principles.

"Let him be, Clara. A boy without spirit's no son of mine. Girl's old enough to take care of herself." He fixed fiercely unsympathetic eyes upon his distraught daughter, who was too shocked by the discovery of her own father's collusion with injustice to protest. "And," he continued, "if there's one thing I like less than a crybaby, it's a tattletale."

So Louise showed him that she did not have to be either a crybaby or a tattletale. Whenever her arm was twisted, her face would flush, her eyes water, but she would not scream. And from an early age the two eldest children were locked in bitter conflict, their every confrontation venomously, hissingly fraught with violence, while little Lorraine, the baby, the perfect image of the mother, a plump, round-faced kewpie-doll of a child, smiled from her neutral corner, too intrigued with the wonder of her own hands to care who was to blame for what.

"Why can't the two of you ever get along? I don't understand,"

43

Clara wept. "We've given you everything, haven't we? Everything money can buy. There isn't anything you could possibly want isn't already yours. So why can't you get along? Like brothers and sisters instead of wild animals." And with her wonderful faculty for not seeing what she was incapable of coping with, she wrung her hands, remembering what never was:

"Why *we* never fought like that when we were children. And there were fourteen of us. Fourteen, mind you. Not three. And we all loved one another. We all managed to get along like brothers and sisters should. Why, when I think how . . ."

And as often as not, the guiding thread led only deeper into the labyrinth.

From the first, Arnie's cruelty seemed almost a part of his physical make-up, the love lavished on him undergoing some perverse chemical metamorphosis to be returned to the world as poison. The more prodigal were life's gifts, the greater the indulgence afforded his every whim, the greater was his need to tyrannize whatever was weaker — insects, animals, sisters. So insignificant were his first victims, so gradual their mounting size, that the phenomenon was seldom noticed, and when noticed, easily dismissed. His face with its glittering, gold-flecked eyes gave the lie to every sinister suggestion. Monsters, after all, did not look like angels.

2

"Damfool Kid!"

That the words had been uttered at all was a measure of the impact the announcement had had — a slip of the tongue somewhat compensated for by the tight control Vince maintained over his face.

Horatio Perkins, principal of the San Oriel Grammar School, removed his pince-nez and massaged the arch of his nose, the sigh he released resonant with weary fatalism.

"I don't believe you! I simply don't believe you." Clara clutched at her knotted strand of pearls for support. "You must be mistaken. Why, my Arnie would never — not in a million years . . ."

"All right, Clara!" Vince cut her short with a sharpness that stunned her. "Let the man have his say." And he fixed their

44

embarrassed visitor with dark almond eyes, the upper lids buried beneath oriental folds. They were clearly eyes that had never been bested in any bargain, and Mr. Perkins felt their full impact.

Already he had made a concession to the family's position in the community by coming to the house rather than sending for them, as he had with the other parents concerned, and he certainly had not, unpleasant though his task was, expected to have the purity of his motive challenged.

"I understand your concern, Mrs. Woods. Mrs. Perkins and I are also parents, and I fully realize, believe me, how painful this must be for you. But certainly not more painful than it is for me."

Clara nodded — in gratitude or confusion, she could not have told which — as she tried desperately to ward off the tears welling in her eyes, her hands still fidgeting with the pearls knotted over her breasts. "Yes, yes, I didn't mean . . ." She was all aflutter, her instincts as a hostess warring with her instincts as a mother. "Can I get you something? A cup of coffee? Tea? A drop of port?" Anything to delay what she had not the courage to hear.

"The man isn't thirsty, Clara, or he would have gone to Costa's, stead of coming here."

So divorced from all affection were his words and manner so lacking in tenderness, she felt herself momentarily more frightened by his rebuff than horrified by her son's atrocity.

"No, thank you, Mrs. Woods. I think we'd best get on with the matter at hand."

And too intimidated to utter another word, Clara responded with a frozen smile.

"As I was saying," Mr. Perkins continued, turning once more to his host and swallowing hard, his composure shaken by Vince's formidable demeanor. The argument was clearly, and most regrettably, being reduced to a contest of wills instead of issues. But after a lifetime spent in the defense of virtue, he had long since steeled himself to find principle soiled by expediency and even clearly defined black-and-white issues, such as the one at hand, meld into ambiguous grays. "What so upset the faculty — and I may say, they are behind me one hundred per cent —"

It was a clever ploy, but Vince Woods was not about to be put off by such words as "faculty"; a bunch of school teachers was a bunch of school teachers, no matter what one chose to call them. Since he had on his own, with very little aid from them and their like — having left school after the sixth grade — attained a fair degree of success, he had come to look upon them with good-natured scorn — which, nevertheless, in no way influenced his determination to see that his children received the formal education denied him.

"A hundred per cent of four is still only four, Mr. Perkins. No matter how you count it."

"Yes . . ." Mr. Perkins continued, the tips of his ears blushing scarlet. It was clearly going to be worse, much worse, than he had anticipated. "As I was saying, we all — the four teachers and I, if you will — agree that what was so terrible was not just the cruelty itself — bad as that was, I'm sure you'll admit . . ."

But Vince Woods was not about to admit anything. So unyielding was his gaze that Mr. Perkins felt compelled to repeat the charges:

"Pouring kerosene over a live animal and then setting it afire. A dog, Mr. Woods! A defenseless dog! In front of the entire student body. Subjecting innocent eyes to such an exhibition of horror! Well, what more need I say!"

Despite the blow, Vince Woods remained impassively in command of himself. There was none of the Anglo Saxon sentimentality in his approach to animals. In his eyes they were merely the instruments and servants of man. If his horses were handsome as well as sturdy, it was only because it was nature's law that form and function, beauty and strength, should go hand in hand. The boy's little joke was, he was quite prepared to admit, in bad taste, but that was hardly cause to blow it all out of proportion. A dog, after all, was still only a dog.

It was Clara who withered before the brutal onslaught. Her flushed and swelling flesh strained against the constriction of her corset, until she felt positively giddy. Drawing a handkerchief from her bosom, she pressed it against her mouth and attempted to stifle the involuntary sobs, but their force was too great to contain. Try as she would she could not connect this cruel man's cruel words with her son, whom she had — such a short time before, it seemed a matter of days rather than years — led to

46

school for the first time, curled and cuffed, and wearing, she remembered as if it had been yesterday, a blue polka dot cravat. A regular little prince. So pretty she could scarcely contain her pride. Only to be set amid the throngs of calico and denim, like any ordinary little boy. A Gouldian finch among the sparrows. Her heart had ached for him. And yet, what was it she could have done? It was the taunting sparrows, naturally, who had won. And so soon. The very first week he had come home, his curls mutilated by his own hand. And as the number of torn poplin suits and linen shirts mounted, he had been allowed, finally, like all the rest, to wear open collars and patched overalls. Like all the rest. So many peas in a pod.

"Would it have been something less had it been a cat, Mr. Perkins?"

Vince's wry thrust threw his adversary momentarily off balance.

"A cat, Mr. Woods? No . . . no, of course not." Mr. Perkins grew flustered, fearful that his iron-clad case was in danger of melting away because of his own inept presentation. "A cat or a dog is immaterial. I said a dog simply because it happened to *be* a dog — a favorite of the children, I might add," he continued, further entangling himself in sentiment, which he knew very well could touch only the mother and thus serve further to harden the paternal adversary. Yet swept up in the rhythm of his own speech, he could not keep the discussion hard on center. "A rather unattractive mongrel they had, as children are wont to do, taken a fancy to. They called him Jimbo, I believe. So you might say it was a kind of school pet. A mascot of sorts."

"I can't see, Mr. Perkins, that the dog's name has any bearing. One way or the other."

Once again the principal removed his prince-nez, and with his eyes closed, he rubbed the arch of his nose.

'As I was saying," he continued, his voice tremulous with both the righteousness of his cause and his own inadequacy to expound it, "What so shocked us was not the cruel act itself, bad as that was, but the fact that it was planned. Planned and then coldly carried out. An execution, Mr. Woods. With a last meal and all . . ."

Vince merely smiled, as if something in the quality of the

boy's imagination, its thoroughness, perhaps, had struck a sensitive chord: a constricted, inward smile not intended for public viewing.

Unable to bear more, Clara rose and walked to the window, keeping her back to the room so that her tears might flow freely and unobserved. She could not order her thoughts. Even her emotions she was at a loss to define. Revulsion, horror, shame, fear, or simply an uneasy, threatened credulity — it didn't matter; she wanted to have done with this cruel scene as quickly as possible.

Why she wondered, gazing through the curtains (they were in need of washing; she must tell Sarah in the morning), why was this unpleasant man so determined to upset her? What had she ever done to him that he should barge into the very sanctuary of her home and raise such havoc with her world? "Of course he didn't act alone," he was saying, and the quality of his voice, at once groveling and condescending, so desperate to maintain a middle course between tolerance and vindictiveness that it vacillated weakly, offended her.

"I don't like to use the term 'gang,' but . . ."

"Then by all means don't use it," Vince responded icily.

Gang, indeed! Clara's shock was fast giving way to a defensive anger. It just went to show how the simplest ideas and actions could be twisted around in a clever man's hands. A sorry lot they were, certainly, but what chance of real companionship did the likes of San Oriel offer anyone with Arnie's abilities and background? Slim pickings, she'd call them.

"Along with your Arnold," Mr. Perkins continued, "there was Manuel Serpa — I believe you know the family — Ignazio Oliviera, and a Ken Yamamura."

For the first time Vince came close to losing his composure. as he pounced too eagerly on the last name.

"You see, Clara! Haven't I told you!" The force of his words lifted him from his seat. "How many times have I told you: that's what comes of hanging around Japs?" And sinking back into his easy chair a different man, renewed and spoiling for combat, he reached into the lamp table cabinet for a cigar, rolling and sniffing several before settling upon one. The ostentatious display and his refusal to offer the box to his visitor a deliberate rebuff.

Grateful that her husband had, after so severely shutting her out, once again brought her back into the discussion, Clara tearfully offered her verification, shaking her head in awed admiration at the wonderful simplicity of the answer: that strange little Jap boy whose father's greenhouses were just beginning to dot the delta of the creek. It was an answer so obvious she could not imagine why they had been so long arriving at it.

"It's not natural; that's what I've always said. It's just not natural. Why, if God had meant us all to mix like that, He wouldn't have been to such pains separating us into so many different continents, now would He?"

"I might've known that Jap kid was behind it," Vince continued, once again cutting his wife short, but so pleased with himself as he lit his cigar that he blessed her with a benevolent smile. "Why, the whole thing reeks of the Yellow Peril. Fancy tortures and the like. What else have the Chinks ever been noted for? Not that my Arnie's any angel, mind you. Wouldn't have him one if I could. But . . .;

"Of course," Mr. Perkins interrupted, a bit queasy at the turn the discussion was taking and not wishing to be considered in any way derelict in the performance of his duties, "the idea did occur to me. Unfortunately your boy denies that Ken was the instigator and has — and for this I must give him credit — quite manfully taken full responsibility upon himself."

"Certainly he denies it." Clara resumed her seat, her tears mastered. "He's afraid of him. Anyone who could do a thing like *that!* Why, there's no telling what he'd be capable of." And she shuddered at the prospect.

"That seems unlikely." Mr. Perkins faltered, not altogether unwilling at this juncture to be led into their corner, if only he might be led with honor. "Anyone his size — why the boy's positively diminutive."

"Size!" Vince snorted. "What's size to do with it? May I remind you, Mr. Perkins — though I shouldn't have to, since you're an educated man — that Portugal, tiny Portugal, once ruled half the world. So don't talk to me about size." And with that bit of chauvinistic bombast, he sank back into his chair, puffing furiously.

"But in the absence of any evidence . . . as long as your boy chooses not — if I may use the expression — to become a witness for the prosecution, I have no alternative but to expel them all. For the remainder of the term," he hastily added, hopeful that the foreseeable termination of the sentence might lessen its impact.

It was effort wasted.

"Now just one second, Mr. Perkins. Just one second there. Before you take a step you may live to regret," Vince added ominously, as he carefully laid his cigar in the ashtray, and braced on the arms of his chair, leaned forward.

All too conscious that he was being manipulated as well as threatened, and for nothing more dishonorable than the performance of his duty, Mr. Perkins blushed.

"I suppose you're aware who it is pays your salary?"

"My salary? I'm not sure I see — why, the school district, of course," Mr. Perkins answered with more dignity than his pittance warranted.

"And where, Mr. Perkins, may I ask, does the school district get the money to pay you?"

"Why, from the taxpayers, of course. But really, I don't see . . ."

"And I suppose you are also aware, Mr. Perkins, who pays a considerable portion of the taxes in this district?" He paused to let his words sink in. "Yes, Mr. Perkins. And if you think for one minute that I intend to sit back and allow myself to be bled white and then be told my only son, my own flesh and blood, can't attend the school my taxes have built — well, you've got another think coming, Mr. Perkins. You've got another think coming."

"But certainly you don't condone —?"

"Condone? Nobody's condoning anything," Vince continued, rising to terminate the discussion." The Jap kid's clearly to blame, and tomorrow you'll have, as you put it, your witness for the prosecution. Rest assured of that, Mr. Perkins."

Mr. Perkins also rose, taking his hat from the table, his damp fingers leaving their imprint on the stiff brim. "Far be it from me to tell you how to raise your own children, Mr. Woods," he ventured, his face an agonizing mask of conflicting emotions, "but I hardly think that's going to do the boy any good. To allow him to shift the blame . . ."

50

"Now, now, you just let me worry about that, why don't you." His smile positively unctuous, Vince placed his hand on Mr. Perkins shoulder. "You've already got your hands full as it is. A whole schoolful of little demons. Don't envy you for a minute. No sirree, not for a minute. Clara," he continued, with his arm by now conspiratorially across the full breadth of the principal's shoulders, "you go find the boy and take him up to his room. I'll see Mr. Perkins here out."

3

Clara did not waste a second of the time allotted between her husband's departure and his return. She had no difficulty locating Arnie. As she suspected, he had been eavesdropping in the winter parlor, where she found him crouched behind a potted palm. Meek and silent he followed her up the stairs and into the sanctuary of the parental bathroom. The stained-glass skylight dappled them like two penitents with petals fallen from some cathedral rose window. Although he had only once in his twelve years felt the sting of his father's violence, he had witnessed enough to know how the old man reacted to all opposition, how suddenly, without any more warning than a flash from the dark eyes, he could change from generous friend to implacable foe, and anyone who attempted to cross him was left shattered against the stonewall of his will.

Offering no resistance to his mother's ministrations, Arnie submitted with a grim wince to the comb run roughshod through his tangled hair and the damp cloth, as coarse as sandpaper, rubbed so hastily over his features that an outside border of dirt still framed the shining interior. A quick glance in the mirror momentarily bolstered his courage. He was not, after all, a hired hand, an illiterate wetback to be bruted about by every tinhorn foreman. But not even a lifetime of indulgence could put him entirely at his ease.

Uneasiness grew to apprehension as his father returned, a long thin branch cut from an apricot tree carried at his side like a riding crop. Arnie studied it, and though his mind was boggled by the sheer lack of precedence, the sour taste of fear scorched his throat. He snuggled against the protective shelter of his mother's skirt.

With a heavy sigh, as though he might be settling down for the afternoon and meant to make himself comfortable, Vince sat on the maple rocking chair and began nonchalantly to peel the reddish bark from the branch, exposing the pale yellow flesh beneath. The smile on his face was deceptively warm and far from encouraging. The smile of a cat tempting a canary to come out of his cage to play. Arnie responded by burying himself even deeper in his mother's skirts.

"Hear that Jap kid's been getting you into trouble at school," his father began as he reached over to drop the bark peelings into the wastebasket beside the maple desk. Then, as the smile grew broader, a malicious twinkle dancing in his eyes, he ran his hand along the slick length of the branch, testing its flexibility by drawing down the tips to form a lopsided O.

"Gee, Pa, who was it told you that whopper?"

Arnie shifted his footing in response to his mother's nudge.

"Mr. Perkins just been here — hasn't he, Clara? — telling us all about your little escapade. How that Jap friend of yours forced you to help him set some damfool dog afire."

"He's a liar," Arnie spat out, then thinking belligerence was perhaps the wrong tack, he termpered his outburst with a more thoughtful, "if he said that."

The switch sliced the air with such suddenness it could be heard with greater clarity than it could be seen, catching Arnie so unexpectedly across the calves that both mother and child yelped as they jumped, their backward leap halted by the wall.

"Vince!" Clara called out, appalled at the sudden violent turn; but ignoring his wife, Vince directed his words to his son:

"Don't interrupt your pa while he's talking. Understand?"

Arnie's face twitched, his eyes liquid bright. "But Ken ain't no more to blame than I was," he ventured gamely.

"Ain't?" Again the switch cut a neat slice out of the air and Arnie yelped. "Here we've gone to all the trouble sending you to school and you're still using ain't like any Mexican cherry-picker. Or Jap florist," he added significantly. "I want to hear you tell the truth and I want to hear you tell it in proper English. Do you understand?" And he drew the switch through his clenched fist to dot the question.

52

"Please, Dear." Clara's voice was shaking. "Don't try to save him. He isn't worth it. Believe me. Any boy who'd do a thing like that — why he just isn't worth it."

"You want me to tell a lie?" He turned to her, his question echoed in his eyes, but before he could read her answer in her face, the switch cut across his legs for the third time. "Yie!" he yelled.

"Careful, Vince. Please!" Clara implored. "You're being too rough with the boy."

"Rough?" He smiled, his face still deceptively benign. "I've only just begun, Clara. Now, Sonny Boy," he continued, letting his eyes fall once more upon his son, "you listen to me. You're going to school tomorrow, understand? And you're going to tell Mr. Perkins in no uncertain terms how your little Jap friend — whatever his name is — made you — understand? *made* you — play that damnfool trick."

"I can't, Pa." Terrified as he was, he was not about to sacrifice his most loyal disciple.

"Can't?" Again the switch cut across the legs, this time catching a protective hand as well. "I don't understand *can't*."

"But geeze, Pa," Arnie pleaded, "he's the best friend I got."

The benign mask fell and in an instant Vince was on his feet, propelled by the rock of his chair, his expression distorted by the explosive force of his words:

"What you mean the best friend you got — huh! Tell me! A Jap! What the hell you think I'm raising? Tell me that! A Jap your best friend! Vince Woods' boy's best friend a goddamn, pintsize, banty-legged Jap! What're you trying to do, make a fool out of me? Is that what you're after? Make a fool out of your old man? You want him to be the laughing-stock of the whole damn countryside? If that what you're after? Is it? Well, if it is, you're in for a big surprise, Sonny Boy. Because Vince Woods isn't about to let you or anyone else make a goddamn fool out of him."

He had his son by the collar now, lifted off the floor, Clara pleading hysterically. It was not a solution she longed for so much as a return to order, to the loving harmony that was now crashing down about her. "Please. Please, Vince! No more! The boy's been punished enough. O, my God! No more!"

Arnie's trousers were ripped open and yanked down, bunched about his ankles, his dimpled buttocks thrust onto the bed so that he seemed, in his nakedness, more than ever her little boy, her baby.

"Vince, no!" she implored, holding back his arm. But without so much as a glance at her, he shouted, "get yourself out of here, Clara," and brushed her aside. Stumbling, she fell against the wall.

"I promise you, you're not going to like this," he added, his voice stern but still solicitous for her welfare. "And I'd advise you to leave before the real fireworks start — because the boy's going to get something he's been asking for all these years." And without further ado, with a vehemence trebled by the years of easy license and laughing tolerance, he laid a red welt across one honey-colored cheek to a duet of screams.

"Clara!" he called out, his own face almost as red as the welt left by the switch. "I warn you: leave the room!"

She dared no longer disobey. Never before had she seen him like this, his voice raised to her, brushing her aside as if she were a total stranger. Her own husband. But experience told her there would be no stopping him now when even a man as gentle and soft-spoken as her father could collapse, exhausted from whipping a defiant son, his breath labored, his face purple with rage. And what she was powerless to prevent she certainly did not want to witness.

No longer could she tell who it was deserved her profoundest loyalty. Her son, perhaps, since he was the weaker, and her own weak flesh called out to his suffering, his screams piercing her to the heart as she fled the room.

In the hall outside she ran headlong into her daughters. Too frightened to speak but too fascinated to flee, Lorraine cowered in the sewing room doorway. Behind her a more sombre Louise struggled to hide all trace of the conflicting emotions warring within her, for the joy of revenge had been so startled by the savageness of its form that her gloating was lost in revulsion. Only two bonfire burning in her cheeks gave any hint of the struggle taking place behind the painted mask of her face.

Clara halted momentarily, but her own tears merely compounded the confusion, added terror to Lorraine's fright and guilt to Louise's revenge. Beyond the reach of all comfort, she was powerless to give any, and without so much as a word of reassurance, too distraught even to attempt speech, she fled to her room.

A gentle breeze billowed the curtains and the room was flooded with the perfume of blossoming orchards so heady it made her giddy. She slammed the windows closed and shut out the light by drawing the drapes. Then throwing herself onto the bed, she attempted with her hands pressed against her ears to muffle the cries reverberating through the house. But like slivers of glass, they pierced the barriers of flesh and bone and continued to find their way to her heart. Our Lady of Sorrows. Every mother's lot. She could not bear the pain another instant. With her head buried beneath a pillow she attempted to drown out all sound, with her own voice crying aloud to heaven, to Sweet, Sweet Jesus, her tearful prayer, so that she would not have to listen, would not be able to hear, until suddenly she became conscious that there was no longer anything not to listen to, that she had somehow reached the calm at the heart of every storm.

An ominous silence as alive as the screams had once been filled the house. Suddenly a door slammed, too loudly to bode any good, but the screams had been stilled and the faint muffled sobbing that now took their place would soon die of its own accord. She could hear her husband run down the stairs, too fast for a man of his years and weight. The outside door slammed, so hard it shook the entire house. A settling silence, then the garage door banged open and soon she could hear the putt-putt of the Model T. Out the driveway, over the bridge, and far away.

The nightmare was finished and she was awake. For a moment she lay, arms at her side, as still as a corpse, listening, a dry ghostly whimpering. The tearful exhaustion that follows pain. It was over. She was still alive.

She got up and smoothing away the wrinkles of her dress she returned to Arnie's room. Outside, she stood for a minute with her ear pressed against the door. She could hear a dull droning, but she could not tell whether the sound came from the room itself or her own ringing head. She tapped lightly before entering, softly calling his name. The hum stopped the instant she stepped inside the room. He was lying on the bed, face down, hushed and motionless, his trousers still down and his buttocks — she let out a cry at the sight of them — fretted with red welts. She moved quickly to the bed. Sitting beside him and leaning over him, she pressed her cheek against his back.

"There, there," she said, tears of relief washing her cheeks, "it's going to be all right. Everything's going to be all right."

"Without answering or turning to face her, he struggled to pull up his undershorts, to cover his nakedness and the scars of his shame.

"Your poor daddy —" She helped him on with his trousers. "I don't know what got into him. I've never seen him like that before. Never. But you mustn't cross him, Dear. He's older and knows what's best for you. So I hope," she added, sitting upright, her whole being keyed to his answer, "you promised what he asked."

Still without looking at her, he shook his head, and there was, she could see, simply in the set of his shoulder, a terrible pride in his resistance, as if there had been something grand in it, something she would never be able to understand, and she knew then that she was only touching him, not holding him, that he was no longer a baby, that something fine and beautiful between them, something she had not shared with her daughters or her husband or anyone else in the entire world was forever gone.

"Oh, Darling!" she cried, once more throwing herself upon him, but it was an empty gesture. He remained unresponsive, rejecting her by his silence as perversely as he had rejected his father's plea.

"Why, oh, why, can't you do as he asks? Why? After all he's done for you! It seems so little to ask. So little."

"You want me to lie?" Turning over, he confronted her with an accusing, tear-streaked face, his eyes, flaming with resentment, searing through her, and suddenly she realized he was confronting her — oh, so unfairly! — with some terrible choice, a choice she had no right, if she could, to make.

"You want me to tell a lie," he repeated and this time there was not even the faintest hope that he might hear his accusation denied.

"I don't know what you're talking about." Her voice remote, her eyes dull, she was no longer looking at him, but through him, at another child, younger, sweeter, a different child altogether, one forever dead, an angel now to be cherished in her memory. "How can telling him that someone else planted such poisonous thoughts in your mind be lying? How? Tell me."

Unable to bear the look in his eyes, she smoothed back his hair, fussing with his person, wiping his tears, arranging his collar, anything to avoid the intensity of his gaze.

"Cause it was *my* idea, that's why. The whole thing was my idea. And nobody else's."

"I don't understand you, Arnie." She shook her head, rising as if she had not heard him. "A boy should obey his father. That much I know. But of course I'm not an educated woman. I haven't had all the advantages we've tried so hard to give you and the girls, so I don't suppose I understand anything. Just an ignorant country girl."

She rose, and bending before the dresser mirror to preen her hair, she could feel his eyes still intent upon her.

"Such a headache you've all given me!"

She turned to him, smiling a sad, wistful, wet-eyed smile that filtered him through a blur of tears and reduced his agony to the picturesque: a young boy learning the painful lesson of growing up.

"But life isn't just a bed of roses. And you have to learn that sometime. There's pain as well as pleasure — "

Empty words.

"Oh, dear, I don't know." She shook her head, sadly, her eyes slipping past him, out the window to an afternoon sky bleached of all color. "I just don't know."

Chapter Two

1

Oh how she dreamed of a world in which voices were never raised, tears were never shed, and every frown could be conquered with a smile! She was not made for suffocating fires of passion. Even unhooked, her corset was strangling her. Once in her room she stepped out of it and into a flowered kimono. But how she had changed! And every change for the worse! Her waist fairly drowned in the encroaching fat, her breasts sagged, her skin, once so firmly golden thinly translucent. And her thighs — like polished alabaster they had been — marred with a spiderweb of purple veins. But after three children — well, considering what they had taken out of her, wonder was she had survived at all. Nursing them with her own life's blood. And what was her reward but pain and anguish?

And fat.

But she could not bear to look, and hiding her nakedness in the formless fall of flowered silk, she moved from the mirror to the bed. She must do something before it was too late, reach out and catch hold of herself, slow the dismal slide into dowdy middle age. Already past thirty. Well past. It had tolled, that terrible birthday, like the deathknell of her youth. And every day since she had become ever more conscious of time bearing down upon her, the years breathing at her back. And now her own breath came only with effort. She was not strong. She had been born with no more than a tissue-thin layer of skin to armor her nerves against the blows and buffets of life. Was it any wonder they had been torn asunder?

"Louise," she called into the hall. "Bring Mamma the box of aspirin powders, will you."

Her head was pounding so, every pulse beat hammering another nail into her flesh.

"Where is it?"

"And just where do you think it would be?" she snapped, her voice shrill with a sudden, stifling irritation, a flush of blood swelling at her throat, choking her so that the words were spat out like poison. "In the medicine cabinet, silly girl. Where else would Mother keep her medicine?"

"All right, I found it, Mamma. In the sewing room."

A sweeter, softer, more delicate version of Arnie, Louise was just as tall as her brother, with arms and legs she seemed not yet accustomed to, long tapering fingers and a fragile frame that was, despite its appearance, both strong and resilient. Her breasts, already at fourteen, were those of a woman, but borne furtively, hidden in the slump of her shoulders. Her hair was held taut off the forehead by a huge taffeta ribbon inappropriately girlish, the bow on the side over the right ear accentuating the almost perfect oval. It was, except for the dark brooding eyes, which now studied her mother with more curiosity than affection, a face of Murillo-like sweetness. Only in her mother's presence did her gaze ever vacillate, a pseudo-shyness founded on the knowledge that no matter what she did or said she would never be able to make up for the long-ago disappointment of having been born a girl.

"And just how do you expect me to swallow them?" Every nerve end smarting, Clara took the box and removed two paper wrappers. "Sometimes, I declare, you act as if you didn't have a brain in your head. Can't you ever, just for once, get something right the first time?"

Without altering her expression, the two small brushfires in her cheeks flaring, Louise waited passively for her mother to finish before she ran out of the room. In an instant she was back with a glass of water. In her eagerness to be done with her duties, she tripped over a pair of slippers beside the bed and splashed her mother's kimono.

"Clumsy girl!" Clara grabbed the glass, brushing aside the girl's hand with a gesture half intended as a slap, and in her haste spilled ever more water.

From behind a mask of perfect serenity Louise watched her mother down her powders, her feelings too tepid for hate. That was an emotion reserved exclusively for her brother, at whom she could never look without a sneer flaring her nostrils. She was simply resigned to reality. Only recently had she made what proved perhaps the two most devastating discoveries of her young life: first, that her mother did not love her, but far, far worse was the inescapable conclusion that her mother was herself not worthy of love: a silly, vain, and selfish woman. An since she was not prepared to apply for her parent's affection by pandering to her vanity or indulging her silliness, Louise was reconciled to remaining unloved.

"All right, now, you can leave Mother alone. She wants to rest," Clara continued, unconsciously. "You can take Lorraine outside with you, but don't play too close to the house. Mother has such a headache. You might," she continued, handing the empty glass back and rewarding her daughter with a wan smile, "run over to see Aunt Belle. Only get me the comforter first, like a good girl. From the closet shelf. And send Sarah up to me before you leave."

Silent, docile, and unsmiling, Louise obliged, covering her mother's legs with a satin comforter.

"Thank you, Dear. Now you can kiss Mother on the cheek before you go."

No one would have been more shocked than Clara herself had anyone suggested there was no bond of love uniting them as they both acted out their charade. The young girl bent forward and planted a formal kiss on her mother's cheek, and then in the doorway turned just as impassively to receive her final instructions.

"Keep an eye on Lorraine. And please, Dear, whatever you do, don't let your aunt feed her anything. You know what a problem it is to get the child to eat what she should. She'll only play with her dinner . . . after Sarah's been to such pains . . . Well?" Her face once again fretted with annoyance. "What're you waiting for?"

"For you to finish, Mamma."

"Well, I'm quite finished. Run along, run alone. And don't forget to send Sarah up."

And lying back, Clara sighed, studying the room as she waited for the aspirin to take effect. How shabby it was becoming! Like her own figure, showing its age. And the color. She'd never like it. But as usual — it was fast becoming the story of

61

her life — always thinking of others, she had allowed her taste to be compromised by expediency. And where did all the sacrifice lead but to sagging breasts and purple thighs! Well, it was time she began thinking of herself for a change. Something gay was what the room needed. Something light. A floral design, perhaps. Pinks and blues. But why, she wondered, biting her lip to stifle the sob caught in her throat, did they have to grow up? Smelling like the morning dew his skin as soft as rose petals. Like a little fish, his mouth sucking the air before the teasingly withheld nipple, so eager the hungry latch of his lips always made her momentarily giddy, a wet warmth stealing over her. But she mustn't think of that. Of the dead past.

An alabaster lamp, perhaps, to mute the evening light and restore to her flesh its lost lustre. Illusion. It was a woman's right. No, her duty. And down with the velvet drapes. Dust-catchers fit for an undertaker's. Satin or taffeta . . .

"Oh, Sarah, Sarah, you can't imagine what I've been through!" The tears welled at the sight of Sarah coming into the room, her blessedly homely face and figure a caricature of concern.

"Imagine? I didn't have to imagine. I could hear. Every shriek and groan of it I could hear all the way down to the kitchen pantry frightening the mice back into their holes."

"It's not like him, Sarah. He isn't like that. You know that as well as I do. Why, he can be as gentle . . ." Her eyes went soft with the memory, her body weak, suddenly, not with pain, but desire, to be held and comforted and entered, her old flesh rocked back to joy and youth with the gentle swing of his gentle lust. "You'd think he was cradling a newborn baby. Why . . ." She smiled, a blush shining through her tears.

"Oh, you don't have to tell me, all the time I've been here, I can see how he treats you: like a queen. I can see it."

"It's true, Sarah, he does. A queen. He's never raised his voice to me before. Never."

"And all that passion wasted," Sarah shook her head, a broad lascivious glint momentarily taking command of her face. "But it's over now. And you can be sure of one thing, the boy's no worse off for it. Make a man out of him, it will. Why, he's had it too soft all these years, what with you and me and everybody else under God's heaven spoiling him the way we do. Not that you or anyone else could help it, and far be it from me to tell you, his own mother, how to say no to such an angel face as his. Why, he'd squeeze tears out of a turnip, he would. Nosirree, there's no woman alive wouldn't spoil the pretty likes of him."

"Go to him, Sarah. See if you can find him. I heard him running down the stairs and out the sunporch door. Just a few minutes ago. Try to find him and see if you can make him understand — because he won't listen to his own mother — that sometimes, for his own good — and it doesn't mean his father doesn't love him. His own flesh and blood!"

"Oh, you don't have to tell me, Mrs. Woods. You don't have to tell me. But first, let me just freshen his own sweet mother up a little. Wash those tears away and fluff those pillows. Why, you can't have Mr. Woods coming home and finding his honey-girl looking like this, with cheeks all stained and hair every which way . . ."

And without once interrupting the flow of words, Sarah washed away the last traces of tears, freshened the bed, and brushed her mistress's hair, leaving the drapes drawn so that her husband might return to find his aging Venus asleep on a bed of flowered silk, her head sunk in swan's down and linen, the cruel traceries of time blunted by the kind afternoon shadows, the theatre of her misery so dimly lit that he would be forced to recreate her once again out of his own best memories.

2

"What do *you* want?"

Panting from the climb, Sarah did not immediately answer, but smiling, surveyed the loft and the slim figure of a boy lying face down on a loose pile of hay against the far wall. The luminous outline of the locked hatch stood out like a naked bulb, white hot, in the shadows. The only other light came from the stalls below, a dim radiance seeping up on the musky odors of horseflesh and manure. A single pulley and hook hung from the central rafter, the rope knotted about a supporting pole. Nearby, the handle of a pitchfork stuck out of a wired bale like a tilted flagpole.

Clutching a bandana-wrapped bundle in one hand, Sarah

struggled with grunting gracelessness onto the loft floor, then, brushing her skirt, she sank onto a pile of hay beside the young boy with sufficient force to set off a tiny firecracker of a fart.

"Whoops!" Despite his determination to resist all beguilement, Arnie giggled. "You stink. Worse'n ever."

"Well, that's better'n howling like the devil himself, as I got wind of not so long ago I've had time to forget. Rattling every pan in the pantry. Why, it sounded like a buncha Spanish dancers having some kinda contest to see who could shake the plaster loose first."

He stifled his giggle.

"Besides," she continued, "I got something here'll soon sweeten up the air." And untying the knot of her bandana, she carefully laid out the four corners to expose a jar and a package wrapped in wax paper cover from a large square, which she held hidden from his view.

"Bet your boots you can't guess what this is."

"Don't have any boots."

"But you do have a sweet tooth, don't you? And who knows better than Frogface herself? Warts and all won't make this taste any less sweet. Just look at it, will you." And she peeled away the wax paper to reveal her prize. "An inch of buttercream frosting. And your favorite — banana-nut."

Shifting himself gingerly onto his side, Arnie reached out silently for the proffered cake.

But Sarah drew back her hand and the gift.

"Can't you even so much as say, 'Thank you, Frogface, for thinking about me in my hour of need'?"

The hand fell and the face hardened, the lips clamped shut. The fluster of bantam defiance was more than Sarah could bear, and she relented, handing him the cake. He accepted it with an animal grunt and quickly devoured every last crumb — thanks enough for Sarah.

"Gonna leave this stinking hole," he mumbled as he crumpled the wax paper into a ball. "Run away." And he tossed the ball into one of the open traps leading to the stalls below. "Maybe go as far as Frisco. And never come back."

"Not even to see old Frogface?"

"For *nothing*. I don't ever wanna set eyes on this stinking old

64

hicktown again. What's that you got?'' he asked, his eyes intent upon the jar in her hands as she sat back on her haunches, her own eyes never for an instant leaving him.

"Some skin cream to take the sting away.''

"How you know it stings?''

A raucous laugh shook her back and forth on her haunches like a hobbyhorse.

"You think you're the first one's ever felt the sting of a switch? Oh, sweet honeyboy, if I could tell you the number a times my buns been beaten raw, you wouldn't believe me. All my pa ever needed to get his whipping hand itchen was a few drops a booze. And I can tell you, sure as you're alive, there wasn't a night of his life he ever went to bed without a drop a something. He woulda drunk the coal oil if there was nothing else.''

Smiling, she uncapped the jar, setting the cover on the floor beside her.

"Well?'' She waited with open jar in hand.

"Well's a hole in the ground.''

"It ain't gonna do no good to cream your trousers. Least ways, I don't imagine that's where the sting is.''

Suddenly alert to her intentions, he wiggled away from her.

"You think I'm gonna take my trousers off in front of you, you're crazy.''

Again the raucous laugh shook her. "Oh, sweet honeyboy! What you think you got to hide's so precious your Frogface can't have a look at it? Nothing you got down there's gonna surprise me one bit, I can tell you, so if you wanna go on stinging, well, you just go right on stinging. Does it hurt real bad?'' Her laugh suddenly swallowed in the contours of her concern, she reached out to touch him.

"Jesus, don't!'' He rolled over on his side.

"See.'' She reached out to unbutton the fly conveniently positioned by his turn. "It does hurt.''

And turning this time to hide the bewildering evidence of his excitement, he was forced to display his bruised buttocks.

"My, my, he did give it to you, didn't he?'' she commiserated as she slipped off his trousers and shorts, leaving him without any defense but to bury his face in a mound of hay. "Well,

65

this'll make it feel nice and cool.''

He squirmed at the first touch of her hand, his shrill yelp ringing from the rafters, but as she continued, barely brushing the tips of her greased fingers over his burning flesh, the groans grew softer, deeper, so gradually it was impossible to tell when precisely the transition took place and the groans of pain became moans of pleasure, the fire from his wounds sinking deeper into some mysterious center of his being.

She giggled softly at the slight lift of his buttocks, rising with the magnet pull of her hand to meet her touch half way. "Well, well,'' she whispered, her own voice deeper as softly caressing as her touch and teasingly suggestive.

The sound of a motor sputtering into the yard brought their idyl to a momentary halt.

"Jesus! The old man!'' His ears alert, head cocked, Arnie lifted his shoulders.

"Shhhhh!'' she whispered, sweeping him up in her arms and drawing him to her as the door of the old carriage entrance rolled open on its iron pulleys, shaking the entire barn as it clanged to a thundering halt. She held him, too surprised to protest, crushed against her while they waited for the car to drive in and the door to close once again. She loosened her blouse and snuggled his head against the pillow of her bare breasts. And before the door had slammed shut and they could hear the footsteps move across the graveled yard toward the backdoor, she had somehow contrived, without once letting go of him, to slip entirely free of her dress. Caught by surprise, as if the earth beneath him had suddenly opened and he had fallen into a sea of warm flesh, he seemed to be swallowed up by her enormous body, drowning in liquid fire. A burst of flame and then darkness, descending as softly as a fall of ashes, bringing with it a peace beyond dreaming. An infant rocked gently to sleep with the silken touch of skin against skin, his head cushioned on a pillow of flesh, he lay beyond reach of all harm, curled in the cradle of her protective arm.

3

She could feel rather than see his face suffused with a radiant

66

smile dispelling the shadow, three dozen pink carnations in his hand smelling fresh as peppermint as he sat on the edge of the bed, his old familiar self again, just as though he had not only a short while before loosed the devil in himself and torn her heart and nerves to shreds.

Tearfully she turned her head into the pillow, but they were tears of relief to have him back again, the husband whose ardor, inexplicably but lovingly when she most needed it, was always fired by those same tears, whose greatest pleasure was to coax her lovingly from sorrow back to joy.

"A shrewd little businessman that Mr. Yamamura." Placing the flowers on the bed beside her and lifting her hand, he stroked it gently. "He may not speakee much English, but he's a shrewd one, all right. No bones about that. But no shrewder than your own Vince, I'll have you know." And he leaned forward to kiss the cheek still turned away from him, his hand slipping under the kimono. He smiled to find her flesh bare without the usual obstructions of lace and elastic. His hand cupped her breast. "All ready and waiting," he whispered, leaning forward to kiss her neck just below her ear. "Aren't you the coy one!" Suddenly dissolving in tears, she turned to him and buried her wet face in his chest, crying clinging to him, washing her pain away in a flood of pleasure.

"There, there." He leaned forward, laying her head back on the pillows, his lips so close to her, his words were scarcely more audible than breath, his hand speaking more insistently than his tongue. "Don't you fret your pretty little head about a thing. You understand? Because everything's going to be all right, Your Vince'll see to that. When's he ever let you down before? Everything's going to be just fine, I tell you, Just you wait and see. And there aren't going to be any more tears, because we're going to shake this old bed silly, you and me. The two of us. You think your old Vince is wearing down, beginning to show the years, eh? Well, he'll show you what no hot-blooded young buck in the whole damn country is up to . . ."

And because she never for an instant doubted that he would, he did. And there were no more tears. For awhile.

Though Arnie did not, in Mr. Perkins' phrase, become a witness for the prosecution, his testimony proved unnecessary. The next day Ken Yamamura himself confessed his sole and full responsibility and the episode was, if not entirely forgotten, no longer discussed. There were other things to occupy them all.

Arnie had discovered in Sarah a new toy. And since the very notion of temperance was alien to his nature, his time and his imagination were, for a good many seasons to come, consumed with finding just how many different ways there were, given the physical limitations involved, to play the same game. Every fold and crevice of Sarah's body was explored with the thoroughness of an archeologist unearthing some ancient tomb rich in precious relics.

Within a month Clara was, as she put it, "up to her ears" in painters and paperhangers, so preoccupied with her renovations that she did not have the leisure to notice the new glass structure rising on the delta of the creek, a greenhouse that was almost sure to double the Yamamura annual yeild of carnations; or, perhaps more important, though less apparent, she also failed to note the subtle changes taking place in her son. He was growing up. That much was obvious. It seemed only natural that he should, in the process, become more secretive, more independent, and where his family was concerned, less demonstrative. It was a part of nature and there was, she knew only too well, no changing *that*.

Chapter Three

1

Belle continued to live in the Bettencourt house — her house now, though the title belonged to Vince. But that was a mere technicality. There had been an understanding at the time of the transfer that the house would remain Belle's for as long as she needed it, and though she felt no affection for her brother-in-law, he was family, and one did not betray one's own. Thus the change of ownership had been for her no more than a formality.

At the bank she was soon doing more work than most of the men for less pay and happy for the privilege. Happy most of all to find herself once again indispensable. Like the indomitable Sarah, she thrived on work and seemed most contented when most burdened. Even the feel of her native soil was enhanced by her daily contact with the world of commerce, and every evening, after she had washed and changed, she strolled through the apricot orchards, past the rows of currant plants, across the small bridge to the barnyard where the dappled grays were stabled. She felt a peculiar affinity to these workhorses, handsome, sturdy beasts suited to toil rather than pleasure. There was a kind of beauty in their strength that the sleekest of racehorses could not match, and when she felt their soft, furred lips on her hands as they munched the cubes of sugar she always carried in her sweater pockets, she felt as close as she had ever come to contentment.

It was here one evening that she first met Olaf.

She had heard talk of him from Vince, who spoke of his new hand with a sniggering condescension not far removed from insult, so that even before she saw him she felt a certain kinship.

A strange and moody northerner whose only words were necessary words, he had appeared from nowhere with a three days' growth of beard and a lean and hungry look. Since the apricots were ripening and the currants already crimson, he was hired and allowed, until his first month's pay, to sleep in the barn.

It was there that Belle first saw him. He was standing framed in the open hatch hooking and shifting the bales of hay, as tall and fine a man as any she had ever seen, his shirt open and wet with sweat, so that it clung to him and rippled like the loose flanks of her dapple-grays. The skin below the burnt V was almost chalky in its whiteness, and his hair glowed like a crown of raked coals. He was a silent, docile worker with a body designed for labor, so slim and hard that she could not tell his age; he might be as young as thirty or as old as fifty, though the truth, she imagined lay somewhere in between. His redness added a fierceness to his expression, as if he were burning from within, and his docility was the docility of the damned, of those who have ceased to resist simply because they have ceased to hope.

Conscious that he was being observed, he paused, and wiping his brow and chest with a red bandana, fixed her with fierce eyes. She did not flinch, but returned his stare with the same look of unabashed admiration that she bestowed upon her horses. Since she had from necessity never been an item in the marraige market, she had always confronted all males with the same frankness with which she confronted her sisters, measuring them against a standard divorced from desire.

Impersonal though it might be, her stare was still oppressive, and startled as much by its persistence as by its frankness, Olaf frowned. His cheeks grew hollow and his eyes — she could not tell their color in the deepening dusk — receded into their orbital shadows. His eyebrows forked suddenly, singeing her cheeks like two pentecostal flames. She had not meant to be rude. With a curt nod she returned on her homeward walk. Idly she reached out to let the branches of the currant bushes rub against the palms of her hands, the sulphur dust with which the leaves were powdered against the mildew forming a dreamlike knee-high mist through which she glided rather than walked, a tall barge on a yellow sea, strangely exhilarated, her cheeks flushed, her breath short, she was moving so fast. Midway through the orchard she stopped.

The trees were burdened with fruit, clustered like golden barnacles on every branch. She reached up to pick an apricot as big as a peach, breaking it in two and smelling it before she ate it. It was still warm from the heat of the afternoon sun and so ripe its juices spilled over her lips. In her backyard the air was thick with the cloying sweetness of honeysuckle. The old house was covered with climbers, its shabbiness disguised for a season in their lush growth, its loneliness secreted away under their profligate blooms. It was summer, she thought, now suddenly, inexplicably depressed. She could feel tears welling in her eyes and a cry choking in her throat. It was summer and she could not bear to see it wasted.

The next day she was uncharacteristically restless, brusquely efficient with her bumbling co-workers and out of sympathy with her customers. All demanding so much more than they were prepared to give, their whining, avaricious voices pinched with mistrust, and she, caged, wasting away, speaking to strangers through brass bars from which there was no escape. Sister Nora in Turlock was already expecting her first, and Belle had promised to arrange her vacation to coincide with the lying-in. Brother Joe, struggling to get a foothold in a garage of his own, was making fresh demands upon her salary. What did she, with a house of her own to keep her sheltered, with enough hand-me-downs from Clara to keep her clothed, with a constant supply of fresh fruit and vegetables to furnish her table, need with money? What was there that she did not already have that she needed to buy? Again and again she was asked to give of herself, yet not one of them since their mother's death had come calling on her without an ulterior motive — a loan to arrange, a child to be watched, a dress to be pinned up, a coat to be cut down, a hat to be trimmed. Not one of them, in all that time, had ever, on an idle Sunday, dropped in just to sit for a minute at the breakfast table and chat about old times, just long enough for once in her life to give her the chance to offer herself before they asked.

When she came home at night and opened the door into her empty house, she could feel her heart contract at the sound of ghostly scurryings and that peculiar, spirit-chilling scent of an ancient, unaired house, the faint, sickening-sweet odor of death seeping still from beneath its blanket of gardenias in the Sunday parlor. The silence that greeted her was the silence of the grave.

In no time at all she would be talking to herself, to the pots simmering on the stove or the plants rooting on the windowsill, to anything that moved or grew or simulated life. Already she had caught herself addressing the carrots being diced on the chopping board as if they too should share in the decisions of the evening, the quantity of celery and onions fit to join them in their pot of stew. And in her bed at night, the window open so that the room was flooded with honeysuckle and jasmine, she was reminded once again that outside in the silver night it was still summer, and she could not bear to have it wasted.

2

The next evening she found her eyes wandering in search of the flaming apparition that had so briefly lit up the dark waste of her life. He was not there. She patted the horse nearest her, gently tugging at its mane, and then burying her hands deep into her sweater pockets, she turned, and feeling unaccountably cheated, walked slowly away.

The evening after he was there again, and she blushed at the sight of him, dismayed at the extent of the pleasure she felt in his presence. June became July and these encounters became for both an evening ritual. When she was for some reason late, he would delay his feeding until he could see her, rushing too fast for a stroll, her proud head high above the currant bushes, fearful that she would be late, and when she arrived, even more fearful that he might spy in her flushed cheeks and glittering eyes the truth: that it was no longer the horses she came to see, but him.

He never spoke to her and he never smiled, but he followed her with his fierce eyes — they were green, she had noticed, streaked with an edge of blue. Nor did she ever speak to him, satisfying herself with a nod and a smile, which was, though slight, somehow different from that bestowed upon the daily line of faces outside her bank cage as though it began so deep down inside of her and expended so much of its force on the long voyage out, there was energy left for only the slightest curl at the corner of her lips.

His silence did not dismay her. She was used to silent men. Nor was she herself given to garrulity. What was there to say that her eyes had not already said? She knew, moreover, without the passing of a word, that he had come to await her visits as eagerly as the horses. There was the same poised alertness of the nerves, the same cock of the ears listening for her steps: the rustle of her skirts against the currant branches, the crunch of her feet on the dry earth as she approached. And he was always there, never close enough to demand a screen of words to separate them, but there waiting for her.

July became August and her sister Nora called. Reluctantly she packed her bag, reluctantly she locked the house, and even more reluctantly she drove the long road to Turlock, over the Livermore Hills, through the Altamont Pass, and into the fierce Valley heat to sleep on a folding bed in the sweltering kitchen, squeezed between the sink and the table, to be teased and fussed over for a night and then forgotten, except to be told before she left how hard times were, how pennies had to be pinched and corners cut until they could hardly see their way clear and wouldn't she, Dear Belle, Kind Belle — but never then Poor Belle — always willing to give of herself, help out just a little? And of course she would — cut her own corners so that theirs might be squared. But her giving was colored by the contempt she had felt at her frightened sister's screams.

For she would have sung such a chorus of hallelujahs to greet *her* son's issuance into the world as would have shamed her spoiled sibling into silence.

She could not join in the family's festive joy. Her mind was elsewhere. She was impatient to be gone, impatient with her sister's self-indulgent convalescence and leisurely recovery, impatient with the loan she could not give with grace, impatient most of all with herself for her so disturbing lack of contentment. She felt a restlessness she had never known before. The ritual of each day was left incomplete, and sleep came fitfully plagued with tongues of fire that were not of the Holy Spirit. And she was frightened.

August became September and she drove the long road back, over the Livermore Hills to the temperate coast and her home waiting in the dark. The lights of her runabout were almost too dim to lead her through the long drive to the shed alongside the tankhouse, which she had converted into a makeshift garage. There was no moon, and she had to strike a match to find the

73

keyhole to the kitchen door. A bucket of pears and apples sat on her doorstep. There was no message. She smiled. Poor Vince must be in a hard way for a favor, she thought, but when she thanked him after mass the next day, he denied any knowledge of the gift, and she was left to her own conjectures.

That evening, struggling to appear casual, telling herself that she was only resuming a ritual almost sacred in its regularity, a habit of too long standing to give her heart any cause to race with excitement, she resumed her nocturnal walk. Olaf was still there. He had survived the summer to become a part of the permanent work force. At the first sight of him she breathed a sigh and slackened her pace to give her heart a chance to settle itself. She answered his nod with a smile, her eyes alive with gratitude and relief, for she had been too fearful to ask, too diffident in any way to link her name with his.

Yet linked their names inevitably were.

"Belle's got herself a beau," Vince said to his wife one afternoon at the lunchtable.

"Belle?" Clara was incredulous. "Our Belle? Who for heaven's sake?"

"Olaf."

Clara laughed at the very absurdity of the notion. "Tease," she said. "Now you leave Poor Belle alone."

"All right, laugh, but just you wait," he continued, smiling. "There's fire left in the old gal yet. All she needs is for the right man to come along and stoke it, and she'll fall for him like a ton of bricks. Mark my words: a ton of bricks."

It seemed unfair that the gossip should have begun before they had themselves spoken a word to each other. It had to come some day, that first word, and when it did, she knew, it would have to come from her. She was beyond anything so calculated as a prepared speech or a contrived gambit to cue an opening line. When the time was ripe, the words would come. And come they did one evening after the first frost.

Bundled in a great wool sweater and scarf, she stood leaning against the corral, lined now with stacks of mildewing cornstalks, the earth rich with autumn odors rising from the steaming mounds of compost. In the fading light she watched the steam of the horses' breath and Olaf currying the shaggy coats, his ministrations answered with ripples of furred flesh. His ears were blue with the cold.

"Ah, you need a scarf, Olaf," she said, surprised at her casual courage.

He paused in his currying to confront her with his solemn gaze. "And who's to make me one, Miss Bettencourt?"

Her face grew as red as his hair and her eyes flushed with tears, but she said nothing more. It was enough that he knew her name and had voiced it.

That evening as she sat on the rocking chair before the kerosene stove, she stared numbly at the knitting in her hands as if it were the cloth of her life, falling stitch by monotonous stitch, a meaningless interlocking of minutes and hours and days; but she had it within her power to transform this piece before her, to give it shape as a sweater or a skirt or a scarf, and she wondered if sometimes her life too might take its shape. But if ever it did, she thought, she would have to be the one to determine its pattern. To make of it that scarf for Olaf.

And when, two days later, it was done, she did not wrap it, for she did not want it to appear as a gift, but as something that had always been rightfully his, something that he might have left, forgotten on the back of a chair or hanging on a hook by the door. So she carried it wound as a muff about her hand.

She was not given to coquetry. The mirror was merely the half-conscious instrument of her morning ablutions, and she never sought in it the secret of her own character. She knew that well enough — or as well as she cared to know it — without any artificial aids. So it did not ever enter her mind to arrange her hair with any more care than she ordinarily used, or to select a dress any finer than the one she ordinarily wore. She was not beautiful, yet there was a sweetness about her face one sometimes sees in nuns, for she had, until recently, raised not great protest, no outcry of the heart to etch its history there. Her passions and her longings had all been buried deep and had only now, dislodged by the shock of her mother's death, begun to work their way to the surface. And possibly because she had already, at twenty, looked middle-aged and her face had scarcely altered since then, people began to think of her as ageless. "Belle," they would say on meeting her, "you haven't aged a day in the last ten years. Tell us, what's your secret?'' And without so much as a gratuitous smile, she would shrug her shoulders and turn away, for though the answer was easy enough, it was too bitter to voice: nothing had happened to her in those ten years to give her any cause to change.

Her cheeks were flushed with the autumn chill, her skin taut and olive-smooth. Her eyes watered, shining darker than their customary gray as she watched Olaf finger the scarf with his large, freckled hands. Kneading it, he stood, unsmiling, gaxing at her. The wind lifted a tuft of her hair loosened from the knot. It curled about her cheek, circled her chin, then fell to her neck, where it sank into the hollow of her throat. He watched it come to rest. She reached to tuck it back in place.

"No, Miss Belle," he said, and she thought for a moment, for that was where his eyes rested, that he meant for her to let her hair blow free, and she dropped her hand. "I can't rightly take it." And his mute, unsmiling gaze was an impenetrable barrier.

What happened next she never knew. She was hot and cold at once. A foolish, shamed, middle-aged schoolgirl. Somehow, without any conscious effort of the will, she was stumbling through the currant patch, the scarf dragging from her limp hand until it caught on a dried branch and pulled her back to consciousness. She tugged at it, then impatiently she let it fall to the ground and ran on home, trying desperately not to listen to the voice that kept saying: he said Belle, not Bettencourt. Belle. Over and over. And for the first time the name sounded without bitter irony — Belle!

Chapter Four

1

"Have *you* ever been in love?"

The question burst out of the young girl with all the bluntness of youth.

Her hand buried in a bowl of breadcrumbs, Belle colored. For an instant she feared she might have been spied upon, to be exposed now to the obloquy of those she most loved, but those, she was also aware, from whom she could in this matter least expect sympathy.

"Why, what a question!" she stammered, but her discomfort proved redundant. Her niece's eyes remained fixed on some distant point, removed in time as well as space, her snug smile curled in upon itself like a kitten before a fire. The question, it was clear, had not been personal, had not for that matter been intended as a question at all, but as a prelude to confession: to the overwhelming fact that she, Louise Woods, was, most irrevocably — though neither hopelessly nor desperately — in love, and she had to tell someone before she burst with the knowledge.

Confronted by her aunt's consternation, the young girl was struck suddenly by the cruelty of her question with its foredoomed negative, and a wave of pity washed over her, momentarily unsettling, but leaving her once again to bask in the sunshine of her own triumphant good fortune; and in an outburst of generosity and affection nearly as cruel as her words, she threw her arms around the older woman.

"Forgive me, Belle. I didn't mean it to sound like that. Anyway, *I* love you. And that's a good deal more than I do a lot of other people," she added, cryptically, as she once again sat down and began to pluck crumbs from the stale loaves. Dressing for tomorrow's turkey.

It was such a demonstration and such a declaration as Belle

was seldom granted. "When have I ever had time for such non-sense?" she asked, flustered with gratitude as she shook the crumbs from her hands, and lifting the earthenware bowl from her lap onto the table, she studied her niece. "But I can see," she continued, *"you've* already found time enough. How pretty you are!" She marveled at the young girl's fresh beauty with an ache somewhat lightened by the pride she felt in the dark oval face, as if she had herself been responsible, at least in part, for its perfection, the dark eyes swimming in seas so white the pupils seemed almost black; and again she blushed at her own middle-age pretensions. "How fresh and pretty!"

"Am I? Really and truly?" Louise's brow furrowed awaited the answer. But Belle could only reluctantly indulge such fancies.

"What questions you ask!"

"But tell me. Please tell me, Belle, am I *really* pretty?"

Belle responded with a shake of her head and a question that was its own answer.

"When was the last time you looked in the mirror?"

"Oh, that!" she replied, more disappointed than pleased. "That doesn't count because it's *me* I'm seeing. How can that help me know what other people see when they look at me? Mamma," she added, her voice and face suddenly pinched, "thinks Lorraine's much prettier." While she herself, she might have added, didn't think the frizzy-haired, fat-faced Lorraine pretty at all. Which left her she didn't know where. And it was a question she so wanted settled, once and for all, so that she might then move on to more important matters secure at least in the knowledge of her own beauty's power to win without words or actions the willing submission of others. For she wanted nothing less than the approbation of the entire world: to be crowned at once both saint and queen. There were moments, certainly, when she felt worthy of such an honor; but there were other moments when she felt herself, of all the world, least deserving.

"What nonsense you talk! What perfect nonsense!"

"But it isn't nonsense, Belle; it's important. Who wants to be an old maid? Oh, dear," she continued in response to her aunt's wry smile, "I don't seem to be able to say anything tonight without putting my foot into it, do I? But that's only because I never think of *you* as an old maid," she added, once again on the defensive though she met her aunt's gaze without blushing. "But more like an older sister. Or best friend. There certainly isn't anyone else I can talk to," she concluded, her eyes once again distant.

"And who is it's responsible for all this foolishness?" Belle interrupted, "or dare I ask?"

The deferred blush blossomed on the young girl's cheeks but she did not demur:

"Henry Ramos."

"Ah, I might have expected as much," Belle responded with a smile that carried its own approval. "But if we don't get moving a little faster with this dressing, it'll have to be saved for the Christmas turkey. And Henry?" she continued, failing to heed her own advice. "Does he —?" She could not bring herself to say love. It was not a word to be bantered lightly even in so serious a conversation.

"Yes," she answered, plucking the white heart from a dry crust and rubbing it between her hands. "Look," she continued, brushing her hands on the sides of her apron before lifting the chain from around her neck to exhibit a tiny gold ring dangling alongside a cross. "His baby ring. See. There's even a tiny diamond fixed in the R."

"And that, I suppose, makes it official."

There was just a hint of mockery in the older woman's smile.

"Well, it'll have to do till he can afford one that fits a little better," Louise answered, smiling herself as she secreted the ring once again under her dress. "Mamma would be furious if she knew, so you mustn't tell her. She's forbidden me to see him," she added. "Except at piano lessons, where she can't do anything about it. Unless she wants me to give up the piano altogether, and she's got this crazy notion in her head I'm going to be a concert pianist. Even though I can't play two consecutive bars the moment I know someone outside the family's listening."

"But why, should your mother object to Henry? He's a fine boy."

"It's because of Poor Julia."

79

Belle blushed, for Clara as well as herself. "But everyone knows how that happened. An accident."

"Oh, Aunt Belle, it wasn't an accident." The young girl was clearly disappointed in her aunt's duplicity. "I'm old enough to know *that* much."

Again Belle blushed. "Yes, I suppose you are. But that was her mother's sin. Poor thing. And they both paid dearly for it. No one can say otherwise. So I don't see why your mother should demand more than God already has."

"Oh, Mamma's afraid, if we have children, they might be crazy, or something. Like her."

"Not crazy, Dear. Simple-minded."

"It doesn't matter." She shrugged. Then giggling suddenly, the girl in her vanquishing the young woman she was trying so hard to be: "Last week Mrs. Ramos left her peeling potatoes in the kitchen for their dinner while she went outside for something — I forget what — and when she came back later, Julia had already peeled the entire sack. Over a hundred potatoes. And the only reason she'd stopped then was because there weren't anymore. Or maybe she'd still be peeling them."

"Poor thing." Belle smiled. "But you mustn't make fun of her. It's not her fault."

"Oh, I wasn't making fun of her. She's really a very sweet person, once you get to know her," she added, more sententiously than she had intended, then swiftly changing her mood, she blurted out:

"What Mamma's *really* afraid of is that Henry isn't going to be a fancy lawyer or doctor and won't be good enough for us. She wants someone that'll put her one up on the Aikens and their stinking old salt works."

"What nonsense," she said, though the claim sounded just enough like Clara to be true. "But just remember, it's you that'll be doing the marrying, when the time comes. Not your mother. Though you mustn't tell her I said so, or she's liable to forbid you to see me as well. And I'd miss that," she added. "I'd miss that very much."

Every inch of counter space was cluttered, every burner blazing. The rattling tin lid was lifted and Belle's face was washed by a gust of steam. In the background Sarah sulked over the invasion of her kitchen.

"I wanna help too," Lorraine demanded, stamping her foot. "If Louise can help, why can't I?"

"Because, Dear there are already more people than the kitchen can hold," Belle answered without so much as a glance at her niece or Sarah. "Already too many cooks."

"And if it's overdone," Sarah huffed, "who gets the blame? That's what I wanna know. Who gets the blame?"

"Then how come Louise gets to stay?"

"Because Louise is helping, stupid," Louise answered. "That's why."

"All right, then, I'm gonna tell Mamma."

"Well, you just do that, Dear." Belle brushed past her in her rush from the stove to the sink with the steaming pot in her hands. "But do be careful of that door or someone's going to have to scrape the sweet potatoes off the floor."

"And two guesses who that'd be. See! What'd I tell you? Overdone!" With a triumphant thrust of a plump finger into the still-steaming potatoes, Sarah surveyed the invaders.

"Oh, do stop fussing and get the bowl," Belle demanded. "Or everything'll be overdone — including my patience."

It had begun simply enough with the usual last-minute rush complicated by the usual bickering. The dining room table was set in full splendor: the best silver polished, the best crystal shined, and the best china laid out on the best linen. A fire burned in the marble fireplace, and the crystal medallions of the new electric chandelier reflected the flames of the two-branched candelabra, which flickered also in the water goblets. Coming late to the table, Belle charged through the swinging door, her apron still half on, and sat down so precipitately there was not time to save herself from Vince's trap. A rude outburst filled the room. Doubled over in malicious delight, Arnie came close to falling off his chair and carrying the table cloth with him. Mortified by her father's crude trick, Louise blushed, her eyes buried in the center bowl of fruit and autumn leaves, her thin lips pinched with disapproval. Clara tittered, drinking in the sweet delight of her family. She liked to think of her husband as one part little boy, a size less awesome than the great man of affairs she had married.

The invariable brunt of her brother-in-law's practical jokes, of dribbling glasses, collapsing chairs, and popping paper snakes, Belle had little cause to be surprised. With stiff dignity she removed the rubber bladder from under her and dropped it without comment onto the floor, where it was left for the tearful Sarah, shaking with vindictive glee, to pick up.

"What's the matter, Belle? Too many *favas* for lunch?"

Belle chose to leave her brother-in-law's question unanswered.

"What's *favas?*" Lorraine asked.

"Horse beans, Dear," Belle answered, unable to resist a dig of her own: "If your father had taken the pains to teach you his native language, you wouldn't have to ask."

"But we ain't natives," Arnie said, regaining his composure. "We're just as white as anyone else."

"Besides, it sounds silly. I only want white meat," Lorraine added, shaking her head and refusing the plate offered her. "And no gravy on the dressing. And no sweet potatoes either." She knew well enough not to ask to be spared the peas as well.

"And what did you forget?" Clara asked.

Momentarily baffled, her pretty mouth dropping, Lorraine studied her mother's face for some clue. The light came slowly: "Oh — *please.*"

"That's better." Clara handed Lorraine's plate to Belle. "I hope *you* don't mind dark meat."

"Anything, anything at all," she answered, accepting the plate. "But if it sounds silly," Belle persisted with her topic, "it's because you don't understand it. Anything you don't understand sounds silly. Why, English must have sounded pretty silly to your grandfathers too, at one time. Both of them," she could not resist adding with a hard critical look at Vince: "Your Grandfather Silva-that-was as well as your Grandfather Bettencourt."

"I wish *I* could speak another language." Feeling very grown up, Louise came to her aunt's defense. "Any other language."

"You're American," Vince snapped. "And I've noticed you at a loss for words with only one language at your command."

"Louise has been meeting Henry Ramos down by the creek." Arnie's announcement brought a quick change of mood.

"Louise!" Clara's voice trembled with injured dignity. "And after I expressly asked you. For your own good."

"We'll discuss that some other time, Clara." Vince cut his wife short. "This is a holiday."

"I could tell plenty of things about you, too, if I had a mind to." Ignoring her parents, Louise directed her full wrath against her brother. "Last night under the bridge, for instance." And with a coltish toss of her head her eyes darted from her brother to Sarah, opening the swinging door into the kitchen with a bump of her well-padded hips.

Arnie made a hasty retreat into silence, but Louise was by no means through with him.

"If you're so anxious for a fight, why don't you go off to Europe and fight the Germans. Or are you only fit to fight girls?"

"He's not going anywhere. To fight anyone!" Clara fairly shrieked. "It's not our war, do you understand?"

"And it's not going to be," Vince declared with a finality that brought the subject to a quick end. "This year or next."

The turkey platter was removed to the sideboard, set between two enameled bronze pheasants, and the dinner commenced without grace.

"There's been a bit of news," Vince announced, taking a bite of turkey and pausing to swallow it before continuing. His smile grew mischievous. His eyes intent upon his sister-in-law. With the offhanded manner of a virtuoso he deftly rolled his bomb right at her feet:

"Olaf's got a wife. And two children . . . two boys."

She did not move or cry out, she scarcely flinched, but her color changed so radically the entire table remained momentarily speechless. But as she neither fainted nor wept nor in any other way gratified their melodramatic longings, the tension eased. Arnie was the first to break the spell with a guffaw. Lorraine was quick to follow with a potato-splattering giggle.

But Belle was deaf to all scorn. Her cheeks burned and her eyes, dazzled by the sudden illumination, brimmed with tears of joy. In a trice the heavy sense of shame that she had borne for days was lifted. She had not been wrong, after all — a foolish, middle-aged schoolgirl. And she could not now imagine what it was that kept her body fixed to its seat when her heart was soaring so.

"In Fresno," Vince continued, though he might have been speaking to a statue. "Without so much as a by-your-leave, just ups, one day, and walks out. Just like he was going down to the store to get himself a cigar and can't find his way back. But the crazy fool doesn't even have sense enough to change his name." He paused to take another bite. "Good dressing, Belle. Don't you think so, Clara? One of her best."

"Yes, Belle, dear. Quite like old times. I wish you could teach my Sarah a few of your tricks. Thanksgiving simply wouldn't be Thanksgiving without it."

Belle gave no indication she had heard. Vince continued his assault. "Always knew there was something fishy about him. Man who won't talk has something to hide. But the law's finally caught up with him. Only yesterday. Louise," he interrupted himself and angrily fixed his attention on his daughter. "For God's sake, quit shuffling your food around. Eat it or be done with it."

"I'm not hungry anymore." Her pallor almost as remarkable as Belle's color, Louise pushed her plate away. For months she had been the staunchest defender of her aunt's honor only to discover now, to her dismay, that the gossip was true.

"There are plenty of starving Belgian babies," her mother admonished, "who'd give their eye teeth for what you've left on that plate."

"Well, send it to them, then," Louise answered. "But babies don't have eye teeth."

Clara looked more baffled than offended at her daughter's insolence. "I don't see what that . . ."

The slap was so swift in coming and so sharp in its report, it startled the observers with almost as much force as it startled the recipient.

"I won't have you sassing your mother." Vince's voice was

sharper still than the sting of his hand. "Understand?"

Louise flinched but made no outcry. The color returned to her cheeks. With a quick, defiant jerk she fixed her gaze upon her brother, her burning eyes so intense they seemed to be etching every nuance of his gloating smirk upon her memory.

Belle also flinched. What had provoked the slap she did not know. She was sure Louise had merely acted as proxy, offered herself to spare another. But her niece was blessed with the resilience of youth; with beauty and love and the promise of a bountiful summer she scarcely needed an old aunt's pity.

Glowing still with an exaltation she was determined not to share by so much as a sign, Belle studied the faces about her as though she were seeing them all for the first time. What was she to any of them but an extra chair at the family table? They seemed suddenly strangers whose deaths she might have beheld with all the resignation of indifference. Only for her niece did she feel any appreciable bond of blood. *Her* affection was still capable of touching her. And for that she might have wept had not her own sense of liberation dried up all tears.

"He refuses to go back — Olaf — and God knows," Vince resumed his monologue, "odd as he is, he's still the best worker I've got. Strong as a whole team of horses. So I'm not anxious to be rid of him. Not by a long shot." He reached over to the sideboard to help himself to another slice of breast. "They've attached his salary," he continued, holding the speared piece of meat over his plate, "and the poor devil's back to spend the winter in the barn. Fortunately for me, he'd rather risk a few chilblains than return to whatever hell it was his wife made for him in Fresno . . . Some more turkey, Belle?"

"No." Belle sat erect, her hands in her lap, her voice calm. "No thank you, Vince. I've had quite enough. Already more than my share."

"What's the matter, on a beauty diet?" Arnie asked and the ever-obliging Lorraine responded with the customary giggle.

"All right, that's quite enough," Clara scolded. "From both of you. And Arnie," she continued, "I want you to eat your peas or there'll be no pudding for you."

"For God's sake, Clara," Vince said, "if you always treat the boy like a boy, how you ever expect him to become anything else? He's old enough to decide for himself what it is he wants to eat.''

So as usual, Arnie neither ate his peas nor forfeited his pudding, and Belle, in the distraction scaled a mountain. Standing dizzily on its peak, she planted her flag, and no one, she was determined — no army of foes nor troops of friends — would ever budge her from it. She knew now what she must do and there was nothing left but to do it.

Chapter Five

1

The moon shone dim through a veil of clouds. Before the prickly silhouette of the monkey tree she raised her astrakhan collar about her ears. Now that there was no longer any cause for coyness, she felt herself suddenly strong. She was forty-four. More than half her life had passed by, and it had not yet taken hold. But there would be no stopping her now.

The air smelled of autumn, of mildewing husks and steaming compost piles. Out to the currant patch she ran. There, still tangled in the bare branches, she found the scarf, damp but otherwise undamaged. Scarcely pausing to catch her breath, she carried it bunched in her hand to her own yard. No lamp burned in the window to welcome her home. Stumbling up the backstairs and through the unlocked door into the kitchen, she lit the kerosene stove and draped the scarf over the clothes rack to dry. Without pausing to take off her coat, she set about to pick out all the burrs and twigs. She inhaled deeply the comfortable odor of steaming wool. As soon as the scarf was dry, she folded it, pressing it still warm against her breasts before laying it on the sideboard. Then lifting the kerosene stove, she carried it to the tankhouse, her solitary figure glowing yellow in the night.

A two-story structure built on a square base, the tankhouse was topped with a windmill pump and a water tank. The lower portion served double duty as laundry room and storage bin. Two zinc wash basins fronted the bottom window, and alongside them on a gasoline stove was a large galvanized container in which the water for washing was boiled. The opposite wall was lined with shelves with quart jars of strawberry jam and currant jelly, each labeled with an inkmarked square of adhesive tape and topped with a wax lid that was in turn protected by a paper cap held down by a rubber band. Garden tools hung from nails on either side of the door and in the corner garlands of braided garlic and onions hung from rusty iron hooks. Stepping over the awkwardly high threshold, she placed the kerosene burner in the middle of the room and climbed the ladder to the loft. In a second she was back down.

Leaving the burner to heat the room, she ran in the dark back to the house, first pausing in the kitchen to change her coat for a sweater and to light a hurricane lamp before climbing the stairs to the second-floor bedrooms. She had not entered the remotest of them in years. They were musty with stale air and dank with buckling, mildewed walls, the floors littered with fallen plaster. From every dank corner, the flickering light of her lamp roused the spectres of children long since grown or dead, as mice, first pausing to scan the intruder with beady eyes, scurried into holes chewed through the exposed laths. Too intent to heed them, she moved from room to tiny room until she found a folding canvas cot with its cross bars and hinges still sturdy enough to bear the weight of a grown man. Quickly she rolled it into a compact but awkward bundle, and, grunting audibly, she dragged it down the stairs and out to the tankhouse, hoisting it by means of the ladder onto the loft. She sank for a moment onto an old sea chest to catch her breath. Her hands were shaking, and despite the evening chill her forehead and neck were damp with sweat. Breathing deeply through her open mouth, she looked about her. She could not remember how long it had been since last she had climbed to the loft. The rough boards were cluttered with chests of every size, brine-stained and dusty with cobwebs. What could they possibly be filled with that was worth saving? The ghostly remnants of her family's past: dried wedding bouquets and the decaying gowns of those who were themselves already long since decayed; tintype albums and velvet boxes coffining locks of hair, a childish curl of her own among them.

Tomorrow she would burn them all; tomorrow she would return to the dead what belonged to the dead. In the meantime she must somehow clear the clutter and move the chests against the wall, stacking them one on the other to open a space before the upper window to set up the cot. One pane was cracked, but that too could be changed. Everything could be changed. Nothing was permanent, nothing endured — except the need to be needed and a thirst for life. Nothing else. Again she returned to the house, standing on the kitchen ladder to get at the sheets and blankets in the linen closet. In an old chest of drawers she found a pair of her father's flannel pajamas, reeking of mothballs but still intact. Nothing was ever thrown away, nothing ever wasted, and yesterday's gown became today's potholder. It was not the first time her frugality had rewarded her.

The bed was made, the pajamas laid upon it, the window screened with an old quilt, and an orange crate set beside it to hold the hurricane lamp; and when all was ready, she paused to survey her handiwork. It would do, she thought. Yes, it would do. It was hardly a palace, but it was not a barn.

So intent had she been that she had forgotten the cold and the hour and the brewing storm, and as she ran once again through the orchard and the currant patch, she stumbled in the dark, her sweater open, her hair loose about her face, the scarf crushed against her breast. At the barn she paused to catch her breath. Her heart was pounding so hard it seemed lodged in her throat. The small side door leading to the carriage stalls was rimmed with light. He was still up. Waiting for her. Before she could fan the hard core of fear burning in her gut like a live coal, she knocked:

"Olaf?" she called. "It's Miss Bettencourt, Olaf. Belle Bettencourt. I want to speak with you. Olaf?"

She was surprised at the firmness of her voice. Though too forced to be natural, like that of an unpracticed speaker addressing an audience, it did not falter.

Her heart continued to pound in her throat and to beat in her ears as she waited, but not for an instant did she waiver. There was a shuffling noise and the sound of a bar being lifted. Held up only by her courage, she stood her ground, as Olaf appeared in the half-open doorway, his hair and wool shirt flecked with hay. He eyed her guardedly. His face was flushed with more than its natural redness, and his scowl was like the growl of a dog that has just been beaten, a broken beast with no defense left but a cracked bark. He had clearly been drinking. His breath was labored and thick with fumes. So much the better; it would make her task that much easier. He did not speak, but his eyes fell to the scarf clutched in her hands.

She blushed at the sight of him, but she would not give way to pity — for him, for herself, or for all the world. There was nothing to do but begin speaking, letting the words come as they would:

"Why you can't, with winter coming on, stay here. No, Olaf, it's not right. Why, the porch posts all need bracing, the roof's beginning to leak — oh, there're so many things need fixing. A thousand things. And I don't much relish, anymore, living out there all alone, what with the world the way it is today, next to the creek. Why, it's becoming a regular haven for tramps, it is. All kinds of strange men prowling about the backyard at nights . . ."

Baffled, he studied her through squinting eyes, rubbing his beard with his hand as he tried to piece together what she was saying so that he could determine what it was she was trying to say, what her glittering eyes and her brisk voice, mounting with a dizzy momentum of its own, could mean.

"And I just thought," she continued, "there's that tankhouse — oh, it ain't much, so you needn't get your hopes up too high, but it's better than this. Oh, my, yes; it's better than this. Why, there's a stove and running water. And you'd be doing *me* a favor, if you came. Yes, Olaf. You can't imagine what it would mean, what a load off my mind it would be, knowing there was someone there. Someone I could trust. I'd sleep easier at nights. And you could work off the rent doing things about the place. Oh, I'd keep you busy, I would. Bracing those posts. And the roof. So you see, you must come. For my sake, Olaf," she concluded, her voice by now close to the breaking point. "For my sake."

She was as surprised as he at the number and force of her words, but they left her too weak for more; too weak to say what she would never, anyway, have been able to say, that she didn't care, that she didn't want to know — ever — how he had been hurt. All that mattered was that he *had* been hurt, as she had, and life was not meant to be lived alone, that even a feast unshared is famine enough to kill the heart of any man. And her eyes pled with him not to shame her again with another rejection, not to cripple her spirit forever by slamming the door against her.

For what seemed minutes he stared at her. The scowl vanished, but his brow remained furrowed as if he were trying to clear his thoughts. He swayed slightly, leaning for support upon the door. A smile hovered about his lips — a furtive, almost boyish grin, for which his lack of equilibrium might have been as responsible as her words. It did not last long. He blinked and his grin was replaced by his customary frown. Without a word, he turned and went back into the barn, but she stood her ground, waiting, thinking it was the longest minute she had ever spent in her life, until he appeared again at the door, lean and gaunt, a duffle bag in his hand, and she released a sigh that was almost a prayer.

"And Olaf," she said, all the excitement in her voice worn down so that it was unduly flat and colorless, "it's cold out. You'd better wear this." And she handed him the scarf.

His eyes moved from the scarf to her and back again to the scarf. Then still without a word, he accepted it, and with a nod that was almost curt in its formality, he wound it about his neck, tucking the ends into the shoulder straps of his lumber jacket.

Smiling, she turned to lead the way. He had brought his lamp with him so that the walk back was easier, through the orchard, its stripped, bare forms silhouetted against the foreboding sky: the skeleton of a world that would a few months hence be flushed by the spring sun but seemed now desolate.

"Time for pruning," he said, his voice natural and matter-of-fact, as though he were merely thinking aloud, making a mental memorandum, so that she had difficulty realizing they were the first words he had spoken. "Should get to it before the rains come."

"I like autumn," she answered, afraid that if she turned to look at him she would laugh or weep, or worse. "The fires burning in the fields . . ."

She smiled at the vision: Olaf raking the pruned branches, the forked brambles catching flame from his hair, the fire lighting his face and chest, orange, crackling in the chill air. The dark coming early, the horses breathing steam, their shaggy coats in need of brushing, owls hooting in the palm trees, steam coating kitchen windows — everything snug and warm. A life that custom would soon sanctify and habit approve. Oh, it was going to be a lovely autumn.

She could hear him lagging no more than three paces behind, stumbling along the unfamiliar path. She was stronger than he. She would lead the way, past each familiar marker, over the path that she had already worn. Soon he too would know it as well as she did, and her heart leapt at the thought. They crossed the wooden bridge that spanned the creek, and she could spy in the distance the light from the tankhouse window. She stopped for a moment to look at it and to marvel anew at her courage. "Almost there," she said, and he followed her under the grape arbor into her yard. At the tankhouse she threw open the door like Aladdin rolling back the stone to his cave. The kerosene stove was still burning and a bank of warm air came out to greet them.

For the first time since they had begun their walk they looked at each other. In an instant everything might have changed and the unthinkable become not only possible, but necessary. A single gesture, a single word, and their life together might have become what it never after had a chance to be. By now sober enough to be acutely conscious of the unsightly stubble that fleeced his face and the cloying sweetness that thickened his breath, he made no move either to enter the tankhouse or to touch her, but blinking with embarrassment, he clutched his duffle bag and waited expectantly, unsure what it was she wanted him to do.

Though she too faltered for an instant, she was not about to relinquish control or leave their destinies to the mercy of impulse.

"Ah, it's beginning to rain," she said, holding out her hand to catch the first drops. "Don't let all the warm air out. It'll be cold tonight. The bed's in the loft, all made and ready. I put an old pair of Pappa's pajamas on top, in case you didn't have any of your own. They've been in the drawer so long, they smell a bit of mothballs. But goodness me," she continued, her voice taking a sudden dizzy rise in pitch, "don't let all the heat escape while I stand here chattering away. Goodnight, Olaf."

And without waiting for an answer, without once turning back, she walked toward the house.

More baffled than ever, he stood before the open door until

he heard the latch of her own door snap shut and saw the light move out of the kitchen to appear a few seconds later as a brown glow through the shade of her room. And shaking his head, he entered the tankhouse. But the threshold was unduly high and he stumbled over it, falling to his knee. With a muttered curse he rose and rubbed his skinned palm along the side of his overalls. Turning once again to the yard, he stared at the glowing windowshade through eyes flaming with resentment.

2

For Belle that night there was only one moment when her courage failed. Her faith was simple. God's law had been clearly laid down and there was no denying or changing it. Olaf was another woman's husband — a fact that could be altered only by enlisting God as an accomplice in that other woman's death.

And the immensity of her commitment struck terror in her heart. She knew her family and her neighbors well enough to predict the consequences of her decision. Her life would become a pitched battle. Without the armor of a free conscience she would crumble at the first charge; with it she could outface the world. And weeping she made her terrible vow.

At six the next morning she knocked at the tankhouse door. She held her breath as she waited, fearful the whole adventure had been nothing more than a lonely old spinster's fancy run rampant, and the sigh that greeted his reply was one of relief as well as pleasure.

"Breakfast will be ready in a few minutes, Olaf. The kitchen door's unlocked. And Olaf, I'm leaving a towel on the doorknob. If you need hot water, you'll have to warm it on the stove."

She marveled at the very ordinariness of her words. Surely too commonplace to feed gossip or germinate scandal. Yet there was in her virtue a giddiness that almost spoiled for battle. She longed in some secret part of her to make the world that had passed her by stand up at last and take note of her presence.

Wary, but no longer capable of surprise, Olaf made his way into the kitchen. In the predawn, the overhead light glowed through a mist of steam rising from the huge enamel kettle into

93

which every serviceable bone or vegetable stalk was tossed. It curtained the windows and filled the air with savory odors.

When the original kitchen had grown too small for the burgeoning family, one wall had been knocked out and an extension added; but her father's calculations had always been haphazard and the dining area was, in most places, six inches higher than the rest of the room. An inadequate level and a faulty eye compounded the error. Capable of extending the full length of the room, the ponderous oak table was now locked in its smallest position. A bowl of walnuts with a brass, eagle's-head cracker sat in the center upon a crocheted doily. Before the only curtained window stood an empty wicker bassinet. Though she dusted it weekly, it had always been so much a part of the room, Belle had not thought of it for years until her eyes now lighted upon it and she blushed at its grim inappropriateness.

Awkward in the doorway, Olaf stood bent with a tall man's stoop, his head bowed like one too familiar with the hazards of low ceilings to greet any new room with his full measure. A tiny paper patch to staunch the flow of blood from a razor nick on his chin stood out in gory relief against his neatly barbered face. The blue shirt underneath his overalls was buttoned to the top button, and his red hair was a shade darker from the water that plastered down the natural curl. He smelled of soap and tobacco. The paper tab from his sack of Bull Durham dangled from the topmost pocket of his overalls.

"Sit down, sit down." She pointed to the table.

Ducking to avoid colliding with the central light fixture, he stumbled over the unsuspected step that separated the dining area from the rest of the kitchen and then stepped back to survey the trap with a puzzled shake of his head.

Belle smiled. "You'll get used to it," she said. "Pappa wasn't much of a carpenter, but I suppose the place'll stand for as long as I need it." She almost said "we".

He sat down without answering, instinctively assuming his own place at the head of the table, and with the craftsman's contempt for shoddy workmanship, he tested the wobble with both hands.

"I'd a had bacon or ham for you," she continued, as she served him a stack of hotcakes topped with an egg, "but it's

Friday and I didn't know if you might not be Catholic."

She watched him quizzically for an answer to her implied question. Nor was it idly offered. The world for her had always been neatly divided into Catholics and non-Catholics. At the far end of town across from the grammar school, there was, she knew as well as anyone, a Protestant church with vague pretensions to Christianity, but there was no resident minister, the Sunday services being conducted by various members of the congregation — which hardly seemed like religion at all, let alone another form of her own. His answer, however, was ambiguous. He shook his head, but at what she could not tell, her question or the food set before him.

"Already more'n I've had in a coon's age — Ma'am."

"Well, you're too thin for the work you've to do. Much too thin." She spoke with the not-to-be-questioned authority of the surrogate mother of a baker's dozen. "But we'll soon have you fattened up." Then suddenly fearful that her possessiveness — the assumption that his welfare was not only her right now, but her duty — might have roused his defenses, she blushed. Turning from the table back to the stove, she added, almost under her breath as she busied herself with the dirty pans: "It'll be a pleasure to cook for someone again. Never could get used to eating alone. Seems almost indecent, somehow."

He did not answer. Eating in silence he gave no indication that he understood how far she had committed herself or how much yet depended upon him and his own commitment. When the meal was done, she again spoke, eager that he might understand without words, for the very voicing of her hopes would be their ruination, and unless he understood and accepted her offer, her future would be as bleak as her past.

"Dinner's not till seven. I hope that's not too late. Pappa always liked to eat by five-thirty, but it's hard, working till five, as I do, to get it any earlier."

"No, Ma'am," he answered, and she turned, still holding the breakfast dishes in her hands, and fixed him with reproachful eyes.

"No, Miss Belle. Belle," he repeated, as if he were testing the sound on his lips, and it did, she thought, for once ring in her ears like churchbells. "That's just fine."

And he smiled, his face crinkling like a schoolboy's until he seemed far younger than his years, the milkwhite skin that undercoated his freckles pink with blushing. She had never before seen him so morning-fresh, a stunning figure of a man in his prime, and something like regret rose to overshadow her joy.

"That's better, she said. "I couldn't stand being Ma'am-ed in my own kitchen."

As she watched him leave the yard, she exulted in the knowledge that he would be there again in the evening, and the evening after that, and that despite their taciturnity, something momentous had taken place. She had become a bride — of sorts — and her own name had caroled the ceremony.

Part III

Chapter One

1

Though little more than two decades old, Wood Acres already speaks of the past and tradition. Built in another century by craftsmen from another and far grander age, the house has grown with the years more gracious and less pretentious. The garish sheen of polished brass has been muted by the acid touch of the seasons. The palms that line the drive are more stately; the bank of eucalyptus along the creek completely screens the road, which has recently for the first time, been paved; and the barbed tentacles of the monkey trees that flank the front porch form ever broader arabesques. Fields of narcissi spring unaided before winter ends, forced to compete with a rich variety of weeds for their existence.

The neat, meticulously trimmed lawns give the whole garden the illusion of care, without, at the same time, tempering the lush wildernesses. And, as Clara has long since learned, illusion is the very food of happiness. The gloss has been tempered by a romantic verdigris, and with the dispensation of time, the entire estate now speaks in the subdued voice of easy confidence.

Vince Woods' small empire has continued to flourish. Scarcely noticed, a war has come and gone and left in its wake a comet's tail of prosperity. The circle of his influence has spread from San Oriel to Hayward, to San Leandro, and as far as Oakland itself. The Bay, however, is a barrier he has not thought to cross. San Francisco is clearly foreign territory. And he does not mean to cross any Rubicon that does not offer the prospect of easy conquest.

His figure has kept pace with his fortune; it too has grown stouter. But the new flesh has erased the traces of age, and he still seems remarkably youthful. With the exception of the elegant mat of gray hair that frames it, the face has changed little.

Although a decade older than his wife, he now seems her contemporary. There are even those who find him more strikingly handsome than ever, a wise and weathered sheik with shrewd eyes glowing like hot coals.

No longer has he to speak in a loud voice to make the world take note; he has only to whisper to be heard. He sits now on committees and boards: he is a director of the Bank of Italy, of the Eden Township Water District, a founding father and first vice president of the Western Fruit Growers Association, and a trustee of the Hayward Union High School District. He has an Oakland broker, but he is apt to make his own decisions, one moment thrilling with his audacity and the next disappointing with his conservatism. But whatever his decision, it is invariably right.

Right also is Clara's behavior, and limited, though certainly "right" is her circle of friends. The only Catholic member of Hazel Aiken's bridge club, she never fails to prove herself one of the "girls" by ostentatiously taking at least one meat canape at each Friday meeting, and the wife of the third Robert to run the Aiken Salt Works treats her with scarcely a hint of condescension. More than ever the grande dame, she too has grown stouter but seems otherwise hardly to have aged; since she had very early adapted herself to the matron's role, it is merely a larger version of herself that she now presents to the world. Her past has receded into a half-remembered dream. There is only her family to remind her: the scandalous Belle, living in open sin with a common laborer, and a plethora of complaining sisters with their shamelessly transparent pleas for assistance. Here also her husband finds her behavior invariably right. Every hint is met with smiling incomprehension; she will not play the king's ear. And when their pleas become insistent, she answers sharply:

"Loan to one, and first thing you know, we're running a family bank. And that's the worst kind."

Once a year her family is entertained en masse at a Fourth of July bean feed when the weather is warm enough to keep them outside safely away from her precious porcelains. Boiling vats of corn, an iced trough of beer, an evening display of fireworks early enough to get the children home to bed on time, and the annual "headache" is over.

But there are other "headaches" that cannot be so easily shaken off. The pain of motherhood, she has come to learn once again, does not end in the confinement of the delivery room.

2

Sunk deep in a bank of pillows, Clara lay spent and panting on the plush sofa, her hand clutching at her throat as she cringed before the insistently solicitous Sarah.

"No!" she screamed. "Don't touch me! Don't you touch me — you — ! you — !"

But she could not wrest out of her dismay words fierce enough to lash the unspeakable creature out of sight and mind, and her very inability to articulate her emotions made them all the more painful.

Undaunted, Sarah stood her ground, self-possessed and ingenuously well-intentioned, her placidity an added affront. It was all too clear she had been born without a sense of shame. Only a moment before had she revealed her depravity, not so much by her dilemma as by her proffered solution — the suggestion that they might allow their son to squander his life upon a creature not worth the tenth part of his own little finger was beyond enduring.

Well in the background and unwilling at first to interject himself between the two women, Vince merely shook his head, marveling:

"What cheek! What magnificent cheek!"

He could not help admiring the girl's pluck, and as for his son's share in the affair, he would have been worried had the boy *not,* at seventeen, shown signs of life. He was surprised only by the boy's choice. He did not relish the thought of any part of him so shabbily domiciled as his putative grandchild now was.

Incapacitated by shock, Clara was never at her best in scenes; she could not snatch victory out of chaos or overwhelm with a torrent of abuse. In an emotional crisis she was apt to disintegrate. Courage and purpose melted in the first heat of battle. She could only gasp, "My stays! My stays!" and blanch white under threat of imminent asphyxiation.

99

Vince, whose wife's stays were as much of a mystery as his son's choice of lovers, was forced to defer to Sarah, who cordially came forward to oblige; but at her touch Clara once again screamed and was spared all further torture by unconsciousness.

Despite her delicate condition, Sarah was still strong enough with Vince's help to get her mistress safely out of her corset and up to bed, where, still panting from the ordeal, Vince studied the pallid form stretched out under the satin comforter.

"We'll have to find a doctor."

Sarah laughed. "Oh, she'll be just fine, poor dear. Just give her a few minutes to catch her breath and she'll be good as new again. Sweet thing." The compelling nature of her own interests in no way lessened her sympathy for her mistress.

"I didn't mean for her." Vince moved away from the bed. "For you." And he fixed her with a look constituted to turn strong men's knees to mush.

It left Sarah unfazed.

"A doctor? For me?" Though the sound of her laugh was stifled in deference to her suffering mistress, its form could be seen rippling through her body like a slice of peach trapped in a gelatin mold. With a last glance at the recumbent Clara, she gently closed the door to the bedroom before allowing her words to spill over, bubbling on the froth of her chuckle:

"You rich folks are all alike, spoil yourself sick with too much care you do. And why shouldn't you?" she quickly added, for she was no bomb-hurling anarchist. "You got the means. So if that's what you want, you're welcome to it. But what would the likes of me do with a doctor? An old workhorse like myself? No sir, Mr. Woods — and no offense, mind you — but I don't hold much store by doctors. Far as I'm concerned, they can keep their needles and pills and welcome to them. It's there, all right." She stopped at the head of the stairs to give her belly a proud pat. "And nothing any doctor's gonna say can change that. No-sirree. It's long past prevention time. An ounce or a pound wouldn't do a speck of good right now. So why make a pincushion outta my behind, big as it is," she giggled, "when it can't do nobody no good?" Again she chuckled, as though in response to some private joke. "It'll find its own way out when it's good and ready, and it won't need no doctor's help for that.

No sir," she continued, more seriously, "you won't catch me running to the county hospital. Like as not, from what I heard, they're not above sneaking someone else's Mongolian idiot into my baby's crib. No, sir, I'll take my own chances, same as everybody else around here, with somebody I can trust. Mamie Gomez'll do just fine."

"All right, Sarah, all right. You just let me handle it. Just let me handle the whole thing." Vince gave her hand a sympathetic pat though her smile seemed to indicate sympathy was the least of her needs. "The right kind of doctor *can* change that. And that's the kind of doctor we mean to find you. Before it's too late," he added with an uneasy glance at her midsection, and before she had time to assimilate his words, he descended the stairs at a livelier-than-usual clip.

Sarah's only weapons were honesty, good nature, and an overwhelming desire to please; but there were limits to what even she would do to please the Woods.

"Oh, Mr. Woods!" She followed him into the living room, stopping at a respectful distance before continuing. For the first time she seemed truly troubled by her plight. Her smile was gone and in its place was something closer to disappointment than shock. "You don't mean that, now, I know. A man with your heart. A fine upstanding man like you. Your own flesh and blood!" Her eyes moist with concern, she shook her head. "No, sir, you don't mean it. I know you didn't mean it. Least not the way I took it."

"And suppose I did mean just that?" He turned to confront her with the look of a prosecuting attorney about to trap a key witness into a betrayal of his defense. "Just suppose for a minute I did. What would you say to that?"

But Sarah remained inflexible.

"No sirree, no doctor's gonna get within touching distance of me with his knife. Cutting out my own flesh and blood! Not on your life. It's not natural, it isn't. Why, just look what happened to Mae Ramos's sister Julia, poor thing. The curse of the Almighty put upon her. And with a crochet hook! Why, just thinking about it's enough to give me the living creeps. A crochet hook!"

He smiled at her naivete. "There are methods today considerably

101

more modern than that. You wouldn't feel a thing. I promise you that much. Mind you, I don't want you to get the wrong idea. I'm not talking about a backroom abortion performed on a kitchen table by some hack butcher. He'd be the real thing, Sarah. A regular licensed doctor in a proper hospital. We'd see to that. And see that you were well taken care of after, too. You wouldn't have to worry about a thing. Not a thing. A little vacation in the big city — and it's not as if you haven't earned one after all these years — and nobody'd be any the wiser. Why, you'd come back fresh as new again.''

"No, sir, it's not natural, it isn't,'' she persisted just as though she hadn't heard a word he'd uttered. "Much as I respect you, and Mrs. Woods — poor dear! — I wouldn't have nothing to do with anything like that. And I know you wouldn't neither, once it came down to it. Not with your own flesh and blood, Mr. Woods. Why, it's murder, that's what it is. Plain and simple murder.''

"Well, then,'' he sank into his favorite chair, a gold plush monster with elephantine arms and a tufted footstool, "there's only one other choice left us: we'll have to find the child a father.''

Sarah giggled good-naturedly. "Oh, Mr. Woods, that part's already taken care of.'' She laughed more heartily. "It's not a father we need. Your son's already seen to that. And a mighty fine job he's made of it, too, let me tell you.''

Vince smiled in appreciation. The girl was either ingenuous to the point of simple-mindedness or, more likely, nobody's fool. He was almost beginning to enjoy himself. There was nothing like a good challenge to make him feel twenty again.

"A drop of port, Sarah?'' He pointed to the liquor cabinet.

"Oh, Mr. Woods, I never could say no to a little port. You know that well as I do.''

"Nor anyone else, eh Sarah?'' He laughed at his own little joke. "A little Port or a little Irishman? They're all pretty much the same, eh, Sarah, once you get down to the bare essentials?''

Once explained, the joke was an even greater success with Sarah than with its originator. The house rang with her bawdy laugh. Her whole person quivered with delight, her breasts heaved, her eyes watered, and the very hairs on her wart bristled. "How you talk, Mr. Woods! How you talk!" And she had to catch her sides to keep her balance. "Your son's own father you must've been, I'll wager, in your day. Why even now — just look at you: in the prime of life. A man like you. Oh, she's a lucky woman, Mrs. Woods is," she continued, shaking her head in frank admiration, her eyes taking shameless but apparently inoffensive liberties with his person. "A lucky woman."

So pleased was he with the reception of his joke, he could scarcely contain his own mirth. "Well, you know where it is," he said, coughing to regain control of his voice, then settling back against his cushion, he lit a cigar and followed her with his eyes as she bent before the liquor cabinet. The spread of her hips drew her skirt high enough for him to catch a clear expanse of flesh above the rolled stockings, thighs as thick as an elephant's, though considerably whiter and softer. As homely and inviting as his favorite chair.

For the first time he was beginning to understand his son's weakness for the ugly creature. She could easily, he imagined, show a man a glory time, tickling his pride while pleasing his body. And the Good Lord knew, there were worse ways to go.

"No need to be shy; help yourself," he continued, his words tilting her hand and filling her glass to the brim. "And since you won't have a doctor, we'll see what we can do about finding you a husband."

3

The search was abetted by Sarah herself. The very largess with which she had bestowed her favors and the openness with which she now named her beneficiaries — indicating on the sly that she might not be altogether opposed to enlarging that list should certain parties be so inclined — gave Vince the only weapons he needed to prevent a scandal. The list was narrowed to the most likely single candidate, and the others were shrived of their sins. Her complicity assured, Vince set about his task with mounting relish.

Pinch-browed and hirsute, Manuel Furtado was even less a match than Sarah had been. His great soft eyes set darkly in a craggy face grew even softer until they seemed about to liquefy as his coarse hand stroked a two days' growth of beard. Somewhere in their depths an incipient idea struggled for release. He was being had again, somehow. Of that much he was sure. But how?

Drowned in shadows, his answer was doomed never to see the light. He was no mathematician. The laws that govern cause and effect were swathed in mysteries of timeless superstitions and customs as old as the land he tilled — which was now as it had always been, another man's.

"Course you're going to do right by her — or by God, Manuel!"

Vince stood in the cauliflower patch, his hat in his hand, his forehead ringed with a band of sweat, his face flushed above his starched collar and tie. He would have suffered sunstroke rather than be caught in the fields by one of the local men in any costume less formal. A well-tailored suit and vest always helped keep things in their proper perspective and gave him an immediate advantage before a word was spoken.

"Right?" Manuel seemed more than ordinarily dense, his thick brows pinched even tighter, as if he feared, should he for an instant relax them, whatever hold he had upon the situation would slip away.

"Right! Marry her, man! Marry her. As it's your duty to do."

"Duty?" He was clearly going to put up a stiff resistance.

"Yes, duty. And you might as well own up to it. You had your little fun, and now it's time for the reckoning. I'm surprised at you, Manuel," he continued, patting the young man fraternally on the arm. "You should've known better, a man like you, that no one gets anything for nothing in this world. Not even a toss in the hay. Or a midnight tumble on the banks of the creek. And it seems — according to Sarah, anyway, and who should know better? — you weren't none too particular just where you took it. Or when. Well, a man pokes around with fire's gonna get burnt sooner or later. And it pretty well looks, Manuel, like you got burnt sooner than later. But those are the risks of the game. You have your little fun and you always pay for it in the end. One way or another. And there's no denying you've had your fun, is there? And some of it, I'll wager, on my own time and my own hay," he added with another pat of the arm and a conspiratorial wink.

"But just to show there're no hard feelings, Manuel — and Sarah, she's a good girl. A hard worker and the best damn cook in town, I can promise you. Why, it's gonna take some doing for us — the missus and me — to get used to someone else's meals after we've been spoiled all these years by the likes of hers. You don't know how lucky you are, getting a girl like that. She'll keep a fine house for you, Manuel. A fine house."

"House?"

"Yes, Manuel, house. Because, as I was saying, she's been with us a long time, Sarah has, and we mean to do what's right by her. Just as you do. No, sir, we don't intend, after all these years, to cut her short without a penny. So you see, things aren't as bad as you might've first thought they were. Not only are you going to get yourself a prize cook and housekeeper, but a little cash on the side as well."

The pinched brows relaxed somewhat, but the soft eyes remained wary.

"How's two thousand sound? Two thousand to help give her — and you, of course — a little start in life. Set the two of you on your feet." And to add force to his words, he took out his checkbook and ruffled the blank checks with his thumb. "Two thousand dollars, Manuel. That's more than you've ever seen all together at one time in your entire life. And by the way things look so far, more than you're ever like to see."

"Two thousand, you say?"

"Yes, two thousand, Manuel. Two thousand government certified silver dollars. And what you do with them's your business. As I see it, a man's head of his own house or he's head of nothing, so naturally I'll make the check out to your name, Manuel, case you got any doubts on that score. Got pen and ink right here with me so you won't have to worry I might forget my promise tomorrow."

4

Two thousand dollars! Sarah hardly seemed worth so much. The price of an acre of the richest land. It was enough to make

Manuel smile bravely at the altar rail in his tight collar and multi-creased trousers; it was even enough to make him overlook the shiny satin mound of the bride's belly, as slick and pure as a St. Joseph's lily, for despite the overwhelming evidence against her, she had insisted upon a white wedding with a wreath of wax orange blossoms and a veil of curtain netting.

Magnanimous to the end, Vince, who had given the bride away, smiled contentedly from his front pew. Two thousand dollars. Why, the sight of the pregnant Sarah as proud as Juno in her white satin was alone worth that.

5

Only Clara failed to be amused. She, of course, did not attend the wedding.

Minus stays, she had returned to consciousness beneath her satin comforter her head fairly riddled with spikes. And there was no one she could blame but herself. How blind she had been! In her very own house to have sheltered one of the devil's handmaidens and not to have recognized the Jezebel for what she was! And there must have been signs. Countless signs. All manner of sly gestures and looks suggestive of abominations she trembled to dwell upon. But worse — and for this she would never be able to forgive herself — to have with her own hands delivered her only son into the arms of the temptress. Her own home turned into a bawdy house! Her very sheets smeared with their sinful lust! Her darling and that fat, ugly — *slut* was hardly, considering the circumstances, too harsh a word.

But try as she would she could not put the two together. One simply did not set diamonds in tin rings — though swine, she supposed, as the Bible certainly bore witness, had often enough been fed on pearls. Although she knew it was wrong even to toy with the notion, she could not — with a sinking, guilty shiver — help wonder what marvelous changes the years had wrought in his slender body since last she had glimpsed it shining from the shower and dripping a puddle on the matless floor. All golden innocence. An ormolu Eros that any lady might, without offense, display leaning nonchalantly upon her mantle clock. Her exquisite darling soiled by the crude touch of a . . .

No! She would not allow herself to think about it. She must rinse her mind of all such thoughts. Bleach out the ugly blemishes and spotless once again sink into soothing oblivion. But the harder she struggled to escape the crude realities Sarah's shameful "condition" had forced upon her, the deeper the spikes pierced, and in her blind haste to get at the aspirin powders, she sent the nighttable lamp crashing to the marble top.

There was no one to scream at, no Sarah to come rushing to her aid, no cool hand to pry loose the imbedded nails, and whimpering she lifted the fringed lampshade with its beaded Venetian scene, fingering the gash, which had severed a black gondola and two pillars of the Doge's Palace. Ruined. It was ruined beyond repair. And biting her lip, she let it fall, lamp and all, crashing to the floor, her head sunk into the barbed-wire brambles of a swan's down pillow.

Agony! She had never known such agony!

But what did it matter? What did anything matter anymore? God knows she had tried, and against all odds, to create a little order in their lives. A civilizing touch of beauty to offset the stench of the barnyard. And there they were, behind her back, all ready to turn her lovely home into a pigsty. She had fed them on pearls and they had repaid her by soiling her best efforts with the smear of their slime. All those precious little touches of her own fashioning: satin valances, beaded lampshades, porcelain parrots — why were they all there? The trouble she had taken, the money she had spent — and all for what? Not, certainly, herself. But that her children might have the chance that fate had denied their parents: to grow up knowing nothing but the best that money could buy. Sheltered in an atmosphere of love and beauty. And what had her best efforts led to?

And turning her head, she let her eyes fall to the lamp in ruins beside the bed. But what did it matter? Let it lie there. Tinsel and alabaster. Why should she shed a single precious tear for a torn shade or a broken pedestal? Unlike her son's innocence, they could easily enough be replaced. And none too soon, after all. She was sick of it. Sick of the silly little gondola, sick of the pastry palace and the glitter moon. Sick of the entire room, for that matter, with its sun-streaked walls and rows upon rows of faded violets. What could ever have possessed her to choose such a pattern? An attack of momentary blindness or more likely the blandishments of some smooth-tongued salesman. Every one out to take advantage of her good nature. Abuse her soft heart. Well, that would all be different from now on. *Trust no one* would be her new rule of life, and there would be none then to betray her.

No, betrayal was everywhere. Even her own taste could no longer be trusted — for how tawdry it had all become, when it seemed only yesterday she'd had the whole thing redone. But those yesterdays had all been years eating away at her life as well as her wallpaper. Nothing lasted. Beauty or youth or beaded lampshades. Nothing. It was simply a marvel how she'd been able to bear it all these years — a room raining violets from every wall. Why, just to look at them made her dizzy. Pattern upon busy pattern, when she longed for the peace and quiet of an unadorned space. Rose, perhaps. She would have it all done over in a dusty rose. The chaise as well. A satin brocade. Tufted. And a fringe of silk. Lovely braided tassles. And the rug — would she dare try anything so daringly impractical as white? Or a Chinese pastel, yes, with lovely strange birds flying across golden skies above fields of sculptured flowers as soft as over-ripe melons. She could almost feel her bare feet sink into them . . .

And without knowing it had happened or when, the pain of past errors melded into the promise of future fashionings.

6

Exhaustion blotted out all dreams but merely postponed the misery. The next morning she woke before dawn with painfully stiff joints: swollen fingers that would not bend and arms that seemed soldered into the shoulder sockets. With an effort she slid her hand over the empty space beside her, the sheet cool and unrumpled. She was alone. For an instant panic seized her. She raised herself on her elbows, and as soon as she had verified the familiar rise and fall of her husband's breath coming from the screened sunporch off the bedroom, she fell back against the pillows with a sigh.

By the afternoon her fingers had limbered, but migraine had

set in, and her appetite seemed to have fled with Sarah's cooking. It would, she feared, be potluck for a long time to come. Vince again slept on the iron bed of the sunporch. So much to his liking did he find the fresh air and the open sunrise that it soon became his permanent summer abode, and Clara's stiff joints were spared the pain of his importunities. She herself received precious little comfort from the sparing. Perhaps if he could somehow tell her without her asking that she was still young and desirable, she might once again, through the magic of his touch, become young indeed, her poor aching body supple with its lost youth.

In the confusion of redecorating, Sarah and her sins were soon forgotten. There were other things to occupy Clara's mind. The painters seemed perversely determined not to give her the precise shade of rose she had imagined. The color they showed her wet turned out, when dry, either too bright or too dull, and twice the room had to be repainted. There were fabrics to choose, workmen to oversee, and the bedroom set to replace, for the old carved monster had proved far too dark and heavy for the pastel rug. There was Arnie's new motorcycle to worry her and there was Louise, voicing liberal heresies like an emancipated woman and encouraging the forbidden attentions of Henry Ramos, to set right. There was, in short — and as usual — more than one woman alone could manage, so that when Vince came home one evening with the announcement that the baby had been safely delivered, Clara had difficulty for a moment understanding what baby it was he was talking about.

"Oh, Sarah and Manuel's baby. A girl, you say?"

"What?" Clara looked up from her needlepoint.

"Immaculata. How's that strike you for cheek?"

Chuckling, he reached into the liquor cabinet for the brandy bottle, and taking it with him, settled into his gold plush chair. "I wouldn't be at all surprised if old Moriarity refused to baptize it till she picks something more fitting."

"Well, it does seem a bit old-fashioned," Clara answered, not sure she understood exactly why the name should so tickle her husband "but then Sarah's an old-fashioned girl. Took months to get her used to the electric stove. And never cold teach her how to make a real American pie. Though there's nobody in the world can make a lighter custard. I hope the poor thing's not going to be called Mac for short," she continued, trying to get her mind off Sarah's cooking and back on to the new baby. "But how *is* Sarah? I hope you told her how we miss her."

Matrimony is a sacrament, and the manifold powers derived from all sacraments are mystical in nature. Sarah's marriage had transformed the sluttish Jezebel of Clara's former nightmare into the respectable housewife of her present concern. In Clara's eyes it would have been cruelly vindictive to force Sarah Furtado to pay for the sins of Sarah Cabral, and whatever faults Clara might have, cruelty and vindictiveness were not among them. Unlike her husband, she had neither the taste for the one nor the talent for the other.

Vince seemed hardly surprised at his wife's solicitude.

"Sarah? Oh, nothing can get that girl down. I'm sure she'll find something to laugh about at the Last Judgment itself. It's Manuel that's the problem. Doesn't seem to take to marriage like he should."

"Well, maybe now he's a father he'll settle down. We'll have to send her something. Poor dear . . ."

Chapter Two

Trinity Sunday inaugurated San Oriel's spring rites. Traditionally the Holy Ghost Parade should have been held a week before, on the Feast of the Pentecost, but that was the day the city of Hayward had its parade. So few were the important feast days and so limited San Oriel's diversions, it seemed a waste for two towns so closely allied to hold their biggest celebration of the year on the same day, and it was not long before some enterprising soul had the happy notion of postponing San Oriel's parade for a week so that its citizens might partake of both celebrations. So successful was the compromise that the other Portuguese communities of the Bay Area were quick to follow, and one could for weeks celebrate the descent of the Holy Ghost simply by getting into a car or wagon and moving on to the next town, to San Lorenzo or Niles or Newark, or even as far away as Pescadero on the coast. Not only were there more parades, but each parade, enlarged by the visiting queens and their courts, was that much grander.

The parade began in the morning with an assembly in front of the *Irmandade do Divino Espirito Santo* Hall, known to all simply as the I.D.E.S. Hall. Long before sunrise crowds of sombre men and gesticulating women gathered, their faces etched as faintly as the last imprint of a worn plate with the stamp of a diverse lineage, the fruit of Prince Henry's dreams. The shrewd Semite, the sensual African, the fair Teuton, and the cautious Oriental all grafted onto a Latin stock formed the face of Portugal in its latest outpost.

Young boys, slender as reeds and sullen as the wind, stood immaculate in white shirts, white trousers, and white silk sashes. Impatient to have done with fussing, they grumbled protestations as they submitted to the last-minute ministrations of meticulous mothers striving to stabilize unruly cowlicks with doses of wave-set carried in purses for just such emergencies. As stiff as storybook dolls freshly removed from Christmas boxes, their hair fastidiously curled, be-ribboned, and capped with communion veils and tiaras of wax orange blossoms, the girls waited primly and coolly in the shade of an adjacent magnolia tree.

As the order of procession was arranged, noisy, sometimes angry, arguments ensued, for each position was ranked, and if Irene Gomez was to be a flower girl, then certainly Stella Cardoza had every right to be one as well, a prospect which was sure to leave Mamie Sousa fearful for *her* position. The enmities of competing mothers jealously guarding family prerogatives were numerous. Because her daughter had once been slighted as queen, Lena Perry had not spoken to a single member of the selection committee for the last twenty-three years, and her case was unique only for the length and unrivalled bitterness of her resentment.

The highest honor given a boy was to carry the silver, dove-topped crown and sceptre of Saint Queen Isabelle. The flag bearers were ranked below the banner bearers and the simple marchers lowest of all. The queen, of course, ruled, and her mother, as dowager, assumed the role of mistress of ceremonies.

Not everyone joined in the festivities with equal enthusiasm. There were those such as Vince and Clara Woods who found the custom too quaintly Old-Country for their tastes. To avoid the crowds of once-a-year Catholics with their cheap perfumes and wretched pomades, Clara took her brood to the early mass to sit in splendor in the nearly empty church, crowded with more flowers than parishioners, with banks of St. Joseph lilies and white roses and callas and snowballs and bridal veil and angel's breath. The sermon then was always blessedly short so that the building could be vacated in time to set up the coronation prie dieus. Religion, Clara felt, was a private affair, and she resented the public infliction of her faith upon her non-Catholic friends, most of whom could not themselves have been driven from their front porch rockers until the last marcher was long out of view. They and their guests formed a kind of reviewing stand, measuring this year's extravaganza against last year's, sure that the present queen couldn't hold a candle to her predecessor, though the new band certainly revealed a good deal more pluck with its Sousa marches than the old. The Woods children did not march, but nothing, not their father's laughter nor their mother's scorn, could have prevented them from taking their position at their front gate well before the parade was to arrive.

The parade began with the hired band playing martial hymns more redolent of cavalry then Calvary. Directly behind the band came the members of various lodges, each introduced by a youth with a banner identifying the lodge, its patron saint, and its town of origin. Two boys holding silk streamers flanked each banner and were in turn flanked by two more young men, one of whom carried the flag of Portugal and the other the Stars and Stripes. Under their ornate gilt sashes the marching men wore ill-fitting dark suits that reeked of history and camphor, their serge seats polished to a high gloss. Every brown, sun-burnt neck was pinched by a high paper collar rigidly unyielding and noosed with a sometimes-spotted and always clumsily knotted silk tie. The youngsters were mostly clean-shaven, but the weathered, foreign-born faces of their elders were invariably plumed with some hirsute adornment, a sloppy soupstrainer or a neatly trimmed Dapper Dan waxed to perfection. There was even an occasional beard, usually white, to dignify the oldest of the oldtimers.

The ladies of the S.P.R.S.I., preceded by a smart drill team led by Mae Serpa and her girls, were dressed in white gabardine and so tightly corseted it was sometimes difficult to tell where busts ended and chins began. Only the splendor of their white shoes was marred by the dust of the gravel road. They in turn were followed by a huge American flag borne recumbent by eight young boys also in white. It had first been introduced five years before as a patriotic expression of America's independence from what everyone hoped would remain Europe's war and was now proudly borne as an outsize declaration of America's victory in that same war, a glory all agreed no other country had any right to share. The bearers' slow progress was interrupted every few steps by solicitous mothers intent upon arranging a ruffle, a collar, or a sash or snapping yet another picture with their black box cameras.

Next came the musical honor guard of the first visiting queen, a trio composed of two saxaphones and an accordian playing the traditional *Alva Pomba,* White Dove. The melody was pleasantly innocuous, but played over and over again with scarcely a pause to mark the point at which one rendition finished and another began, it soon became hypnotic. The visiting queen was flanked by two attendant ladies-in-waiting, her splendor somewhat diminished by the absence of train-bearers, which were allowed only on the day of her own coronation, so that she had to carry the train of her cope thrown over one arm. She was, some were cruel enough to note, chewing gum, but the parade was long, the pauses were frequent, and few found it in their hearts to censure her.

The local queen came last of all, her arrival heralded by flower girls, some bearing wicker baskets of St. Joseph lilies, others scattering rose petals. Their number was limited only by the fecundity of the townsfolk in any given season or by an individual family's ability to finance a costume worthy to compete in splendor and workmanship with all the others. Few would not willingly have suffered malnutrition rather than that their little Lydia be allowed to march in a dress less gorgeous than Geraldine Freitas's — which was gorgeous indeed, with so many ruffles the envious matrons could only estimate the yards of stuff poor Mr. Freitas had had to pay for, to say nothing of the hours his wife had had to spend putting it all so marvelously together.

The queen herself shimmered in satin beaded with a thousand artificial pearls, her plump figure rather daringly uncorseted so that highlights flickered from every glossy bulge. Her hairy forearms were hidden under elbow-length gloves and her cape, the collar of which rose above her head, was edged with a rabbit fur so luxuriously thick and soft it might easily have been mistaken for ermine. Her crown was borne in the gloved hands of a sober-faced boy in white whose hair, oiled to a midnight blue, out-glossed the satin of his queen.The train bearers, a boy and a girl just out of their cradles, were apt at any moment to desert their post to turn to familiar faces on the sidelines, and when coaxed to return, let the precious yardage drag carelessly in the dust so that the fur lip was soon more gray than white. As the musicians of the hired band clustered on the front stairs of

St. Anthony's to smoke, to joke, or to nap in the spring sun, the overflow crowd strained to push its way through the jammed front porch to see the young maiden crowned at high mass by a grim-faced Father Moriarity, who looked upon the spectacle with ill-disguised distaste as a pagan rite that must somehow be tolerated for the Greater Good.

After the final benediction the reassembled parade returned by a different route to the I.D.E.S. Hall. Here in the tiny chapel separated from the main building by the refreshment stand and festooned with green and red bunting, the queen placed the crown and sceptre on the flower-decked altar for the worship of the multitudes. Throughout the day they made their way in pairs to kneel before it with considerably more devotion than that bestowed on the tabernacle itself. A white dove was loosed from its cage, but instead of flying through the open doors of the chapel, it settled on the rafters and had to be shooed to its freedom with a broom, its delayed flight greeted by the cheers of the assembled throng.

In front of the chapel the auction tables were already set up. Here the women displayed their handicraft and the men their produce. Embroidered linens mixed with caged pigeons and chained goats, and crocheted doilies starched as stiff as cardboard served as lace collars to pyramids of loquats and cherries.

Though he ignored the parade, Vince Woods never missed the auction. With the not inconsiderable advantage of ready cash, he never failed to walk away with the best bargains of the afternoon. Today he is elegantly dressed in brown English tweed faintly flecked with scarlet, one of the few men present with either the means or the imagination to free himself from the tyranny of black — the single suit that must serve for feast, wedding, or funeral and is almost a badge of peasantry. His expensive stomach is held in the firm grasp of a tight vest crossed with two gold chains, one of which holds his watch and the other a gold penknife. A row of cigars juts from his top pocket and a diamond stickpin adorns his tie. He carries a walking stick in one hand and with the other guides his daughter Lorraine through the crowd. To distinguish her from the marchers, she wears pink, the lack of ruffles on her dress compensated for by the richness of the fabric. At this approach the crowds part, hats tip, and the weathered faces grin broadly. Whenever he stops to speak, the men always stand a little straighter, their hands pumping the air as if they felt the need to crush their hats against their chests yet still retained enough pride to keep their respect, though fulsome, just short of obsequious. For it is spring and there will soon be plenty of jobs. Dropping Lorraine's hand, Vince squats to his heels to inspect a calf tied to the chapel stairpost, feeling its hind legs and checking its teeth.

"What do you think it'll bring?" he asks a farmer standing nearby.

The farmer shakes his head and rubs his chin. "Wouldn't dare say, Vince," he says. "Wouldn't dare say." But the word goes round that Vince Woods is interested in Oliveiera's calf, and the more timid of the would-be bidders, unwilling to antagonize the great man, shift their interest from the calf to the goat.

Before the refreshment booth Arnie struts with a princely swagger, his old friend and sycophant, Ken Yamamura, whose father owns the green houses on the delta of the creek, close at his heels. He laughs at Arnie's jokes, points out the sights, and accepts the overflow of his friend's bounty with a gratitude that comes near to groveling. Behind the booths, their sleeves rolled up, their ample figures swathed in canvas aprons, the cooks bend over huge cauldrons of mint-flavored *sopas*. Sarah Furtado, nee Cabral, the hairs bristling from the wart on her chin, her curls tied down with a blue bandana, sweat glazing her cheeks, spies a familiar face and calls out:

"I've something sweet for you, my pretty, if you save me a dance."

Arnie blushes — for he can blush — his Apollonian features teased by a fall of hair, which he quickly brushes back with a rake of his fingers and a toss of his head.

"Sweet as shit," he answers, poking his friend with his elbow. Ken doubles over with laughter.

Sarah answers in Portuguese, which she very well knows Arnie cannot understand, but the women helping her do, and by the bawdy quality of their laughter he knows he has been bested. Still blushing, he moves out of her view and in passing pinches a girl on the arm. With an outraged squeal, she whirls about. "Oh, it's *you!*" she says with a haughty toss of her pretty head.

116

"I might've known." And she and her friends, their sneers untempered by restraint, move out of the range of his fingers.

Glancing over her shoulders to be sure that she is not being followed or spied upon, Louise Woods follows Henry Ramos past the private hedge to the rows of tables set up under the grape arbor, where the free *sopas* is being served. He is wearing a large white sweater too heavy for such a warm afternoon, but he wants to show off his red and blue block letter, a large M prefixed by a small ST. He has curly hair parted in the middle, which gives his most collegiate face a somewhat fatuous symmetry saved from silliness by his open, eagerly friendly expression and the obvious intelligence of his eyes. Just finished with his freshman year at St. Mary's College, he has been chosen cheerleader and is capable of a little swagger of his own, though he draws the line at pinching girls; as the town's single bona fide intellectual he has a position to maintain of which he is almost painfully sensitive. As they seat themselves, they look about secure in the knowledge that the envy they inspire is well deserved, for they are both young and beautiful and clearly the children of prosperity. The sound of the auctioneer's voice can be heard above the din of the servers and the diners so they know they are at least temporarily safe from Vince's scrutiny, but before they can be served, Louise rises. Her Aunt Belle has entered and a hush falls on the gathering.

She is alone. She is always alone in public; no one has ever seen her beyond her garden gate in Olaf's presence. Her appearance has changed considerably. Though she looks no older, she looks, somehow, more than ever the spinster. Her carriage, which had formerly been erect, is now positively rigid. There is a defensive haughtiness about all her gestures. Her dress is too tightly buttoned too high, her sleeves are long and her skirt, unyielding to the post-war fashions, still falls to her ankles. The only flesh that one can see is the flesh of her face and that is still remarkably free of wrinkles.

Blushing, Louise takes hold of her aunt's upper arms and kisses her on the cheek. Belle smiles and returns the kiss, but it is clear that their former closeness has been strained and she shrinks from the too obvious solicitude. She shakes Henry's hand without removing her gloves, nodding her head and simply voicing his name as greeting.

"Won't you join us, Miss Bettencourt?" he asks, not so much a man of the world that he does not also blush at his words.

"No thank you, Henry," she says, looking about her for a ready excuse to spare the lovers her ponderous presence. "I'll sit here with Mae Dutra for awhile and chat. You and Louise stay where you are."

And Mae Dutra, who looks anything but pleased, but does not dare, all by herself, to go so far as a public rebuff, ungraciously makes room for the notorious Belle Bettencourt to sit beside her.

Arnie enters with Ken a few steps behind, like a royal retainer who knows his place. The princely walk is even more arrogant, his tight hips swiveling on their narrow axis. Everyone knows him but the smiles that greet him are less than warm. He spies his sister at the far end, but unwilling to pit himself against Ramos, as he calls Henry, he spares her his attentions and plops down on the nearest bench alongside one of his father's workers.

"Lo, Joe," he says, reaching into the little man's comb pocket and lifting out a package of cigarettes nestled there. Joe watches him without smiling, but he raises no verbal objection. Arnie offers one of Joe's cigarettes to his friend and, taking one himself, returns the pack to the little man's pocket.

"Well, aren't you gonna offer me a light?" he asks, as the cigarette dangles, unlit, from his lips.

Without taking his eyes off his plate, Joe reaches into his pocket and finding a large kitchen match places it on the table beside the boy. With a wink and a shrug, Arnie picks it up, lights his own cigarette, then leaning across the table, holds the still burning match before Ken's.

Relieved from the cauldron to wait on tables, Sarah winks at Arnie. A moment later she appears with a plate piled with a double helping of the mint-flavored beef. As she leans over to serve him, her breast, not altogether accidentally, for old time's sake, presses against his shoulder.

Inside the hall the dancing has begun — the *chamarita*. The saxaphonists and the accordianist have been joined by two fiddlers,

118

and the groups begin to form, the elders sitting on the benches that line the walls. It is not a complicated dance, and except for the music, which is decidedly foreign, not unlike a square dance, so simple, in fact, that even the clumsiest of farmhands after a couple of draughts of homemade wine can make a fair show; sometimes, if he is properly drunk and his partner properly nubile, he may even add a few bawdy turns of his own with his bandana slung underneath his hips.

As it grows darker, the mood changes. The paper lanterns over the raised dias that acts as a stage are lit. The musicians and the dancers rest for awhile, sitting on the floor. An old man comes forward with a large black-and-silver guitar. He takes his coat off and hangs it on the side of his chair. His sleeves are held up with two rubber armbands and his trousers by frayed suspenders. His white hair is still ringed with the mark of his hat and his eyes are moist with the tears that never cease to flood them. He begins to play, his head bent so low over his instrument he seems intent upon deciphering some secret message whispered too softly to be heard above the music his fingers make.

A woman comes forward out of the group of dancers. She takes a black shawl that has been lying on top the upright piano in the corner and wraps it about her body. Suddenly she throws back her head, and the flickering lights of the paper lanterns expose an agony every bit as private and intense as childbirth. She is singing.

It is a strange song, alienating each in a private sorrow. For as long as the music continues, couples cease to be couples and become strangers, their hands, though touching, insensate. No one looks directly at the singer for more than an instant. Throbbing with echoes of a Moorish lament, her murky-rich contralto is so taut that high notes, caught in the throat, burst like sharp fragments of glass. It is fado — a song of mourning for lost times and lost loves, for dreams that have died and for sights that are no more.

When the song is finished the applause is perfunctory and in no way measures the intensity of the broken spell. The woman takes off her shawl and resumes her place in the crowd. Someone calls out something in Portuguese. There is scattered

119

laughter, mostly male; the mood has changed and the musicians once again take over.

"I hate that kind of music," Louise says. A practical girl, she is not given to nostalgia for a country she has never seen. "She wasn't once on pitch," she adds as they make their way through the hall door.

"If you spoke Portuguese it would make a difference." There is a note of censure in Henry's voice. More chauvanistic than she, he is fascinated by all things Portuguese; it is a penchant she is more than willing to tolerate as long as it stops short — far short — of an actual return to either the Old World or its ossified attitudes. It is the undertone of condescension that disturbs her.

"Well, that's hardly *my* fault," she snaps, then regretting her sudden, inexplicable sharpness, she takes his arm, holding him back to slow his pace. Ahead of them in the shadows a solitary figure trudges along the gravel path. Though the street is dark, the walk is unmistakable: sober and purposeful, the figure strides rather than strolls, alone in the dark, her purse hanging from one hand almost lost in the folds of her skirt.

"Poor Aunt Belle," Louise whispers with just a touch of that contempt the whole feel for the lame.

"Do you think —?" Henry begins but has not the courage to finish.

"Think what?" Louise's temper is already alert. More than casually conscious of her family's faults, she is, outside the family circle, even with Henry, the first to champion their cause.

"Well, that Olaf and she . . ."

Again he cannot bring himself to finish, but there is no need; his meaning is clear.

"Oh, Henry! How can you? Belle!" Tickled rather than offended by the absurdity of the suggestion, she crushes his arm against her side. "Why, she must be fifty, for goodness sakes."

The idea seems sufficiently ludicrous to both of them to stem all further speculation, and Henry answers her squeeze by putting his arm around her shoulder and drawing her closer to him, bending to brush his lips against her neck. With a sudden squat and a skip, she slips away from his hold and once again takes his arm.

120

"Someone's liable to see us."

"Oh, Loo, it's dark enough."

"It'll only be that much nicer if we have to wait," she says, and too intent upon the promised alliance for more words, they head for the creek in silence. And the solitary figure before them becomes just one more shadow in a night already filled with shadows.

Chapter Three

1

Aware that she was being followed, Belle would not look back, nor would she hasten her steps. Although the night was dark, she knew there was nothing to fear. No one would harm her. Nor would anyone rush to intrude upon her privacy; that much at least she was sure to be spared. As she crossed the footbridge over the creek she could see the yardlight waiting for her, and all the pain of the afternoon and evening was dissipated in its warm glow. She was in her own yard where someone cared enough for her safety to light the way for her, and as she passed the tankhouse, she longed to knock on the door to thank him so that she might end the evening with the sound of one kind and loving voice, but her life was circumscribed by an extensive code of unwritten laws. She never entered the tankhouse when he was in it. She made his bed and changed his linens and gathered his laundry always after he had himself left, and though the prohibition had never been more than tacitly agreed upon, it had been sanctified by habit, and she feared now that any break in the almost inflexible routine that their life had assumed might serve as the impetus, which once set off, could never again be contained. She had borne every cruelty of the afternoon with fortitude, but a touch of kindness, she knew, might be the ultimate cruelty, dissolving her in tears against his chest. And if she, who had the blessings and the benefits of God's grace, proved herself weak, how then could she expect him to remain strong? For his lack of faith had become over the years more painful for her than his possession of a wife — though she could no more have discussed the one than the other.

His dinner dishes were stacked in the kitchen sink waiting for her. Without taking off her hat or coat, but simply removing her gloves, she rinsed them with cold water from the tap, and, lighting the burner under the kettle to heat the water for washing, she sat down at the table, still in her coat and hat, and waited for the water to boil. She would have preferred — a thousand times preferred — to stay at home and share his meal of leftovers with him, but she knew that such a gesture on such a day would have been interpreted as cowardice. Or worse, an admission of shame. And for fear of that, she had stayed longer than she might ordinarily have and braved every last sad song. An evening of fado as cheerful as a lover's wake. She could not free herself from their lugubrious melodies, as waiting for the kettle to whistle, she looked back upon their life together; and she knew that she would not — given the circumstances — have had it any other way.

Almost immediately their life had assumed a routine so lacking in variety or excitement, so staggeringly monotonous to all but the two concerned, that it should have been proof against all gossip, but gossip was a way of life in San Oriel. It took the place of the dramas that could not be performed for want of a stage to play them on and for want of actors to act in them. There was no cinema, such as it then was, within less than five miles and only the wealthy as yet had radios. Where there was no theatre, the people created their own, and nothing Belle or Olaf could have done, or failed to do, could have prevented them from becoming dramatis personae in the living theatre of San Oriel.

The drama of their lives was only incidentally connected with the facts of their life, that every morning they shared breakfast, and every evening dinner, after which they sat about the table, with Belle doing most of the talking, Olaf's sentences limited for the most part to brief declarations of fact or of action: "Hauled two tons of cots today," or, "The early rain's ruined the tomatoes."

Of such small bits and pieces was their life constructed. The routine varied little from that of others in the town. Their life together was possibly more placid than that of their more volatile neighbors. Not for any lack of emotion. But since they had not the luxury of loving, they could not afford the luxury of quarreling. Yet they *were* different. They were not married and they could not marry and thus nothing they could do together, from the most ordinary routine to the most refined ritual, could

124

fail to be of absorbing interest to their neighbors.

There were, Belle found, things harder to bear than talk. It was difficult at first as she passed him sitting in his chair or bent over the fire in the stove, stoking the logs of cherrywood or apricot, the form of his strong, slender back outlined by the taut shirt. She would be overcome with the urge to touch him, like some ache in the bones of her hands, which she would then rub across the face of her apron, rubbing, rubbing, as if she might thus wear away desire. But here as well habit proved her salvation. They almost never touched, more careful of contact than strangers on a bus. And the force of her chastity soon worked its enchantment upon him. It stifled the first timid advances, drew the shades on his bewildered questioning gaze, until desire was soon proscribed by a taboo as sacred as that against incest. And he became less her lover than her son.

Every action became, as soon as it was performed, a part of the ritual of their life together, and every novelty soon assumed the force and comfort of habit. The hours of his entrances and exits, the schedule for bathing in the great lion-clawed tub, the rack upon which his towel hung, the ashtray that appeared with his coffee, the toothpick that signaled his departure — all had been formalized their first week together and had never been altered. The same was true of their late and leisurely Saturday breakfasts and the solitary Sunday mornings devoted, on her part, to mass, and on his to sleeping off the bout of drinking that invariably followed the most controversial of all their rituals — their Saturday night in the Sunday parlor.

It was hardly a room to be taken lightly. Even those who, like Clara, had left their heritage behind experienced in it an atavistic sense that great and unusual things were about to happen, that only a day among days permitted their intrusion upon memories too sacred to profane with their living presences. That Belle should choose such a room in which to entertain such a man every Saturday from seven-thirty to nine-thirty seemed, to her family at least, the true measure of her defection.

What in such a setting they could possibly have found to do — or given the personalities of the two concerned, to say — became a matter of obsessive interest, not only to the family, but to all of San Oriel. They were closely observed for any hint that might cast light upon the mystery — which was, in truth, no deeper than the box of dominoes stored in the drawer of the shawl-covered, picture-ladened table, their every move chaperoned from every wall by eyes too fiercely intent to have allowed the least breach in the family's honor. But so simple a solution suggested itself to no one, and would, moreover, have satisfied no one, for gossip feeds best upon fiction.

It was noticed and reported that Belle never, for a single Sunday, failed to receive the sacraments. But even here she left room for ambiguity. For she had in her makeup a streak of perversity, a stubbornness every bit as unyielding as her brother-in-law's. She might, as was customary, and considering the near proximity of her home to the church, almost obligatory, have confessed on Saturday afternoon, or better, if her conscience had been clear, omitted confession altogether. Instead, she chose with unfailing regularity to wait until Sunday morning before mass to shrive her sins before the assembled congregation. By this public act, she deliberately courted speculation. For whatever else they had come to believe her capable of, sacrilege was not included, and certainly if her relations were, as the family never ceased to claim, blameless, she could very well, like most of the other communicants, have confessed on Saturday.

What it was she confessed on Sunday morning only Father Moriarity knew. Olaf, the only other person who might have solved the mystery, never, not even during his ritualistic and joyless weekend drunks, allowed her name to cross his lips in public. Thus they might very well have braved the storm roused by their defiance of the social conventions had not each won the enmity of the single man capable of crushing them. Belle was the first to offend, and the instrument of that offense was his own daughter.

2

"I don't care what anyone says, they're innocent." Louise rolled up her napkin and stuffed it through a silver ring.

"Unfortunately the jury happened to disagree with you. Of course," Vince continued, "they haven't had your advantages. They aren't enrolled at the University of California. So naturally they don't have access to your inside information."

"It's not a question of 'inside information.' The trial wasn't fair. Everyone knows that." Or everyone with any sense, she wanted to add but had the good sense not to. "It was already decided in the newspapers long before the jury was picked."

"And you, I suppose, want to change all that. The whole damn system. Throw it all out and begin over again. With a woman president, no doubt."

"Oh, there's no arguing with you." Louise pushed her chair away from the table, the sickle-tips of her new bob trembling. "It always comes down to the same thing. Just like the unions. Because someone happens to believe a worker's entitled to a living wage, you think he's out to overthrow the government. And what does being a woman have to do with it, anyway? Are men given exclusive title to truth and wisdom?"

"There's no need to get excited, Dear. I'm sure your father knows what he's talking about. After all, he's been around a good deal longer than you have." Clara rang the silver bell beside the water glass. "This Lydia simply isn't going to do," she continued. "Things just haven't been the same around here since Sarah left." And once again she rang the bell impatiently.

"If it isn't sex it's age," Louise muttered against the background of her mother's complaints. "Hasn't anyone around here ever heard of logic?"

The real argument, which ran like a turbulent under-current throughout the seemingly placid course of the dinner, did not concern Sacco and Vanzetti, but his daughter's recently bobbed hair, a mutilation in Vince's eyes almost as shocking as murder. Why, she might as well have hacked off her breasts and have done with it. And there wasn't any question in his mind about the source of his daughter's radicalism.

"A school for revolutionaries — is that what they're running up there in Berkeley? Defending anarchists and bomb throwers! I suppose the next thing we'll be asked to put up with is the spectacle of you marching down public streets with some sign, defending common murderers."

"The point is," Louise continued, straining for self-control, "that they *aren't* murderers. They didn't kill anyone and they're being persecuted now simply because of their political beliefs. No one's denying they're anarchists — but you don't send a man to the electric chair just because he happens to believe in a different form of government. Our system isn't perfect, you know."

"Nothing's perfect, Dear, but you don't go around throwing bombs to change things," Clara interposed. She could never get the names of the two men straight, which was the shoemaker and which the fish peddler, and she couldn't see why they should have such a disruptive effect upon her dinner table.

Ignoring her, Louise rose.

"Where are you going? We haven't had dessert yet." Clara fixed her daughter with a troubled look.

Louise stood behind her chair, her pose and expression rigidly under control, as Lydia, the latest in a long succession of maids, strolled casually through the swinging door to clear the dinner dishes. "I'm going upstairs to change clothes." Then, attempting to sound off-handed, "I'm meeting Henry later."

Lorraine followed every word, her gaze moving from face to face. Absorbed in the drama, she was unconscious of her finger probing her nostril until she felt the sting of Clara's hand and a whispered,

"We don't pick our nose at dinner table."

Clara turned from Lorraine to her husband, but did not have to speak. The message was clear, and as soon as the too-curious Lydia disappeared behind the kitchen door, he rose to the challenge, the calm of his voice countered by the sharp chill of his gaze.

"I thought your mother expressly asked you not to see Henry anymore."

"I'm twenty-one — or almost — and I suppose I can see anyone I want to." Though she tried to plane down the rough edges, her speech came out bristling with splinters.

"So! You're twenty-one, are you? Your own boss now, is that it? Well, then, will you please tell me why I should be wasting *my* hard-earned money to send you to the university? Turning my own daughter into a Red with my own funds? Only a fool sets fire to his own house. If you're twenty-one and so blessedly independent, you can damn well pay your own way. Why don't you, for a change, consider how exploited I've been all these years, instead of my workers? Not one of which, by the way, has ever dropped dead from overwork. And exploited by my own, I might add. Not strangers."

"Oh, Daddy, you wouldn't!"

"Oh, wouldn't I! As long as you're living in this house at our expense, you'll do precisely as we ask. Twenty-one or no twenty-one. And I'm asking you now to sit down and eat your dessert with the rest of us. Because you're not seeing Henry Ramos. Tonight or any other night."

It was no longer a question of the Ramoses but of his rights as a father. If a man couldn't expect the respect and obedience of his own children in his own house, what was left?

The simple act of cutting her hair, for which fashion had initially been far more responsible than any desire to declare her emancipation, was having unforeseen consequences; Louise remained for the moment speechless, gripping the back of the chair.

"I really don't see, Dear, why you're so determined to get involved with that Ramos clan," Clara said.

"I wasn't aware they were a 'clan.' I thought they were a family. Rather like our own, for that matter. From the same country with the same religion." Her knuckles on the back of the chair shone white.

"A bunch of speculators," Vince huffed. "Tom Ramos doesn't know beans about business."

He took a cigar out of his coat pocket and noisily unwrapped it.

"Can't you wait, Dear, until after dessert," Clara ventured, her concern for her husband's excessive smoking provoked by his doctor's warning.

"Why should I wait until after dessert when it's now I want it?" he snapped, then turning once again to his daughter, he broadened his attack:

"Every penny comes in goes out. On show or some damnfool speculation. Diamonds for Mae and parties for everyone. Get rich quick — that's all they think about. Like everybody else these days. How to get rich without having to work for it. A lot of paper empires they're all building. Well, let me tell you: it takes a good deal more than guesswork and a nose for gambling to build a solid fortune."

"You sound as if you're afraid he's liable someday to be as

rich as you are."

"You're mighty sure of yourself, young lady." Controlling his anger, Vince lowered his voice: "Where Tom Ramos is concerned, I'm afraid of nothing. Why, he's the softest touch this side of paradise. Every hardluck Johnny within miles knows that. A halfway convincing sob story and before you know it, he's *paying* the rent, instead of collecting it. And once you get a reputation like that, you might as well throw in the towel."

"And weren't the rich instructed to give to the poor? At least it seems to me I read that somewhere."

Vince smiled. "And saints, I suppose, go around having their hair bobbed, rushing off to the beauty parlor to keep up with every fad. I don't notice you giving your sheets away to sleep on the floor."

"For one thing they aren't mine to give."

"Damn right they aren't. And I'm glad you recognize that fact."

"And those parties, Dear." Clara did not like the turn the conversation seemed to be taking. "Even you must admit no lady — and Mae certainly thinks she's one, way she dogs herself up for Sunday mass. You'd think she owned the church and the rest of us were there at her invitation. But you can be sure, no lady would allow such carrying-on under her roof. Bootleg whiskey for everyone. And the noise! Landsakes, you can hear it clear across the creek. Like a bunch of wild Indians on the warpath. People their age! Oughtta be ashamed of themselves."

"I don't see what the Ramoses and their parties have to do with anything. It's Henry I want to marry. Not his family."

"So it's gone that far has it?" Her father met the threat.

Holding her knife like a standard planted in the table, Lorraine sat even more erect, her commitment to the drama absolute.

"Of course it's gone *that* far. Why else would I put up with scenes like this every time I want to see him?" Her eyes filled with angry tears. "Would you like it better if I told you I just wanted to sleep with him?"

"Louise Woods!" Clara's hand came down hard upon the table, upsetting Lorraine's standard and bringing a sudden choking halt to her giggle. "That does it! I never thought I'd live to see the day. Vince," she turned to her husband, "I think you're right, the university *has* done something to her and it's about time we put a stop to it. She never used to talk like that. And in front of your sister. To say nothing of your own mother and father. I don't care how old you are. I won't have any daughter of mine using language like that in my house. Do you understand?''

She would not cry, nor would she bow the weak knee to her parents' will.

"I'm sorry, Mother. I'm sorry for your sake I was ever born. And Daddy, too. I'm sorry, But I can't for the life of me see what it is you have against Henry. And please! Don't give me that tired old story about 'poor simple-minded Julia.' We wouldn't have to open many closets in our own family to find a few skeletons hanging around. At least Henry's trying to make something out of his life. Not like some other young men I could mention.''

"Just what young men you referring to?''

Vince felt the weight of his years bearing down upon him. Suddenly old and tired. Even the cigar tasted vile, and he stubbed out the stump, half unsmoked, in the ashtray.

"Just exactly what do you know about this young man isn't already common knowledge round here?'' he asked without waiting for her reply.

"It's more than the knowledge that's common.'' She took refuge in innuendo.

"Won't someone please tell me what's going on?'' Vince looked from his daughter to his wife and back to his daughter, his face ruddy, the mask of civility cast aside. "Why am I always the last one to know what's going on in my own household?''

"Why don't you ask him yourself? Since you're such a fine judge of character, you shouldn't have any trouble at all seeing through his lies. They're transparent enough.''

"Listen, young lady, I've had just about all the insolence from you I can take for one evening. Are you or are you not going to sit down and eat your dessert like we asked?''

"No, Daddy, I am not.''

"Well, then, you can damn well resign yourself to not going back to the university next fall. Looks like two years have already been two years too many.''

131

Louise flushed. Her back stiffened. That her father's threat was real she did not for an instant doubt, and that conviction made her all the more determined not to give in. There was, after all, a difference between filial honor and slavery. And as she confronted her father's gaze without flinching, she thrilled at the grandeur of the sacrifice demanded of her.

"All right," she began, her eyes brilliant with defiance, her beauty momentarily dazzling, touching even her father, whose own emotions were sufficiently ambivalent to temper his anger with exaltation, "if that's the way it must be, that's the way it'll be. Because I'm going to marry Henry Ramos. Even if *I* have to do the proposing. And nothing either of you can say is going to change my mind."

And with a snappy turn, she marched from the table with stiff dignity, her dessert uneaten, her father's imprecations snapping ineffectually at her heels.

3

So full was she with a sense of her father's injustice, Louise rushed through her aunt's screendoor without knocking, only to come to a shocked halt. It was not so much Olaf's presence that startled her as the way they both started, like guilty children, at her entrance. In his haste to scramble to his feet, Olaf knocked over his chair.

She blushed — for them rather than herself. "I'm sorry," she said, "I didn't know . . ." And her attempt to excuse her surprise visit merely compounded her confusion.

"That's quite all right." Belle rose, attempting to cover her embarrassment with a smile so forced it might have been a fissure left by some seismological upheaval. "We were just finishing." She began stacking the plates with neat efficiency. "Since we don't have someone to cook for us, we don't eat as early as you folks," she added half reproachfully as she moved to the sink to deposit her load. "Join us for a cup of coffee?" she asked without turning.

Her aunt's repetitious and insistent use of the first person plural forced Louise for the first time to see them as the two halves of a couple. Ignoring the invitation, she remained transfixed

132

by Olaf's glowering eyes.

Without a word, he moved away from the table, granting her in passing a curt nod. Still too surprised to return his gesture, she shuddered inwardly as he brushed by. His clothing exuded an odor as bitter as his expression. Vaguely Lincolnesque, his face might have been redeemed if his eyes had revealed a touch of Lincoln's humanity instead of scowling mistrust. A touch of the poet, perhaps. Instead, he was all earth and grime, muscle and sweat and brooding silence. And once again the mystery of her aunt's predilection troubled her. Though she had never — until this moment — doubted that their relationship was anything but chaste, she had never been able to imagine why anyone, let alone someone so special as her aunt, would jeopardize her good name for a man who, despite his flaming hair, revealed all the warmth of a Norse winter. But greater than the mystery was her resentment that anyone at all should have come between her and the aunt she had loved far more than she had ever loved her mother — or anyone else, until now.

Making no effort to stop him, Belle followed Olaf to the door, calling after him a request clearly intended as one more declaration of their union, as if she were, in her own way, saying to her niece: *Yes, my dear, he comes even before you.*

"You might look after the Ford, Olaf, and see if you can figure out why the motor's skipping. Well, Dear?" She turned back into the room and defensively confronted her visitor.

"Nothing really." With a sigh and a shrug Louise sank disconsolately onto the nearest chair. "I asked Henry to meet me here so he wouldn't have to run into Daddy." And taking the cup intended for Olaf, she studied the coffee as she stirred it, oppressed by an acute sense of her aunt's shame.

"I'm going to marry him," she announced with such a lack of excitement Belle looked up, troubled.

"I would have been surprised if you had told me you weren't going to." Reclaiming her own cup, she sat beside her niece. "So why, since you've finally made up your mind, would you sound so unhappy?"

"It's Daddy."

"Ah . . .!" There was a volume of shared sympathy in that *ah:* pages upon pages of childhood's bitter anguish blotted by

133

her own soft breasts.

"It's my bob that set him off," she said, touching the ends of her severed locks with a coy blush. "He thinks I'm trying to declare my emancipation. And if there's one thing we don't need around the house, it's an Emancipated Woman." She made a halfhearted attempt to belittle her father's opposition by mocking it with her mimicry.

"Yes, I noticed." Inspecting the new cut with a baffling lack of curiosity, Belle gave no sign of approval or disapproval — or indeed, of any real interest at all in how her niece chose to wear her hair — and the young girl's blush deepened.

"He sees it as just one more manifestation of the 'Red Menace.'" With forced jocularity she tried to expose the absurdity of her father's position, interpreting her bow to fashion as a tribute to Lenin rather than to Irene Castle. "He's already stopped my allowance, and he means to keep me from returning to the University in the fall," she continued. "So I'll have to live at home again where he can keep his eye on me. He even rather grandly threatened to disinherit me if I go through with it — the wedding, I mean. It's already too late to do anything about the hair. Though I'm ready at this point to have it all cut off," she threatened not very convincingly.

"But what can your father have against Henry?"

"Oh, it's not Daddy, really. It's Mamma who's put him up to it. Not that Daddy has any love for the Ramoses. Or anyone else who might get in his way."

"Still poor Julia?"

Louise nodded. "And it's all so silly. Just because her mother tried to force an abortion. With a crochet hook," she added, shivering visibly.

"Well, the Emancipated Woman is blunt, if nothing else."

For the first time Belle's smile seemed not forced and for a moment they came close to sharing their old intimacy.

"I prefer 'honest.' Facts are facts and they have to be faced. Running away from them doesn't get you anywhere." Then suddenly remembering Olaf, whose chair she occupied but whose existence she herself preferred to ignore, Louise blushed again.

Since the gap caused by her niece's embarrassment was so

easily bridged, Belle responded with more force than was perhaps called for: "Yes, facts do have to be faced. You're right there."

"But I'm not really worried about the marriage," she continued. "Daddy'll come around to that eventually. I'll see to that. In the meantime, he'll keep me out of school and out of cash. Just to test my will. When he should know, by this time, how much of his own blood I have in me. Why, at this point I'd marry Henry even if I didn't love him."

"But you do, I hope?"

"Yes. Fortunately." She looked at her aunt and blushed again. She had meant to ask her, if she might, in the interim, until the marriage, live with her. There was no lack of space, a whole hive of empty rooms, but Olaf's presence, it was all too clear, made such a move impossible, and she hated the strange man for further complicating her life.

"Well, then, what are you fretting about? You're in love with a fine boy, he's in love with you, and you're going to marry each other." She shook her head, unable to give her niece the sympathy she seemed to be demanding. "Don't ask for too much," she added. Then fearful that her remark might be read as a demand for pity, she quickly turned from the girl's insistent gaze.

"But I'll be his prisoner. For a whole year. Until Henry gets his degree. Without even a penny to buy myself a new dress, let alone fill my hope chest."

"Well, then, get yourself a job." There was an edge of impatience in Belle's voice. "That's easily done. You type, don't you? Then come to the bank with me. Inez Cardoza's expecting and she'll be leaving in another week or so."

"Oh, Belle!" Louise threw her arms around her aunt's neck, so thrillingly simple was the solution after all. Her father would be furious, and nothing, absolutely nothing, could delight her more. "You're still my favorite," she said. "Still my Belle."

Belle stiffened, a reflex so spontaneous it might have sprung from repugnance. There was such poison in that "still" that Louise drew away, covering her confusion as well with a perfunctory kiss.

4

"What's wrong with you tonight?" Henry asked, drawing

135

back from her unresponsive kiss.

"Oh, everything's so complicated," she answered, letting her head fall back against the seat of Henry's roadster and enjoying, more than just a little, the new sense of playing a role in life's drama. "Belle and Olaf. And everything. I had another fight with my father tonight," she said, sitting up straight to avoid the smoke from the cigarette he had just lit. "That's a nasty habit," she added, fanning the smoke with her hand. "You have no idea how awful it makes your mouth taste."

"About me again?" He ignored her comment on the taste of his kisses.

"Yes. It all started over my hair, but that was only an excuse to get him worked up so that by the time he got to you and your family . . ."

"So what's wrong with my family now? Aside from Julia?"

"It seems they give too many noisy parties."

"So? And is that against the law?"

"Well, yes, as a matter of fact, it is," she answered, laughing, "since nobody pretends whiskey isn't served."

Henry blushed. "Just because *your* father's too stingy . . ."

He would have been less defensive if he were not himself so subject to embarrassment at the spectacle of his parents' Prohibition bacchanals. Try as he would, he could never get used to the sound of his mother's earthy laughter at someone else's dirty joke.

"Well, you have to admit, it *is* disgusting, sometimes, the way they carry on. People their age."

"You're not calling my parents disgusting, I hope."

"Of course not. But the people who come to their parties — all middle-aged and acting as if they were twenty. Drinking too much and laughing too loud. And dancing those ridiculous dances in skirts so short *I* wouldn't be caught dead wearing one. And I can tell you, my legs are a darn sight better looking than any of theirs."

"Prove it," he demanded with an arch leer as he drew back to allow room for a demonstration.

"Oh, Henry, you're as bad as my father. It's impossible sometimes to talk to you seriously. About anything."

"Just because my parents aren't the stuffed shirts . . ."

"See." She sat up with her head over him, the moon silvering his unhappy face. "We always get side-tracked. My father does the same thing whenever we try to discuss politics together. He always takes everything I say as a personal attack — upon him or whatever he stands for — and instead of listening to what I have to say, he attacks my motives. Or tries to justify his own. We can be talking about anything — Sacco and Vanzetti, for example — and before you know it, it isn't them we're talking about anymore, but us: what he thinks a daughter of his should owe him. And how can I attack a system that made him what he is today without also attacking him? It's almost as if I were accusing him of personally shooting down strikers and pulling the switch on the electric chair."

"I'll bet he'd like nothing better."

"You seem to forget, sometimes, he is my father. And I love him." She pushed herself away, straightening her hair with a toss of her head. "Despite everything."

"And I love my parents, too. So where does that get us?" He too moved away, leaning his back half against the car door.

"Oh, Henry." She moved closer and caught his hand in a gesture of mollification. "You know I like your parents. I really do. Your father, especially, you can't help liking him. It's just that — well, they seem like such children sometimes. Trying so hard to have a good time. As if they were afraid it was all going to end tomorrow."

"Well, maybe it is." He looked at her intently but made no effort to draw her closer. "And if it does, your father isn't even going to have a party to remember. You know what really gets me about him? How anyone who produced Arnie has the unmitigated gall to object to me as a son-in-law! Well, how the hell you think that makes me feel? He thinks I'm out to marry his precious daughter just to get my hands on her inheritance."

"Well, you won't have to worry about that anymore." She bit her lip to control the smile induced by the memory of her father's words, like a speech memorized from some Victorian melodrama redolent of abandoned daughters cast out into the storm and death-bed reconciliations and so out of touch with the times it was more comic than terrifying. "He's already disinherited me. You can't imagine how grand it made me feel," she added with a chuckle; then with the air of making a momentous announcement, and one designed to inspire an equally momentous gratitude:

"He won't let me go back to Cal next semester — just because I told him I intend to marry you."

"The bastard!" he said, but his smile carried more weight than his epithet. He was clearly flattered.

"Don't talk like that. Please. Right or wrong, he's still my father."

"Father or no father, I'd like to tell him he can take his goddamn money and shove it . . ."

"Henry!" She held her hand over his mouth. "There's no need to antagonize him. He'll come round. Once he sees he can't break me, he'll come to my side. I know him better than you do. I know him better than anybody does, for that matter. That's what gets him so upset: I'm so much like him he can't bluff me the way he bluffs everyone else."

"If I really believed that," he said, somewhat disappointed by her practicality at a moment when passion should have swept away all discretion, "I'd think twice before marrying you."

"Well, it's true: I am like him," she answered, not without pride, as she snuggled against his chest. "I get everything I set my sights on." And with the barest suggestion of a smile that softened all her features and flattered him into believing that he, out of all the world, was the single thing she now had sighted, she became suddenly vulnerable and inviting.

"Then I'm doomed," he answered and accepted the invitation of her lips.

Chapter Four

1

Vince Woods did not brook interference in his family affairs. There could be no question who had abetted his daughter's rebellion, but unless he chose to publicize his quarrel with his daughter, he must temporarily postpone his revenge. That the future would give him ample opportunity to employ it he never doubted. Nor did he doubt the means it would take. It was merely a question of waiting for the right moment.

He did not have to wait long.

Even during the darkest days of Prohibition, Costa's Corner was never entirely dry. The barroom itself was innocuous. Its glossy mahogany panels, its brass rails, and its etched mirrors all reflected the tender faces of the town's young sipping cherry phosphates or an occasional stranger thirsty enough to adulterate his palate with two-per-cent beer. In the rooms beyond, which had once bedded traveling salesmen, one could always find ample reserves of the best Canadian whiskey smuggled from the Mendocino Coast, or for those who couldn't afford the best, a thick red wine more lethal than most.

Here one fall Saturday Arnie arrived. On foot. But that was merely the latest of the indignities he had recently fallen victim to. Dropped from Berkeley after a single semester so dismal it doomed any prospects of an academic future, he had responded to one of his father's rare displays of wrath by leaving home and taking a job no better suited to the world of high finance than to the university, and he was soon forced to return home to work for his father. Not as a job foreman, but as a mere hired hand to take orders from men he had from childhood treated as underlings. The prodigal son had returned, and instead of feasting on the fatted calf, he had been sent out to feed with the swine.

Since the underlings who were now his associates comprised a good portion of Costa's patronage, Arnie's presence was more tolerated than welcome. Sensing a new lack of permissiveness in the father, the men were less intimidated by the son. No longer did they disguise their contempt. He had been offered the world on a silver platter, and he had sent it back to the kitchen.

Their contempt merely bolstered his bluster. He veritably swaggered as he made his way past the pool table, upsetting the chalks in his progress and giving the tin-shaded oil lamp over the table a swing with a flick of his finger, his slick Valentino hairdo coating the low ceiling with the sheen of its effulgence. In the dimly lit inner sanctum he slouched onto the first available chair and called out his order loudly enough for every patron in the house to hear: "A double a the best Canadian you got. And a chaser of ginger," he added, somewhat more softly. Then settling back he took inventory of the customers, his eyes picking out a ruddy little man at the dart board.

"You should a heard The Old Man tonight when he found some damn fool left the water tank going." He spoke to no one in particular and loud enough for all to hear. "There's a lake in the backyard wasn't there yesterday." And he smiled at the man who might have been responsible and would certainly be blamed.

His public conversation at Costa's was not infrequently about the "Old Man," his voice half boastful, half scornful: *"My* Old Man,*"* with too lingering a stress on the possessive pronoun to give any real bite to his mockery.

"You was in the tankhouse when I left," the man at the dartboard retorted. A tiny, wiry man with skin burnt a muddy red and tiny black eyes as small and shiny as currants, he was married to what was certainly the biggest woman in town, a dark-skinned, kinky-haired Amazon who lived in perpetual terror of her miniscule husband's mighty temper. "Why in hell didn't *you* turn it off, 'thout waiting for the Old Man to find it?"

"Cause, Little Joe, I wanted him to find it. Jesus! Look at your teeth. How can you chew that stuff's beyond me. Black shit."

"*Wanted* him to find it?" Joe ignored the reference to the Mail Pouch was tucked into one cheek. "Why'd you want a thing like that to happen?"

"So's he can see what a bunch of leadass bastards he's got working for him. That's why. Eatin up my goddam inheritance like that." With a broad smile that was almost ingenuous, he slung his leg over the side of his chair and took one of his father's cigars out of his pocket to light. "Jesus! Know what my old man told Old Man Aiken down at the salt works today?"

No one knew and no one apparently cared to know what Old Man Woods told Old Man Aiken, for they all, without exception, turned their backs upon the narrator before the tale was finished.

Arnie was well into his third double before Olaf arrived.

Every Saturday evening shortly before ten o'clock Olaf made his entrance. There was never any variation in his routine. He never came earlier or drank less or left later one week than he did any other week. He was a harmless but persistent Saturday night drunk who attacked a bottle of whiskey as he attacked everything else, with undoubted strength, with silent vigor, and with a moody, not-to-be-questioned determination. He never joined the conversation or the poker game or the dart board. He drank. That was his sole reason for being there. And he drank in silence. But there was an underlying hostility to his silence. He seemed to drink with only half his attention, the other half cocked against the expected affront, ready for firing.

As he made his sullen way into the room, all conversation ceased for a moment and the curious eyes followed him to his customary corner table. A single voice greeted his entrance. Sensitive to the blot upon his family's honor, Arnie seldom let an opportunity to cut Olaf pass, but he had always before played his dangerous game with just enough caution to keep the cocked gun from going off. The other patrons, who could recognize a lethal weapon when they saw one, were perfectly content to allow the man to brood as solitarily and silently as he chose.

"I said, hello, Olaf." Arnie's loud iterated salutation sounded the alarm bell. All activity ceased while Costa behind the bar, his huge walrus mustache bristling with trepidation, signaled a warning with both hands. There was no sound save the click of billiard balls from the next room. His back to the group, Olaf ignored the greeting and bolted his first drink. There was nothing on the table before him but a bottle and a glass. So familiar was the house with his routine, he did not have to order. He merely placed his bill on the table and it was quickly replaced with a bottle.

Had his aunt chosen to live in public sin with some local counterpart of Al Capone, had she mothered a gang of notorious safecrackers and bankrobbers or run a fancy bordello with a stable full of expensive fillies, Arnie would have found little to complain about. He might even have boasted of her achievements. It was not the sin itself that offended him, but its smallness. To have sold his family's honor for anything so insignificant as this scrawny renegade from his own family was a pill too bitter for swallowing.

"What's the matter? Cat got your tongue, Olaf?"

Arnie caressed his glass with his thumb and forefinger. The swagger returned to the tilt of his chin and the tilt of his chair, and had he been content to let it go at that, he might also have swaggered out. But he could never deny an attentive audience an encore. Certainly no one but Costa was encouraging restraint. Like caged cats, the silent onlookers waited for the meat to be thrown to them.

"Guess you'd need to put one on too," Arnie continued, still with a casual look of concern, "if you'd a had my old Aunt Belle hanging on your neck all night."

Olaf was up so fast his chair banged to the floor. Arnie did not have a chance to prepare a defense. Like a bale of hay caught in the pinch of iron tongs, he was lifted out of his seat and flung against the far wall, falling limply to the floor. The screaming pain in his left shoulder was echoed only faintly from his lips. Dazed, he shook his head, unable for a moment to focus his eyes or his forces. Then he had his knife out, the long blade glistening under the swinging chandelier as he cowered, weapon in hand, awaiting Olaf's advance.

From behind the bar, Costa came running, his stubby arms flailing the air with such vigor he seemed to be swimming against a rough current. "All right, men. All right. We don't want no cops. No cops."

But it was already too late. The moment the knife appeared, a nearly hysterical Minnie Costa had the Hayward operator on the line. The sheriff's office had already dispatched a car and Costa could do little more than run around, rounding up bottles

142

and drinks, as the hungry cats, forming a wide circle, called for more meat. Before the door had finished swinging, Costa was back, his arms brimming with bottles, to pass out the innocuous two-per-cent beer, mumbling, "On the house. It's on the house. Don't worry, it's on the house. Drinks for everybody."

Quietly Olaf wrapped his jacket around his left forearm, moving steadily toward his prey, his green eyes glaring under their pentecostal brows. With a feint of his cushioned arm, he caught Arnie's wrist. A slight application of pressure — a simple matter of weights and balances. And strength. The knife fell to the floor and with it the last vestiges of Arnie's courage. Whimpering contritely, he offered no resistance. Without a word, Olaf lifted him, spat on him then dropped him to the floor and, walking out of the room, walked into the arms of the sheriff.

2

Had the damage been less extensive, had Arnie's clavicle not been broken, had the Costas' financial existence not been threatened, the affair might have ended there. But it did not end there.

Employing a disguised voice that succeeded only in exposing her own lack of temerity, Minnie Costa called Belle Bettencourt.

'Thank you, Minnie. I'll attend to it," Belle answered, her voice registering neither surprise nor anger.

With prompt and prim dignity she appeared shortly after at the Hayward courthouse to post bail. As the officer on duty watched, his face rigid with forced solemnity, his manner stiff with arch politeness, Olaf followed Belle down the cement stairs to the old Ford convertible parked at the curb. With her hand on the door handle, she scanned the gathering clouds. "Looks like we'll have rain before morning," she said.

"Yes, Belle, it does." Olaf answered. "A real storm brewing."

Again after the affair might have ended had not an enterprising reporter, languishing from lack of news, published the following paragraph in the next evening *Post Enquirer* under a headline almost as long as the article itself:

143

BANK DIRECTOR'S SON INJURED IN BARROOM BRAWL

Mr. Olaf Throndson, 52, of San Oriel, was arrested last night for drunken and disorderly behavior at a local restaurant run by Frank Costa, also of San Oriel. Bail of $100 was paid by Miss Isabel Bettencourt, sister-in-law of Mr. Vincent Woods, director of the San Leandro branch of the Bank of Italy and president of the Eden Township Water District. Mr. Woods is also the father of Mr. Throndson's victim, Mr. Arnold Woods, who suffered a broken clavicle in the fracas. No charges have yet been filed.

If he had chosen, Vince Woods might have forgiven much. Secure in the knowledge that Arnie had more than likely earned it, he could easily have overlooked his son's injury. What he could not overlook was the resulting publicity. He did not like being made a fool of in public print. In the face of such provocation no one could call his response vindictive.

3

"Now I know very well, Dear — we *all* know and understand there's nothing at all in what folks been saying. But even so . . ."

Clara got no further in her prepared speech.

"Well, then, there's nothing for us to talk about, is there?" Belle lifted the lid on the pot of soup and sampled a taste from a wooden spoon. Her cheeks glistened from the gust of steam. "I've nothing to do with what 'folks say,'" she continued, wielding the lid and spoon disconcertingly like a sword and shield. "Nothing whatsoever."

But it was unfair to unlease her full wrath on Clara, who was obviously acting as her husband's stooge. "Vince sent you, didn't he?" She clamped the lid on the pot and turned to confront her sister.

"Yes," Clara responded. "Yes, he did. And rightly so."

"Well, then?" She stood with one hand on her hip: a woman at her stove, too busy to idle the afternoon away.

"Belle, you make it so hard." Clara's plea was blatant, but Belle had no intention of easing her sister's cruel task — for cruel she knew it would certainly be if Vince had not had the courage to deliver the blow himself.

"Why should it ever be hard for two sisters to talk to each

other, Clara? Unless," she added, the ring of an old authority embellishing her words, "one means to do the other a wrong."

"A wrong, Belle?" As Clara moved away from the stove, the sloping floor caused her to tilt the upper portion of her body back, giving her a curiously stagy stance. The house reeked still of the past that was over now and best forgotten: poverty in a brawling, teeming kitchen; the meatless dinners off chipped china, kale and horse beans and codfish until she couldn't bear the smell of them. "What wrong?"

"That's for you to tell me, Sister Clara."

"Oh, Belle, I don't any longer know who's in the wrong." She sank onto a chair beside the table. "All I know is poor Arnie's in a cast. And after all we've already been through with Louise. Course, you've no children of your own, so you . . ."

"Well, he wouldn't be," she snapped, reddening, "if like some other people he'd tend to his own affairs."

"Vince had to let him go."

The words came out so naked, Clara herself blushed, but she wanted to get the scene over as quickly as possible. Before she burst into tears or said something they would all be sorry for.

"Let him go? Let who go?" Belle was momentarily nonplussed, the wooden spoon idly stirring the air.

"Olaf. Vince had to fire him. Why, after that article . . ."

"Ah . . .!" The spoon fell against her apron. She did not stagger, but she seemed for the moment to have the wind knocked out of her. She studied her sister's face as though the latter were a stranger who had just given a clue to a startling identity.

"Why do you tell *me* this?"

"Why, Belle, what a strange question! I really don't understand you, sometimes. I really don't." Clara shook her head. "Vince thought, naturally, considering . . ." Her hands fidgeted with her hanky, dabbing her lips, her face as vulnerable to sudden and drastic change as unfired clay.

"If you think I'm going to beg, Clara Bettencourt; if you think, for one minute, I'm going to get down on my knees before you — well, you've got another think coming." Belle seemed suddenly to tower over her younger sister.

With the demotion to maiden status the years were wiped away and Clara was once again a little girl quivering with resentment at the inequities of life, conscious that *her* lot, above all others, was a difficult one, that her pains were somehow more penetrating, her bruises more lasting, her punishments more undeserved; and Belle — a great unfeeling ox of a sister dispensing her spare diet of commands and rebukes in place of sympathy. Really, she could not understand how, for such a man, Belle could now drag her own sister through the wringer like this.

"If Vince has anything to say to Olaf," Belle continued, her voice once again under full command, "he can say it to his face. Like a man, Clara. And not send his wife to do his dirty work for him."

"Oh, how unfair you are, Belle!" Clara struck her breasts and her eyes watered at the injustice of her sister's attack. "He will. He will. He means to tell him tonight. But right now, he's thinking of you, Belle. Can't you see that? Trying to make it easier for you. Not sparing himself, as you seem to think. But you. It's you he's trying to spare, Belle. And I think you owe him an apology for that."

"No, Clara," she shook her head. Her face flushed, her eyes burning with hot tears, she spoke as though she had not even attended to her sister's words, "I'm not going to beg. Why, there's plenty a work to keep him busy right here, if he can't get another job. And I suppose Vince will see to that. Yes. He never does anything half way, does he? A new chicken coop to build. And I've been meaning to make the vegetable garden bigger, to open up the . . ."

"Belle!" It was Clara's turn to be stunned. "You don't mean to say — after what's happened — you intend to keep him on here?"

"Keep him, Clara?" Belle's glance slid off the side of her sister's face to a fly crawling on the wall behind her. "There's no 'keeping' him. This is his home for as long as he chooses to stay. That's all. But I can't 'keep' him. He's a man and free to go as he pleases. But as long as he's here — and I tell you frankly, Clara, as I've told nobody else, I pray that's as long as he has breath left in him to breathe God's good air — he'll always have a bed to sleep on and a plate to eat off at my table. And you can tell that to your husband."

"I didn't mean to say this, Belle." Clara stuffed her handkerchief back into her bosom; there'd be no need of it now. For once in her relations with her sister moral authority was clearly on her side. No longer was she little Clara Bettencourt bending to her big sister's imperious will. "Believe me, I hoped I wouldn't have to say this, but you force me to, Belle. You leave me no other choice."

"Yes . . .?" What is it I force you to say, Clara?"

"I must remind you, Belle, it isn't any longer yours."

"What isn't mine?"

Even bolstered by moral authority Clara could not take a direct route; but she was close enough to the mark to make her meaning clear:

"You know very well, after Mamma got sick, if Vince hadn't been there to help out."

"Ah . . .!" Again the wind was knocked out of her. Her face went white and her hand trembled. "So it's come to that, has it?"

"Yes, Dear, I'm afraid it has. The house isn't yours. To bestow on Olaf or anyone else."

"And what wrong, you ask! What wrong! I should think it would be hard for you to say it. Thirteen children there were, Clara, not counting myself. To dress and bathe and bury. Thirteen children. In Pappa's house . . ." For the first time her voice came near to breaking. "And if after that — if you could still find it in your heart . . ." She shook her head, but no more words would come.

Moved to pity despite her resolve, Clara moved to take her sister's hand, but Belle rejected the offer and turned her face to the stove.

"Belle, believe me. No one wants to . . ."

"You'll have to excuse me, Clara." Belle wiped her eyes with the back of her hand then braced herself, her shoulders back, her chin out, her voice steady: "I've got to get the roast on. Olaf," she concluded defiantly, "has the appetite of a workhorse."

4

Belle's initial reaction to her sister's visit was more angry than fearful. Though stunning, Clara's threat had been idle, for they knew her well enough to know that she would never leave voluntarily, that if they did in fact mean to take possession of *her* house — for such it was and always would be, despite any laws to the contrary — they would have to carry her out, feet first, with the entire town as witness. She had nothing to do with laws and deeds and rights of way. It was her father's house, built with his own hands, and she had more than earned her right to live in it — with whomsoever she pleased under whatsoever conditions she chose — for as long as she lived. And that was precisely what she intended to do.

Vince would do everything in his power to make her life difficult, but he would stop short of actual eviction. Nor would he, she was sure, in any way interfere with her own job at the bank. Such a course he would have the foresight to see might end by costing *him* money. And that was another risk he would not be willing to take.

It was only later, when she began to consider what Olaf's reaction to his dismissal might be, that her courage faltered and anger gave way to fear.

Chapter One

1

"Tell you what I'm going to do, Frank, long as you're so anxious to get in on the market. I'll give you a thirty thousand mortgage on the Alvarado ranch. Ten years at seven. How's that suit you?" Vince leaned back in his usual chair at Costa's Corner, his thumbs stuck into his vest pockets so that his hands hung limp on either side of his stomach like two pink fins.

"It's worth fifty."

"Sure it is, Frank, and if I was buying it, I wouldn't dream of offering less. But it's just a friendly loan, Frank, and in a year's time, with your luck, you'll have it doubled. You can pay me back and still have thirty thousand to play around with."

"Know something 'bout the market nobody else does?"

"All I know's what I read in the paper. And hear from my broker. And he's all for putting everything I own into it. Lock, stock, and barrel."

"That so?"

"Chance of a lifetime, Frank."

"Then what's holding you back?"

"Well, you see, it's this way, Frank." The chair comes down, the hands rest upon the table, the head bent forward in an attitude of easy confidence. "I've already made my share and I figure it's time you younger boys had a go at it."

"Vince must be losing his touch," is the word in Costa's back room. "The old gambler's playing it cautious."

"That son a his. Nuff to break any man's spirit. Damn fool kid, could be sitting on top the world now."

"Tell you what I'll do, Harry, since you're so set on cashing in with the rest. How's a twenty thousand mortgage on the Decota ranch sound to you? Usual terms: five years at seven and a half."

"It's worth thirty, thirty-five."

"Sure it is, Harry, and if I was buying it, that's what I'd offer. But I'm not interested in buying. Got all the land I can handle."

"What's old Vince up to, collecting mortgages right and left? Know something the rest of us don't?"

"Losing his touch. Seen it coming way back. That son a his done it. Broke the ole man's spirit."

There was no question he was slowing down, the old ticker giving him a pause or two, the old peasant in his background whispering caution. It was too easy. He could not trust anything that allowed every damn fool in creation, without any effort or craft, with nothing more than the courage and instincts of a gambler, to make as much in a single season as he had earned in a lifetime. Land, his forefathers whispered, is the only real basis of wealth, the only foundation of empire. So he built on land.

But the stumbling block to all empire builders is succession, and the thought of his son fired him with such resentment that he demonstrated himself in his reaction his son's true father. Stronger than ever became his need to prove himself, to show himself before the world as a man set apart, a lord of the land and nature's own nobleman. There was an added harshness to his orders; his language coarsened, his jokes became more ribald, his affection more impulsive, his gifts more extravagant.

"Oh, Vince!" Clara's face was puckered with delight. "It's lovely! But why?" Her hand trembled as she held her almond-shaped dinner ring to the light, the diamonds sparkling in their lacy platinum setting. The smell of security lingered in the room in the still summer air. Amber bulbs glowed through silk shades and preened the glossy feathers of porcelain birds. Outside, real crickets chirped, and moths, lured by the light, besieged the window screens. "It's not my birthday. Nor our anniversary. And it's certainly not Christmas. Come now," she placed her newly-ringed hand on his, giving it an affectionate squeeze, "what mischief have you been up to?"

Her smile was only superficially suspicious, its underlying trust apparent. Where gifts were concerned she remained a child. They needed no logic other than their own existence. Her joy in possession amounted to a passion. She regretted only that she had not herself been allowed the pleasure of selecting it, of moving from store to fine store, fawned upon by the elegant young men in their immaculate shirts and beautifully fitted suits, like so many magi bearing the velvet-lined trays in their delicate hands to lay on the table before her their feast of jewels. For almost as great a thrill as possession itself was the process of possessing: To sign her name with a great flourish of purple ink — Mrs. Vincent Woods — told her all she needed to know what it was to be a queen.

"Sold some TransAmerica for Harry's mortgage and had a little left over I didn't know what else to do with." He beamed in response to her tearful kiss. "And I couldn't help notice," he continued, "the other Sunday in church, how you kept eying Mae Ramos's. So big she couldn't get her glove over it and had to flash it for the whole parish to see. Well, you didn't think I was going to stand for that, now, did you? And not do something about it?"

"Oh, Vince how you talk! I didn't even notice." The lights in her eyes as dazzling as those in her ring and reward enough for his wit.

"Now you two can flash your messages back and forth right over Moriarity's head."

She giggled appreciatively. "How you talk! How you do talk!"

Chapter Two

1

Having mastered Sarah's instructions in the simple arithmetic of love, Arnie was soon ready for algebraic complications; but despite his early indoctrination, Sarah's obliging accessibility had spoiled him. Her unfailing good nature and uncomplicated enjoyment had made an ordinarily complex subject appear altogether too simple. Gratification had come so easily he was unprepared for resistence, and he was never able to transform a reluctant refusal into eager acceptance. As a result, the catalog of his conquests was shamefully slender, and with Sarah no longer available, his frustration became increasingly more acute.

Nor could he any longer find satisfaction in mere sexual release. He could feel life at its fullest now only when it was placed in jeopardy. Danger was fast becoming the most enticing lure, fear the ultimate pleasure. But even that was dulled by the sense of his own impregnability — that, and a last-minute reticence that he could never overcome — an unwilled, atavistic evasiveness as strong as life itself, some force which told him: Fear must have its orgasm in death.

2

He met her in a speakeasy in Niles, the girl with the listless eyes and the taunting tongue who dared him to please her, to make her laugh or cry — she didn't care which. Someone more bored than he.

The nearly empty room was murky: two weak bulbs glowed through dusty paper lanterns. She sat against the far wall, one arm slung limply, like an empty holster, over the back of her chair. Wax-covered winebottles disgorged burning candles, their pallid flames teasing the slumbering darkness.

152

Never before had he met anyone like her. Her monumental indifference was an incitement to rape. She was shielded by a contempt that seemed to encompass all of creation. She led him on only to stop him short with a mocking, Prove yourself. She answered his embraces with indifference, his brutality with scorn, and his force wilted before her steely smile. He no longer even cared what she looked like, that her breasts were niggardly mounds, her hips boyishly slim, her complexion sallow, her hands damp. Her lips, a knife-slit of scarlet sallow, across her white face, were exceptional. She would not even tell her name.

"One laugh, Buster, one real, gutsy laugh and I'll teach you things you didn't know were possible," she challenged, and he accepted her title as mistress to worlds yet undreamed of.

The bare orchards stretched across the false dawn of a gray February morning. Plum blossoms languorously sweet; soggy china lilies and paperwhites growing wild on the borders of the road promised spring. Between the rows of bare trees, shavings from the furrow shone slick black. There was not a sound. The rain, fine and cool, a thick mist hovering.

"Where's your coat?" he asked, snapping the top button of his leather jacket.

Without answering, her eyes closed, she raised her face to the sky. Her skin was quickly covered with a beaded net rent with the red slash of her lips. He tried to plant a kiss on her neck. She pushed him away and fixed him with tired eyes.

"Well? Are we going or aren't we?" So tired she was held up only by the force of her will.

"Where the hell's your coat?"

"Why?"

"It's raining, for chrissakes."

"So, that's what it is — rain. Good. We both need a bath."

"Jesus, you're crazy."

"Yeah . . . and don't forget your galoshes, Sonny Boy. Or Mommy'll get after you."

"Shit! Come on. I'll take you for a ride you'll never forget."

And he did.

Her slim thighs astraddle the back fender of his English motorcycle, her short skirt hunched high above her knees, her face pressed in sleeping repose against his leather jacket, indifferent to

153

the icy dimples formed on her cheek by the silver studs, she held him with so light a touch he had to look back to see that she was still there: for all her bravado frail and frightened and as light on the wind as a dandelion thistle. He had found someone more fearful than he, someone for whom tyranny might become benevolent, someone whose weakness might give him strength, someone whose willing submission might teach him love — if he could catch her.

If he could fasten all the loose springs, screw his head tight on his shoulders — he was drunk with rotten liquor, his head reeling, but not fast enough to numb him. If only . . .

The soft rain became sharper, the gentle breeze a gale as they sped off to meet the dawn.

"How's that?" he called, half turning his face.

A wet strand of her short hair stung his cheek, her only answer. The speed and the wind and the cold cleared his head, power in the clasp of his hands.

"Feel like laughing yet? Or crying?"

"I feel nothing. Nothing at all. Sonny Boy on his Christmas scooter."

And the words flew away like a ribbon loosed on the wind.

"I'll knock that mocker out of you yet," he said.

And he did.

A series of speeding snakecurves and he could feel her hand clutch tighter as the cycle slithered and slid along the wet pavement.

"I'll catch you yet."

His heart singing. He and the world were young and youth was power. He could feel it swelling in him, massive and hard. There was more power in his body than in all his father's wealth. He could do such things — !

"I'm lighter than the wind. But do! Do — if you can."

The mockery was gone. Worn thin by the wind. The ribbon of her voice a silken thread that he might snap or knit again into something new and strange.

"On top of Mount Diablo?"

He would do such things — !

"On top of Mount Diablo."

Full throttle, impatient, he could not wait. From a slick of oil the sun came tumbling too soon. Spinning, they were sucked into a cyclone, lighter than the wind, she flew, her only cry a startled: "Whee!"

3

Fear had lost at last its power to thrill. It became instead, a paralyzing terror. Imprisoned in a plaster cocoon as white as death, he must labor forth in pain. Over him a gray spectre hovered. Constrained by his cocoon, he screamed for the release that came on a sharp point pressed into his arm. Slowly he sank into euphoria. Numb to all save for one conscious point beyond the reach of drugs where he could still feel her wet hair sting his cheeks, her parted lips like a bleeding lance wound on an ivory crucifix.

The odor of incense, sumptuous as an oriental night, mixed with prayers chanted from some faraway minaret:

Mea culpa, mea culpa, mea maxima culpa.

The taste of holy oil cool on his fevered lips: the milk of paradise. He was dying and he didn't care. It seemed at the moment a beautiful thing to die and the oil on his eyelids mixed with his tears. Weeping for his own wasted life.

Immense in the doorway, Father Moriarity intoned:

"God's grace may see him through."

A rustle of silk, a tearful whisper. Sweet sobs. Familiar odors seeping through the incense and the disinfectant into the half dormant center of his being.

"Oh, pray, Father. Pray."

The dark baritone wrath of the Lord rumbled on:

"If we expect miracles we must first offer God a helping hand. I hope this proves a lesson to the boy."

A lesson? Yes. But how to read it?

It was no more than the ghost of her son Clara saw as she sat silent and helpless, a patch of needlepoint untouched on her lap, a rosary entwined about her swollen fingers. As he had grown up he had grown away, and he was most real to her still, not as this monstrously patched and plastered body suspended from a tangle of pulleys, ropes, and weights, but as a little boy in a poplin suit, his dark eyes aglow with wonder. She could not now imagine what doom-driven curse lay upon him, what it was he could so

155

have wanted or needed when he already had everything. What had they ever denied him? What could he have asked for they would not have given?

"We can do no more than pray for him" Father Moriarity's kinky, rusty hair, parted in the middle, peaked above his ruddy temples like the horns of prophesy. "It's out of our hands and in God's now," he continued in a sepulchral whisper that sent shivers tripping down her spine, "and it's for you to search deep into your own conscience, Mrs. Woods. As his mother. Leave no stone unturned, no corner unlit. For remember the words of Our Lord: It is far easier for a camel to pass through the eye of a needle than for a rich man to enter into the kingdom of Heaven."

The ageing Father Spinoza's recent replacement, Father Moriarity had a penchant for quoting the Bible that Clara found positively Protestant. What meaning had money in the face of death? How did her wealth lessen her suffering that he should throw it now in her face?

Intimidated as much by the priest's overbearing manner as well as his size, Vince stood in the gloomy sterility of the hospital corridor, his whole life threatened suddenly with meaninglessness. Against the Irish he had nothing in particular. They, he supposed, had their place as well as anyone else. It was simply that that place was not his place, and religion at its best was tribal. He sought something deeper and more fundamental than ritual: the consolation of the known. Every sacramental crisis drives one back to the sensitive core of his being, and no change of name or language or daily habits could alter the primordial fact of Vince's nature, the race memory that no surgery can alter. He was a Port, descended from the ash farmers of Pico, men whose names had long ago been buried with their bodies on an island he himself had never seen.

Dull and tediously discursive though good old Father Spinoza's sermons had always been, he had never failed at the important moments. At baptisms, at weddings, at deathbeds, he knew instinctively that his most important duty was to make of life's great moments transcendental experiences, to transform the copulation of two animals into the sacrament of love and the death rattle of a wornout body into the trumpet sound of the soul's deliverance. There was comfort in his very faults, in his stumbles with the liturgy, his food-stained cassock, his broken English. In short, his shared humanity.

Father Moriarity was too much the priest ever to be a good priest. Never for an instant did he allow one to forget that he had been anointed by the bishop's own hand a minister of the gospel. He was the shepherd, his every gesture promulgated, and those he served mere sheep. His harsh words still echoing in Clara's ears, he disappeared down the hospital corridor, the *grande-dame* swish of his skirts saved from the ridiculous by the overwhelming size of the aggressively masculine body, better suited to the quarter-back shufflings of a college football team than the mannered choreography of an ecclesiastical ballet.

'Camels are all very well,'' Vince huffed, "but it's the rich man he comes to when the roof is leaking or his church needs painting. There's never any talk then about the eyes of any needles."

"The man has no delicacy," Clara sobbed. "No sense of finesse. To speak like that at such a time."

"And the Pope sitting up there in his palace," Vince grumbled, his threatened emptiness filled now by his mounting anger. "Like the Emperor of China, choking on his own jewels. I don't see *him* selling his crown to feed the poor. Not on your life. Well, Moriarity can damn well get him and his cardinals through the needle's eye if he has a mind to. I'll manage on my own. Same as always."

Never until now had Clara thought much about God. When she did think of Him, she saw Him as a large, bearded, white-haired gentleman not altogether unlike her husband costumed for some fancy-dress ball. Religion was merely another habit in a life filled with habits. Nor could she respond to her pastor's gaudy metaphors and doomsday rhetoric with more than awed distaste. No one, certainly, and least of all the man himself, had ever felt compelled to listen to Father Spinoza, whose sermons had always sounded like the aimless wanderings of a simple and prosaic soul half-heartedly in search of meaning from poetry too deep for human understanding. His successor, whose thundering voice commanded attention, had a way of fixing his eyes upon individual members of the congregation at the most

157

unexpected moments, as if his altogether tasteless and lurid threats of damnation had some sinister personal intent. So the slightest indisposition, the least hint of a headache — and the very thought of those icy gray eyes peering through her was enough to trigger a migraine — kept her home from mass.

Yet if God had His place, it was, certainly, with death. And she stormed heaven's gate with her prayers. Checks were sent to the Franciscan Fathers for a round-robin of masses. Bells rang, clouds of incense rose, and a fiery forest of candles burned before a host of plaster saints. Clara wept and beat her breasts; she fingered her rosary, she chanted her litanies, but the smoke from the vigil lights she burned and the incense from the bene- dictions she had sung only increased the migraine. Her ankles as well as her fingers began to swell. It was, the doctors said, arthritis.

Shrouded in the same mysterious Greek and Latin liturgy, the ritual of the hospital, she discovered, was not unlike the ritual of the Church, its solace, if less permanent, more immediate. Its ministrants spoke to her, certainly, with far greater delicacy:

"We're going to pull him through, Mrs. Woods. Never you fear. He's coming along just fine. Why, before you know it, we'll have him up and around good as new again. So it's time you began to think about yourself for a change. Yes, I don't want to mince words with you, Mrs. Woods. If you don't begin devoting a little more time to yourself, it's going to be *you* we have to worry about. Not your son. Why, just let me have a look at those fingers."

The scrubbed hand held her wrist with a feather touch, the golden hairs bristling from the bottom joints of his marvelously white fingers, the pink nails polished to a lacquer finish. And at his cool, sterile touch, she felt her spirits soar, her pain lessen. How clean he smelled, in his white smock, his closely shaven cheeks scented with cool spices! How quietly he moved, how gently he spoke, his eyes liquid with concern. Here was a man worthy of his priestly calling; and as Arnie healed, she took to her bed, comforted by the soothing, Christ-like ministrations of a soft-spoken apostle of Hippocrates.

It was there that Sarah found her.

4

"What have they done to my honeygirl?" Eyes rolling heavenward, she wrung her hands, a saint contemplating the apotheosis of martyrdom. "Who could have been so cruel as to leave you in such a state?" She moved to the bed, a general about to take command. "But don't you fret your poor sweet head, Sarah'll have everything shipshape in a jiffy. Just like old times." And bracing her former mistress's back with a strong arm, she removed the matted pillows, fluffing them lightly and smoothing the sheet, deftly tucking the loose edges under the mattress. Then she stepped back to survey her handiwork:

"There, that's more like it. That's the way I like to see her. But how are you, Mrs. Woods? How's my poor sweet honeygirl?"

She had come to visit but she fully intended to stay.

"Oh, Sarah Dear, you don't know . . ." The voice whimpered on the brink of tears: "You don't know what I've been through."

Sarah did not disappoint her.

"Don't know! Don't tell me what I know and don't know. Why, sakes alive, I've got eyes, haven't I? She shook her head, marveling, hands once again clasped, great cow eyes brimming with tears. "I've only to look at you to see what a wringer you've been through."

"And with no one to help. They come and they go, Sarah, you wouldn't believe it, too fast to keep track of their names. You can't imagine what it's been like, no one knowing where anything is. No one thinks about anyone anymore but themselves. And I'm left to cope. In my condition! Would you believe it! Even Louise — that selfish girl! I suppose you've heard. Hasn't everyone? Working at the bank and living in an apartment in Hayward. Two unmarried girls keeping house away from their families! Well, I ask, what can people be expected to say? As if we couldn't afford to pay for our own daughter's keep! And at a time like this, with Arnie coming home and no one here to help."

"Well, don't you fret your sweet head for one second longer because your Sarah's back. And back to stay."

159

"But Manuel, Sarah?" Her face tremulous with delight and expectancy. "What'll Manuel say, taking you away from him like that?"

"Oh, that one!" Sarah snorted. "Well, we don't have to worry about him no more. No, M'am. We're not all lucky like you, Mrs. Woods, to find a prince for a husband. A real prince. My *paisan* — bless his black heart — he's up and left me. With nothing to remember him by but a baby girl and a mailboxful of bills. And good riddance to him, I say. As long as I've got these two strong arms to work with, no daughter a mine'll ever go hungry. No sirree. Not while her mother's still standing she won't. But there's no crying over spilt milk, I always say, and here I am. Just like old times."

Or almost. There was Immaculata now to consider. Though Sarah continued to live at home, the child was quick to insinuate herself into the household, eating her meals in the kitchen and spending her days playing in the house or garden. She was a sturdy, healthy child with thick, strong bones and handsome features, fudge-brown eyes and provocatively full lips. Sarah herself had grown coarser, her mustache more pronounced. Fatter and better tempered than ever, she was so unstinting in her devotion that Clara was soon once again completely under her thrall.

She could not, certainly, have borne the strain of Arnie's return had not Sarah been there to welcome him home. With purring solicitude, Sarah bathed him and shaved him and powdered his casts. The metamorphosis progressed. Daily he emerged ever more finished from his plaster cocoon, until the only ostensible evidence of his ordeal was a scar running from temple to midcheek.

He was relieved, at first, that he had never learned his companion's name. It would, he thought, be easy to forget a nameless girl who was only a pair of listless eyes and a wounded mouth. But as his bones knit and his strength returned, he began to feel cheated. They had raced the sun and lost. And there were moments now of blinding lucidity when he knew that he would never be anybody but his father's son. And that knowledge was more painful than a butcher's table of broken bones.

She haunted his dreams, the girl with the listless eyes, but every time he reached out to catch her, she disintegrated into a thousand star-tipped filaments lighter than the wind. He could not even catch her with a net of statistics; root her firmly to the earth with a name, a birthdate, and a family — all of which might then easily have been buried with her broken body. Her anonymity kept her alive and transformed her into a myth. It was she now, as he slept, who held him in her wet embrace; she whose cold hands brushed his lips; she who, when he woke, dissipated on an echo of mocking laughter. And he was afraid.

He too resorted to prayer. When Father Moriarity came with the Easter viaticum, he closed his eyes and received the host on a reverential tongue. It was, however, only unleavened bread that he tasted and *her* presence was stronger than Christ's. His faith departed with the tinkle of the altarboy's bell ascending the stairs to his mother's room.

No, there was but one father and Vincent was his name.

Chapter Three

1

"Well, Belle," the dreaded scene began, the words apparently as hard for him to speak as for her to hear, "guess the time's finally come."

She could not control the quiver in her voice: "Time for what, Olaf?"

She already knew the answer and was braced for his reply: "Moving on."

Though armored in her resolve, she was nevertheless dazed by the first blow. Momentarily too overcome to speak, she merely shook her head, silently, fearful that if she gave in to weakness now, if she dissolved in tears, their life together was over. And that blank prospect she was not willing to face. Scorn, contumely, bitterness, even shared poverty she could bear with a light heart and an easy step — she was, after all, used to hardship and asked of life no gift of luxury. But a solitary walk to the grave she was not strong enough to bear.

"Ain't nobody going to give me work around here. He's seen to that all right. 'Cept for part-time seasonal jobs. And it's February, Belle. February. No one needs a new hired hand in February. Summer's a long way off," he added, as if pleading for her to make it easier for him. But she would not spare him.

"No, Olaf." Rising from the table, she found her voice again. "For better or for worse," she said, turning in the middle of the kitchen floor to confront him, seated still at the head of the table, so sombre he seemed a judge listening to the final plea for the defense, and at her borrowing from the marriage ceremony, his whole face burst into flame. "Yes, Olaf, I took you, when you came here, when you came to live with me, for better or for worse. I thought you understood that. We both understood that. And so far, up till now, it's been better. It has, Olaf," she challenged the lift of his brows with a defiance so

shrill, she seemed almost to be attacking him. "In spite of everything, we've had a good life together. Don't deny me that. Oh,
please don't deny me that."

Her fierce resolve seemed for a moment about to give way
before an onslaught of tears, but with a majestic lift of her chin,
she dammed their flow. "What can't be helped there's no helping," she continued, the near hysterical pitch of her voice
returning to a cooler, more natural contralto, "and the less said
about it the better. But we have had a good life together, you
and I. And you don't think now, just because we've had a little
trouble — yes, *we*, Olaf. Don't think I don't know what that
fight was all about. I know what Arnie is — no one knows better
— and I know what you've had to put up with. Well, don't think
now, just because we've had a little trouble, I'm about to let you
go off and leave me here all alone. To let you desert me like that
without putting up a fight. No, Olaf. No."

"Belle!" He shook his head. "You don't know what you're
asking, Belle."

And from his lips her name still rang in her ears like churchbells. She knew she had won, but it was a hollow victory echoing
the sound of his own defeat.

"Yes. Oh, yes I do. I know, I know, Olaf." The tears were
brimming over the lids, but she thought by refusing to recognize
them she might cancel out their existence. "It's selfish of me, I
know that, Olaf, but I've got a right, for once in my life, I've
got a right to think of myself first, and before I let you go,
before I do that, I'll go into the streets, Olaf, and tell anyone
willing to listen what never was. I'll drag my name through
mud, Olaf. I'll tell them such things and do such things, they'll
have food enough to feed their talk the rest of their lives
— before I let you go."

And every reiteration of his name fell upon him like a blow.
She was bludgeoning him with her virtue. He could not, if he
had wanted to, find the words to oppose her.

She was still speaking, and speaking for him now, skirting the
subject, dancing around a fire too hot to touch, shielding his
pride with her words, feeding him lies that he must, if there was
ever to be any living with himself, nourish until they grew fat.

"I know what you're thinking, Olaf: there won't be work

164

enough to keep you busy. But there will. There will. Why, there's that patch of land near the creek. Be perfect for tomatoes. Might even sell the excess. And asparagus and corn. Why, we can grow anything on this land, Olaf. You know that, how rich it is. A regular Eden, my father used to call it. And we won't have to buy anything, but beef, sometimes, and clothes."

He shook his head, baffled, as if the problem confronting him were too great for his simple mind to encompass. "I didn't mean to hurt the kid. You know that, Belle. I never asked nothin from nobody — 'cept to be left alone sometimes. It's hard, Belle."

"Yes, Olaf, I know."

She sat beside him at the table, and breaking all precedent, placed her hand on his. His large hand under hers seemed small and fragile and, though rough with toil, still the hand of a frightened boy, his flesh next to hers curiously cool, despite the images of fire that had since their first meeting haunted her dreams. But even here the mark of her daring was one more measure of his defeat, one step closer to the final loss of his manhood. She could touch him now because the fire had died and there was no longer any danger of burning herself.

"It'll be Saturday every night, Belle." Again he shook his head, his eyes focused on the bleak future. "Every night."

She knew well enough what he meant. Every man must have his solace — not to compensate for his labor, but to withstand the terrors of his leisure. But even a whole week of Saturdays was a prospect pale before a lifetime of solitude, and she was prepared to take the risk.

2

And the risks seemed at first minor, more farcical than tragic.

The following Saturday a delegation from the S.P.R.S.I. appeared in her backyard. She was not accustomed to visitors, casual or otherwise, and these were far from casual, so formidable were their starched smiles and their scarf-crossed bosoms. Quickly surmising their intent, Belle kept them standing in the yard wrapped in their coats, the wary concern of a roaming white bantam rooster, and refused to ask them in even to warm themselves before the kitchen fire.

Minnie Costa, who had the crown of Queen Saint Isabelle enshrined in her home for the month of February, and whose husband had been fairly frightened out of his wits by a visit from two federal agents alerted by the unwelcome publicity, had threatened to burn down her house with the crown in it, rather than relinquish the crown, as it was scheduled for the month of March, to Isabel Bettencourt. And wouldn't Belle, the ladies wanted to know, reasonable as she was, want to avoid a scandal, though they, of course, knew — and each in turn cast a wary glance at the tankhouse and Olaf scowling in the doorway — there was nothing at all in what folks were saying; but wouldn't Belle be willing to let Lena Oliviera have the crown instead and take her turn sometime later in the year? But Belle, reasonable as she was, would not listen to their reasons. March was her month and March it would be. And March it was.

A week later, the same ladies, dressed now in white suits, their bosoms crossed with their gilt-edged green and red sashes, came bearing the silver crown to be placed on an improvised altar of lilies and paperwhites. After the recitation in Portuguese of the Five Glorious Mysteries of the rosary and the Litany of Saints, all except for the noticeably absent Minnie Costa, whose house, after all, had not been burned and whose husband was still dispensing the best Canadian in his back rooms — sat stiffly on the mohair furniture to sip their glasses of port, their eyes searching furtively, but insistently, for any evidence of bacchanalian festivities. But they found not so much as a crushed pillow. And Belle in her triumph was as awesome as an armed Athena fighting the battles of her wounded darling.

But fight as she would, holding the world at bay, she was still powerless to heal Olaf's wound. The first weeks were consumed in a fury of activity, and when the real tasks ran out, he manufactured new ones, loosening shingles so that he might fix them, pruning trees that had already been pruned, stopping occasionally, and then frequently, to stretch himself and pull out his watch to see how much longer he had to go before lunch, how much longer before his next cigarette, how many hours before Belle came home and it would be dinnertime, how much time before sleep and tomorrow came and he must look again to find

166

how much time was still left to him. And there was always too much. The fury slackened. Dry timber burns fast.

He began to haunt the creek. For hours he wandered through the exposed gut of the town. Once he got as far as the Bay, but he found it too open there, exposed to the sky and the sun, the lavender salt flats checkering the distance. He preferred the hidden recesses choked with foliage where he must tunnel through the underbrush or climb over the debris carried on the spring floods — the broken branches of fallen trees, scattered refuse, and the waste of all their lives. Bottles and cans and blossoming chestnuts mixed with the curly red leaves of poison oak. An old sofa caught in the trunk of a bay tree, its rusty springs jutting through horsehair. A battered car door; the broken wheel of an old carriage; a wicker chair, its front legs crippled; and everywhere — bottles; bottles that had cured the sick or poisoned the unwary. Blue bottles and clear bottles, brown bottles and white bottles, flat and round and square and cylindrical — there was no end to their number or variety. All used up. Here and there a septic tank dribbled a slick path down the irregular bank, its foul course fringed with a wild growth of grass. Then for awhile the underbrush became so lush, the primordial beauty was unmarred by a single visible rusting can.

Occasionally, coming upon a small sandy beach, he would lie down; stretched out stiff, his legs spread, his arms at his side, he would let the sun warm the blood into a moment of forgetfulness — until the pain became keen again, and reaching into his back pocket he would draw out the wine flask, drinking with his eyes shut, his head thrown back, listening: a horse-drawn wagon, its iron wheels clanging on a paved street and the faraway sad cry: "Rags, bottles, sacks; rags, bottles, sacks." Somewhere a woman's voice calling: "Har-REE! Har-REE!" Footsteps over the bridge. A sudden unexplained laugh. Then quiet. A mockingbird trilling, too sweet, too sweet. And he must take another long draught and trudge even deeper into the undergrowth. Over the iron trellises of the Southern Pacific bridge with its chalked exhortations illustrated with crude drawings as fanciful and ritualistic as African sculptures he crawled, then onto a steaming soft mattress of compost from the Yamamura nurseries, the banks covered with cascades of rotting carnation

167

shoots. Nearby a small dam of sand-filled sacks formed a pool deep enough for swimming, though only minnows and tadpoles now occupied it.

It was a lonely place. Seldom did he meet anyone in his explorations. Most of the creek's visitors were furtive: children surreptitiously embracing under the scrawled totems of the bridge; itinerant artists and roving poets scribbling their libidinous works; an occasional tramp rifling through the debris for some redeemable find, a dented kettle, a chipped plate, or fuel for his evening fire.

3

No action was taken to deprive Belle of her house or her job; there was no need. Olaf's disintegration was punishment enough. She could see him daily slipping away from her and she was powerless to save him. Powerless even to slow the process.

And for her, too, it proved a time of crisis. The necessary breaks in the ritual of their life together left her without a form to follow. At the mercy of chance, she became a victim of her own chaotic emotions. Taboos that had once seemed sacred were broken with an almost casual lack of regard. But they were not broken with impunity; their toll was paid in the long, fitful nights.

Again and again the faint, strangulated cries of a sick child pierced the wall of her sleep, and leaping from her bed, her heart pounding so loud she could hear it, she would catch herself rushing to an empty room, through an empty house. "Poor little thing," she would mutter, sinking back onto the bed. "Poor little thing." And the next moment of consciousness would find her body tense, her legs jerking convulsively, her heart racing. Rising on her arms to ward off her attacker, she would once again find herself shaking off phantoms, alone in an empty house. But she was not alone; the house itself was alive with more than memories. She could hear the boards breathe, she could hear the mice scurrying across the plaster-strewn floors of the upstairs bedrooms. A strange tattoo as regular as a heartbeat challenged her imagination, until following it with her ears sweeping the walls of her room she traced it to the knob of an open door bouncing like a ping pong ball off the trembling house — a study in perpetual motion. Never for an instant was it still. With every gust of wind the walls groaned and the windows rattled, with every calm the floors settled, the ceiling sagged, and the braceboards sighed.

She too became a prisoner of time. She could not sleep without a clock within reach. At every waking she would reach for the light to read the message of her fate: only two o'clock. Four more hours to go. An eternity. Each finite piece of an infinite whole measured off with another dull tick: a grain of sand dropped from the beach of the night. Tick. Then four o'clock. Two more hours to go. Only two — when the sound of her alarm would find her too heavy to rise, ready at last for the sleep she had throughout the long hours of darkness so effectively resisted. And once the night was over, she found herself even less prepared to meet the day and Olaf's doom-filled eyes.

The times were hard, their enemies strong, yet it was too easy, and she too honest, to lay the blame anywhere but at their own feet. For her sister's cruelty or the world's scorn she could not be held responsible, but for the actions of her own heart she would plead neither poverty nor circumstances. She must scratch out the cause buried in her own conscience until the raw wound smarted. She knew then, in her selfish concern for her own salvation, she had condemned her lover to a hell from which he was powerless to extricate himself. And that knowledge had become her own hell.

4

"I had no right," she sobbed, beating the ledge of the confessional with her fist. "No right to deny him what every man needs."

"Not *every* man." Filtered through the dark screen, Father Moriarity's voice came to her dark with reproach.

"Ah, but *you* have God." She made no effort to disguise her voice. There was no pretense that her identity was unknown, yet she needed this cover of the confessional to bare her soul even to her pastor.

"Every man has God."

He knew by the unusual hour, the end of a long and trying Saturday afternoon, that her need was acute, and weary though he was, he struggled to rouse himself from the lethargy induced by his long hours of entombment in the dark, musty box; but the mounds of soul-shriveling pettiness, of forgotten prayers, missed masses, and onanistic orgies fairly suffocated him.

"But every man hasn't been given God's grace," she protested. "Some are weak and their weakness cries out to be loved."

He cleared his throat. "Are you not, perhaps, talking now of yourself? Of your own needs? Rather than his."

"Ah, Father, Father . . ."

With a, "Hush, hush, Belle!" he cautioned her to lower her voice for fear there might still be lingering in the dusky shadows of the church some tardy eavesdropping penitent, and without removing his ear from the screen, he lifted the curtain that topped his Dutchdoor and swept the empty pews with his eyes.

"After all these years!" she continued in the same loud whisper as though she had not heard his interruption. *"My* needs!"

And he knew by the almost hysterical shrillness of her cry that she was no longer after counsel, but license. She did not want his advice so much as his imprimatur upon her sin.

"The only need I have is to see him whole again. Everyday — everyday I watch him die, bit by bit, piece by little piece . . . I had no right," she continued before the priest could finish clearing his dry throat, intent now upon its own crying need for the customary five o'clock whiskey, "no right to deny him what might have given him the strength to believe in himself as a man."

"Even at the peril of your own soul?"

"Even at the peril of my own soul!"

"Oh, Belle! Belle! Get down on your knees and pray to God when the devil is out to have his way with you, putting such notions into your foolish head. Pray! And when you've finished praying, pray again, until you have banished Satan and all his cohorts — in whatever shape they may take."

"My whole life has become one long prayer to save him, Father."

Stirred back to life by his own eloquence, he continued,

unaware of her interruption: "And who knows what glory God is preparing for you? What rewards to bless your constancy —"

"I don't want glory!" she fairly shrieked, her voice echoing throughout the church.

Tumbled from his pulpit by the fury of her reply, the priest succumbed once more to fatigue. Again he cautioned her to lower her voice, and again she continued as though she had not heard:

"I am a simple woman, Father. I don't ask for glory. All I ask is that he be given the strength to live out his life as a whole man. A whole man, Father. And I know God will forgive me for what I must do. Must, Father."

"That may very well be," he answered, speaking now with the voice of a judge handing down his sentence; "no man can circumscribe God's mercy. But with that resolve, I hope you understand, *I* cannot give you absolution. I ask you, before you leave," he continued, fearful that his own great need to be released from the confinement of the dark little box might have precipitated her fateful decision, and anxious to ease his own conscience by extending his torture, "say your usual prayers at the altar rail. Commune privately with God for a few minutes. Give Him one last chance. And I'll wait here until you've finished in the event you should change your mind. God bless you," he added as she stumbled blindly, numbly, out of the confessional and up to the altar rail.

The light filtered through the amberglass windows cast long golden shadows. In the dusk the sanctuary lamp burned brighter, glowing scarlet as Christ's own blood. Kneeling, she studied the stained-glass window over the high altar: Christ in the Garden of Olives preparing to shed his blood as an act of love. The message was clear. How much greater, then, to offer that which was infinitely more precious than life, to give, not just her flesh and blood, but her very soul!

She left the church in a state approaching exaltation. Running past the confessional and down the front stairs, she hurried home like a saint to her martyrdom, lifted beyond pain by a mind-conquering sense of her selfless gift. Even the sky was lit with tongues of fire, and he was standing once again in the open hatch of the barn, a beautiful lithe animal in his prime, winged

171

now in her memory with the rays of the setting sun.

The orchards were broodingly dark in the dying light. She rushed past them into the gravel circle of her backyard. The tankhouse door was shut, its window dark. Shedding her coat as she mounted the stairs to her kitchen, she called out his name. But there was no answer. Opening the door, she discovered him sitting in the kitchen shadows, broodingly silent, unshaven, hollow-eyed. She flicked on the light, blinked at its glare, then plunged to earth a broken old woman.

She was capable of anything to save him, but she was not capable of shaming him, so deeply had he already been shamed. Without an insult too deep for him to bear, she could not offer to his broken body what she had denied to his splendid wholeness. For any solution so simple the time had long since passed. It was too late now for her to be anything but his nurse.

Chapter Four

1

On and on he rode, the wind in his hair, the rain on his face, up the bare rocky spine of Mount Diablo, up and up he climbed, chilled by the cold gray menace and the wet embrace of his lost lady, over the shoulder and into the deadly mist that shrouded the top — forever beyond his reach. The scream tore at his throat, but the lance at his side pinioned his flight. An insect mounted on the point of a pin. Trapped.

The sagging wiremesh of the upper bunk prevented a sudden bound. The scream still tearing at his throat, a billyclub pressed into his side, he confronted the curious eyes of the white-uniformed guard. The nightwatch.

Bewildered, he looked about, scanning the even rows of brown-painted iron bunks, tiered, one on top the other, each weighted with a sleeping bundle. Recognition came with a sickening spasm. He sank back onto his pillow, a tiny, hard mound scarcely large enough to cushion his head.

"Easy, there." The voice impersonal, but not hostile. "Everything all right?"

"All right," he answered, blinking awake, his hands now behind his head, his undershirt damp with sweat.

But that was a lie. Nothing was right; rather, all wrong. Life always promising more than it ever intended giving. He must have been drunk — or mad — ever to have imagined there was any easy escape from parental tyranny. To be his own man at last. What a laugh! Now was he less than ever his own.

The promised pagodas strung with silver bells — where were they? The bare-breasted dancing girls? The swivel hips? The slender palms? Their only reality in the wet dreams of the hundred droning bodies, sounds in the night no more melodic than the flatulent rumblings of the stucco Cyclops that housed them — San Diego Spanish.

173

And once again the enormity of his act weighed him down. Six years! He had signed away six years of his life, celebrated his sister's marriage by selling himself into a bondage that made his father's tyranny seem, in retrospect, the lenient benevolence of a fond warder. Instead of his own man, he had become the indentured slave of the United States Navy.

2

"Six years, it's a long time, Vince. And there's no use pretending I don't miss him."

Clara in her dressing gown reclined on her satin chaise, a mirror dangling unused from one hand, her face, creamed for the night, bland in its nudity. "And with Louise gone now, why, the place seems almost empty. If I didn't have Sarah to keep me company . . ."

She sighed, then sighed again as she lifted the mirror to her face. Her glasses lay on the table beside her. Too indolent to reach for them, she was forced to draw what picture she might from the blur, the shining forehead of her greased face looming from the silver shadows: the image of her naked skull, as if she were already dead and peering from another world through the glass top of a coffin.

"Vince!" she cried, gripping his arm as though her husband, who might dare anything, might also, before it was too late, halt the advance of time. His strong arm steady beneath her grasp calmed her so that her exclamation, eased of its terror, served only to bridge the gap from action to answer.

"Do him good." He bent over and kissed her neck. "A little discipline for a change."

Kinder than her mirror, her husband's eyes reflected only the woman he had married, younger than he and by now too comfortable for regret. The only beauty that counted was that which gave pleasure, and she pleased him, her enduring loyalty the single untarnished tribute to his dream.

"Teach him a thing or two about life."

"But he's so young, Vince, to be so far from home. Look at this." She removed a letter secreted beneath a tangle of hairnets and hairpins on her dressing table and handed it to him. "The

174

second already this week. He's learned his lesson, Vince. "I'm sure of that. So you mustn't be too hard on him. Six years! Think what that means. Six years! At his time of life."

"Make a man of him." Nothing made him feel so old as thoughts of his son. "That's what he needs. A little discipline."

3

Six years! Six years of petty, menial tasks, six years of drilling. Of nightwatches and deck-swabbing and hull scraping. Six years of slavery. Working all day, until stiff and aching, heavy with sleep, he must roam the silent night alone, looking for God alone knew what — but *something!* Lonely and afraid.

The letters home became more frequent, pleading: this time he had really learned his lesson and learned it well. Get him out of this scrape and he would settle down. Once and for all. Get him out of this and he would do anything they asked of him. Anything.

His sister Louise had shown the way. The outcast prodigal welcomed back into the fold, she had exposed the old bugger at last, shown that, like everyone else, he too had a crack in his iron facade. She had even, before she mounted the altar, wrung from him his reluctant blessing, and though he had looked as glum as any pallbearer, he had still led her up the aisle.

Well, he too would call the old man's bluff. Stare him down and he'd come whimpering back, open-armed, to claim his own. Blood was thicker than water. And to prove his good intentions, his willingness at last to give up his wild exploits and matriculate into the adult world of middle-class morality, he followed his sister's example and married.

Chapter Five

1

Tall and efficient, harshly angular, with the flat hips and long sturdy flanks of a swimmer, large, uncoordinated features — huge, wonderless eyes and full, unsensual lips — and a low, soft voice that seemed, for all its resonance, curiously sexless, Marge Dalrymple was an unlikely bride. She had been touched first by his beauty, which was all the more wonderful alongside her own plainness. She was touched even more by the false bluster of his arrogance.

"Yes? May I help you?"

Her first words were brisk and unfriendly. She had spied the swagger as he made his way through the door. At the counter he noisily crumpled his attempts at composition and let the yellow balls fall carelessly to the floor.

"Let me get his one," she had said to the other girl. "What're the odds he's out to break some pregnant heart with a soft hammer?"

"He can break mine anytime he wants to," her companion had answered, an appreciative leer no more enduring than a flash-bulb lighting up her face. "But go ahead. My book's already filled for the week-end."

Possibly because she was herself so plain, she had a positive "thing" about these strutting peacocks, these dime-store Valentinos, as she called them, and a very nice way of puncturing their pretensions with a little jab of her wit; but the message thrust before her was so blunt in its appeal — SHIP OUT NEXT WEEK STOP SAVE ME BEFORE TO LATE — that she looked up from the telegram to the face.

The cruel lips quivered, their ends tucked pathetically into the pocket of his cheeks; the hard eyes grew soft, pleading, as the peacock actually blushed, the subtle tint of his cheeks far more appealing than any garish spread of feathers. And she too blushed, first for having so unfairly misjudged him, then for intensifying his embarrassment by witnessing it. The naked plea seemed to be directed at her:

SAVE ME!

"There are two *o*'s in 'too.'" She made the correction with her pencil hoping that her tone had been matter-of-fact rather than smart or pedantic.

"Thanks." He blushed again.

"Regular or night letter?" She smiled — warmly, she hoped. He shrugged his shoulders. "What's the difference?" Then encouraged by her smile, he confided, "Never sent one before. Never been away from home, as a matter of fact."

"Where is San Oriel?" She hoped to ease his embarrassment by drawing him out, her curiosity roused by the little-boy-lost look of the frightened eyes, meltingly brown. She was even touched by the transparent bluster of his words: "My old man owns half the town." A little boy desperate for status.

A casual encounter, it should by all odds have ended there, but despite the forbidding efficiency of her manner, Marge was not altogether lacking in romance. She read all the currently fashionable novels, and though she sneered at its pretensions, she would no more have missed the cinema on Saturday night than she would have missed religious services on Sunday morning. There was in both her devotions a lack of discrimination. She went to see "the pictures," rather than to see *a* picture, as on Sunday she went to church, rather than to any particular church, to a Methodist, and Episcopal, a Presbyterian — to whichever was at the moment handiest, most convenient, or most conducive to a particular mood, her choice more often determined by the quality of the windows and the choir than by any doctrinal difference. It was this same lack of discrimination that transformed her smile of recognition the next day as she spied the handsome young man with the tragic eyes and the boyish smile.

She had been running for the bus to take them off the base. At the door he stepped aside to let her on. She smiled. "Hello, again," she called over her shoulder as she mounted the steps and sat on an empty double seat, tucking her coat under her so that the space beside her might look invitingly spacious, her

178

heart oddly racing. On the window side she turned just as he came down the aisle to look at him, her eagerness, she hoped, less apparent than felt. He answered her smile with his own. It was marvelous, she thought, how the face changed. From Apollonian hauteur to bucolic charm. Once again she was touched by some hurt in the eyes still cyring SAVE ME!

"The girl from the telegraph office," he said, taking the empty seat alongside her.

"Yes," she answered, unduly pleased that he remembered her. "The boy whose father owns half of San Oriel," she rejoined and they both laughed.

Slouching slightly in her seat to appear smaller, she played with the tortoise shell handle of her purse, snapping it open and shut. She longed to say something smart and memorable, but she could for the moment think of nothing at all save the warmth of his thigh alongside hers. "I see you're carrying a map." A stiff, undistinguished beginning, but better than none. "Can I help you find something? I'm not a native, but I know the city pretty well by now."

Had she not been so comfortably plain, he might have raised ugly defenses, but her church-going wholesomeness precluded any suggestion of a pickup. She was so clearly a "good" woman that she was, though not altogether unhandsome, sexless. As all good women were: those who ran households, raised children, flattered their husbands and pampered their sons and generally made life warmly worth living; as those, in short, men married, in glaring contract to those men chased.

He had to think before he could answer, for he had no plans at all. "The zoo. I thought I might give the old zoo the once over."

"That's easy enough. We both transfer at the same stop."

He stood up when they arrived — too soon, she thought. He let her off first, tipping his head and touching his hat in token salute. For some reason she inspired his best Sunday school manners. Far from home, he enjoyed playing the *grand seigneur* patterned on his father, taking her arm to help her over the curb to await the arrival of their respective cars.

"Say," he said, still holding lightly onto her elbow, "how about you joining me? It gets sort of lonesome," he added, "not knowing anyone."

Had she been a likely target for seduction he would never have managed the invitation.

"Well . . ." Blushing until her eyelids brimmed, with surprise as well as pleasure. "I really shouldn't . . ."

She could hardly be said to know him, yet he seemed, for all his dangerous good looks, harmless enough. Just a homesick boy achingly lonely. It was a state she could well sympathize with, having herself come to San Diego to get as far away from her family as possible, without friend or relative to help her catch her bearing or find her way. The first few months had been desperately lonely, but she had never regretted her decision. It had given her a certain pride in her ability to care for herself. Girls who got into trouble, she was convinced, were girls who asked for trouble.

"Monkeys aren't much fun alone." He gave her elbow a gentle tug.

She had dared to defy her family, so why shouldn't she continue to dare? The world belonged to the brave. And the beautiful, she might have added, but for the sting.

"Well, all right, why now? Yes, why not?" And with her heart once again racing madly at her audacity, she slipped her arm through his, partly to steady herself, but so natural was the gesture, he beamed with pleasure, as though he had just been granted a touch of home. "I'd love to go to the zoo with you."

2

"You know," he said over their after-dinner coffee, their hands resting on the checkered tablecloth, close but not touching, "it's the first day since I arrived I haven't felt like blowing the whole damn place up. God how I hate the dump! The end of the world. Whatever made you wanna settle down here?"

"Oh, it isn't so bad," she protested, sympathetic but compelled to offer a defense, "once you get used to it. The weather's ideal. Why, it was so warm last Christmas people were actually swimming in the ocean. And the poinsettias. I'd always thought — from Christmas cards, I guess — they grew in the snow. It's strange seeing them — whole trees of them —

blooming in the bright sunlight. Right alongside the cactus. And not a flake of snow in sight."

She might have spared her breath. It wasn't San Diego he disliked, but the Navy. All prisons have a sameness about them, and he viewed the town through a grate.

"Marge," he said, testing the feel of her name on his lips. "Marjorie Dalrymple. That's some label to be stuck with."

"Yes," she admitted, smiling, "it does have a rather silly lilt to it, doesn't it? But I won't be stuck with it always." Her laugh was awkward. "I hope."

And it seemed only natural that she should, simply for the improbable fun of it, test the sound of Marjorie Woods. It had a cinematic ring to it. Then catching sight of herself in the mirror over the cash register she blushed, once again her awkward self. *She* did not want to be the subject of conversation, gangling Marge Dalrymple, girl giant.

"Won't you ever stop growing?" her mother used to say, shaking her head like a disgruntled shopper stuck with a piece of defective merchandise. "I wanted a little girl, and what did I get? A gangling goose. Come now, stand up straight. As long as you've got to be tall, don't make matters worse by slouching. Round shoulders won't make up for a flat bust."

And she wanted to slide down in her chair, to perch, like some contortionist, on the small of her back so that she might seem, of all things, a demure little flapper, with round pink cheeks and bee-stung lips. A Clara Bow of the boondocks.

"The scar on your face," she asked, longing but not daring to touch it. "How did you get it?"

"This?" His eyes grew brooding and vulnerable as he himself touched his cheek. "It's a long story." And he looked away with self-conscious drama.

"Tell me."

"You won't like it. A girl like you."

"And just what do you mean: a girl like me?"

"Don't get me wrong. It wasn't a cut or anything like that. Just the opposite. A nice girl. Someone who isn't — fast. I just don't wanna shock you. That's all."

She blushed, not sure she should be flattered. Apparently her virginity was as obvious and impenetrable as Joan of Arc's armor.

"I think you're bragging," she challenged. "I don't shock easily. Even when it comes to stories about — as you call them — fast women. What was her name?"

"She didn't have a name. Or at least I never found it out."

"Ah, then she must have been *very* fast," she gave her brows an arch lift, "to have come in and gone out of your life without time enough to leave her name."

"It doesn't matter anymore what she was. She's dead."

The starkness of his answer was all she needed to convince her she must have the whole story. Nor did it take much coaxing to get him to oblige.

Even censored as it was, the story came to her filtered through the screen of her own reading, the characters softened in a Bronte-like mist: a wildly handsome Jazz-age Heathcliff driven by strange and uncontrollable desires; a nameless, doom-driven Cathy destined to haunt him forever after. So moved was she by her own version of the tale and so touched that he had been willing to share it with her, she forgot for the moment her own gangling person. Unable to find words sufficient to express her emotion, she placed a comforting hand on his.

And he too was curiously touched. She seemed to him the epitome of every spinsterly school teacher who had ever forgiven him for carving his initials on a desk top. She was as homely as a winter fire, and though a missionary at heart, one who set for-giveness above reformation. Raw material for a wife. And he was greatly in need of some dramatic gesture to startle his father into action.

She made only one nearly disastrous gaff during their first eve-ning together. As they were getting ready to leave, she put her hand on the bill. She was used to going out with young men who expected her, as a working girl, to pay her own way. The town seemed filled with single men who wanted nothing more than her company, a sisterly shoulder to cry upon, a Platonic dialogue on the relative merits of Norma Talmadge and Gloria Swanson, neither of whom she was sure had ever had to pay *her* way.

"You really must let me take care of my share. I know how little they . . ."

"*I*'ll pay." He didn't even attempt to soften the brutality of his reply or the brusqueness of his rise from the table. "What do you take me for, some goddam gigolo?"

"I forgot," she tried to make a joke out of it. "Your father owns half of San Oriel."

"The old man's got nothing to do with it. This happens to be *my* money I'm paying with. Not his."

The awkwardness was eased by the walk back to her apartment and the lovely warm darkness thick with the tropical sweetness of angel's trumpets and jasmine. To give him the added security of looking down upon her, she slipped off her heels, walking in her stocking feet. It seemed a daringly Bohemian gesture, for the "roar" of the twenties with its shattering of conventions had reached San Diego as only a faint rumble.

She was surprised at the inexplicable, but flattering, urgency of his request to see her again. Then remembering the first part of his telegram: SHIP OUT NEXT WEEK, she didn't even try to be coy. She put him off only long enough to give her an opportunity to get downtown to buy a pair of the shortest, stubbiest heels she could find. If she couldn't be Clara Bow, there was no reason she had to be Marge the Amazon.

When she offered her hand in parting, she was pleased that he had, like a perfect gentleman, made no attempt to kiss her goodnight. Or so she thought, until alone in her own room, she first regretted being denied the chance to refuse, and then regretted even more the chance to submit.

Chapter Six

1

"But Vince, *can* something be done? Or are we simply to sit back and watch him sink deeper and deeper into this mess?"

"Something can always be done. If you have the time and the contacts. And the money."

"Well, then, I think you'd better take the time and go to San Diego." Still clutching the awful telegram, Clara spoke rather more testily than she was wont to speak to her husband. "At least you can look her over, if nothing else. I dread to think . . ."

What kind of a girl, she wanted to ask, would marry a sailor. But remembering that sailor was her own son, she contented herself with conjecture rather than outright condemnation.

"Why, there's no telling *what* she might be."

"Well, it's too late now to do anything about that part."

"Too late? How too late? He only said he'd married the girl. He didn't say anything about marrying in the Church. And certainly, if it had been a proper ceremony, he'd have made that clear enough. But he didn't so much as mention a priest. And what's her name — Dalrymple?" She screwed up her face as she let the strange letters fall from her lips like seeds from some unsweetened lime. "That certainly doesn't sound Catholic to me. We'll simply have the marriage annulled."

Vince smiled at his wife's naivete. It was, after all, one of her more endearing charms; it left her always at his mercy, and her abiding faith, even in the face of defeat, could deflect the severest blows to his ego.

"On what grounds, Clara? Even if you please the pope, there's still the law to contend with. They might not have had a priest, but they damn well must have had a marriage license. And you can be sure, whatever kind of girl she is, she'll get herself pregnant fast enough to seal the bargain. If she wasn't already before the ceremony took place. Once that happens, it won't matter how the knot was tied. With or without the pope's blessings.''

"But he simply *can't* support a wife and raise a family on a sailor's pay. Our own grandchild. You'll simply have to give him another chance, Vince. And I promise you, on my sacred honor — and you know I've never lied to you in my life — if this doesn't work, if he doesn't settle down to business and begin, the instant he gets back here, to make something out of himself, I'll be the last person in the world ever to ask you to come to his rescue again. I swear that. Though he came out of my own body, my own flesh and blood, we'll cross him off our books. Like any other bad debt. But how can we do that — his own parents — before we've done everything in our power to help him save himself? After all," she concluded, her face going mushy with imminent tears, "he's the only son we've got. The only one." And the last frail remnants of composure were swept away on a flood of tears.

2

Two days later, Vince Woods was standing in the palm-decked, white-pillared lobby of the Ulysses S. Grant Hotel. Dressed in his traveling best, a board-of-directors, country-squire tweed altogether out of place in the near-tropical setting, he made no attempt to disguise his surprise at the entrance of the bridal pair coming arm in arm to greet him, embarrassed smiles pinned on their faces like paper cutouts. His son's swagger was held in check by the sheer weight of his bride anchored on the crook of his arm, her eyes still glazed from the speed and improbability of fortune's recent twists and turns.

Whatever it was Vince expected, this awkward grinning giant of a girl with no more grace or style than a trombonist in a Salvation Army band was certainly not it.

Too bewildered even to guess what was expected of her, Marge stood with hand extended, her white kid glove as heavy as an iron gauntlet, her knee slightly crooked.

Her husband's challenge spared her from any further need to act:

"Well, aren't you going to kiss the bride? After all, like her or not, she's the only daughter-in-law you're apt to have. Unless you've been holding out on us," he added with a sly wink his father chose to ignore and his wife failed to comprehend.

Though Vince could not begin to understand what his son could possibly see in this gangling, sexless girl, all angularities and clumsy, well-minded intentions, he was quick enough to recognize that she might be just the catalyst Arnie's life needed to give it some durable form. Every teacher's nightmare most improbably mated to the very model of a classic schoolmarm. And considering the mind-boggling range of possible alternatives with which his son might have presented him, Vince could ask for no more.

"Oh, I like her fine. Just fine." And his welcoming embrace was not stinting in its warmth.

The ritual kiss of both her cheeks sealed whatever doubts she had. Her decision, wild and hasty as it may have been, had been the right one. Of that she was now certain. And by the time her father-in-law escorted her into the dining room, she had already fallen in love with him.

Like most men of accomplishment, he gave off an aura of familiarity. He could not walk through a public room without drawing every eye to him, the interrogatory glances trying vainly to place him in some celebrated slot. So convinced was he that he was somebody, it seemed only natural to those who watched him that that somebody must then be identifiable.

Once seated, he dominated the conversation with the ease of a man who has never for an instant suffered the anguish of self-doubt, and Marge, who had — remembering her own family — dreaded a series of long, agonizing silences interspersed with muttered banalities, was charmed. Herself the child of a mush-willed father and a domineering harridan of a mother who believed children should be raised and husbands subdued as horses are broken, she admired nothing more than a man who knew how to take command. And since Vince liked nothing better than to play the commander, they seemed destined to get along. He ordered the waiters and everyone else about with a flair that no one would dare countermand or take offense at.

With an off-handed "never trust these hotel cooks with anything but steak," he ordered filet mignon for everyone with such benign authority that Arnie's defense of his wife's right to make her own choice embarrassed her:

"No, no. I *adore* filet. Even though I can almost never afford it."

"Well, *he* sure as hell can. That's why he always likes to order it. To make all the waiters think he's Mr. Bigshot himself."

Vince's first response to any attack was always a smile.

"Well, Sonny boy, when you can afford to do the ordering yourself, I'll be more than happy to step aside and let you take over. Long as you can serve up something more appetizing than cold egg salad on stale bread."

"Still the same old Daddykins I remember." Arnie's smile was ironically affectionate. "I'd almost forgotten. But if you wanna play that game, it's all right with me. And for starters," he continued, perversely, since he would far rather have had the steak, *"I'*m going to have the chicken."

"Oh, Arnie!" With a glance at the impassive waiter, Marge placed a mollifying hand on her husband's. The tension of his clenched fist startled her and she felt herself suddenly caught up in the pull of some ancient malice.

"Let him be." His own smile playfully teasing, Vince patted Marge's other hand. "If he wants chicken, let him have his chicken."

With a cruelly analytical smile, Arnie waited for the culminating cut he knew was sure to follow.

"It'll be the first time he's ever voluntarily offered to save me a dollar. And I'm the last person in the world's gonna object to that."

Arnie's teeth-gritting silence was the first evidence of his growing maturity. For once the stakes were too high to risk sacrificing the jackpot for the easy trick. His marriage had had its desired effect: it had startled the old man into action, but that action remained unfinished.

"He'll be all right," Vince continued, speaking to the troubled Marge, "once we cross the border and welcome you into the family with a magnum of the best French champagne."

It was clearly a truce offer, and Arnie was quick to accept it:

"Now you're talking."

"And tomorrow . . ."

"Yes?" Arnie's interest was keen. "And what about tomorrow?"

"Well, that remains to be seen. I've already made a few contacts. But we'll have to see yet, when the proper time comes, what the going price for freedom is."

And the father fixed the son with eyes that made it abundantly clear, whatever the price was, he expected a full return.

"It seems," he continued, "your doctor thinks someone with a history of asthma like you shouldn't be confined to the close quarters of a ship for any length of time. Away from land and proper medical attention."

"Asthma? I never even had whooping cough."

"Well, you damn well better develop at least a slight wheeze by tomorrow morning."

Arnie smiled. "Enough champagne'll take care a that."

"Well, for once I won't say no. You don't want them to think a fully qualified doctor like old Dutra might somehow have confused his records. And it seems, sometimes — even the navy doctor agrees — a history of asthma isn't always clear, if some patriotic young man so anxious to serve his country's willing to do anything, even lie, to get himself into uniform."

"Why, you old fox."

For once there was no pretense or irony in their shared affection, and Marge, basking in the embrace of smiles, was so pleased at the sudden switch from hostility to open affection that she gave up trying to follow the bewildering conversation.

"You know," Arnie continued, "maybe I will have that steak after all."

There was considerably more ebullience than malice in Vince's laughter. "I thought it was too much to hope you might spare me that dollar. I was even thinking about having it framed. For your heirs, case you have any."

"Well, we'll see what we can do to expedite that, eh, Marge?"

But Marge, whose comfort vanished in her sudden blush, was incapable of responding.

"You can be damn sure," Arnie continued, apparently enjoying his bride's embarrassment, "I'll take care a *my* end."

"I'm only gonna lay down one condition," Vince continued,

finding his daughter-in-law's discomfort altogether commendable, "The first boy's to be named Vincent Woods the Second."

Arnie whistled. "Get a load a that 'Second,' will you! It's a long, long way from Pico, eh, Pa?"

"It's a long, long way from nowhere." Vince seemed suddenly displeased with something. "I was born right here. In the good old U.S.A. Same as you."

"Sure, Pa."

Suddenly everything had changed, and their always-mercurial relationship once again moved from affection to irony. Only this time it was the father who had exposed his vulnerability and the son who held the advantage. The real prize, the latter suddenly realized, was not Arnold Woods' discharge from the United States Navy, but Vincent Woods' immortality.

"Anything you say. You just do your part. And Marge and I'll see what we can do to oblige you about the rest. Only — Vincent? Don't you think that sounds a little old-fashioned for the fast-moving twenties? And maybe — who knows? — I might, when the time comes along, just wanna have a little Arnold Junior running around the house."

"And maybe," Vince's dark eyes smoldered, "some cocky young stud too big for his bell-bottom britches may find himself serving out every last day of those six years he signed himself up for."

There was little humility or intimidation in Arnie's answering smile. "Just kidding, Pa. Course we mean to name the kid after you. But one thing I can also promise, there won't be *any* kids till I'm outta the goddam Navy. So there you are. We both of us got a little capital invested in this affair. Haven't we? 'Less you happen to wanna buncha kids named Ramos taking over. And wouldn't that be something? Vince Woods beaten in the end by old Tom Ramos. Yes, sir, I'm sure looking forward to that steak."

Chapter Seven

1

The day had begun so well. The house, the tree, the fire. The handsome old man and his beautiful family. Like an advertisment for the American Dream: two generations from peonage and already princes of the land. A Cherrywood fire burned on the grate and the huge fir tree was ablaze with lights mirrored in the German ornaments. And seated on his plush throne, the old sheik himself, his black eyes alive with mischief, his thick gray hair crowning his noble face, his large stomach adding majesty to an already majestic figure.

Marge made no attempt to hide her pleasure; she was clearly dazzled. Not even the blatant bafflement of her in-laws at her plainness could spoil her delight, and the only shadow cast upon her entrance into the family came from her own husband. Like the protagonist in some child's game who had tagged her "it," he seemed, as soon as he had drawn her into the circle, anxious to disassociate himself from all responsibility for her presence there. As she took his arm to flaunt her own credentials as a bona fide member of the family, he slipped free of her hold and walked brusquely away. Then with his arm around Hyacinth Meek, Lorraine's suave beau, he headed for the dining room liquor cabinet, where the legendary supply of Canadian imports was stashed behind doors carved in elaborate imitation of some Gothic altarpiece.

Once her daughter-in-law had been openly slighted, Clara seemed prepared to welcome her with true warmth.

"Come, Dear, sit here and tell me about your trip." Clara moved over to make room on the sofa, but distracted by her grandson Tony, his eager hands intent upon an alabaster ashtray, she quickly forgot her own request.

"No, no, Dear. Mustn't touch Nanna's things." Clara caught the child's arm. "Since you bring him here, Louise," she snapped, her always precarious nervous system already strained to the limit by her son's long-delayed return, "you've simply got to keep your eye on him. He's just at that stage now where he gets his hands into everything," she continued, half apologetically, to Marge.

"Since I bring him!" Louise's defenses bristled. "Certainly you don't propose I leave him home! On Christmas Day!"

"Easy, Loo," Henry Ramos cautioned as he swept his child into his arms. His black-rimmed glasses and neatly trimmed mustache contrived to give him before students only a few years his junior, the authority of age. Older still was the expression of weary resignation, the ordeal of a holiday dinner with his wife's family to be borne with stoic passivity.

"Of course not, Dear," Clara mollified her manner. "But you simply must keep an eye on him. That's all."

"*My* children aren't going to be allowed to monopolize everyone's attention." Virtually surrounded by pregnant women, Lorraine felt herself at a distinct disadvantage.

Lousie blushed. "Have them first, before you make any such wild claims."

"Please, Dear!" Clara hoped with her mock horror to smooth over the ripples of antagonism that were already, so soon, rumpling the surface calm. "Let's at least wait till after the ceremony." And she bestowed an arch leer upon the awed Marge, whose features were locked in a smile paralyzed by good intentions.

Vince rose from his elephantine throne to commence the formal festivities. Tugging at the points of his vest to smooth away the wrinkles and checking his gold watch, more out of habit than curiosity, he moved to the Christmas tree, mumbling as he stooped to pick up two tinsel tubes, wrapped like oversize party favors:

"Well, well, what have we here?"

Chuckling to himself, he handed one of the tubes to Louise, and since his son, having discovered in his sister's beau a mutual love of poker as well as whiskey, had moved to the gameroom, he handed the other to Marge. Then with a heavy man's light-footed skip, he stepped back to view the unveiling.

"Is this *all* I get?" With untempered petulance Lorraine

studied the five ten dollar bills stuffed into the Christmas card just handed to her by her mother. "Not even *one* package?"

"Really, there's no pleasing anyone." Clara's reply was unaffectedly churlish. "You specially asked for money, didn't you? To complete your hope chest. And I told you already last year, after you returned everything I'd been to such pains to choose for you . . ."

"I didn't return the silk scarf," she pouted. "It just doesn't seem like Christmas without at least one package to open in your own home. That's all."

"Next year," her father's fond smile forming a strong contrast to the biting sarcasm of his voice, "I'll give you the money ahead of time and you can wrap all your own gifts fancy as you like."

Then he turned, with unconcealed impatience, to watch Louise parsimoniously remove the tinsel from her tube without tearing it, folding it neatly so that it might be saved for future use. Already supporting three and a prospective fourth on a very slim salary, she had become almost fanatical about budgeting all expenses in order to demonstrate that a childhood of affluence need not necessarily lead to an adulthood of extravagance. But she seemed now, in the light of her father's impatience, to be deliberately torturing him.

She soon repaid him in full. The large architect's blueprint adorned at the top with the legend *Ramos Bungalow* in her hands, she bit her lip, blushing until the tears rose before she could bring herself to her feet to throw her arms around her father's neck.

"Oh, Daddy! Dearest Daddy, thank you. Thank you." She made no effort to stem the flow of tears, gilding his cheeks with her gratitude. "I couldn't bear to have another child in the cramped little apartment. Without even a yard to hang the diapers in. Our own house," she continued, sinking back into her chair and sharing her pleasure with Henry, whose embarrassment at the moment exceeded his gratitude. Payment of one sort or another, he knew, was sure to be demanded.

Pleased enough with her reaction to spare her, at least for the moment, any reference to her husband's inability to furnish her with a place fit for a daughter of his to live in, Vince basked in her gratitude.

Marge, who had felt it politic to wait until Louise opened her gift, was confronted now with an identical plan. Not so readily given to tearful demonstrations, she could only mutter, "Oh, Mr. Woods!" and quickly call her husband to come relieve her from the clumsy burden of solitary gratitude.

"I'm right in the middle of a game, damn it." Arnie's reply issued from the gameroom, where a Tiffany shade, like an inverted fruitbowl, glowed over the green felt of the billiard table.

Marge flinched.

"But, Dear," Clara called, delighted at the opportunity to demonstrate the superior drawing power of *her* authority, "we're opening our presents."

"Don't worry," Vince added, to Marge's horror, "he'll be in here soon enough, touching me for the money to pay his losses."

"I heard that."

Arnie made a sullen entrance into the living room followed by Hyacinth Meek, whose midnight blue curls, fastidiously parted in the middle of his forehead, shimmered with brilliantine.

"I'm afraid it's Arnie who's been taking me."

Hy's magananimous smile testified that his losses had been a matter of good manners rather than bad playing. One does not fleece one's hosts at their own Christmas party.

"Don't tell me I'm not gaining another son but another loser as well."

Though Vince's shaft was clearly directed against his son rather than his future son-in-law, Lorraine was the first to take offense.

"Oh, Daddy! That isn't fair." She latched onto her intended's arm. "Anyone can see Hy isn't a loser. Why, his family practically founded the town."

"And have been going to seed ever since," Louise muttered to her husband as the two of them studied the plans for their new home.

"Your father's just having his little joke, Baby Doll. Don't take offense." Hy's white teeth flashed his good will. "I certainly don't."

His whole manner seemed designed for a banner heading: Idol of the Silver Screen. His fingernails were lacquered, his starched cuffs were held together by out-sized gold nuggets, and his hair was arranged to give an air of meticulous precision melding into dapper nonchalance, as though he meant to make the most of both worlds. He had clearly spent as much time with his toilet as had his frizzle-haired flapper, whose flame-covered, flame-patterned dress, its irregular hem exposing fat, dimpled knees, seemed itself designed to "set the town on fire."

"Oh, Hy! I know Daddykins better'n you," she answered, kicking up on heel as she nuzzled her wrinkled nose against his cheek.

"What the hell you on my tail for?" Arnie confronted his father with fractious intent.

"Arnie, just look." Marge caught his hand. "What your father's giving us."

The price for his son's freedom had proved higher than anticipated and the gratitude returned a good deal less than expected. Thus Vince's resentment, given months to smoulder while Arnie, apparently preferring to live at his wife's expense rather than his father's, continued to delay his return, was more than a retort to a single insolent remark:

"Well, you haven't proved to me yet you're man enough to get yourself out of your own scrapes."

Arnie shook loose his wife's hold. "Why're you so goddam anxious to start something, that's what I wanna know? You been on my tail all day. From the minute I got back."

"Please, Vince," Clara cautioned. "It's Christmas. Don't tease the boy."

The plans still open on her lap as the infant Tony, trapped between his father's legs, tried to use the blueprint as a drum, Louise interrupted:

"Certainly you won't object if we make a few changes."

"Changes?" The old man's temper was growing short. "What changes?"

"Well, for one thing, I notice there's only one bath. And if the new child's a girl, as we hope, we'll have to be able, someday, to add an extra room. Along with an extra bath."

"So it isn't good enough for you!" The words were directed

to his daughter but the appeal was to his family. "Here I go to all the trouble to surprise you — and nobody can say we haven't been generous, your mother and I — and offer you a house to live in. Which is a damn sight more than anyone else has done. Including your husband, I might add. Or his high-living family. And it isn't good enough for you."

His expectations vindicated, Henry nursed a wry smile. He would have plenty to say later, alone to his wife, but for the time being he meant to hold his peace. His contempt for his wife's family left no room for shame. Not certainly for the shabby state of his finances, which were, after all, the product of a social system that rewarded gall with gold and intelligence with dross.

"Oh, Daddy, don't be like that. Of course we're delighted. And we're not asking you to spend another penny."

Vince snorted his disdain, playing the role of wronged father with Shakespearian relish.

"But it would be so much easier," Louise went on — "save *us* money, in the long run, if we built the house with all possible contingencies taken into consideration. And that would include plans for expansion. At our own expense, of course," she was quick to add.

Arnie whistled. "Get the 'contingencies'!"

"Your sister-in-law doesn't seem to find *her* gift lacking."

"Oh, Daddy, don't draw her into it. That isn't fair. Naturally *she's* not going to say anything."

"Then why must you?"

"Because I've know you longer." She smiled, attempting once again to mollify him with an affectionate press of his hand. "And we're more alike, the two of us, than either one might care to admit."

Vince's sole answer was another snort.

"But what difference," Louise persisted, "can it possibly make to you, if you're going to spend so much money, if we move a closet from one side of the room to another and build a door where you have a window? We're the ones's who are going to live in the house and I can't see . . ."

"You'll take the house as I give it or you won't take it at all."

She knew her father's moods well enough to know that further argument was futile; that his reason could never be reached once his emotions were aroused. Adept as he was at worldy affairs, there was still a part of him that remained forever a stubborn child who could not bear to be bested in anything.

The entrance of Sarah, bearing a tray of champagne punch garnished with orange slices and maraschino cherries, brought the discussion temporarily to a halt.

"Christ, I need real drink." Arnie disdained the proffered glass. "When I want a fruit cocktail, I'll eat a fruit cocktail. But right now I need something with a little more bite to it. Join me, Hy?"

Hy needed little encouragement, and as he passed up the dribble glass set aside for him by his joke-loving host to follow Arnie to the dining room liquor cabinet, Sarah turned to her master with the confusion of an actress who has missed her cue and remains paralyzed for fear any step may be a misstep. Vince nodded in Henry's direction, but already too well versed in his father-in-law's pecadilloes to be so easily tricked, Henry ignored the plea in Sarah's eyes to indulge the old man and reached past the offered drink, leaving the dribble glass to stand in solitary isolation on the tray.

Vince smoldered.

"Sarah, Dear, take one for yourself," Clara said, adding, "And bring Immaculata in. I think there's a little gift for her here."

Sarah, whose bright, shining face almost as red and irregular in its contours as the clusters of toyon berries, indicated she had been helping herself in the kitchen, shortly returned with her daughter in tow and a dainty cup scarcely half full shimmering in her hand.

A sturdy, large-boned, nose-picking six-year old, Immaculata moved like a wound-up toy directly to the mistress of the house, first extending her head to receive Clara's benedictional kiss, then curtsying as the package was placed in her hand. Acutely conscious of a large and not altogether friendly audience, she turned to her mother for guidance.

"Well, open it child. Open it and let everyone have a look at what you got."

Timidly tearing the paper, the girl extracted a fuschia-colored sweater, and letting the garment dangle from her hand without a sound or a change of expression, she again turned to her mother before either registering delight or expressing gratitude.

"Well, what do you say?"

"Thank you, Mrs. Woods, thank you, Mr. Woods," she recited, mechanically kissing each upon the cheek, as Lorraine in the background could clearly be heard muttering:

"*I* didn't get a sweater. Or anything. Course I'm only a daughter and not the kitchen help."

"I hope you like the color, Dear." Clara held the sweater in front of the girl to check its size. "If not, your mother can always exchange it for you."

But Sarah would never have presumed to challenge her mistress's taste, and as soon as her hyperbolic delight had run its course, Clara read aloud the verse from the card with all the fervor of an unrecognized poet giving a public reading. Then rising stiffly with a grimace intended to call attention to the arthritis no one had cared enough to inquire about:

"I think we can finish our drinks at the table."

And delicately dragging one slightly swollen foot, she led the way into the dining room. At the foot of the table she braced herself on the upholstered back of her chair.

'Arnie, Dear," she continued, directing traffic with sweeping flourishes of a multi-ringed hand flashing diamonds, "you'll sit here next to me. And Marge, I think between Arnie and Louise. And Henry — there, I suppose that'll do. But Lorraine, if I let you sit next to Hy, you've got to promise to pay *some* attention to your food. Poor Sarah's been sweating in the kitchen all afternoon over a hot stove and I won't have you hurting her feelings by leaving your plate half picked over."

Lorraine blushed, Hy beamed, and Marge smiled her blessings upon the young lovers.

"Just a second, Marge." Louise forestalled her sister-in-law. "Before you sit down," she added as she drew out Marge's chair and lifted off the rubber bladder hidden by the fall of the lace cloth. "Oh, Daddy! And on Christmas Day!" She gave her father a severe look as she handed the inflated bladder to Sarah.

"I don't —?" Bewildered, Marge shook her head until Sarah,

pressing a fat upper arm against the bladder, shook with laughter in response to the rude report.

Vince smiled, his chagrin at his daughter's intervention somewhat abated by Sarah's lusty laugh.

"Don't worry," Arnie responded, not altogether pleased at his wife's rescue. "It's the old man's way of initiating you into the family. Everyone comes into the house has to be treated to at least one of his little jokes."

"Arnie, I've told you a thousand times." Clara grew instantly cross: "I won't have you using that expression. You may be a married man, but while you're in my house, you'll abide by my rules and show your father the respect he's due. Do you understand?"

"Where're the houses to be built?" Louise asked as Sarah, still shaking from the aftershock of her laughter, served the fruit cocktail. "Or dare I ask?"

"On the other side of the creek. Next to Belle's place."

"By the way, how is old Belle?" Arnie asked. "And her red-headed beau?"

Most of the other diners took a sudden and keen interest in the floral patterns garlanding their service plates. Hy studied his manicure, polishing an imaginary dull spot on the nail of his little finger, as Marge, bewildered, searched the averted eyes for some clue to the identity of the people under discussion.

"My mother's sister," Arnie commented for his wife's benefit, then added, with a wink at Hy: "An old maid fierce enough to freeze the balls off almost anyone but . . ."

"Arnie!" Clara exclaimed, appalled. "Really, I should think, at the family dinner table . . .!"

Marge blushed. "I don't know what's come over him," she stammered, her hurt eyes focused, pleading, on the glass clutched in her husband's hand. "I'm afraid the excitement of seeing you all has gone to his head."

"That's not all that's gone to his head." Louise attempted to freeze her father's chuckle with an icy scowl.

"She doesn't speak to us anymore," Lorraine quickly joined in. "She hasn't stepped foot in this house since Daddy fired Olaf. She even changed her pew so she wouldn't have to sit next to us in church."

"Will the deeds come with the houses?"

The single member of the family who still maintained open relations with the disgraced Belle, Louise hoped to divert the subject away from her absent aunt.

"Deeds?" Vince looked up from his turkey, his smile culminating in a frown. "You won't need any deeds. The house'll be built on land already belongs to me."

"Ahhhh, so it isn't us you're building the houses for." Louise sat back, pushing her plate away from her as Tony on his highchair began to beat his spoon against the tray.

"Why, whatever do you mean Dear?" Surprised at her daughter's remark. Clara failed to catch the point of the dispute.

"If we're not to be given deeds, they won't be our houses, will they? And of course that's your privilege. There's no obligation for you to give us anything at all. And I might add, we haven't asked for anything. But please, let's call a spade a spade. A loan is not a gift no matter how much tinsel it comes wrapped in."

"Would you rather continue to pay rent?" Her father was growing ever more contentious.

"Of course not. But it seems to me to smack somewhat of dishonesty to pretend to give us something you're only going to let us use."

As Tony persisted banging the tray of his highchair, Louise lifted him out and stood him on his feet. "Now you stay here, alongside Mommy," she admonished.

The child looked up at her with wide, wondering eyes, and then, falling to his knees, immediately crawled under her chair.

"What difference can it possibly make? Clara felt her daughter, as usual, deficient in gratitude and quibbling now over distinctions which hardly warranted comment.

"Well, for one thing, if we're going to put our own money into keeping the place up and adding onto it, it would be nice to know it was ours, and not going to be taken away from us the moment I say or do something doesn't happen to please you."

"You're saying a good deal right now doesn't happen to please me."

Her father's scowl was fierce, but it failed to intimidate.

"Yes, and I'm sure I'll say a good deal more," Louise answered, the blood rising to her face as her husband across the table tried to caution temperance.

"Can't we discuss something else for a change? This subject's getting boring."

Ignoring Lorraine's sensible plea, Vince challenged his oldest daughter: "All right, say it."

"You want to be able to control us," she continued, making a concerted but not altogether successful effort to keep the pitch of her voice under control. "To have something to hold over our heads as blackmail."

"Easy, Loo." Again Henry cautioned restraint, but his wife was well past all temperance.

"And you would, you know," she continued, ignoring her husband. "You would blackmail us with anything at all that happened to upset your narrow Republican outlook."

"All right, so what if I would? Someone has to control you. Because you're not any of you capable of controlling yourselves."

"I resent that." Louise's eyes flashed fire. "What have I ever done that you have a right to be ashamed of? Name one thing."

"What you're doing right now. What I do for one I have to do for all. And you should know that without forcing me to say it."

"And what do you mean by that, I'd like to know?" asked Arnie.

"You know very well what he means," Louise snapped, then turned back to her father. She realized now her terrible mistake, discussing at the family table what she should have broached to her father alone, out of her brother's hearing but she had already gone too far to stop herself. "Just because one of us is unreliable doesn't mean you have to punish all of us for his sins."

"And just who you referring to?" Arnie's ire was up.

"You! Of course. Who else? If you weren't already so drunk, you wouldn't have to ask." Louise's contempt was flagrant. "Why can't we simply have whatever it cost you to get him out of the Navy, since you insist upon fairness? Giving to all what you give to one. And without any strings attached to it. Deeds held over our heads to blackmail is with."

"Listen, you, you —" Arnie faltered.

"Here they go again." Lorraine turned an exasperated face to her fiance. "Like cats and dogs. I swear, I'm never going to have more'n one child, so there won't be all this bickering. And if you want anymore," she added, tears of shame streaking her kewpie-doll cheeks, 'you'd just better marry someone else.''

"But Baby Doll," he protested, patting her comfortingly on her hefty thigh, "it's you I want. Not kids."

"Do all families fight like this?" Clara directed her question to Marge, who was for the moment too stunned to reply, though she felt the question demanded a comforting affirmative. But how could she say that, no, there were families that smothered each other with silence and stunted their children in cramped little cages of good manners? But she was saved by the diversion of an impending disaster.

"Oh, dear — the child!" she cried, half rising from her seat.

With the alacrity of a ballerina in her prime, the arthritic Clara was out of her chair, but too late to prevent the porcelain parrot from crashing to the floor. Tony's head was missed by a fraction, but Dresden's finest was shattered on the parquet floor.

"Naughty, naughty child!" Clara shook the screaming boy by the arm, at the same time soundly slapping his limp hand.

"Mother!" Louise was on her feet. "He's only sixteen months!" And she swept her child into her arms.

"Yes." Clara clutched the largest fragment of the broken parrot, her halo of tight curls atremble. "It's you whose hand I should be spanking. You! You naughty, clumsy girl."

Louise could feel herself shrink, the years shriveling around a hard core of adolescent resentment.

"Yes, you'd like that, wouldn't you."

Clara stood erect, her eyes brimming with tears. Then with an imperious lift of her chin she hobbled back to the support of her chair. Marge reached out to help her with a steadying hand.

"What an impossible child!" Lorraine's comment broke the momentary lull.

"You just keep your remarks to yourself, young lady," Louise fairly shrieked.

"Loo, Loo." Henry was up and at her side cautioning his

wife, whose eyes were flashing now with more fire than he would ever be able to handle.

She turned to him, trembling, momentarily undecided, as if she might in an instant vent her interrupted fury upon him. Then dropping her head against his chest, she burst into tears.

"Why do they always make me behave like this?" she sobbed. "Why do I always start to shout and scream the moment I enter this house? I'm not like this, am I? You know I'm not like this."

"This is the last one." Clara resumed her seat. "The last one. We'll have no more Christmases after this one. No more. I simply can't take any more. My nerves can't put up with it."

Vince rose with the petulance of a child who has just watched the sea carry away his sandcastle. He left the table.

"But Vince," Clara pleaded, "we haven't had our dessert. Where are you going?"

"To my room. Before the lot of you send me to an early grave."

With head bowed, one hand pressed over his heart, he made his exit, followed by the silent gaze of the assembled family.

"Vince!" Clara called after him, real alarm in her voice. "Is something the matter? You're not ill, are you?"

"Just sick to death of all this squabbling."

Dazed from such a rich display of what she could only assume was Latin temperament, Marge followed her father-in-law with her eyes, his shoulders borne with the dignity of a defeated general. For an instant her eyes moved from his back to the mirror over the fireplace. She blinked, it was impossible, she thought, a trick of lighting. But, no. The old man was smiling. There was no mistaking it. And then meeting her glance in the mirror he actually winked at her.

The room seemed suddenly to explode with light — from the candles burning over the table, from the flamebulbs flickering on the chandelier, from the colored lights of the tree and the fire on the hearth, all reflected from china and crystal and porcelain, from shredded tinsel and blown glass ornaments, mirrored and multiplied and magnified a thousandfold to focus on the mantle mirror and leave her momentarily blinded. She had seen what she should not, that much she knew, and shamed at this insight, she dropped her eyes once more to her plate and the unfinished meal she could no longer even pretend to eat.

Chapter Eight

1

"Have you stretched the wire for the chicken coop yet, Olaf?"

No longer did they look at each other when they spoke.

"No, Belle. Haven't got round to it yet . . . Will one of these days. Right soon."

The stubble of his beard, darker and coarser than his hair, hid most of his face. The cheeks were gaunt. The eyes no longer burned, but glowed, sparked still with an occasional flash from old fires.

"Well, why don't you keep it till Sunday and I can give you a hand?"

She sat beside him on an old apricot log propped against the tankhouse and with a face devoid of emotion surveyed the ruin of her garden. Half the spring planting was limp from lack of water, the artichokes were covered with aphids stunting the new growth, the corn had not yet been planted, and the asparagus was already going to seed unharvested.

"Must be hard to stretch," she continued, her voice steady, but as dry as the earth. "Without someone to hold it up for you. Dryer opens next week," she added, straining for a matter-of-fact tone. "With Brentwood cots. Tom Ramos, I hear from Louise, will be needing men to load the trucks."

She said no more, for her ministration, while he was idle, unemployed, and fast becoming unemployable, were only added affronts.

"Soon be time for cocktails," she concluded, rising from the box and leading the way into the kitchen.

It was a new ritual, a last desperate effort to transform his vice into a sociable pastime. While changing his bed one Saturday she had discovered a bottle stashed away under his mattress. Careful not to expose it, she had finished making the bed, but she could not forget the furtive cache. It was not the drinking she minded so much as the fear that he might ultimately be reduced to begging or stealing to maintain the myth of sobriety. So she had placed a whiskey bottle prominently on the kitchen shelf beside the radio.

"Help yourself to a drink before dinner," she had said, when he left the bottle untouched and unremarked. "I'm too light-headed for one myself, but you go ahead."

Her collusion, however, only served to remind him once again that he could no longer even fall alone: if she could not hold him up, then he must drag her down with him. Or snap the chain that bound them.

When, after their dinner the bottle remained untouched, she changed her tactics. If he must drink, she was determined he would enjoy at least one drink with his head held high and in company.

"Well, even if you won't," she had said, "I think I will have a little cocktail. Might be just the thing to relax me. Sure you won't join me?"

And fearful that, if crossed, her own strong will might lead here where his weaker one had already gone, he had consented.

But if his head was held high, it was merely to sneak a hasty gulp from the lip of the bottle before reshelving it. For soon, even in her own kitchen, he was resorting to subterfuge and secrecy, the need for which seemed as strong as his need for the drink itself. While still maintaining the fiction of a single "cocktail" before dinner, he would wait until her back was turned to color his chaser with another shot — a desperate game aided by her own reluctance to catch him in the act.

From the faucet of the sink a flour sack filled with steamed currants hung suspended over a pan. As Olaf carried the glasses to the kitchen table, she gave the sack a twist. A crimson ooze appeared at the tight knob. She scraped it into the pot with the blunt edge of a knife and let the sack unwind. The crimson faded to a light raspberry color. She was making the jelly more out of habit than need. For the joy had gone out of everything. The jams and jellies and preserves were all meant to please others, not herself. Alone she might have lived on soup and bread. The tankhouse shelves were still filled with last year's unused jars.

He ate almost nothing now. The fanciest roast was greeted with the same apathy as a warmed-over hash, her pies left uncut, her cakes untasted.

"Another slice of meat, Olaf?" she asked, a speared slice in her hand ready for his plate. She tried to keep her eye from testing the level of the bottle, but everytime she lifted her head, it was there, like a thermometer registering the health of the evening.

He shook his head. "Nuff here, Belle." His mouth was full as he spoke, chewing listlessly what could be swallowed only with effort. "Already more'n I can manage."

She did not badger him, and the speared slice was dropped back onto the platter. "Well, you can have it tomorrow for sandwiches," she added, knowing full well that he would more than likely satisfy himself with a hunk of bread and a slice of cheese washed down with the thick, almost black wine that was now the only product of his own handiwork.

A knock on the backdoor and the sound of her name stilled their labored chewing.

"Come in, Henry," she called from the table without any effort to warm her words with a note of welcome. "The door's unlocked."

As Henry Ramos made his way into the kitchen, Olaf attempted to rise, but quickly clamping her hand on his, Belle held him to his place, commandingly. Keeping her hand on his, she seemed almost maliciously to be drawing Henry's eyes to her gesture. He blushed at its effrontery, and Olaf seemed momentarily to have ceased breathing, his empty eyes unfocused, his mouth open, his gaunt cheeks gray.

"I think you'd better come, Belle." Breathless from running, Henry could not lift his eyes from the linked hands frozen on the table before him, but his voice was urgent. "They've already started."

Roused back to life, Olaf rose. Roughly breaking her hold, he tore his hand free, and before she could so much as protest, he himself spoke:

"Think I'll got for a walk, Belle."

"No dessert?" she asked, and ignoring their visitor, she too rose, keeping her eyes on Olaf, who refused to meet her gaze.

207

"Made you some bread pudding with raisins. Kind you used to like."

"Not tonight, Belle. Maybe later. Before I turn in."

His voice was hollow, its lack of all inflection denying the very promise it offered. And reaching for a toothpick from a glass in the cupboard, he walked past the transfixed Henry Ramos and out the screendoor, stumbling on the scraper before the first step. Following him to the door, Belle caught her breath. Instinctively she reached out her hand though she was too far away to catch him. But he quickly righted himself on his own and headed with a slow shuffle toward the shed. His back was stooped, the shoulders folded in like the wings of a sick bird. Half hidden by the screen, she watched him duck behind the shed and appear a moment later, his hand now clutching a brown bag in front of him as he headed toward the creek.

She bit her lips, and moving back into the kitchen, she was momentarily baffled by the presence of Henry Ramos, still standing fidgeting in the middle of the room. She answered the plea in his eyes with a blush.

"They've already begun, Belle," he repeated. "I can almost feel them myself."

"How far apart?" she asked with a coolness that chilled him.

"Why, I don't know, ten, maybe fifteen minutes."

"All right, Henry, no cause to be alarmed. You go back to her. I'll be right along. In just a few minutes."

But as he left the kitchen, she made no effort to follow him. The wine bottle was still uncorked. She poured a few drops into Olaf's empty glass and tasted it. It was sweet and strong. It burned her throat, slipping down like hot honey. There was time, she knew, still plenty of time, and she poured a little more, just an inch in the bottom of the glass and sat down on his chair.

"Oh, dear God," she said, but left her prayer unfinished. She no longer knew what it was she wanted. From God or from anyone else.

2

There were times when his wife terrified him. Fortified by her fierce virtue she would not bow even to the inevitable, and he

208

knew, as he watched the unequal battle, that it would always be he who must bend before her. Pleasure, she seemed to affirm, must be paid for in pain, and the fierceness of her passion was now more than balanced. She could not exult in the one without also embracing the other, and she threw herself into her labor with the same eager relish with which she had thrown herself into his arms — with which, in fact, she threw herself into all her moods or activities, into her bouts of house-cleaning or her displays of temper, attacking a soiled carpet with the same torrential energy with which she attacked a political or religious adversary, her drive shaming his easy — "Latin," he liked to call it — complacency, a lightly cynical view of the world that made, ultimately, all virtue meaningless, all effort ineffectual: nature was supreme and nature did not change, though it might, temporarily, assume a disguise.

He could see the pain wash over her like some electric current, he could see it twist her in its vise, until the cords on her neck stood stiff and her eyes fairly popped, her hands tugging at the twisted towels wrapped about the bedposts, and still she would not cry out. Behind her, sturdier than the bedposts, Belle held onto her forearms, while old Dr. Michaels, his sleeves held high above his wrists by two garters on his biceps, slowly, nonchalantly, shook powder into his rubber gloves. There was no sound save a sigh as each contraction let loose its wrenching hold in preparation for the next. There was no outcry, only the terrible grinding of her will, like the growl of a dog that will not relinquish a bone held between its teeth; and each contraction caught him in its cruel bind, wrenching his nerves until he felt *he* must cry out. He could have borne her screams more lightly than her awful silences.

"There's no sense you being here, Henry."

Belle's sense of propriety was offended by his presence. His attendance could serve no purpose and he moved from the bedroom into the kitchen. The excitement of fatherhood had already been tarnished by the colic cries of his firstborn disrupting every routine from sleep to thought so that he could not concentrate upon a single task without the anguished cries drawing him back to the cradle and the realization of his own captivity. Only three years married and already, one by one, like the stays of a barrel, binding his freedom, confining his will, limiting his thought, the matrimonial ties bound him ever more securely, narrowed his reach and therefore restricted his grasp. His doctorate seemed now further away than ever: *The Portuguese in Brazil* held in abeyance by the all too pressing demands of the Ramoses in San Oriel; even the chance of a Brazilian adventure had been vetoed before it had had time to tease his dreams.

"If you think I'm going to raise my children in a jungle, you're badly mistaken. If you're so crazy to go, go! But leave me and the children behind."

She would not even grant his startling proposal the dignity of her tears.

"Don't you mean, you and the child?"

"No, I mean — the children!" She flung her answer at him, her cheeks flushed with the drama of her announcement.

"Oh, God, Loo! Not again. Already."

"Already."

The wind was taken out of his argument.

"Don't you have any of the spirit that moved your ancestors to cross the unknown seas?"

"None whatsoever. And why should I? The spirit that moved our ancestors was hunger. They weren't chasing wild dreams, they were looking for food to feed their children and we already have food enough right here. In our own backyard."

"Our children!"

Again he could feel the seismic force of her contractions seize him and he was drawn once more to the doorway. Belle's eyes met his. She had her own old-fashioned notions about a husband's place at such a time. Poor Belle. She seemed in her own body to be sharing the labor, the tendons on her neck rising with each contraction, her diaphragm straining encouragement. It was a mystery, her eyes seemed to say, that no man can share and no woman forego. And as the child came forth, glistening and wrinkled, into the light, her own exhausted sigh blended with her niece's.

"A boy," she breathed, bending over the back of the bed. "It's a boy — and praise God, all of him there."

The child's first cry was echoed in the distant whistle of a train.

"Oh, dear, I wanted a girl." Louise turned her face, puffed and wet, into the pillow. "I did so want a girl," she repeated, without rancor or resentment, smiling wanly as though a joke had been played upon her.

Belle lifted the infant out of the doctor's hands to bathe it.

"Oh, the poor dear." She held the child lightly before her in the cradle of her hands. The whistle, nearer, grew more insistent. "Yes, yes, isn't it awful?" she said, wrinkling her own face in response to the infant's red-skinned howl, louder than the incessant, and by now frantic, hoots of the train. "Go ahead and cry your poor little heart out."

Henry moved to her back, pride in his parentage overwhelming the last traces of resentment. "Welcome to the world, little Vasco," he said, and with a timid finger he touched the sole of his son's foot. "Such as it is," he added with the tone of one of the world's reluctant lovers.

"What's that?" Exhausted as she was, Louise rose on her elbows, as the grinding screech of iron rent the night air, a cataclysmic mating of metal against metal. In the aftershock the room was silent for an instant, listening. Even the infant pressed against his great aunt's breasts, ceased to howl, his puffed eyes squinting against the overhead light.

"The train," Belle said. "Must've been an accident."

"Sounds like my evening may not be over yet." With weary fatalism the doctor resumed buttoning his vest and then reached for his coat from the back of a chair. "Better get myself over there and see what's happened."

"If everything's all right here," Henry said, paternal pride fast giving way to curiosity, "I'll ride along with the doctor to have a look."

"Yes, yes, go along," Belle encouraged. She longed now to be left alone with the infant and these first few precious moments that were always hers.

Henry bent over the bed to kiss his wife on the forehead. She reached up to touch his cheeck with her hand.

"I don't like the name, Henry."

"What name? Vasco? Why, it's a beautiful name. The pride

of Portugal.''

"But we're not living in Portugal.''

"And a part of my family,'' he added, rising stiffly. "The Old Man. And my brother.'' And he seemed suddenly almost a stranger to her in the tone of his reserve.

The doctor took her hand. "A brave girl,'' he said, "a brave girl, Louise. Couldn't have been easier. For me, at any rate,'' he chuckled. "And I leave you in good hands. Why, I'll bet Belle here's delivered almost as many as I have. Right, Belle?''

"Almost, Doctor.''

She placed the baby in the bassinet already prepared for it and followed them out of the room, pausing in the bathroom to let the hot water run. From the back porch she carried the tiny zinc tub into the bathroom. She tested the water's temperature with her elbow then carried the full tub back into the bedroom and placed it on a covered table beside the bassinet. She lifted the child, carefully cupping the head in one hand, and dipped it, gently, into the water. It howled its protest. "There, there,'' she comforted, not so much speaking as communicating on a sub-lingual level with soft cooings and cluckings. Reassured as much by the pacific rhythms of the wordless sounds as by the liquid warmth of the cotton sponge dribbling onto its chest, the infant ceased its howling and rowed the air with tiny clenched fists braceleted with red wrinkles. The puffed lids opened, blinking against the light; two clouded black dots appeared. Each crease of flesh was probed with a cotton swab and the child lifted, dripping, onto an open towel. Blotted dry, he was oiled and powdered. There was nothing the least out of the way in the ritual, nothing peculiarly personal out of the way in the ritual, nothing peculiarly personal or unique in it, yet it was performed with all the solemnity of a sacred service, a dipping into mysteries as holy and awesome as the transubstantiation of the foetal bread into the body of life.

The faraway sound of a siren thrilled the night air with its tale of violence and disaster. The train, she thought, and thought no more. Louise lay drowsing on the bed. Wet wrinklets of bobbed hair fringed her forehead. Belle laid the swaddled baby on the table, dipped a gauze pad in the bath water, then gently ran it over her niece's forehead, washing the hair away from the face.

Without opening her eyes Louise smiled. The older woman studied the younger. How beautiful she looked! An after-birth calm; radiant with the sense of her great accomplishment: the vindication of all suffering. The pain, she knew, was nothing; she longed for that too; she would not be denied any part: to be torn asunder by a pain so intense it could purge the body of all poison and leave one spent with the gifts of life.

Once again she lifted the infant and this time nestled it in its mother's arm. Louise smiled, lifting the blanket off the face to inspect her son.

"Vasco," she said, testing the name. "Oh, Belle, I don't like it. Not at all."

"Why it's a fine name, Dear. The Old Man would be proud. And Mae."

"But the living shouldn't be saddled with the dead," she said, and baring her breast, she lifted it, teasingly, caressing her son's chin with the nipple. Though the child appeared to be sleeping, its mouth opened, the lips already sucking the air long before they found their mark.

"But they are," Belle answered, "whether they ask to be, or not."

So absorbed in her task was she, Louise had already forgotten what remark of her own her aunt could be commenting upon. "Oh, Belle —!" she said and said no more, her face resplendent. Belle bent over the bed to kiss her forehead. A car stopped at the front gate and a moment later the backdoor opened.

"Henry," Belle said, answering a question that had not been asked as she primly squared her shoulders, but Henry did not make his expected appearance in the bedroom. She listened: there was no sound of any movement.

"That you, Henry?" she called into the hall.

"Yes, Belle," he answered, a faint, unsettling echo of shock distorting his words.

Quickly she moved into the kitchen. He was leaning against the door, reluctant to relinquish his support.

"What was —?" she began, but left her question unfinished. His damp forehead glistened in the overhead light as ghastly white as the underbelly of a beached fish. "Why, Henry, you look as if you've seen a ghost."

213

"I have," he answered, shivering visibly so that she rushed to support him until frozen by the sound of his voice:

"Belle —"

It was too full of sympathy for comfort. Gooseflesh rose on her forearms. She took a deep breath, fortifying herself with a shaft of air, which alone seemed to hold her up. There was no need to say his name; there was no one else in all the world who belonged to her. She raised her hand to ward off the blow. Awkwardly Henry moved to take her arm, but her reflex seemed almost a rejection of his support.

"It's Olaf, Belle," he seemed suddenly embarassed, shaken out of his own shock by the cumbrous imbalance between his desire to comfort her and the inadequacy of his means. He was not physically demonstrative; it was not his style. He could not take her in his arms. She had always held herself aloof, shielding her private heart against intrusion, and there was not, as with his wife, a child's memory of untroubled intimacy. She did not cry out or collapse, and again he was astounded — his ego shamed — by the silent acceptance of pain, when nature seemed to cry out for some loud and shrill release. He pulled out a chair for her, but she remained oblivious to it.

She stood for a moment stunned, her hands clutching her elbows, swaying slightly, as though cradling an imaginary infant. "You can't say God won't forgive a driven man," she said, her words almost inaudible. Her eyes intent upon his.

"No, Belle," he answered, reaching to ease her onto the chair. But once again shattered by a fleeting recollection of the crushed body, he was himself in need of support.

"No one durst say God won't forgive a driven man." She sank onto the chair, shaking her head. "No one."

He moved to the pantry to pour her a glass of brandy, as much to satisfy his own need as hers. She accepted it without comment. Cupping the glass in both hands she peered into the amber depths.

"I had no right," she whispered, shaking her head. "I had no right."

"Right, Belle?" he answered, fearful for a second that he was about to become privy to some unseemly confession, and hoping to forestall her, he added, "'No one judges you, Belle."

214

She lifted her face to look at him. For an instant she seemed baffled as to his identity; then sensing his embarrassment, she bolted her drink. She shivered and placed the empty brandy glass on the kitchen table. She donned her old wool cardigan which sagged practically to her knees. "I'll leave you to take care of things tonight, Henry," she said, speaking now with a different, but more familiar voice. "Everything you'll need's on the table next to the bassinet. I'll be over in the morning. But I'd like, tonight, to be alone. You'll understand, won't you?"

She was her old impersonal self again: efficient, helpful, and considerate, but distant and forbidding.

"Certainly, Belle. And if there's anything I can do . . ."

"Yes." She turned. Her hand was already on the screendoor, on which a large moth, lured by the porch light, was transfixed. "You might see about getting him a plot. In the Protestant cemetery," she added. "It hardly seems right," she continued, "but I guess there's no helping that. I've got some savings so you won't have to worry. I'd appreciate that very much, Henry."

"Be glad to, Belle." He moved to help her down the stairs but she forestalled him.

"Take care of Louise," she said. "And the young one. You'd better call your mother; she'll be waiting. And Clara too," she added, slipping off her sister's name with clinical impartiality. "I'll see you in the morning."

And with firm steps she moved alone into the dark orchard, stumbling occasionally over a large clod. The rustle of summer foliage whispered to her. There were voices all about, but no one to speak to, no one to touch, and high above, stars that would never be reached. She looked up into a patch of the dark sky framed with the irregular silhouette of even darker branches, and as he had first come to her out of the night in images of fire, she saw him now as a great comet, a ball of flame blazing like the sun just before it sets.

"Yes," she said, whispering back to the leaves, "Oh, yes!"

Part V

Chapter One

1

Two identical stucco cottages now occupy lots excised from the apricot orchards. Squat, square, and unadorned, they are obviously economy models designed for mass production. The more westerly of the two is fronted by a lawn blotched with patches of brown rot and fringed on two sides by the skeletal remains of a garden. Two acron-topped cement portals span the gravel drive that leads to a backyard strewn with car parts, rusted tools, and broken toys. Among them sits a child's playpen, its rows of maple bars as rigidly joyless as any other prison. Ruin and neglect are evident everywhere: in the garage door that has fallen victim to a hasty getaway and hangs now from a single hinge as well as in the iron grate of the barbecue pit crusted with the charcoal remains of the single meal ever cooked over its coals.

Architecturally as unimaginative as its twin, the other house is already virtually hidden under a lush growth of bougainvillaea, wisteria, and trumpet vines, its future privacy assured by a planting of cedar and pine. Twin hawthorns span the driveway, hiding the pretentious pillars under umbrellas of green foliage and pink blossoms. The skeleton of a new room rises creekside, threatening the integrity of the original square. Although the question of the deed has never been resolved, the Ramoses have chosen to act as if it has. To reward the care with which they have tended their garden the old man, in a typically unpredictable display of generosity, has sacrificed another row of his apricot orchard for its extension, and the gound has already been rolled for a second lawn and the hole dug for a lily pond. Hidden from the street and the backyard wisteria arbor by the garage and a glasshouse, a more practical green garden leads to a miniature village of chicken coops, rabbit hutches, and pigeon cotes which furnish the family's main source of protein, beef being a rarity reserved for special occasions.

The times have, without question, taken a turn for the worse. Each week sees the entrance of some dilapidated wreck piled high with rolled mattresses and bouquets of tin utensils. Bursting with two-headed children, freckeled and stark, their wan faces wizened into premature old age, the ancient Fords and Chevies chug and sputter through clouds of dust; for wherever they go, the new arrivals bring the old land with them. It falls from their cars, it falls from their possessions, it falls from their clothes. Even their skin is pitted with dust, their bodies, eroded by the dull granules, rough and scaly.

Though these strangers with the soft, slow voices come from many states, they are all, with equal impartiality, labeled "Okies," and neither the Portuguese, who are still the majority of the population, nor the smattering of Irish, English, and Scandinavian who make up the rest, feel that they have any more right to be enrolled in the local census than the migratory Mexicans who steam in with the summer heat to pick the cherries, apricots, and pears.

Although the population has swelled, the number of houses has remained relatively steady, and the newcomers are left to their own devices. A few are lucky enough to find homes vacated by death, and multiple families now share quarters that lonely widowers once found cramped. Every empty chicken coop, every vacant garage or tankhouse, whitewashed, fitted with glass, wiring, and rudimentary plumbing and rechristened a cottage or duplex, has been rented. Beneath every bridge that spans the creek, hoboes sleep, sheltered from the rain by steel girders and concrete, until the rising floods send them on, unlamented, to drier refuge in some other town.

Yet there are enough familiar objects to offset whatever changes have occurred. The earth is still rich, green in winter, except where the furrow turns it glossy black, and white in spring with the dazzling glare of orchards in blossom. With little encouragement, the fruit still swells, beautiful to the eyes and touch as well as taste. There are many poor, some poorer than others, but so there have always been. No one starves. Strange men come begging at back doors for enough work to earn them an evening meal. Grateful for scraps that were once thrown to stray dogs, they are not often turned away. They are fed, sometimes grudgingly, but they are fed, and always in silence, their names unknown, their histories etched on their faces, to obvious for retelling. But for the families who have now come to think of themselves as "oldtimers," the Great Depression of the thirties was most often spelt with a small *d*.

2

"I don't know what we'd do without her," Clara declared as Sarah produced from seemingly nowhere the teak stand for the blue porcelain vase then disappeared behind the swinging door to the kitchen, leaving her mistress once again to marvel at perfection: "My greatest treasure. But you were saying, my dear . . .?"

The plain antipathetic girl her son had married always made her feel strangely uncomfortable. Without looking at her, with eyes fixed instead upon the gladioli, whose stiff and unyielding forms refused to submit to the role demanded of them Clara tried to avoid Marge's stance of moral superiority that put her so on her defenses. As though a woman of her years and standing should have to defend herself to anyone!

"It wasn't really important." With scarcely a tremor of defeat ruffling her voice, Marge gave up as futile any further attempt to enlist Clara's aid. It was now all too clear: Whatever must be done to rescue her husband she would have to do herself. Without any help from his family.

As Clara remained preoccupied with her flowers, Marge turned with bland distaste to a polychrome statue of an apple-round, pink-skirted peasant shining fresh and nubile from her packing case and newly ensconced under a potted palm in the corner bay of the living room. Standing some three feet from its table base, it cried out to be noticed. Leaning one almost-white hand upon a brown marble rock, her Carrara bosom straining every marble stitch of her pink bodice, the chill beauty peered with hip-swelling elegance into a Carrara pool.

"From Florence." Clara laid aside the last recalcitrant gladiola and joined her daughter-in-law before the latest arrival. "That's in Italy," she appended as she ran a possessive hand over the pink skirt.

"Yes. I know where Florence is."

Marge's chilled constraint was dismissed with the same ravishing smile Clara might have bestowed on a waiter who had just retrieved a fallen glove.

"Marv'lous colors, don't you think? Such craftsmen!" She stepped back for a wider view, her head shaking incredulously. "You've no idea! Whole shops filled to the rafters with such treasures. Every one of them fit for a museum. But you haven't seen it with the light on." Eyes dancing with delight, she reached behind the palm for the switch. In an instant a school of gilded fish swam into the illuminated pool.

"Of course," she added, more baffled than hurt by the ponderously silent reception. "it's far more beautiful at night . . . when the room's dark."

Though she knew full well that a compliment was called for, that Clara's delicate health was nursed best on capsules of praise meted out to everything that was hers, from her son to her dress, Marge could manage only a dry and noncommittal:

"It must have been fascinating — your trip."

Fascinating? Clara flinched at the affront. It had been a good deal more than that. Over and above all other considerations — the delights and encounters any first-class tourist might have been expected to reap from so comprehensive a tour — the trip had capped her husband's career with a stroke of fortune so breathtaking in its consequences that it had stunned even him. Two days out of La Havre on their homeward voyage, news reached them of The Crash — nearly six months after Vince, unwilling to gamble with cards he could not himself hold and watch, had reluctantly, and against the advice of his broker. extricated himself from the swelling market and invested a considerable portion of his capital in high interest, short-term mortgages made out to those who were only too anxious for the ready cash to take up the game where he had left off.

It had taken Clara scarcely a week to discover that those to whom she had once deferred now deferred to her. For months on end, blind to the worried wrinkles fretting familiar faces, she had held court, the center of every gathering, the crux of every conversation. It seemed impossible that she might ever exhaust her storehouse of anecdotes or weary of expounding upon the windows of Chartres and the floorshow at the Lido. But now in the face of her daughter-in-law's rebuff, she found herself for the first time since her return at a loss for words, the whole marvelous adventure flattened with a single pinprick.

"Yes, fascinating . . ." Clara reddened as she switched off the light and the gilded fish sank once again into their marble depths. Then letting her eyes fall to the ugly, flat walking shoes and the thick ankles of her guest, she gave way momentarily to easy pity. For after all, what could this graceless, sexless girl know of beauty? How could she help finding anything so lovely an affront to her own person? It was no wonder the husband of such a wife, faced with such a dearth of softness, was tempted to play the philanderer.

"Arnie's been a wonder of late. Vince is so pleased. Yes, he is. So pleased. And it's all your doing," she gushed as she might have to a mendicant workman left standing too long in the rain. "We don't forget that. It's your doing, my dear."

"If my husband . . ." Marge could not finish what she had intended to say: that if his present behavior were anything to marvel at, she shuddered to think what his past might have been.

Sarah's head popped through the swinging door of the kitchen.

"You want I should set another place for lunch?"

Like her mistress, Sarah had a facility for re-creating the past and then remembering the altered version to the exclusion of all others. Marge was now "family," and therefore, in Sarah's eyes, subject to the same unquestioned loyalty as every other member. If Sarah's tone lacked graciousness, it could be attributed solely to the younger Mrs. Woods' obvious distaste for what she called "spicy dishes."

"You're more than welcome, my dear." Clara's intentions were warmer than her words. "Course you may not like our . . ."

"Thank you," Marge interrupted, "I'm more than sure I'd like it," she continued with a timid sideway glance at Sarah, "but it just so happens I promised to have lunch with my husband. My husband," she repeated, standing taller than ever and for once proud of her height, so that she departed with a smile adding dim lustre to the dull features.

"A strange girl," Clara said, greeting Vince, who came in through the backdoor as Marge exited through the front door. "I think she isn't happy here with us. And after all we've done for her. She hasn't put it in so many words, mind, you, but I know she means to take Arnie away. Back to San Diego, I suppose. Though the Good Lord knows what he'd do there. Specially now with jobs so hard to find even college graduates are happy for a broom to push. I think you ought to talk to him, Vince. Find out what it's all about."

"Let him go, Clara." Vince took his place at the head of the table. "And good riddance," he added, breaking off a crust of French bread with more than ordinary violence.

"Sometimes I don't understand you, Vince. Let him go? Why, with times as they are . . ."

"The times are as you make them," he snapped, his arrogance supported by the sure knowledge that men who had once hoped to beat him at his own game were now grateful to act as his menials, happily performing for him tasks they would have disdained to perform for themselves when the land that was now his had been theirs. "If he can't find a job, don't blame it on the times. He's a bum now and in the best of times he'd still be a bum. But you don't have to worry: he isn't going anywhere. Why should he, when he's already got a free meal ticket right here?"

Clara's face lost its focus, the eyes fragmented, the voice faintly tremulous:

"That's his trouble, Vince. You have no faith in him anymore. And he knows that. He can sense your — yes, your contempt, because you don't even make an effort to hide it. And it would be so easy to let the boy know — make him feel that you believe in him again. The way you used to. And give him some of his old confidence back."

"No, Clara." He shook his head with the finality of a man who has written off a bad debt. It was his wife's prophetic image: a bad debt destined to bring no return. The birth of Bonny Jean instead of Vincent the Second was just one more sign, if any more were needed, of heaven's foreclosure.

"Trouble is I had too much faith when there wasn't cause for any. But that's water over the dam. Guess what Louise is up to," he continued, a new anger giving fresh life to his old body, "out canvassing votes for Roosevelt! What do you think of that? And to top matters, Hy tried to touch me for another loan today. Seems his Baby Doll ran up more bills than he can take care of all on his own. Course, he didn't say boo about his own gambling debts. My God, Clara!" His eyes flamed with resentment. "I'd like to have done with the lot of them! The whole damn lot! Ingrates all."

"Vince! You don't mean that." Storm clouds gathered, threatening. "Now you know you don't mean that."

"You're the only one, Clara hasn't let me down. The only one. And Sarah, here," he added with a dramatic change of mood, giving her ample ham an affectionate swat as she bent over the table to place the bowl of codfish before him. "Worth more than the whole damn lot of 'em, you are. Wouldn't trade you for a brace of new daughters, Sarah. No sirree."

"How you talk!" With both fists planted on her hips, Sarah shook with unaffected laughter. "How you do talk, Mr. Woods! But start. Start before it's cold." And she hovered over them, a beneficient spirit waiting to feast herself upon their praise.

The clouds quickly dissipated in the sunshine of their laughter, and Clara, her incipient tears turning to tears of joy, soon joined them. *"Balcalhoa!"* she exclaimed, as if she hadn't been smelling it for hours. "Oh, Sarah, what *would* we ever do without you?"

Chapter Two

1

"No, sir." Little Joe of the tobacco-stained teeth stood his ground. "I'll say it again: you ain't half the man your pa is."

Impassively the silent men gathered about the other tables at Costa's Corner watched the confrontation.

"A tinhorn Mussolini," Arnie mumbled and washed down his garlic sausage with a glass of beer and then rinsed the beer with a chaser from the brandy flask kept snug in a leather pouch cut with a fourpoint guage: quarter full, half full, damn fool, boozy snakes.

He had been a damn fool ever to think he could work for his father and now needed the "damn fool" point to face up to the old man, whose youth seemed to be renewed every time he matched himself against his son and won. Hands down.

"A tinhorn Mussolini," he repeated.

"Talk's cheap. Say it to his face. Go on up to him and tell him straight on: No man can live on the wages he's payin. May'be he'll listen to you. Cause he sure as hell won't listen to us."

"And what if I do? How's that gonna help you?" He washed down the last drop of beer with another swig of brandy and then capped the bottle, playing with it as he leaned back in his chair, smiling at the little man who stood before him with just the slightest hint of deference in his bantam defiance. "You know what he'll tell you? 'Well, Joe,' he'll say, 'you been a good worker all these years and I'll miss you. But business is business, Joe, and if you think you can better yourself somewhere else, why you just go somewhere else. Cause I got men out there begging for your job, Joe. Just beggin for it.' And what you gonna say then? Eh, little Joe? What you gonna say then?"

An uneasy laugh rose from the adjoining table and little Joe frowned, caught in the bind of a real dilemma. For the very quality that kept him working for his "starvation wages" was

225

the quality he most admired in the old man and the lack of which he despised in the son: strength that cannot be moved by sentiment.

"I'd tell him, maybe, with all his money he still couldn't buy himself a man for a son. That's what I'd tell him."

Arnie made a sudden movement, half rising to his feet, but sank once again onto his chair, his smile contemptuous.

"Shit, Joe, if you was half my size . . ."

Costa behind the bar smoothed his bristling white mustache with his fingers, and unconscious gesture that capped every crisis.

"You'd tell him nothing, Joe," Arnie continued, speaking to the other tables as well as Joe, who had been spokesman for all. "Like all the rest, you'd take another cut in wages and thank him for being so generous and not making it more. And you know it. Why, you'd lick his ass clean if he ever ran outta paper. Cause you need him more'n he needs you. And that's the way it's always been. He holds all the cards. And when he doesn't — well, he cheats a little. But he always wins — my old man."

Arnie rose and stuffed his flask into the back pocket of his jeans, letting the shirttail hang over the bulge, the beginnings of a pot pulled tight by a thick, silver-studded belt that gave his profile a cupid's-bow outline. The once refined sensuality of the face already coarse, the flesh slackening, the lips set in a permanent sneer.

"Always," he repeated.

"Well, he ain't gonna take it with him," a voice at the next table remarked. One of his companions added. "That's for sure."

Arnie smiled. "And that's just what I'm banking on, boys. That's just what I'm banking on."

"The sooner the better," a young man murmured, but Joe was quick to turn upon him:

"And how you think that's gonna help you? So the old man dies. So the only difference is the farms'll be worse run. And before you know it, you won't none a you have jobs. They'll bulldoze the orchards for houses. And without orchards, who's gonna need a dryer? And where your wife and kids gonna pull in that little extra to tide you over till spring then? That what you want? Hell, I'll take the old man, tight as he is, any day.''

And with that the bantam Joe walked out of Costa's, and untying the horse's reins from the gasoline pump, took his seat on the wagon. Arnie followed.

"You oughtta be in politics, Joe," he said, lying back on the wagon bed face up. "That's where you oughtta be — in politics. You'n Roosevelt. Gonna change the world all by yourselfs. Shit! All you gonna change is a few names and faces. No matter what you call him, a sucker's still a sucker. An a flunky's a flunky." His stomach shook, rocked by a contemptuous chuckle. "You're wastin your time, Joe, cause when you were born, your name was writ down: Joe Pinto, Flunky. And you ain't never gonna change it, Joe, cause it was writ in indelible ink. Yes sir, indelible ink."

And laughing, Arnie covered his face with his straw hat, then pillowing his head with his hands, he gave himself to a drowsy slumber.

2

It was hot and dry, the sun lost in its own brillance, flashing like foil from a white sky. The food and the brandy fired his veins. His own skin lay on him like a heavy blanket on a hot night. Without raising himself he responded to the rough bounce of a pothole on the gravel shoulder.

"Jesus, Joe, can't you drive this goddam thing on the road!"

Joe made no answer. An old Chevy drew up alongside and a lean-faced man leaned out of the driver's window:

"Know anywheres roundabout a man kin get work?"

The accent was not local and the voice flattened of all hope. Behind him — and there was no counting them, they seemed so many to be crammed into so small a space — stark-eyed children stared, their sombre faces capped with hair the color of cornsilk, its sheen dulled with dust.

Without looking his his interrogator, Joe shook his head:

"Not if you was willin to work for ten cents an hour."

Without another word, without a thank you or a damn you, the head once again turned toward the road the car moved on, stuttering from every orifice.

"Jesus, look at 'em! Packed in like animals. A buncha albinos."

"If they'd a been cats, they'd a been hollerin' for food," Joe answered, flatly, without pity, long since having learned that for a poor man in a poor time pity is a luxury.

"Right as usual, Joe." Arnie once again lay back on the wagon bed, musing to the open sky. "Man without money's worse off than any animal."

The wagon drove through the dryer gates, past the seed flats, to the rim of the orchard, where the two men jumped off and Joe tied the reins to the nearest tree.

The dryer was a great open shed with a gently sloping corrugated-tin roof built over a concrete floor. Four rows of work tables were divided into two aisles, each centered by a pair of iron tracks. Flat cars, stacked with the full trays of cut apricots, were pushed along a complicated network of interlinking tracks, first to the sulphur houses and later to the fields, where they were laid end-to-end to dry in the sun. At each work table four fifty-pound lugs, each stencilled with the legend: VINCE WOODS, linked on the bottom by a garland that spelled out San Oriel, were set before the cutters — women and children of every age. Some worked in teams, a mother cutting the cots into a collander, from which a child then spread them carefully onto the tray, flesh-side up. The leftover slop and pits were carried to the puncher, who, as soon as the refuse was deposited in the appropriate containers, punched a number on the ticket pinned to the top of the worker's apron. Nothing was wasted. The slop was sold as swill to local pig farmers and the pits were spread out to dry on great trays in the open air, later to be sacked and sold as fuel.

The sound of Portuguese dominated. Knowledge of the language formed a kind of aristocracy among the workers and added to the rivalry among the various tables, the position of which determined one's rank in the hierarchy of cutters, one's relative worth established by one's nearness to the puncher. Year after year the same tables were used by the same women, their positions jealously guarded and fought over, with the wife of the chief foreman receiving first place at the first table. Since a box filled with small cots could take twice as long to cut as the same box filled with large fruit, there was a constant lookout for any evidence of favoritism, for the men who answered the call of "Box" were not above saving the largest, firmest apricots for their own wives and daughter, their blatant injustices greeted by a cacophony of outraged cries and shrill name-calling that at least once a season ended in a fruit-throwing free-for-all, but seldom more than superficial bloodshed — an occasional knife wound or broken nose. The fastest cutter working at top speed under the best conditions could cut two boxes in an hour. For each box she was paid ten cents. There were always more applicants than jobs, the positions meted out on the basis of one's seniority in the community, so that there were few newcomers.

As Arnie made his entrance, a woman shouted in Portuguese. To tease those who had not the good fortune to be bilingual, the ensuing laughter was louder than it need have been. Pretending to ignore the commotion, Arnie pulled in his gut and hoisted his trousers, his strut by now more suggestive of lassitude than sensuality.

Through the shed he moved out to the open field spread for acres with the drying fruit stuck to the crude pine trays by a honey-sweet, rubbery excretion. One could determine by the color how long the cots had lain in the sun. Those just removed from the sulphur houses, swelling with juices, were almost yellow, while those already shrivelled dry and ready for scraping into packing cases were a darker-than-pumpkin orange.

The door to one of the sulphur houses was open, gagging him with the smell of burning brimstone. Hell's pit, it was the worst duty in the place, and the men who filled the sunken cans and tended the fires were branded like pariahs with a coating of yellow dust. The bell calling an end to the lunch hour had not yet rung. Time still for a smoke. He moved to the open, tin-topped shed beyond the sulphur houses where the empty trays were stored for the winter and worked his way through the maze of stacked trays. The supply was already more than half depleted so that the hollow areas formed tiny, brown-walled rooms. Secret bed-sized cubicles made for seduction. The bell clanged, an old-fashioned school bell provoking thoughts of hooky. If he were lucky he might escape detection for hours and wear off his resentment in sleep.

Stretched out on top of a stack of trays from which he could spy any intruder without himself being detected, he unbuckled his belt and the top two buttons of his jeans to let his stomach spill out with unselfconscious relief. He lit a cigarette and massaged the mark on his skin left by his belt, reaching deep to rearrange his sex, already swelling with an unfocused but persistent lust. In Polynesia, he had heard, a man's virility was judged by the size of his belly. As round and smooth as a ripe mango, the fat man there was king, pressing his ponderous weight on some slim, brown-skinned lovely squirming supple and slippery beneath him. The best of two worlds: one lust feeding another.

A warm breeze blew through the cool shade. Stretched out on his side, he scanned the field before him. The outhouse door opened and he was treated to a free show of thigh as a young girl reached up her skirt to smooth the elastic top of her underpants. Muriel Vargas. He whistled softly, jumping down from his perch with surprising agility, and buckling his belt without bothering to button his trousers, he inched his way to the edge of the shed before the narrow passage past the sulphur houses.

Sweet Muriel. He could smell her before he could see her, a heady odor as thick as the scent of magnolias, her dark eyes provocative enough to distract attention from the coarse nose, which would in a few years' time be as gross as her mother's. Kinky brown curls peaked coyly from the points of the red bandana that bound her head, accenting the firm, forthright jaw. Her wrists were thick, her hands large, the fingers stained from the fruit, the thumb and forefinger of her left hand criss-crossed with darker stains marking the thread-like scars left by the knife.

What she lacked in grace she made up for in vitality, and she carried her full breasts with a pride that was infectious. The shape of her hips was hidden under a gathered cotton skirt, the sides, where her rubber apron had not afforded coverage, smeared with a brown, gelantinous paste that would have to be boiled out. Since nothing so distracting would have been allowed to mar the proud perfection of her breasts, her ticket was hung from a large safety pin attached to her waist. It was this Arnie caught as she rounded the corner of the shed.

Stopping abruptly but silently, she eyed him with sullen mistrust as he took out a chrome-plated punch from his trouser pocket, first twirling it temptingly on his index finger before lowering it to her ticket to punch out a number.

She frowned, inspecting the ticket to check that the mark was official and not a dimestore copy which might possibly cost her the forfeiture of her own hard-earned punches. There was no mistaking the elaborate asterisk-tipped V.

"Just one?" she taunted with a toss of her head contrived to thrust her breasts into greater prominence. "Afraid you'll bankrupt the old man?"

"What'm I offered?" Without pressing he ran the punch over the ticket at the same time maneuvering her against the wall of trays. "We ain't handing out punches for nothing, you understand. Me or the old man. We each gotta get our little profit someway. So take your pick. An' you can be sure a one thing," he added with considerable swagger, his eyes dropping to his crotch, where his distended sex was menacingly apparent. "*I* ain't gonna short change you."

"Talk's big anyway." With a shrug more invitational than contemptuous, she looked about to see that they were not being watched.

"Two," he called, as he punched out another number then held the punch over the next. "Nothing's to stop me from going right down the whole goddam row," he continued, "if I," he added, leaning forward, "was . . . to get . . . some kinda . . .- encouragement."

And without waiting for a reply, he fell on her, brutally trapping her against the wall with his weight. A tactical error. At the touch of his lips, she bared her teeth and pushed with both arms against his shoulders, celebrating her release with a stinging slap across his face.

He caught her arm by the wrist, holding it above her head as once again he pressed her against the wall of trays with his body.

"You'd rather cut cots, I suppose?"

"Yeah. I'd rather cut cots. Let go, Buster!"

As she struggled unsuccessfully to free herself, he trapped her leg between his thighs, foiling her kick.

"You sure got a touch, lover boy. A real touch. Jesus, you and your old man between you must think the whole damn world belongs to you. Well, here's one piece of it you ain't having no part of.''

She was too intent upon the struggle to be aware of consequences, angered, certainly, but exhilarated as well. Her own lust was roused, but fiercely disciplined by injured pride, which would gladly have given what it would not allow to be taken.

"Jesus, what a fiery little bitch you are!"

Arnie's face was red with the struggle, his lust by now explosively, burdensomely heavy. A fat man't sultry lust with more steam than fire in it.

"What you gonna do if I just take it?"

There was a plaintive, almost whimpering undertone to his bluster. Weakness enough to win her contempt.

"Just try it! And I'll crush your balls bloody, Buster.''

"Then I'll have to . . .''

It was he who screamed as her teeth bore down on the hand clamped to her mouth. He leapt back and she ran just far enough out of his reach to enjoy his pain with impunity.

"You goddam little wildcat!"

Standing bent forward with both hands on her hips, she spat out his blood with her scorn, but seeing they were observed, she whirled about, and with a laughing toss of her head that loosened the bandana, crowning her suddenly with a thick mass of brown curls, she skipped over the tracks between the sulphur houses and ran back to the dryer shed.

"What the hell you looking at?"

Arnie covered his bleeding hand with a handerkerchief as little Joe watched, his face an impassive mask.

"Your pa's out front looking for you.''

3

At least once a day Vince made an appearance at the dryer, his irregular arrivals contrived to catch everyone off guard. Dressed in a once fine but now hopelessly spotted suit and a bankers's straw hat, he made no allowances for the weather. On the hottest day of the year his vest was as tighly buttoned, his collar as uncompromisingly stiff, as on the coldest. Occasionally standing under the afternoon sun he could be seen to remove his hat to wipe his forehead with a white linen handkerchief, which was then carefully folded before being returned to his pocket. It was as close as he ever came to recognizing the sun's power to influence his style. Whenever possible he preferred to give the impression that it too was merely another employee working, like everyone else, for his profit — as more often than not it did.

With few words he moved among the cutters, careful always to respect the finely drawn aristocracy that divided them one from the other. To the foreman's wife he nodded and touched his hat, to the next table he merely nodded. Occasionally with an oldtimer or a pretty girl he would stop to make some comment which was invariably greeted with broad smiles or blushing giggles.

With the foreman following a few steps behind, Vince moved from table to table, stopping before a new worker to inspect the tray. "Keep 'em flat," he said, straightening a few of the apricots with his fingers. "Keep 'em flat or the juice all runs out in the sulphur house." He looked at the unfamiliar woman. "New around here, aren't you?" She nodded. "Okies," the foreman added. Vince responded in Portuguese, and a wave of giggles washed over the surrounding tables. The woman neither blushed nor smiled, merely stared at him with an expression saved from total vacuity by a suggestion of fear. Standing on a box to reach the tray, her barefoot daughter spread out the apricots, patting them level with the flat of her hand. Vince nodded his approval, smiling as the child bent over the tray to reveal a total lack of undergarments. Again he spoke in Portuguese, ostensibly to the foreman but for the obvious benefit of the surrounding tables, a remark in which the word "cu" played a prominent role and the laughter was louder than ever. The foreman's wife shrieking her delight.

Hiding his injured hand Arnie appeared at the end of the shed. Vince stopped to light a cigar, first offering one to the foreman to signal his dismissal. Then strolling alone to the end of the shed, he joined his son, walking wordlessly past him out to the field.

"What's this your man tells me about you wanting to move?"

Without looking at his son, he surveyed the expanse of trays as lovingly as a collector inspecting his private Van Goghs, his appreciation of the scene's intrinsic beauty considerably enhanced by pride of ownership.

"That's Marge," Arnie muttered, shuffling uneasily. "She's got some idea in her head — wants to get away. Back to San Diego, maybe. Keeps harping at me, if maybe we sold the house and..."

"The house isn't yours to sell." For the first time Vince looked at Arnie. "Just remember that. I own the deed and I mean to keep it that way. What's wrong with your hand?" He studied the blood-soaked handkerchief.

"Cut it." Arnie made no attempt to elaborate.

"Not working, I warrant." The smile was cruelly ironic, his once-lavish indulgence replaced now by a contempt so strong that by gloating on it, he had come to enjoy it. And goddam! Button your trousers. Stranger'd never be able to tell you from some Okie, way you dress around here."

Seething with an almost binding resentment, Arnie neverthe-less unbuckled his belt to button the top of his jeans without another word awaited his father's dismissal.

The object of his interview achieved, Vince called Joe, await-ing orders at a respectful distance but well within hearing range. Joe's face, however, carefully concealed any emotion but respect.

"Do something about the boy's hand here. Maybe you'd bet-ter give him some light work for the rest of the day. Scraping out in the field. Sun'll do him good. Sweat off some of that fat."

"Look who's talking about fat!"

Vince smiled, arching his back as with both hands he patted the sides of his vest. "When you can afford to support one of these is plenty of time for you to have one of these. Not before. Right, Joe?" And winking at his second-in-command, he moved back into the shed.

"Shit," Arnie mumbled as soon as his father was out of hear-ing range, then wordlessly he followed Joe to the sulphur vat, wincing as the little man rubbed the wound with a soft yellow rock to stanch the flow of blood.

"Maybe I oughtta get a goddam rabies shot."

But Joe would have none of it. "No, sir," he nodded his

head, his smile cracking creases in his dry face. "Not half the man your pa is. Not half." And with a dry, joyless chuckle he patted his own flat belly.

Chapter Three

1

"Off, goddammit! Get off my back!"

He plowed his way through the kitchen door, upsetting a dining room chair on his way. With an outstretched palm Marge deftly blocked the slam reversing the swing, and followed him, pausing to right the chair before moving into the living room. Already sprawled on the maple sofa and with every intention of provoking her, he struck a kitchen match across the side of the coffee table and lit one of the cigars filched from his father's office cache.

She flinched at the affront but would not allow the spark to set off the explosion he longed for. Steadfast in her determination not to be diverted by petty recrimination, she would not allow him to provoke her to tears or rage, which would only give him the excuse he wanted to stomp out of the house.

With visible forebearance, she sat on the edge of the chair opposite him, her stiff back bent forward at the hips, her hands clasped prayerfully on her knees, her whole body tense as a trap about to snap shut. A formidable, righteous, giant of a schoolmarm instructing him in the seven deadly virtues.

"We can't stay here any longer; that's all there is to it. For all our sakes. Mine and the baby's as well as yours. We can't continue like this."

"Sure." He nodded his head. His shoulders latched onto the movement and soon his entire body was rocking in a mockery of acquiescence. "Sure, we'll leave, all right. We'll leave. Only just how far you think we'll get on what we got? Which is just about as close to nothing as you can get. Unless you been holding out on me? Keeping a little getaway fund out of household expenses."

"How do you suppose I could save anything out of what little you give me? When there isn't enough to pay the bills we already have."

"Well, then, you got your answer right there. I already told you, for chrissakes, what the old man said: the house isn't ours to sell."

"All right, then, we'll manage some other way. We're not helpless."

"Manage!" He snorted. "You make me sick with your goddam *manage's*. There's a Depression on, for chrissakes. Or ain't you heard yet?"

Sucking deeply on his cigar, he leaned back and covered the room with an angry sweep of his eyes. His chintz prison. How he hated its snug pretense, its lying promise of comfort that consisted of nothing more than glorified prison fare, thin pillows over hardwood. A pathetic attempt to transform the staple-maple of Monkey Wards into the All-American Dream Home. A little white cottage in the country. Snug and comfy. Everything about the room a goddam lie. Neither a palace nor a dump. A fussy, folksy compromise with too many ruffles and too many bows. Better a whorehouse or a slum. A real dump where he could wallow and play the swine with relish. But like his wife's virtue, this neat, colorless room sought to tie him down to the bareboard necessities, to break his spirit with fasting, and brand him forever as second rate. A common laborer with uncommon pretensions. While he was being eaten alive with longings a king's ransom couldn't satisfy.

"Nothing's impossible," she retorted, adding a lame, "If we make the effort. Where there's a will there's a way."

"Oh, Jesus! What a phrasemaker I married! You actually make that up? On the spur of the moment? All by yourself? Shit! 'Where there's a will there's a way,'" he mimicked. "If you can't come up with something better'n that, forget it."

Despite her resolution tears seemed imminent. "I'm only trying to save what's left of our marriage." She squared her shoulders with the defensive self-righteousness that was her best shield against tears. "Of course, if that doesn't seem to you . . ."

"Saving's for missionaries." More disturbed by her obvious misery than he cared to be, he cut her short. "Where would I get a job? Doing what? Collecting garbage?"

"Why not — if there's nothing else? It's honest work."

"Thanks for nothing."

Encouraged by the relative mildness of his reply, she continued to woo him:

"We'd find something, there's bound to be something, there's always something. We only have to look."

"Yeah, but something's not enough."

There was a hint of the old beauty shining through the waste of his defeat and her heart reached out to him. He was all she had. And Bonny Jean. She could hear the child's muffled cries through the closed bedroom door, but there was another cry more immediate to answer. Aware that any move toward reconciliation would have to come from her, she rose and sat beside him on the sofa, placing her hand on his. He did not reject it. If he could only come to terms with his own weakness, as she had, and let her strength suffice for both, there might still be hope.

"We'd make it enough," she encouraged and for a moment he seemed almost prepared to believe her.

"Sure." He shook his head, in bafflement as well as rejection. "Where'd we live? Give up a free house for rented lodgings? It doesn't make sense."

"But it isn't free. Can't you understand that? You're paying for it. *We're* paying for it. Right now."

The baby's cries grew more insistent. Once again the prison bars clanged shut. He could hear the turning of the locks. Soon it would be too late. His wife: the jailor; his daughter: the heaviest, most confining of all his shackles. And for that too Marge was to blame. A boy might have given him half a wedge to pry open the old man's heart. And purse.

"Can't you see that? Unless you get away from him, unless you make a life of your own, without him whittling away at your self-respect every chance he gets, it'll always be the same. I've seen it, how he plays you off, one against the other. You against Louise and Louise against Lorraine and all against all. Like some mad scientist playing around with guinea pigs in a cage, provoking them to attack another for his own sick pleasure. Needling them until he's had his fill. And then, when he can't any longer stop what he's begun, he turns against the lot of you. I've seen it. And it frightens me."

"Now maybe. But not always."

He rose abruptly her hand rudely cast aside like an old stick he had finished playing with.

"What do you mean by that?"

Rejected, she seemed suddenly overwhelmed by the prospect of defeat.

"He's not going to last forever."

"But that's vile!" She too was on her feet, but he would not look at her. "If he's already brought you to that point. Waiting for your own father to die!"

"Yes, goddammit, so *I* can live," he cried. "Can't you do something about that goddam kid?" And he once again stormed through the house and out the backdoor.

Dazed, she followed him, willing even yet to forgive — if only he had said "we," if only he had made her as well the beneficiary of his father's death.

"Where are you going? Arnie!" Held back at the screendoor by her daughter's persistent screams, she called after him.

"I'll be back," he yelled over his shoulder. And he was gone.

2

"It's all right, all right." She bounced the child in her arms. "Everything's all right now." And the cries were smothered against her breast. "All right," she repeated, a formula designed to soothe her as well as her child. "All right."

But nothing was right. The Bronte-like mist through which she had once viewed her husband, his imperfections blurred in a romantic haze, his gypsy boldness softened by a little boy's bluster that had seemed at once both touching and brave, had long since dissipated in the presence of her flesh-and-blood Heathcliff. Only when he was gone — out of sight but never out of mind — did his attractions any longer seem apparent and her own guilt most acute.

Yet she could not understand now what it was she had done or failed to do. She had never pretended to be what she wasn't. She had made no false claims, employed no deceptive arts. She had come, a stranger, into their midst, and accepted their strange ways as well as their strange God, to Whom she had kept her promises but before Whom she would always feel herself the naturalized alien speaking clumsily in a borrowed

240

tongue, so that she could no longer even pray with native grace. She had accepted — or certainly tried to accept — his mother's indulgent frivolities with uncritical tolerance, his father's teasing barbs, never far from insolence, with stoic fortitude. She had done her best, but her best, apparently, was not enough. As wife she had proved a miserable failure.

"All right, all right," she coaxed, giving the child her other breast. "It's all right now."

The child, she was aware with an increasingly bitter sense of shame that kept these rites secreted from the world, was far too old to be breast fed. Yet she could not bear to wean it away from her own flesh, which would never again, it seemed, to know in its very cells, nurse life. Never again feel the tender wet touch of love. Never. And that knowledge poisoned her whole existence.

On the maple coffee table the copies of the *Saturday Evening Post,* the *Ladies Home Journal,* and *Redbook* lay unopen. There was no faith left to animate the brave, long-suffering heroines. The plain, tiny, frightened women who blossomed late under the warmth of tardy smiles were just that — always tiny. Little Jane Eyre and her brooding blind Rochester. Frail Cathy withering away like a bud of dried lavendar blown across the moors. Small and helpless. In all her reading she could not recall a single sturdily efficient Amazon who had ever been wakened from her dreams to find herself a dewy-eyed nymph borne on the lusty shoulders of a panting satyr.

And as she gazed into the closet-door mirror filled from top to toe with her stanch figure, she could read there the bleak and lonely future, her shoulders square and rigid for the burdens they must bear, her breasts filled now with the only life they would ever know, her face puckered into a protective severity, her eyes lustreless from their Lenten fare. The only lovely thing about her: her gangly child cupping her breast with dimpled hands, the face so like her father's, Marge blushed at the sight; and the warm purr of lust that suffused her with languor.

She laid the baby contentedly in its bed and prepared herself for sleep. The last escape left to her. She could not even force herself to do the dinner dishes. What could one more mess matter in the chaos that was now her life? And as she passed the mirror

241

gaunt in her nightgown the spectre of a fresh spinsterhood rose to haunt her: the old maid schoolteacher she had always sworn she would never allow herself to become. Barren and unloved and bitter for all that. Her child both burden and lover; and one day, if she were not watchful, if she were not ever vigilant against the hungry demands of her own heart, it would be bled dry by her own deep thirst of every drop of affection, and then, when there was nothing left to give, made to feel guilty for a failure it would be powerless to remedy, substituting for a love it could not feel a resentful, grudging pity that would all too soon transform itself into hatred. And she was even more afraid.

3

Restless, she stirred, stretching in her sleep. Longing. An emptiness never again to be filled. Except in dreams. In that twilight world halfway between sleep and waking where nothing was what it seemed to be and the ephemeral granted substance.

Shadows in the room, the air thick with hostile odors. She stirred. She was not alone, but trapped still in the paralysis of sleep, she could not escape. Her slumbering desire suddenly given monstrous shape. Panic blossomed as a silent scream choking in the throat. A warm heaviness she could not shake suffocated her. Awake now to the full horror of naked flesh brutal in its uncoordinated haste, she cried out, "Oh, God! No!" and tearing herself free from the slimy tangle of limbs, her heart racing, longing turned to loathing, she fled to the sanctuary of the bathroom.

There were things worse than neglect, a pain more dreadful than longing, a fear more terrible than solitude.

He had come back, as she had known he would, if only because there was no other place to go. Reeking of whiskey and sweat. Without so much as the whispering hint of an invitational tenderness, he had hurled himself upon her. An act of love that was the antithesis of love.

"I won't have it!" she screamed, slamming and locking the bathroom door. "I won't!"

"I'll break it down. Goddammit, Marge, I'll break it down!"

Behind the rattling door she cowered, too ashamed to turn on the light, her heart racing so fast, frightened as much by the suddenness of her wakening as by his brutality. Her skin clammy with the memory of his body tearing into her. She stepped out of the torn and spotted remains of her nightgown and stood naked in the dark. She longed to bathe herself, inside and out, to wash every last trace of his touch and scent from her body.

She moved to the window and raised the shade. The moon provided all the light she needed. Cool and blue. At the sink she rinsed her mouth, then drank deep. Her thirst slaked, she felt better. Her heartbeat slowed to a more temperate pace. On the other side of the door his fury gave way to indignation:

"You're my wife, for chrissakes. My wife!"

"But not your slave," she hurled back, wishing she had been strong enough to hear him out in silence.

Her bathrobe hung from the hook on the door. She slipped into it. Her nakedness covered, she felt her strength renewed. She could hear the child now crying above the shouts and felt suddenly ashamed of her part in the squalid melodrama. She would not, she could not, continue to live like this. But she must not dramatize. There had been too much drama already. Her fear, she knew, was uncalled for, a flattering tribute to the man she had once thought him to be. He would not harm her. Or the child. She knew that. All bluster and pretense. His instinct for self-preservation was too great for him to trust for long any weapon more deadly than neglect. His whole strategy was based upon retreat. He would desert her before he would harm her. He was, she should have known by now, least dangerous when most offensive. Why then was she cowering?

From shame. From her own sticky shame.

Swinging open the door, she turned on the hall light, and drawing her vestal robes about her, raked him with her eyes, so startling him with the suddenness of her offensive, he staggered against the far wall, visibly shrinking from the light as well as her gaze.

"Well's about time," he grumbled but made no attempt to touch her. His slick pot shining silver, its whiteness, against the sunburnt arms and neck as stark as the underbelly of a fish.

"Cover yourself," she ordered with chilling contempt. Then to cap her disdain, she turned her back upon him. "You look *disgusting!"*

As he moved to follow her into the bedroom, her hand on the doorknob barred his entrance.

"You're not coming in here."

Again he staggered. "What do you mean, not going in there? It's my room too."

"Not anymore it isn't."

"A wife's no right . . ."

Dismayed, he shook his head, more baffled than offended at the affront, but powerless to counter it, his lust withered. He wanted only to curl up against the maternal body and there, under the protective shelter of its warmth, sink into a dreamless sleep. Safe from all harm. Shielded from all terrors.

"Don't talk to me of rights." There was not a quiver of uncertainty in her voice, firm with the strength of its own righteousness. "Until you can prove yourself man enough to love me as a wife, I'll be no wife of yours."

The door closed on his face. "Shit," he muttered so softly it seemed no more than a whispered sibilant hissed from the spout of a cooling kettle. There wasn't steam enough left for a fight. Though the door was not locked, he made no effort to storm it, but turning off the light, he stumbled through the hall into the back guest bedroom. Pulling off the chenille spread, he wrapped himself in it, Indian fashion, and without pulling down the blankets curled up on top of the bed. "Shit," he muttered again, as he drew his knees against his chest, chilled suddenly by one of those moments of blinding lucidity that too often follow the delusive grandeurs of intoxication:

His wife had not rescued him, had not saved him from military slavery or paternal wrath, not, by her virtue, fashioned the boy into a man or rid his sleep of dreams. She had merely trapped him forever in failure.

Chapter Four

1

This time she did not sit outside on the upper deck but remained in the central salon, her large black purse on her lap, both hands clamped firmly over the clasp. She was dressed entirely in black, but so lacking in affectation or elegance was her costume that its absence of color seemed hardly the result of anything so calculated as public mourning. Fierce and unyielding, her eyes were fixed on a point directly in front of her. Not once during the entire trip did she look to the right or to the left, but sat as one fossilized in her own thoughts. She was clearly not a tourist but a woman with a goal.

As the boat docked, the groan of the pilings startled her to action. She rose precipitately. Her eyes responded to the gentle lurch of the deck with a momentary flash of terror. Regaining her balance, she bolted diagonally to the stairwell, her body tilted forward, and clasping the brass rail with a gloved hand, she descended at a hasty, purposeful clip. Not until she was well into the Ferry Building corridor did she pause to catch her bearing. Stopping as abruptly as she had begun, she squared her shoulders and threw back her head like a soldier on inspection before proceeding at her customary brisk pace. There was no problem about direction; she merely followed the crowd through the ticket gate and out onto the Ferry Building Plaza.

Only for an instant did she pause to give the City a cursory glance. She was neither awed nor frightened, accepting it as she accepted the sky and the earth. She had nothing to do with cities or faraway places. The world, she knew, was small, not because she had studied it in any geography text, but because she had observed enough of life to know that all places are circumscribed by one's own being, from which there is never any escape. To her, San Francisco and San Oriel were one, for she was, in both, Belle Bettencourt, and until she could find some means of release from the prison of her own person there was no retreat in all the world that would not, the moment she set foot in it, become San Oriel.

Father Moriarity had advised a streetcar, and there was certainly no lack of cars circling the great square at the foot of Market Street. But never having ridden one before, she felt more secure on her own two feet. She was not up to coping with the multiplicity of decisions and confrontations this simple act would entail, and once again she inspected the rough map her pastor had drawn for her. It seemed an easy matter and she was used to walking. Without further hesitation she crossed the plaza and began her journey up Market Street. Maintaining a steady clip, she walked with her head slightly bowed. Her eyes swept the path clean before her. At each intersection she paused to check the streetsign with her map, her anxiety mounting with each new unfamiliar name until, finally, at the foot of Sutter Street, the name on the marker coincided with that on the map. Her spirits rose. From there it was a simple matter: a half dozen blocks with only a slight incline to take her breath away.

The day was gray and the wind damp but the effort of walking against it kept her warm. Soon she was standing before the store window. Once again she drew her map from her purse to double-check the name and the number with those written down. They were the same. And clamping her purse shut with the map in it, she entered the store.

The balding, nattily dressed clerk, his ruddy Irish face almost lavender in the dim light, greeted her with considerably more deference than her unimposing person would have been granted in any of the neighboring emporiums. Although he was virtually surrounded by the artifacts of his trade — rosary-beading plaster madonnas and Spaniel-eyed portraits of the Christ — his consideration was less than spiritually inspired. He was not so much bending his knee to the blessed hope that the meek shall indeed inherit the earth as quite simply responding to the shrewd instincts of a man who has come to learn that the proprietor of a Religious Art Goods store can ill afford to underestimate the spending potential of little old ladies in black, no matter how threadbare their costumes. It was perhaps something in the way she held her purse so firmly, with both hands clamped over the clasp, as if she feared someone — he, possibly — might snatch it from her, that first alerted him that she had not come merely for a rosary or a missal.

"And just exactly what kind of statue did you have in mind?" he asked in response to her inquiry, awkwardly blurted out in a voice too loud, as one beginning a scene that has been so often rehearsed in the mind's ear that the actual speech has about it an air of uncertainty.

"A corpus," she answered hollowly, looking at him with the intensity of one speaking to the deaf.

"For an altar crucifix?"

"No." She shook her head. "A crypt."

"Ah, then you'll be wanting something lifesize, I imagine."

"Yes," she nodded, mechanically responding to the shake of his head, "lifesize."

"It's not the kind of thing we ordinarily keep in stock, you understand. But I can show you one of our catalogues." His voice rose an octave in response to the thundering crash of her spirit. "And I'm sure we'll be able to find something to please you. If you'll be so kind." And bowing, he pointed the way to a faded plush chair fit for a bishop.

At a loss to hide her disappointment, she was at first reluctant to accept the seat, until taking her by the elbow, the clerk personally, even somewhat forcefully, led her to it. She sat, but her spirits remained stunned, for against all reason she had hoped — after the years of skimping and saving, after the for-feited vacations and the hours of overtime, after the long hungry evenings and the dark lonely nights — now that she was finally taking the first step toward the completion of her pro-ject, that she would be able to take the statue back with her — though it would have required a box the size of a coffin and a complementary number of pallbearers to carry it.

"Most of them, you'll see, come from Spain," he began, as he leaned over to pull the chain on the lamp beside her, pausing to interject a question:

"You won't be wanting one with real hair, I suppose?"

His voice was blandly noncommittal, his face and manner that of a mortician helping the bereaved select a coffin lining.

It was a question she had not be prepared for, though she

did remember, now that she was confronted with it, that there was indeed in Hayward a crucifix with a wig of real hair and a crown of dired and braided bougainvillaea branches, the cruel thorns obviously merely painted plaster and not at all what it pretended to be. No, she thought, she would prefer something without real hair.

"I think you're wise," he added, hovering over her as she flipped the pages of the catalogue. "There's always the problem of maintenance. Keeping the wig up and all that. It's easy enough to dust plaster, but wigs have a way, very shortly, of looking tatty. Not unlike an old furcoat."

But she was not listening. For turning the page, she responded with a heart-skipping chill that made her almost faint to some quality in the slender torso more expressive of pathos than that which emanated from the lovely, almost serene face, which might, except for the gaping wounds, have belonged to a slumbering Endymion. The instant she saw it she knew that she had found her monument. So certain was she of her choice that she refused even to be dismayed by the price, which might otherwise have staggered her. And she answered the request for a deposit by opening her purse, and over the startled protests of the clerk, counted out the full amount. For she knew, once she had seen it, that she would never be satisfied with a substitute, that anything else would of necessity be less than perfect, and above all else she wanted this culminating act of her life to be, as nothing before it had ever been — perfect.

2

But her every act, it seemed, was destined to become a source of controversy. No sooner did the workmen appear to lay the foundations for the crypt than the parishioners rose up in outrage. Informed that their pastor had not, as they feared, committed them to a financial burden their pockets could ill afford, they turned from outrage to dismay — until the identity of the donor transformed dismay once again to outrage. How dare she throw up her scandalous past in their faces!

Only Louise Ramos, however, had the courage to confront Belle in person. Her own disapproval was in no way connected

248

with Olaf. It was, in Louise's eyes, primarily a question of taste. So severely tempered by the Puritan ethic had her own Catholicism been, she found these literal re-creations of Christ's passion that her ancestors relished repugnant — morally as well as aesthetically. Glorifying the physical minutiae of suffering, they exalted the body at the expense of the spirit. Even more fundamentally, Belle's folly called into question the very nature of Christianity itself.

"But Belle, you of all people!" she pled. "How can anyone familiar with suffering feel Christ's purposes are best served by so unnecessary an extravagance?"

But Belle was not to be swayed. "Who, my dear, has any right to speak for Christ and His purposes? You or I or anyone else?" And she stood rigid in her doorway, her formidable person denying welcome.

Forced to stand on the back porch amid the clutter of clay-filled containers, a few petrified stalks the only reminder of the life they had once fostered, her niece continued undaunted, "One doesn't have to be a theologian to know — at such a time at this, with people starving on all sides: children forced to beg for their next meal; with the entire nation, for that matter, in the throes of depression — with so many injustices crying out to be righted, certainly our first duty — as the Bible tells us — is to feed the hungry and clothe the naked."

"Duty? Louise Ramos! Don't you dare speak to *me* of duty!"

"Oh, Belle, do be sensible. It's simply because you've always been so level-headed that we have to wonder what's come over you. Can't you see — yes, I hate to say it, but the whole mad project smacks of vanity. Why not, if you have the money to give, give it to the Poor Clares! Where it can be put to some practical use, instead of . . ."

"No, Louise." She would not allow her niece to finish. "You're wasting your time. And mine. Extravagant it may very well be, and the fruit of my vanity, as you claim. But it is, after all, *my* extravagance. And for once in my life — vanity or no vanity — I mean to indulge myself. I don't expect you — or anyone else — to understand. You with your husband and children — how can you? But this happens to be the one thing in my life

I've touched that is going to outlast me. And not you or anyone else is going to take it away from me. Though that, I'm happy to say, is no longer in our power to decide. The money,'' she concluded with a glacial disdain intended to freeze out the last member of the family with whom she still maintained a semblance of intercourse, ''has already been spent. It's no longer mine to call back. So you see, my dear, like the rest of the world, you'll just have to learn how to put up with your old aunt's foibles.'' And without waiting for a reply, she backed into the kitchen, closed the door, and turned the key. And the sound of the bolt slipping into its slot marked her final retreat into solitude.

3

As her confessor and spiritual mentor, Father Moriarity remained her last link with the world of the living. He alone shared her enthusiasm for the project. He was desolated when the corpus failed to arrive in time for Holy Week so that the grand opening had to be postponed from the more dramatic Good Friday to the summer feast of Saint Anthony. He had been gifted with a sure sense of liturgical theatrics and was apt to judge the effectiveness of any religious service much as a theatrical producer judges a play, by the box-office receipts. Thus he could not fail to mourn such a lost opportunity. He knew that once the furor died down the crypt would become what, in his wilder flights of fancy, he liked to think of as a potential Lourdes. Nor would the whispered innuendos lessen its public fame; many and mysterious were the ways of the Lord and they were not to be questioned.

4

This night had been a long time coming. For so many months and years had the project gestated, it had come to mean so many different things, had taken so many different shapes, assumed so many different features, until it seemed, finally, to have more reality than her own being. She herself had become merely the medium of its fulfillment, so that there was, now that

250

the hours of her deliverance had come, a sense of unreality that she could not quite fathom. Buried deep lay the fear that the very excesses of her longing doomed her to disappointment. And she was overwhelmed with doubts. Perhaps the whole venture had been, as her niece intimated, a monument to self-pity and nothing more. Perhaps she had meant, as her neighbors claimed, only to justify herself before the world and transform her lover's sordid end into something beautiful, a sacrifice transcending the body's means to suffer it.

Though she had fasted the entire night before, so keen were the doubts that assailed her, she refused the sacrament on the following morning. The further extension of her fast throughout the day sprang from nothing more spiritual than need; her throat tightened and her gorge rose at the sight of food until her long fast left her giddy and subject to secret terrors. Loneliness fed upon her flesh to mock that more paltry hunger for the fruits of the earth.

Not until it was dark did she leave her house. She was dressed, as always for mass, entirely in black. She had fortified herself with a single glass of brandy, which had coursed through her like the living fire and bolstered her courage; but it had also, on her empty stomach, left her excessively light-headed. No publicity had been given to her request, so there were no eyes to spy her stumbling through the night. No one saw her, as she climbed the sacristy stairs, lose her footing and fall, crashing to her knees. As the housekeeper's dog sounded the alarm, she crouched in the dark. Her hand on the rail, she listened to the hollow bark, like the cracking of dry wood, her heart racing furiously. A thief in the night, she thought. The kitchen light of the parish house went on, the screendoor opened and closed again, then the light went out. Soon the barking died as well and she stumbled to her feet. One silk stocking had been torn, but what had the likes of her to do with silk? Pausing for no more than a casual ordering of her dress, she reached out to try the sacristy door. It had, as promised, been left open, and slipping in, she sighed her relief.

She dared not turn on the lights for fear of alerting some passerby. She was used to the dark. For years she had been more at home in it than in the light of day. Guided by the faint red glow from the sanctuary lamp, she felt her way to the altar rail. The air was heavy still with the odor of gardenias and incense left over from the morning obsequies for Tom Ramos. Something lay on the floor. She stooped to pick it up. A fallen gardenia blossom, fallen from some spray, the soft petals eerily reminiscent of flesh. The lifeless flesh of the dead. She had in her day laid out enough brothers and parents to keep the feel forever fresh in her memory. Shuddering, she dropped the flower and moved up the center aisle, through the swinging doors into the vestibule. Father Moriarity had throughtfully left the crypt lit for her. By now her fear had grown voracious and her will seemed paralyzed. Tottering on the threshhold, she peered down the cement stairs that led to the wrought-iron gates. but she could not bring herself to move. A chill permeated her bones. Her throat was dry and her tongue lay heavy in her mouth. She tried to swallow, but there was nothing to swallow. She longed for another drink, just one more to warm her stomach and steel her courage. She clutched her purse as the last hold onto the familiar and forced herself to take a step. Her legs seemed as brittle as glass. Shakily she made her way down the five stairs that led to the tiny anteroom. The effort left her winded and she paused to catch her breath. Giddier than ever, she seemed about to faint, and reaching out to catch hold of the free-swinging iron gate for support, she found herself suddenly precipitated into the inner chamber. Taken by surprise, she reached out dizzily for support, but there was nothing to break her fall, and she crashed to the floor, her purse noisily spilling its contents over the terracotta tiles.

The pain was at first intense. Kneeling, she held the injured wrist in her hand and cradled it against her breasts. The light coming from a single concealed amber bulb seemed to emanate from no particular source, and she felt for a moment as if she had startled herself awake by her fall from a dream. She struggled to focus her eyes on some reality that would keep her awake and safe from the unknown.

She had broken her wrist, she was sure of that. And for the moment pain was the center about which she gathered her forces. So insistent was it that only gradually did the body, bathed in the errie light, begin to take shape. Viewed through an iron grill intended to protect it from the depredations of the curious, it lay slumbering and indistinct. Just for an instant she could not imagine who or what it might be, and once again a dreadful thrist assailed her, burning like fire in her throat. Tears further hampered her vision. Startled by her own outcry as she moved her hand, she momentarily mastered them. And her pain as well as her fear was washed away in a flood of joy.

Struggling to her feet, she grasped the iron grill and sank into the wooden kneeler. Her head fell of its own weight against the back of her hand, which held tight to its iron support, the injured hand curled limp against her breast. The dizziness was gone now. In its place there was a lightness that seemed not of the body. And her eyes saw with a fresh clarity that illuminated the very shadows, so that as she studied the recumbent form before her, beautiful beyond all believing. The slim torso appeared to be breathing. It was, she knew, only a trick of lighting, the flame flickering in one of the red glass vigil lights which the priest must have lit on the rack against the wall, but she didn't care what means God chose to speak to her. It was breathing. And she longed to reach her hand through the iron grill to touch it, but something, modesty perhaps, or fear, held her back. It was enough to know that he lived. She was as sure of that as of her own being. He was not dead. There was no such thing as death. She knew that now. They were all there with her in that small chamber — Olaf, her father, the tiny, pigeon-breasted baby clutching at her finger, even her poor demented mother babbling away in a language only the angels could understand; they were all there living in the living body of their Savior. She made no effort at all to stem the flow of her tears. They washed over her in torrents of joy, carrying in their wake all the waste of summer, for she knew now she need never again be alone.

Part VI

Chapter One

1

"Old man's lost his touch."

"That son a his. Damnfool kid! Coulda been sittin on toppa the world, stead of laying in the gutter."

"Hear tell the ole ticker's giving him a pause or two."

"More family troubles. Hy and Lorraine. Carrying on like they was fit to be tied. Won't be long afore the gutter's overflowin with everybody's dirty linen."

"That bad already, huh? Well, just goes to show, money ain't everything."

"Last time I saw the kid, looked older'n the ole man. Pulled out every last tooth. And a pot on him, I swear, big as a bay window."

"Seen it coming way back. Nuff to break any man's spirit."

He could hear the whisperings like some buzz in the ear he could not shake, some bee burrowing into the wax,

"That son a his . . ."

"Broke the ole man's spirit . . . ."

The burlap tents flapped in the breeze. A dead city pitched on the outskirts of the empty dryer flats. The migratory Mexicans, who had steamed in with the sudden onslaught of summer, out in the fields gathering cherries.

His cherries.

There were deaths worse than the final one: the death of faith. There was nothing any longer for an old man to believe in. Only the god of life and lust that stirred in him still. Even his country had joined the list of betrayers. Tricked him into a blind faith it had not deserved. And the war that should have ended in six months, a pygmy crushed in a giant's embrace, moved instead from disaster to fresh disaster. From carnage to carnage.

Franklin Lucifer Roosevelt to blame. A nation of steel defeated by a scrap-iron navy. *Our* scrap-iron . . .

The dreamer lives in the future, but his age precluded that. Since the only sure future was death, his sole refuge from the oppressive present lay in the past.

A city of burlap and patched canvas and the sun-browned timber of fruit trays, the rough boards stenciled with jellied ringlets where the drying cots had bled. Stung by nostalgia, he moved through the deserted city, like a father leading his son, the spectre of his own young self, by the hand. A slender boy with a wooden sword defending his fortress — burned by the hands of envy. He could still smell the stench of their flames, the despoilers out to bury the dreamer in the ashes of his own dream.

But certainly it could not have been he — that boy. As young as the spring with hopes brighter than the sun. It seemed at one and the same time that he had never been young and that he had never grown old, that he was today still the youth he had some-how never been, the past and the present so blurred he could not separate one from the other so that neither seemed any longer real. The smell and feel of burlap so redolent of aching dreams, he could scarcely bear the weight of his own footsteps, his movements retarded by the spectre of his spent youth. A ghost moving through the cemetery where his own childhood lay buried.

Through a burlap flap pinned open by a rusty nail, the sheen of flesh dazzled. Sitting cross-legged on a grass mattress, an adolescent mother suckled a pinkbrown infant, its pinched buttocks dimpling her bare arm. He stood transfixed, his eyes moving from her charred gaze to the exposed breast as the sun shining through the frayed burlap gilded her shoulders. Fascinated, he studied each detail with all the wonder of discovery: the aureole of gooseflesh around the raspberry nipple and the single long hair curled about the lavendar tip, wet still with a smear of milk.

His mouth went dry. His throat constricted. If she had been alone, if there had been no child so achingly helplessly young, he would merely have tipped his hat, and without a second thought, have moved out of the sack city, back to his car and his chores. But she was not alone and he was powerless to will himself away.

His coat was open so that the gold chains crossing his vest complemented the sheen on her shoulders. She made no move to cover herself, and as he made no effort to leave, she chuckled softly without embarrassment, a tickle of sound bubbling from her throat. In mocking invitation she lifted the free breast and gently squeezed it until a white drop oozed from the pinpoint duct.

Numbly he stepped inside and dropped the flap behind him, letting the rusty nail fall to the earth. His earth.

So incongruously stern and sober was his face — a young boy masking diffidence with belligerence, a role made comic by his white hairs — she giggled uneasily. He frowned at her mockery, and there was majesty enough in the scowl to strangle her mirth. Through the aureate haze they confronted each other. Neither spoke. He stood for a moment undecided as well as speechless. Then resorting to the most natural, the most persuasive language he knew, a reflex action that required no gift of tongues, he removed his wallet from the inside pocket of his coat, and taking out a twenty-dollar bill, he tossed it onto the bed.

With the silent fall of the green bill, her apprehension vanished. Unruffled, she studied the money, crisp and flat, and like most of the bills he carried, suspiciously new. With one finger she flipped it over, to check, perhaps, there was not trick involved, that the marvelous numbers were indeed the same on both sides. More than her husband made in a week.

She seemed to know, without surprise, what was expected of her. Rich gringos did not scatter bills for nothing. There was no terror or shame in her knowledge, and though certainly no eagerness, very little reluctance. It seemed, her whole demeanor said, a small thing to ask for so much and no more meaningful than breaking bread together.

Freeing herself from her suckling charge, she laid the infant in a box of rags. Cheated of its meal, the child howled its protest. Expressionless, the girl picked up the bill from the bed, folded it, and carefully tucked in under the beer bottle used as a candlestick on the orange crate table. Perfunctorily she dropped her skirt, and stepping out of the mound of clothes, she stretched out, listlessly, her hands behind her head, on the mattress of dried alfalfa.

His lust was as real as her indifference; her very lassitude stoked it. But it was an old man's lust. It burned through him like a combustive fire smoldering for years in some dank attic corner. It parched his throat, it paralyzed his joints, and flaming through dry timber, it died as fast as it had begun.

The hasty spasm on the burlap bed left him breathless. And something more. His thumping heart rose to his throat, swelling, until he gasped for air. His hand moved to his neck, fumbling, but there was no collar choking him. He lay back on the coarse bed, white and sweating, the skin on his thin legs, infant-soft, netted with a pale tracery of blue.

There was no future but death.

Catch hold, he thought: simply a question of holding tight to will miracles. But blinded with both terror and pain, his eyes bulged from their sockets and he could find nothing to catch hold of. He was slipping.

No future . . .

His heart seemed at once about to burst and to crush him in its bind. A fullness in the chest, strangling him. He was falling from a great height, sinking, time more elastic than the bed that cushioned him, each second stretching into a promised eternity.

Concentrate! He must concentrate.

"That son a his."

"Broke the ole man's heart."

"Laying in the gutter."

"Nuff to break any man."

"On toppa the world."

A chorus of taunters setting the torch to his dream. Well, he wasn't through yet. He'd show them all. Simply a matter of will. Nothing more. He was young still. Young and strong. With years of life left to live. No, he would not give in. He would not die. He would not! And his entire being focused on the pulse swelling in his ears. Again he reached out, blindly, and this time he caught hold of some fortuitous outgrowth to break his fall. The bind loosened, his breath returned, and with it, sight. His eyes focused on the gold-speckled ceiling where the sun was eating its way through the worn canvas and dappling his own white flesh. The sun of life.

And through it all, the hungry, kicking bundle of flesh continued squalling on its bed of rags.

Cowering at the other end of the bed, the young mother watched with wonder, her knees clapsed against her breasts, she compressed herself into a package small enough to avoid his gray touch. He struggled to speak, lifting his head and pointing. She moved away from his finger and cowered against the burlap wall, almost toppling her tent in her effort to escape his touch.

"Baby," he gasped. ". . . stop . . . screaming . . ."

Whether she understood English he did not know, but she seemed at last to understand his intention if not his words. Almost with relief, she rose. Stepping over him without touching him, she picked up the baby from its basket, a rag-filled box stenciled: VINCE WOODS, San Oriel, and once again gave it her breast. Instantly the shrieking ceased and was replaced by a soft, gentle slurping. Mother and child. The mystical pair reunited.

Afraid still to move, Vince turned his head to watch her bounce the child feeding where he had himself only a few minutes before so hungrily fed. The taste of sickness in his mouth.

"Better," he sighed and sank back against the rustic mattress.

At home in her nakedness, she moved silently about the tent. Scarcely more than a child herself. Fifteen, perhaps. Her youthfully tiny hams, waffle-patterned from the burlap, quivered loosely, her dull eyes fixed on the vanquished warrior rising wounded from the dead. With animal casualness she scratched herself. Following her hand, he inspected the secret parts of her body. She was alive with considerably more than the remnants of his lust.

Disgust conquered fear. He rose, Then suddenly dizzy, he sank back onto the bed. Sitting, he caught his head in his hands. She made no effort to help him, but pacing with her child, never once removed her eyes from him. There was a slight flutter in his chest. Then still again. His breath came easily, his dizziness found its ballast. Alone and still sitting, he worked his way into his trouser legs and his shoes. Then rising once again, he slipped his suspenders over his shoulders. He was all right — his head clear, his pulse steady. Perfectly normal. His forehead banded with the cold sweat of relief. He had exaggerated its importance, surely. A little shortness of breath, that was all. Still a young man with years of life left to live. Rich and strong. He tied his necktie without the aid of a mirror and buttoned his vest, checking to see that the gold watch was still in his pocket. He attached the fob and chain across the wide expanse of his stomach, the fragile blue veins now covered with a sturdy brown tweed. He brushed his hair back with his hands then ran a comb through it. Dressed again, he felt himself once more the man of the world. A lord of the land. Vincent Woods.

Defying the auguries of disaster, he lit a cigar. He puffed contentedly before he made an effort to speak. Then in the slow elementary Portuguese he always used when speaking to Mexicans, he made clear the need for her immediate departure, and placing three more bills on the orange crate, he left.

2

In vain he tried to wash away the memory of his encounter with a hot bath, for the shame lingered. It had been on every level a disaster. He could taste the fear of death festering in his foul breath; he could feel his lust transformed now to a persistent, maddening itch, its fire mocked by the burning ointment.

The following day he was relieved to discover that the tent had been razed and the family gone. A nameless stranger, she would soon be forgotton. Only a bad dream brought on by summer's heat. An autumnal lark. A rich man's brief sip at charity's breast.

Chapter Two

1

"MEEK DIVORCE TRIAL ANYTHING BUT"

But *what?* Clara wondered, mystification at the strange head-line vying with her chagrin. With a cramp of her swollen fingers, she crumpled the newspaper. How could they! How *dared* they! Her cheeks burned with shame and resentment, when it was they, and not she, who ought to be ashamed. Whose cheeks should be branded with blushes. Parading in public print obscenities no decent woman would dream of practicing in private! What was the world coming to when marriage was made a mockery of? Every eye free to read what once would never have been allowed to be printed. There was simply no shame left.

It was the war — there could be no question of that — spreading its poison over the whole world like some cloud of germs. Infecting everyone and everything. Killing! Bombing! Cathedrals in ruins, palaces in flames — and for what! Screaming madmen all. Roosevelt included.

And yet she could not, though she had a grandson in uniform sitting on a ship somewhere in that great mass of blue that spilled over the globe, entirely believe in the war's reality. The whole gory mess seemed to her rather like those overlapping cello-phane charts in the doctor's office of skeleton, viscera, muscles, and skin that were meant to elucidate diagnosis, but more often than not compounded mystery with more mystery. Having in her youth disemboweled enough fowl to have a fair notion of what lay beneath the body's surface, try as she would, she still could not relate that slimy reality to her own person. She had been created in God's image, not a chicken's.

Like an outburst of uncontrolled flatulence, the war's reality seemed a kind of shocking rudeness best overlooked. It was not healthy to dwell on death and madness. And no one, certainly, not any longer, at any rate, believed there was the remotest danger bombs might fall on California. And Lord knows, bewail it as she might, *she* was powerless to do anything either to hasten or delay its end, and she wished people would spare her the gruesome details.

Nor could she for an instant understand her husband's strange preoccupation with every minute twist and turn of every battle's fortune. An obsession that had led him to give over the management of all but the most important details of his own affairs to others so that he might, for hours on end, sit before the radio with globes and atlases spread about him, to follow the war's progress as though it were merely an endless football game, and wraped in a blanket of gloom he would not leave the stadium before the final gun sounded.

Today, however, it was not the war news that interested her; nor would it, she was confident, be the war news that would most rivet her neighbor's interest. She might be unschooled, but she was familiar enough with human nature to know that even at the worst of times gossip outranked all other news. Which of them had, even a week before, heard of Saipan? But they all knew Hy and Lorraine well enough and every last word of *that* article, she knew, as well as she knew that night would fall and the day follow, would be read and re-read, and then with rumor added to fact, be passed over back fences, meat counters, bridge tables, and partyline telephones, a veritable tornado of whispered innuendo, until two naughty, shameless children, who both, granted, deserved to be publicly whipped, would be transformed into monsters scarcely fit to continue living. It seemed inconceivable that the judge — and such a fine, upstanding old gentleman he looked — would allow his ears to be affronted by accusations and counter-accusations not fit for a French novel, let alone a court of law.

Though there could be no question where the real blame lay. Certainly no one who knew them could doubt that, and there lay her only comfort. Poor Lorraine! Where could she, sheltered as she had always been with the best that money could buy, have picked up such shameless practices, except from her husband? And a Meek at that! It was almost enough to make one laugh. A fine family *theirs* turned out to be! Which only went to prove once again: there was no judging a book by its cover.

There was scarcely a sancturay safe from invasion. Even the cool musty shadows of the Roxie were subjected to the ear-shattering beastialities of warring nations airing *their* obscenities before the eyes of the entire world. No sooner was she lifted, airily light, on the arms of Fred Astaire, whirling dizzily across glossy expanses of polished marble in a dream world of misty gauze, than the dream was shattered by the crude thrust of a bayonet. Nor could she align her faltering memory with the scenes she saw now flashed from the newsreel camera. Behind the marching armies and the screaming patriots she could glimpse a half-remembered building or square, a *Chocolate Soldier* setting, its charm trampled under the deadly symmetry of goose-steps and guns.

"It's more than I can bear, Doctor. Sometimes — at night — the pain! It startles me awake. And I lay there for hours on end, thinking: What is it we did wrong? Just where did it all begin? If you only knew what it's like to be a mother and watch your family fall apart. Oh, I could bear it well enough alone, but when I look at my husband and watch him every day grow more and more bitter, their terrible squabbles wearing him away —!"

She looked out the window of the lakefront office with its gumwood moldings, its plush chairs and pastoral oils, and just the faintest odor of disinfectant to remind her that is was not, after all, a social visit, a lover's tryst, but a professional call she was making. Outside on the lake a swan glided into view followed by its mate, both riding the water like a royal tandem. A peaceful sancturay it seemed after all the noise and bustle of the outside world.

"You've got to think first and foremost about yourself, Mrs. Woods, or I refuse any longer to be held responsible for the consequences."

She received the doctor's pronouncement with a secret thrill a younger woman might have reserved for a declaration of hopeless passion.

"Anything, Doctor. Just tell me what it is I have to do and it's done. Anything at all . . . within reason."

"Now I'm going to give you something," he continued, fixing

her with soft, tragic eyes, which seemed at the moment filled with compassion enough to encompass all of suffering humanity, as he patted her fingers with a meticulously manicured hand. "It might work and it might not, but we're going to try it for awhile. It can't do you any harm, and it just might turn the trick. It's not on the market yet," he added with a significant furrow of his elegant brow, "so you can imagine it's going to cost you just a wee bit more than an ordinary bottle of aspirin. But your health comes first, Mrs. Woods. Without that, as you all too well know, nothing else counts. If *you're* not up to par, well then, your whole family's going to suffer. So by helping yourself, you're really helping those you most love."

"A thankless love," she blurted out, shaken by a quickly stifled sob.

"Hush, hush, Mrs. Woods." He too had seen the afternoon paper. "You know you don't mean that. There's nothing personal in these matters," he added vaguely. "Divorces. They always have a way of taking care of themselves. Why, in a few weeks' time, who'll know the difference?"

She had never smelled anything so marvelously clean as his person, like the finest, most expensively packaged English soaps, his hands shining pink from the scrub brush. Their touch cool and dry and infinitely reassuring. He made her feel once again like a child, a young girl, coyly virginal, until she longed, with a child's innocence, to curl up against him and lay her head against his chest. His voice so softly comforting. He might enter one, she imagined, like a ray of light, so gently, with an ethereal glow, spreading its soft illumination . . .

Tall, slender, and immaculate, he was on his feet.

"And I'll be expecting you again next week for a full report. In the meantime, don't you worry, Mrs. Woods —" a comforting hand about her shoulder as he helped her with her sable wrap — "We'll soon have you fit as a fiddle."

Weightless, she floated across the parking lot, and with hands free for the moment of all crippling pain, she clasped the steering wheel of the old Packard as it coasted regally down East Fourteenth Street like a royal barge, a clumsy, dated luxury burning up precious gas coupons. She had wanted to turn it in on the latest Cadillac model, but they had decided, she and her husband, to keep the old car as part of their personal sacrifice to the war effort, and now that the war was continuing long past anyone's wildest dreams, nothing new was to be had for love nor money, and they were stuck with the old monster.

Though one would never guess from the traffic that there was a war on. Where, she wondered, amazed and just a little indignant at the constant flow of cars, did *they* get *their* ration coupons? Certainly they couldn't all have private pumps for essential vehicles. Trafficking in the black market, no doubt. But that was just one more measure of the state the world was coming to. There was no question the war was poisoning everything.

But what was past help, as Poor Belle used to say, was also past thinking about. She had only one consideration now: to get home in time to spare Vince.

And there was, suddenly, so much to hide from him. So many crosses to bear alone: clandestine meetings with a son who seemed old enough to be her contemporary; the secret passing of checks pinched from household expenses to support a second family spawned on a creature she shuddered to receive, let alone call daughter, a shamelessly tight-sweatered, rayon-slacked doxy with bottle-black hair and a bust that was not to be believed. Another import from a French novel. Her own son's wife! The threat of whose public visits was enough to blackmail her into betraying her husband's strict orders: "Not another penny. Let him work or let him starve. But not another penny does he ever get from me."

It was more than any woman alone should have to bear.

2

The afternoon paper was not at the gate, and she feared she had arrived too late. Her fears were confirmed as soon as she entered the house. A brooding old ram, his hands on the arms, his body sunk deep into the cushions of his easy chair, he scowled at the world. His color, she noted, was not good — and little wonder, she thought, as her eyes fell to the paper open at his feet.

"Oh, dear, you've seen it then." She took off her hat and placed it on the newel post. "I was afraid you might."

He reached over to turn down the radio beside him. It was on now all day, a strident background to every conversation.

"Course I've seen it. Damn fools!"

She came over the offer a comforting pat to his hand. It was distressingly chilly.

"Are you feeling cold, Dear? Want a comforter?"

"Cold? Why should I be cold? It's summer, isn't it?"

She took no offense at his tone. She knew him too well to question his devotion. And certainly there was cause enough for irritation.

"Well, no one can blame us." Dropping his hand, she moved to the mantle mirror to fluff out her lavendar curls. "We did everything *we* could."

"That's a laugh." His snort loud and contemptuous. "Everything we did still wasn't half enough."

"But Vince," she turned to him, her face troubled by the bitter self-castigation of his words, "it's silly to blame ourselves. Why . . ."

"Silly, is it? Then who the hell should we blame? Tell me that. Why, we might as well let them keep every goddam one of them at this stage of the game."

"Keep what, Dear?"

Baffled, she inspected his face, momentarily alarmed by what she found there, a grayness of the cheeks, the drawn skin held together by the sheer intensity of his anger. He certainly wasn't well. It might be best, if she could manage it, to get him to bed and away from the radio.

"The goddam island!" he shouted, then took refuge in a surly pout: "Thought you said you'd read the paper."

"In the doctor's office. But I don't understand." She shook her head. "What've Lorraine and Hy to do with an island? There isn't something I don't know, is there?"

"Lorraine and Hy? What the hell they got to do with anything? It's the goddam Japs I'm talking about."

She had to turn away to hide her smile of relief. So he hadn't seen it after all. Time yet to spare him.

"And they've done it all with a tincan navy. Roosevelt's navy, mind you. Built from scraps *we* sold them." He reached into the cabinet beside his chair for a cigar, angrily crinkling the

266

cellophone wrapper. "He gave them the ships, so he might as well turn right around and give them every goddam island in the Pacific they haven't already taken."

She gathered up the afternoon paper, folding it neatly and depositing it under her arm as she bent over to kiss him on the forehead.

"Just don't get yourself all worked up, Dear, over something you can't do anything abut. It's not good for you. We've done our part. All *we* could do. Certainly no one can blame *us* for having put That Man in the White House."

He lifted his watch from his vest pocket: three minutes to four.

"Remember now, the doctor said no more than two cigars a day. Where's Sarah? In the kitchen?" And touching his shoulder in passing, she left the room without waiting for an answer, mumbling something about roses as she disappeared through the swinging door.

He rose to turn the radio louder. Something somewhere had gone wrong with his America, a betrayal more personal than that of his own family: the mightiest power of the world running like sacred rabbits from a bunch of pint-sized Japs! Only to buy back in blood what was given away without a scrap. Too little coming too late at too dear a price. He tallied each downed plane, each sunken ship. Sometimes smiling to verify his ill opinion of the world, which had, it seemed, grown feeble along with him, he attended to the sepulchral prophecies of every dooms-day commentator, barking his own unheeded commands into the offending speaker. With impotent fury he hurled his invec-ives against Washington, London, and the General Staff — all staffed by fools. Or worse, downright traitors.

During station breaks and musical interludes, he collected him-self to search out the miniscule dots on the Atlas: Guadalcanal, Tarawa, Eniwetok; but he had difficulty keeping the Gilberts separate from the Marshalls and the Marshalls from the Solo-mons. There were simply too many and the Pacific too vast. One beach looked like every other beach. Mind not as sharp as it used to be. An old man whose wisdom went unheeded.

A sudden painful contraction in his chest caused him to sink once again onto his chair, an icy band momentarily blindfolding him. From the buzzing blur of sound as the blindfold melted he could make out a familiar voice:

"Latest reports from the front . . . casualty estimates . . ."

The radio.

Suddenly he had had his fill of war. Too old to be preoccupied with death and the dying. Not healthy.

Man without a future has only the moment. Look to the sun — eating its way like flame through burlap.

An instant of panic. He did not want to die. Not yet. Merely the strain of the war drawing the cord tight. The shame of too many defeats suffocating him. A contraction of the chest, an internal swelling so great he feared all organs at once must burst, and letting fall his cigar, he moved to still the droning voice. Silence the war. He had had his fill.

But his hand would not reach, and as he attempted to rise, the chill of terror held him down.

Easy, he thought. Relax. Steady himself. Or terror itself would be the cause as well as the effect. Nothing to fear but fear itself. Where had he heard that? But he was above fear, a man made to rule. A warrior tested on many fields. Yet he could not rule his heart, could not command his irregular pulse back into line. With fumbling fingers he loosened his collar, and throwing back his head, breathed deeply, reaching for the air like a drowning man breaking through the surface of the sea with a periscope of puckered lips.

Such the sun!

He closed his eyes, and the voice droned on. Louder.

Somewhere men were dying, but where precisely he no longer cared. Blood spilled on the sands of strange islands with names he could never keep straight. Men with the smooth, hard flesh of youth. Drowning in tropic swamps, their bodies sucked by leeches, torn by shrapnel. But it was a distant carnage. Faceless, nameless, rotting without stench, the dead could not move him. Numbers without names; names without faces. There was carnage enough in a single death if one were himself the dying.

Yet he *was!* — and always had been. Memory was eternal: without a remembered beginning and therefore without an imagined end. Now, at this very moment, he was. How then was it possible that he could not be? No, death itself was not possible.

The voice, he knew, lied. Yet he was afraid. Afraid most of solitude. Death only a deeper isolation of the spirit. The ultimate solitude. And he could not bear to be alone.

Clara, he called. The last remaining loyalty. More mother now than wife. The mouth opened, the tongue moved, but no sound came.

Clara! his heart cried. But his voice was already dead.

Frantically he scratched at his chair, and jerking forward his foot, he knocked over the stool with its pile of Atlases topped with a ring of keys. With a noisy jangle they crashed onto the stone hearth. And still no one came. No one heard. He was alone.

He looked about the room. Everything was in its place: the liquor cabinet with its crystal decanter, a jewel of light flashing on the silver label; the tiny woodcarving of an Italian peasant — where had they gotten it? Florence? Rome? Naples? — his grinning face creased with time as well as pleasure, the silent music of his concertina filled with the joy of life. How long had it been since he had last looked at it? Last seen it for what it was, a tribute to all life? His life. Changeless and eternal. Mother and child —

But that was something else. His mind would not order itself. Another matter altogether. Another time and another place.

The stained glass above the stairs tinted the walls with its autumn colors. A cobweb marred the far corner. Sarah growing slack. Too busy now gadding about to tend to her proper duties. Always something to keep her busy. Too busy now to tend to *his* needs, his three-thirty tea and his five o'clock brandy, and the evening massage of legs, tired now from too much sitting so they jerked at night, startling him awake at all hours.

Why wasn't she here to help him? Time for his tea, goddammit! He wanted what he wanted when he wanted it, and not some other time. What good were servants if they failed to serve? Another ingrate among ingrates. All out for everything they could get. Leeches all, sucking the blood of life from him. No blood of his anymore. Disown the lot of them. Clara alone gave more than she took. But she too was failing him now that he needed her. Couldn't she understand that? Feel his need crying out to her?

The stairs leading to his room. He had only to mount them to find his bed, impressed through the years with his own image, imbued with his own door.

His eyes scanned the room. Everything was there, everything in order, everything familiar. Everything his. The clock ticked, birds sang, the sun shone. Trees that he himself had planted cast their shade on his windows. And his wife, he saw, with a sudden lift of his spirits, was there, and Sarah too, out in the garden, their form muted by the Venetian lace curtains: Clara seen through a curtain of flowers, holding shears in her gloved hands as she cut her roses and laid them gently, one by one, in the wicker basket Sarah held. Clara in a lavendar dress and a straw hat to shade her against the evening sun, unafraid in the garden, comforted him.

Nothing had changed. Only his imagination. Battle fatigue. Soon be time for tea. He had only to wait. Hold out a few minutes longer and Sarah would be here, all smiles and fat quivering hams. His eyes fell on the teacup sitting on the table beside him, a residue of leaves and sugar. But how was it possible? How could he have forgotten? Maybe it was yesterday she'd been late. Yes, yesterday. But if today was today and he'd already had his tea, where, then, was his brandy? He looked at the clock: not yet five. He could have sworn he was listening to the five o'clock news. Nap-time then. The needlepoint pillow and the folded crocheted afghan waiting for him on the nearby sofa. Only a few yards away. He felt easier now that he knew once again where and when he was. Everything was as it should be. Everything fine. Everything in order.

In the gypsy tent on the burlap bed — there death had been possible. Death in betrayal. But not here. Not in the moment of his absolution. Mother and child. Husband and wife. How could he have betrayed his own flesh? For she was he. He saw that now as he had never seen it before. Vince and Clara. One flesh for so many years. Flesh that still clung even after the death of lust. The only lust that mattered. It was he out there gathering roses in the garden. Impregnable in the sun. Unafraid.

He would not die.

Death had nothing to do with crocheted afghans and silver-labeled brandy decanters. Death had nothing to do with his house. With him. Old? Why, he was still young. Hadn't he only the year before been to the senior Tom Ramos's funeral? Young Tom's old father. But young Tom had been dead for years now. That was another Tom. Another generation. Over ninety the old boy had been, and still walking without a cane. And Inez Cardoz. Already a mother long before he himself had been born and still going strong. Over a hundred, people said. And still able to read and get around by herself, even if the house did smell like a cave of dead bats. An unaired tomb. Alive still, she was, shuffling about in her carpet slippers, and that's what mattered. Alive. Why, there were years left, each one filled with a feast of months and weeks and days. Age simply a matter of perspective. Next to Old Lady Cardoza he was a mere boy. And what had she ever done in her hundred uneventful years to earn more than he?

Young!

And he smiled at the memory of Inez Cardoza scolding him with a shake of a bony finger for snitching almonds fallen from her tree. A mere boy — but king already of his gunnysack castle.

The pulse settled itself. The pain was gone. A swirl of smoke rose from the bronze ashtray, filling his eyes with tears. A new and deeper pain. Dry burlap burns fast, like an old man's lust. In an instant, his kingdom reduced to ashes. A sudden blaze, a swirl of smoke, a residue of ash.

But that too had been another time and another place. Only his cigar smoking still in its tray. Good way to set the house on fire. Be a pretty fix now, at his time of life, to have to begin all over again. Get used to new surroundings. Too old to change his ways.

He stubbed out the forbidden cigar. Give them up too. He had lost his taste for smoking. Even the best of them smelled now of dead bats and rotten burlap. A habit that had long since ceased to please. Too paltry a pleasure to cost him so much as a single minute of life.

". . . enemy losses estimated at over . . ."

The damn radio! Who had turned it on again? Moment of silence all he needed. Naptime. And then his brandy to give the old ticker a boost.

Tea at three-thirty, brandy at five. Nap after four o'clock news.

Yet still the voice droned on, speaking of the young who had died and were dying. How little they knew what they were giving up! Just as well, or there'd be no one left to do the fighting. It was the old who knew best the value of life; the treasure of youth.

But what was the war to him? Thousands of miles away. He would give that up too. He had lost his taste for the war as well. It was life that mattered. His trees. His flowers. His Clara picking roses —

Yet that voice!

"Shut the damn thing off!"

The sound of his own voice startled him. But it was a joyful sound as filled with hope as the cry of a newborn infant. His tongue had freed itself. His heart was steady. He was better. It had passed. Whatever it was it had passed over him, and he was free at last of its hold upon him.

He rose and shakily turned the radio knob. Blessed silence. It rang in his ears like the backwash from a crash of cymbals. The war had been stilled. Now he would have his nap, for he was tired and shaking. And this evening — this evening, when they were alone together, just the two of them, as they had so often been. Almost fifty years it must be! — he would tell Clara how the picture of her cutting roses in their garden had comforted him. This evening . . .

And halfway to the sofa, he paused, his eyes turned inward as if searching his memory for some forgotten name buried in the dust, his lips moved, struggling for one last time to form the words: "I am . . ."

But no sound came.

Chapter Three

1

Vince died too soon to see his country's honor vindicated. His death, however, spared him the dissolution of his empire and the sight of his orchards tumbled before the bulldozers. The land was all he had ever understood. It had given him his strength, his riches, and his single contact with the Infinite. It had been more than the promise of gold he had seen in the annual renewal, as for weeks of aimless midwifery, at the touch of a single dawn, his orchards cast off their Lenten shells and burst into bloom. It had been for him a rite older and more sacred than Easter.

For his Christianity had been as formal as his costume. A symbol of his respectability and station. An outgrowth of a continuing heritage passed through the narrowing and distorting lens of history. Stripped to the buff, he was as pagan as any son of Pelops. And the rites of spring were the only promise of immortality he understood. The eternal return.

Yet if his ghost returned, it found little that was familiar to haunt. What the bulldozer missed the axe caught. A rambling ranchstyle high school, as plain as Wood Acres was ornate, now stands on the denuded land. Gravel has replaced the lawns; concrete, the flower beds; and a steel fence, the bank of eucalyptus. The house itself, trimmed to a more manageable size, stripped of its ornamentation, and covered with asbestoes shingles, squats awkwardly on the shoulder of a busy highway. A large neon sign above the porch identifies it as "Paradise Villa." Beneath, in somewhat smaller print, the legend is expanded: "Dinners $3.00 and up — Banquet Rooms for Parties." Colorful tin circles nailed to the veranda columns announce monthly meetings of the Rotarians, the Lions, the Oddfellows, and the Soroptimists.

For San Oriel, which had grown with the war, has burgeoned

with the peace. As fast as trees can be felled, houses rise. Cramped, jerrybuilt clusters of undried lumber, they warp after a single summer and age after a single winter, and the new becomes old almost before it has time to become familiar. Elsie Grubb's Grocery has been wiped out by a Lucky Supermarket vast enough to supply a Napoleonic army; Costa's Corner is no longer even a corner but a cloverleaf ramp onto the Nimitz Freeway. The stately mansions have fallen. The fortunate ones. Others have found new uses.

Topped with a cement stag, an artificial mountain replete with waterfall now fronts the Aiken home, which has been stuccoed and rechristened the Bide-a-While Chapel of Memories. Its single spire robbed of its bell, its circular window boarded over, its crypt a storage room for bingo tables, old Saint Anthony's has become a parish hall. Next to it stands a new and larger church of poured concrete and steel masquerading as Mission adobe.

Here, for those with sharp eyes, Vincent Woods has his memorial — an altar of pink Italian marble, on the lower right hand corner of which his name is carved in Roman letters. The gift of his bereaved widow.

2

With more grace than most, Clara accepted the inevitable. Within minutes of the awful discovery there was a doctor as well as a priest by her side, and since the man who had once been her husband was past all help save that which heaven could bestow, and heaven's help is hardly subject to time, both concentrated their attentions upon her.

More immediate and therefore more comforting than Father Moriarity's assurances of celestial recouplings were the miraculous new drugs that helped to bridge the transition from wife to widow. The first terrible hours were passed in a blessed daze — a soporific numbness that allowed her only lucidity enough to purchase a new black wardrobe. To her considerable dismay, she found that, drugged and bereaved though she was, she could still be concerned about the cut of a dress or the set of a hat. But in that concern lay her own best hopes for a tolerable future. The "business" of death spared her momentarily from thoughts of death. There was, conveniently, a prescribed ritual to follow: duties to delegate, condolences to answer, ceremonies to perform; and this ritual gave form to her grief. The very formalities of the funeral served as the necessary crutch to hobble with a semblance of dignity into the new role life and thrust upon her. At least the public side of her grief remained decorous.

There was still the private ordeal to get through, but here as well an aid appeared. Throughout the turmoil of riotous emotions, Sarah's bland, unruffled presence stood out like a rock island in a stormy sea. Quietly efficient and every bit as at home with the mysteries of death as with the mysteries of life, she proved herself, as so often before, not only "one of the family," but its one indispensible member. Voices were raised, tears were shed, and psyches were lacerated with unprecedented lavishness, but the torrential passions crashed against the solid Sarah with no more noticeable effect than waves washing over Gibralter. it was she who reminded them that even in the presence of death, meals must be cooked and served and eaten, that beds must be made and medicine taken, that clothes must be pressed, dressed hooked, and hair brushed. That life, in short, must go on.

And under her guidance life did go on. It was not, however, until after the funeral that Clara found the leisure and the solitude to appraise her loss with any degree of fullness. Except in their relationship to specific persons or objects, such abstractions as Life and Love and Beauty had never had any meaning for her. Her sables and her pearls were beautiful, but of what precisely their beauty consisted (aside from the telling proof of their price) was a question as remote to her nature as a discussion of the Doctrine of the Trinity or the Immaculate Conception. Comfort came, not from obstruse dogmas, but from specific rituals.

Without the elaborate and extensive ceremonies with which the Church cushions the living from the shock of death, she might never have survived her ordeal. Not since her father had died when she was a mere child had death presented itself in anything but its most benign form: rest for the departed and relief for the living. The only deaths that she personally had had to contend with, those of her demented old mother and Poor Belle, had both been viewed as proofs of God's mercy, and any show of grief had been precisely that — a show. So that once the theatrics of her husband's burial were completed, Clara was left to her own devices, vulnerable to a host of new and hostile emotions. And Death ceased any longer to be an abstraction.

For the first time in her life left to sleep alone, she contemplated the vast emptiness of her house. Never before had she been so conscious of its size. In front of her very eyes the rooms seemed to expand, as if, with the omission of a single person, the house had grown twice as large. And as she marked each step through each silent, empty room, it seemed no longer a home but a mausoleum of memories. Every cornice, every nicknack, every window seat and every fireplace harbored recollections too poignant to bear without pain. And for the first time she was struck with the full extent of her loss.

It was the longest night of her life. Not even her pills helped. Instead of obliterating they merely distorted. Minutes lengthened into hours, hours into years, and the phosphorescent hands of the bedroom clock seemed, after a decade of waiting, to have moved but a single digit.

She was in her old home again, a fair-haired young girl flustered with resentment but too much the victim of her own expectations to stand up for her rights:

"Well, tell me: has he or has he not come to propose?"

"Oh, Belle —!"

"Then the kitchen will do," her sister replied, and the squalid little room seemed to mock her with its echoing: will do, will do, will do.

"I see no reason to open up the parlor unless you know for sure he's come to ask for your hand."

"Come to ask? But who is there to ask — except me?"

"Mamma, of course."

"Mamma! You're not going to let him see Mamma, are you? Oh, Belle, please! Not yet. Give him just a while longer. And not the kitchen, Belle. Please not the kitchen. Just like — like —"

"Like what? Are you afraid he'll see us like we are? Is that what you're afraid of? Poor Cinderella. Well let me tell you, I already seen the house he was born in, and believe me, it wasn't

276

no palace. Far from it. And if what we got to offer isn't good enough, well, you'd just better set your mind to look elsewhere for someone to march you to the altar."

Princely proud and slender, his stiff collar rising to his chin, a huge pearl pinning his silk cravat, every inch of him bespeaking his superiority, the honor his presence paid to her house — their *kitchen!* — a twinkle in his haughty eyes as he smiled down upon her — her prince, her savior.

Awed she stood, her hands, peach-stained from pitting all day at the cannery, hidden behind her back.

"Oh, Belle, no! Not now. Not tonight. Please, Belle!"

Poor Belle, grown grotesque in her righteousness, the perpetual children clinging to her skirts: the wicked witch of every fairytale smashing dreams with her own earthbound reality.

"You could leave the house without Mamma's blessings? On such a night! Oh, Clara, Clara, your own mother!"

Not tonight. Not yet. Not now. Spare her. Spare him. For one more night. Her night. Leave this night to her.

The kerosene lamp frescoed the walls of the pantry with their grotesque silhouettes as Belle led the way through the long, narrow bathroom; and throwing an old towel onto the wicker hamper, she thrust open the door into the camphor-filled room. Then smiling, she stepped aside to let them pass.

But it was not her shriveled old mother buried under a mound of crazy quilts who lay on the huge walnut bed, but her own Vince covered with a blanket of gardenias, their perfume overpoweringly sweet. Her prince grown old, with waxen hands clasped over his belly, a pair of gold-rimmed glasses clamped over his closed lids —

He was dead, she realized at last. Dead! And there was no way ever again to call him back, to throw herself into his arms or lay her troubles at his feet, no way ever again to share her love except through her own death, and she was still too filled with leftover life for that. She did not want to die. Only to sleep. To lose herself in the sweet oblivion of a dreamless slumber. And though sleep would not come, morning came, and with it Sarah to rescue her from morbidity.

277

Together among the African violets of the morning sunporch the two women sat on the wicker sofa, both garbed in such deep mourning it would have been difficult, at first glance, to tell which was the widow and which the companion. But the finest dressmaker would have been at a loss to transform the likes of Sarah into a duchess. Neither pleas, insults, nor bribes could induce her to subject her fulsome figure to the iron-maiden rigors of a corset. Nor would she dream of scrimping her lusty appetite. For she had, in her middle years, arrived at the firm conviction that the Almighty had yet to create the man who was half so delectable as a buttercream-covered chocolate cake, and she now indulged this latter-day passion with the same unstinted vigor with which she had once pursued the former. So despite the fashionable cut of her black faille frock, Sarah's figure remained irredeemably plebian.

There were some who called it gross — though Clara was not among them. Her need precluded fault-finding. There was even something comforting in Sarah's great size. Clara scarcely any longer thought of their relationship in terms of mistress and servant. Sarah was her "companion." And if the outside world insisted upon prefixing the new title with a gratuitous "paid," neither took particular offense. Indeed, so happy was the balance between giving and taking, their relationship proved invincible.

Since Immaculata had followed her soldier husband into the mysterious wilds of Mississippi, Sarah did not hesitate to accept Clara's tearful plea to move back in. And to mark the full extent of her altered status, it was not the maid's room off the kitchen that she now occupied but the upstairs bird's-eye maple suite that had once been Arnie's, its magnificent sleigh bed formidable enough to bear her great bulk.

Since the morning sunporch was designed to catch the first rays of the winter sun, it was in summer used only in the afternoon when there was none of the intense heat of the afternoon sunporch. Here the two women sat before a wicker table piled with tiny cards and black-edged envelopes. As Clara picked up a card and dictated the pertinent information, Sarah scribbled in a spiral notebook the name of the contributor, appending after it

in her large childish scrawl a description of the floral piece con-
tributed along with its estimated cost. The completed card was
then dropped into a hatbox on the floor for future filing and
another card chosen.

"Well, it seems to me," Sarah huffed after the last entry,
"*they* could well afforded a standing piece, instead of a mere
spray. Way they throw their money around."

"Yes, it does seem odd, doesn't it?" Clara was quick to
agree. "And if my memory serves me, I recall, when her father
died, we sent quite a grand piece. Gardenias and carnations, I
think it was. Yes. A beautiful white wreath filled with a heart of
red carnations. Why I remember quite distinctly how shocked I
was when Vince — poor dear — showed me the bill. After all, it
wasn't as if they were family. And we hardly owed *them* anything. And here they return our extravagance with a simple spray
of gladiolas not worth five dollars. Mark it four-fifty," she
ordered with curt finality. "And next funeral comes along she'll
be satisifed with a simple mass card."

Sarah shook her head at the incorrigible ingratitude of mankind.

"Well, it just goes to show. But comes the time, *I* wouldn't
send so much as a card. Nosirree. But knowing you the way I
do, too good-natured to hold a grudge, you'll probably end up,
same as always, sending another wreath. Who's next?"

"Mamie Dutra."

Again Sarah's ire was roused.

"Why she bothered to send a spray, when she was already, all
by herself, brighter'n a bed a spring flowers is beyond me.
Shameful, I call it, wearing a colored print to a funeral. And
such a funeral."

"Yes, I couldn't help but notice. But poor thing, maybe she
didn't have a black dress, and we could hardly expect her to go
out and buy a new one just for us."

"Well, she coulda covered it with a black coat, couldn't she?
Even if it was hot enough to sweat the fat off a pig's behind.
Lean-bacon weather my father used to call it."

"Oh, Sarah, how you talk!" Clara laughed. "Poor Mamie, it
was nice a her, things being what they are, to send anything.
What with her mother — already five years it must be since her
stroke. Just laying there like a vegetable, I hear. Poor thing.

Well, one blessing we gotta be thankful for, poor Vince didn't linger.''

"Bless God for that," Sarah answered, fully prepared to join her companion in a refreshingly therapeutic cry when the door-bell dammed all tears.

"Oh, dear, who can that be now?"

Clara dabbed her eyes as Sarah peeked out the window.

"Father Moriarity. In skirts," she added with a significant lift of her heavy brows.

"Well, we both know what that means, don't we?" In an instant the mealy-soft Clara became as iron-head as her husband on similar occasions. "Coming to draw just a little more gold out of the camel's eye, I warrant," she continued. "Well, I'm afraid this time he's going to find the eye's gone dry. There'll be no more golden tears shed for him in this house."

There were, she was beginning to discover, as lawyers and brokers and priests kept calling, to say nothing of the numerous members of her own family, all manner of traps set to snare the new widow. But her husband had proved the best of teachers, and she paid homage to his memory by not allowing herself to be trapped by any of them.

Religion, which had proved a comfort when comfort was most needed, would not become an obsession. She would not, like Mae Ramos, allow herself to be transformed into a pious little churchmouse. It was not any longer a question of grati-tude, but of outright exploitation. For she had already demon-strated herself more than grateful. The proper number of masses had been ordered, the proper donations made. She had even committed herself to pay for the new altar of the new church to be built the instant the war was over. She would not allow her tender emotions to be so far abused to intimidate her into giving another penny. If the new church needed a new organ as well as a new altar, it would have to come from some other likely source, for as far as she was concerned there need be no hymns sung at all.

"You don't suppose he coulda seen us sitting here, do you?" she asked.

"Not unless he came walking up the yard on stilts. Course, knowing that one, I wouldn't put it past him."

"Well, then, Dear, I really see no purpose in listening again to what I've already heard so many times. I know just what he's going to say before he opens his mouth. Why don't you tell him I had such a headache I took a pill and went to bed. And I'll sneak upstairs the back way."

Among Sarah's many virtues was her absolute conviction that the lies she was asked to tell to spare her mistress became, in the telling, somehow true, so that by the time she answered the door, she was shaking with indignation at the bell which had so rudely disturbed her mistress's rest. So convincing was she the terrible-tempered prelate, who could spy out the secret masturbator in the most cherubic of altarboys, found not so much as a revelatory flicker of an eyelid to make him doubt Sarah's words.

"He says he'll say an extra prayer for you tonight."

Sarah's comment was offered without any editorial comment, verbal or facial.

At the head of the stairs Clara's smile of relief was swept away as her eyes lighted upon the empty gold chair.

"Oh, dear! It always gives me such a start. Every time I look at it, I half expect to see him sitting there. Just like always."

And as Sarah rushed up to help her, the deferred tears flowed with refreshing ease, while Clara, leaning heavily upon the stout supporting arm, hobbled down the stairs and onto the sofa.

"Now you just rest yourself here a minute and I'll be back in no time at all with a little something to cheer you up."

And good as her word, in almost no time at all, Sarah was back, a silver tray in her hands, the ice clinking against the crystal containers of two whisky sours.

"Just the way you like it: a little on the sweet side," she said, placing the tray on the coffee table, then pulling out the huge linen handkerchief she kept handily tucked in her belt, her great breasts hovering with protective warmth above Clara's face, she coaxed the tears away:

"There, there, Honeygirl, we've had tears enough already. And how," she asked, without interrupting the warm flow of words as she blotted the tears and fluffed the pillows, "do you think all this grieving's about to help him? Why, just suppose he's got his eye on you up there — and don't for one minute think he hasn't; he's got his eye on you, all right. You can be sure a that. Do you think he wants to see his honeygirl, her face all streaked and twisted just like some old circus clown? Why, just look at yourself. A regular sight you are. And you've got to keep yourself up, if only for his sake. It's no more'n he'd expect."

It was a formula that never failed.

"Yes, yes, you're quite right. Hard as it sometimes is, the living have to go on living." Clara leaned forward to put Sarah's hand. "But I don't know what I'd have done without you, my dear. Dear Sarah. You've been so good. But I'll make it worth your while, I will. Yes, I will. Don't think I'll ever forget what you've been to me, Sarah. During this terrible time."

And a fresh flow of tears was halted by Sarah's reply:

"Hush, hush, now. All Sarah's interested in is seeing her honeygirl happy once again. Like God intended her to be. That's all I want."

"Oh, yes, my dear, I'll remember, I will."

And she did.

4

It was Sarah's ingenuousness that made her, in the eyes of Clara's most immediate heirs, so formidable a foe. Had she from the first plotted to win an inheritance, she might best have come off with a year's salary. But so completely did she and Clara come to serve each other that the bond which united them was nothing less than love. In the eyes of each the other was the single person whose existence was most essential to her own happiness. So that by the time Clara made her twofold announcement that the family home was to be sold and that Sarah was to be given equal standing in the latest will along with Clara's own children and become, thus, entitled to a quarter of the estate, Louise, Arnie, and Lorraine, even if they had been capable of concerted action, which they most certainly were not, could only have jeopardized their own precarious standings by open antagonism. Already summarily excluded from their father's will, they soon laid their protests to rest in the inflexible glare of their mother's eyes.

No one was more surprised by the announcement than Sarah herself, and despite the malicious hints that such a declaration might tempt the conniving servant to hasten her benefactress's end, no one desired Clara's death less than Sarah herself. It had been Clara's profound need to be cared for and fussed over, as well as Sarah's equally profound need to expend her bountiful warmth upon some appreciative household pet, be it lover, daughter, or mistress, rather than money that had made lovers of them; and need continued to play a far more important part in their relationship than any illusory fortune.

For as the weeks passed into months, Wood Acres grew daily larger and more decrepit. It was a museum piece that made Clara herself more than ever conscious of her own age, as if she were, like her house, a curiosity to be gaped at.

After each rain storm new windows failed to open and fresh leaks appeared. The wind loosened shingles and the plaster of the master bedroom was soon streaked with waterstains. Nor was the plumbing all that it might have been. Washers corroded, faucets dripped, and drains clogged. During the first heavy frost, the furnace pilot went out, and the two women, bundled in furs and too fearful of an explosion to attempt a remedy on their own, shivered through the morning in a chill that left them sneezing for days after. Even memory, Clara soon decided, could best be served elsewhere.

The club that was to become her new home had never, in her memory, failed to be prefixed in the press with a flattering "exclusive." It was also expensive. But as Clara was quick to point out, "You only get what you pay for."

For years it had been her favorite downtown luncheon spot, a place to entertain and if necessary impress her friends. A mint-green paradise with gilt Louis Seize moldings and crystal chandeliers weeping from the twin eye sockets of every ceiling, the Oakland City Women's Athletic Club was clearly designed for the genteel elderly who had never, even in their freshest youth, been remotely athletic. Plush, noiseless carpets of a neutral beige covered every parquet floor, and gigantic bouquets of dried hydrangeas, withered to a dusty mauve, sat upon every ornate console table. Above the placid, invariably empty tile pool was the true center of the building: a dining room of peace-treaty proportions. Here the linen-covered refectory tables burgeoned with unseasoned beef, gelatin salads, fruit compotes, and pastel desserts, along with the requisite calorie counters and sugar substitutes.

In a three-room suite with a view onto the lake Clara and Sarah took up residence surrounded by the choicest of Clara's bibelot and furnishings. Furnaces never failed, faucets never dripped, ceilings never leaked. Room service took care of all needs. There were elevator men to take them up to the cocktail lounge for their nightly whiskey-sour-a-little-on-the-sweet-side and elevator men to take them down for their morning stroll around the lake; and there were doormen to greet at least one of them by name: "Morning, Mrs. Woods. A bit nippy today"; and there were smiling and efficient, if sometimes palsied, waitresses to tempt them both with an empress's choice of delicious dainties:

"Just a taste, Dear. It'll put roses in your cheeks."

"How you talk!" Clara would laugh. "What need have I for roses in my cheeks? A woman my age."

"*Your* age! I only wish *I* had as many years left me as you have."

"How you talk!"

The transition from country to city and from home to club proved far easier than a lifetime of habit might have portended. Indeed, so soon did *The Club* become *Home* that she could scarcely imagine a life outside its precincts. Even memory benefitted from the move, for aging as she was, the past of necessity became an integral part of the present. It was, however, a past refined.

The plush salons never lacked attentive ears. Settled on satin sofas, the beautiful ladies with the soft, gentle voices set up their easels and prepared their palettes. Pastel artists, they painted only in muted colors. Red became rose, blue, lavendar. With the gentle touch of a frail finger, imperfections were smoothed away and the portraits of their husbands, arranged like so many enlarged postage stamps of heroic founding fathers, were held up for the admiration of all.

With every fresh attempt to capture him for her new friends, the real Vince sank deeper into his grave. The more she talked of her grief, the less she felt it. She had fathomed, she knew, some secret, but one so fragile words would destroy it. At peace now, she not only accepted age, she actually came to enjoy it. Pain she had always had, the swollen fingers and the swollen ankles, but with Sarah hovering over her like a guardian angel, she could follow it now to its logical end, total passivity.

She discovered that she could close her ears as easily as she could close her eyes. With the bribe of a small but steady monthly allowance Arnie was inducted to set up housekeeping in Mexico, too far away to be heard at all. And when her daughters bickered, she no longer listened. She heard only their endearments, saw only their smiles. At family gatherings, hers was always the softest, most central seat. She was old, she must be waited upon, fussed over, listened to, and if she repeated herself or lost her way, it was for them to lead her back, for them to greet her with kisses, to comfort her with sighs; for them to shield her from all blows to shelter her from all storms. And when the voices rose, as rise they invariably did, she slipped unnoticed into her dreams, which were now, as they had always been, like her evening cocktail, a little on the sweet side.